MASTER of the GAME

WILLIAM TEPPER

Master of the Game

Printed and bound in Colombia by Imprelibros S.A.

ISBN: 0-9747644-0-X

Published by Synergy Books

Synergy Books

2525 W Anderson Lane, Suite 540
Austin, Texas 78757

Tel: 512.407.8876
Fax: 512.478.2117

E-mail: info@turnkeypress.com
Web: www.turnkeypress.com

For all those who died by such evil hands,
and all those who are about to.

Peter Simmons died that day, on his seventeenth birthday.

The fire spread quickly about him as the flames climbed up the walls to the ceiling. The wooden beams had already commenced a staccato crackling as their trapped water vapor exploded. Peter knew only extreme heat could cause that. He was surprised how rapidly the small cabin had turned into an inferno.

I have set the fire too soon!

Peter leaped up from the space between his two slain parents. *There is not enough time*, he lamented, racing from the house to the shed where a teenager lay unconscious. The boy was the right age and build. The rest was unimportant.

How could I have made such a dumb miscalculation?

There could be no turning back, no second chance, his parents were dead and the house was burning furiously. Peter rushed back with the boy on his shoulder. The full wrath of the firestorm awaited, yet, it drew him with a hypnotic siren's call.

The beams tumbled in about him. Peter fought them off as he pressed forward. Searing pain shot through him in intense waves, subduing his will, seducing a simple desire to flee. Why had he chosen to voluntarily walk into hell? Why? Peter purged those weak thoughts. He had to endure.

The boy was laid between his parents. *It's done.*

Peter sighed in relief, as a nervous hand felt for a face that was gone. Skin seared off; raw tissues were spilling out, and the foul stench of scorched flesh filled his nostrils.

Charred in the cauldron of his own hate, Peter Simmons died that day.

Now, I can be anyone and still remain no one.

Simon lives!

SEVENTEEN YEARS LATER...

Mary Splitorf was so excited Wednesday, English Lit day, that she got up a full hour early. Not that English Literature meant anything special to her, hardly, but David sat next to her in class. Mondays, Wednesdays, and Fridays required some extra preparation.

David was tall and dark and *oh soooo good looking*. He was like one of those male hunks in a magazine, thin yet muscular, making his clothes look *oh soooo good on him*. They were expensive clothes too, and stylish, not the baggy jeans and sweatshirts the *kids* wore. David was an older man, *maybe in his late twenties or even thirty!*

A nineteen-year-old freshman at USC, Mary was slender and blonde, an attractive girl with a pleasant face and disarming smile. She never spent much time or energy on makeup or clothes, but for David, Mary felt the need to do more.

She busied herself in front of the mirror with her makeup, trying to decide which look would be best. What to wear was another decision, but that would not be made for at least half an hour.

The Splitorfs lived in Riverside, a thirty seven-mile drive to USC. Mary's old Volkswagen Rabbit rattled toward school, past the guard station, and into the parking structure near her class. She was late, a little too much fussing this day. Mary rushed into the classroom. *Thank God!* David was there; the whole drive in she worried that he might not be. Mary sat down, concerned that she was too flushed. They exchanged big smiles. All was well.

It was the third week of class. David had not been there the first week. A *complete Geek* used to sit next to Mary, putting her in serious jeopardy of getting an "A". Then, suddenly, there was David. Mary never asked for an explanation, just thanked the kindly Gods of love and romance.

They got along wonderfully from the first, writing each other cute little notes, making small jokes, and giggling cautiously. There was even some touching, nothing sexual of course, just hands and light brushing, but Mary knew that it was meant to lead to bigger things.

She had expected David to ask her out long before, but he did not. Mary feared he felt her too young. *More makeup needed, more adult looking clothes.*

They settled into their normal routine of writing playful little notes in their notebooks. Neither of them had heard a word of the lectures all semester.

About twenty minutes into class, David wrote in his notebook in big letters, "Want to have lunch with me?" *At last!* Mary drew a discreetly sized heart followed by the word "to" and an exclamation mark.

They left in David's car, a brand sparkling new Lexus. *I knew he had money too!* Mary thought she had gone to heaven.

Mary Splitorf was never seen again.

From the Preface

To this text I humbly bring over twenty years of experience and experiences. Together we shall attempt to challenge the impossible, to understand the mind of the serial killer.Of serial killers, little is known, much is unknown, and the rest is speculation. To date, we can rely on only two certainties. Serial killers kill. And, they will not stop until someone stops them.

- Into the Mind of a Killer, John Hightower

Once more Frank Wycheck passed under the sacred arches of St. Matthew's. He entered the old church not to get out of the rain, but because he had run out of places to turn. Rainwater was dripping from his head and down his nose as Wycheck slowly trudged down the old church's long aisle.

He was shivering and cold, wearing clothes that were drenched all the way through. Huddled under an overcoat soaked heavy, he toiled to drag it along with him. Wycheck had been this way for hours, walking, walking, walking.

He cast his eyes upward and around, taking in the old church as he paced further down the aisle. Not much had changed since he was here last. The church was in sad disrepair, its once ornate lavishness barely discernable.

St. Matthew's was built long before his time, when well to do parishioners generously anted up. The church was like the neighborhood, first shiny and new, then, through time, neglected and allowed to decay. Now both lay rotting, forgotten and abandoned by a society that had progressed to the next shiny new thing.

If a church was to provide sanctuary, if it was the place for the weak and weary to take refuge, then Wycheck knew that St. Matthew's was surely God's house. On a pew to the left, was a homeless man settled in for the night, sleeping soundly, passed out. St. Matthew's was always lenient that way.

Wycheck paused to look at the man. He had smelled him several rows before seeing him. The nauseating odor of feces, urine and countless layers of dried sweat haunted Wycheck as it transported him back to the blackness of his own darkest days.

The homeless man was curled up tightly on the pew, buried under layers of torn filthy clothes rescued from assorted trash bins. For a moment Frank Wycheck envied the man. At least for this night, he was content and resting peacefully.

Wycheck tugged at the man's overcoat, disdainfully searching for the man's bottle. Of all things, Wycheck knew, it had to be there. Ah, there it was, cradled in his arms, precious to him, like a baby. Only one third full though, no matter. As long as there was any liquid left, the man was as rich as he needed to be.

Better than anyone could, Frank Wycheck knew this man. Better than any other journalist certainly. Wycheck knew the neighborhood; he knew the church; he knew the pews. One last time he glanced down at the man, wondering if he had ever occupied that very same spot.

Frank Wycheck was known for his insight, his uncanny grasp of the seamy side of life. He understood the streets and those who inhabited them. He made them alive for his readers. His words brought the streets to millions.

But Wycheck did not need insight to know this man. For frozen in time, just a few years past, he was this man. Raised from the depths was Frank Wycheck. He had spent two full years in oblivion, looking out at the world from the inside of a bottle. Not education, not talent, not the love of family could help him. Only this church, blessed St. Matthew's, and Father Romero were able to rescue him. Now here he was, again.

A little further down the aisle was a shopping cart, overflowing with old clothes and assorted junk, all of someone's worldly possessions. Wycheck moved more quickly, curious to see whose they were.

A small woman, worn far past her years, filthy, and with her own aroma, was bent over and rocking slowly. She was not awake and not asleep, not of this world and not of any other. She failed to take notice of him, though Wycheck stared at her intently.

He was familiar with this woman as well, and all the others like her. They were like his Molly. Molly had been his sometime companion in those lost dark days. She was the one and only person he shared his bottle with.

On the cold days Molly would lie close to him, and on occasion he would burrow through the many layers of soiled clothing to partake of her. Molly never minded, well, she never objected.

Frank Wycheck thought he had left those days far behind. He drove a Porsche now instead of a shopping cart and wore Armani instead of discarded rags. He had a home and a warm bed waiting for him. He was rich; he was famous. He had come far.

Since the dark time, he had driven past St. Matthew's hundreds of times, never once thinking of entering. The neighborhood had become his office; the streets provided his inspiration; the desperate, despicable and bereft were his source material. He had become an observer only. And he was a reporter.

Now Wycheck realized that he was never that far removed. Good fortune did not change a man any more than his clothes did. Frank Wycheck was in danger of being dragged back, back to the depths, by one insoluble problem.

Immeasurable stress had thrown him down into the barrel before. He could feel its weight forcing him down again. It was in desperation that he returned to St. Matthew's. He needed an answer to his problem, one that he was incapable of solving, and one that threatened to destroy him forever.

Near the altar, Wycheck saw a priest, sitting and bent over some writing. *Lucky*, he thought, *usually this late at night no one would be here.* He did not recognize the man, but then why should he? It had been years.

"Is Father Romero still here?" he asked the priest as he was almost next to him.

The man looked up at him calmly. "Father Romero died three years ago."

Wycheck was disappointed and saddened and then embarrassed. The old priest had died and he had not even noticed. For a moment guilt supplanted some of his torment. *Three years!* Father Romero was the one who lifted him up and helped him when no one else could.

Frank Wycheck thought back, trying to recall how the old priest had done it. He remembered a hand being outstretched to him, an offer to listen, and then they would talk. They spoke many times, and in time, the miracle. Father Romero brought him back, appealing not to his faith, that had been long lost, but to his intellect. Father Romero made him want to return to the world, realize his potential, live again.

The good Father, through his patience and wise counsel gave him incentive to renounce the bottle forever. For the addictive personality though, it was always preferable to substitute one addiction for another. The new crutch became cocaine, but it worked. For a time, Wycheck was better than ever, actually at the very top of his game.

Wycheck lamented that Father Romero was not there to help him again when he needed him so.

"I am Father Reyes," the priest said. "Perhaps I can be of help, my son?"

The priest was Hispanic, as Father Romero had been, bilingual no doubt, a logical requirement for the neighborhood. And, he had a warm soothing manner about him.

"I'm not sure anyone can," answered Wycheck, for the moment staring into Father Reyes' pleasant face.

"Really?" The priest raised a doubting eyebrow. "Judging from your clothes, you are much better off than the rest of my tenants."

"Not all problems have to be financial, Father."

"Quite right, my son. Forgive me. You look cold and wet. Come, let me take your coat." Father Reyes got up from his chair. He put a comforting arm around Wycheck and quickly separated him from his heavy wet overcoat. "You have time to stay, don't you, to let the rain die down and your coat to dry. You can spare a few moments for God to listen to your troubles. What have you better to do?"

Wycheck listened to the words dance forth from Father Reyes' lips. The lyrical Spanish accent, they came out more in song than in sentences. Everything about the young priest was soothing, reassuring, calming. The man was good and one thing Frank Wycheck had always appreciated was talent.

"Nothing, Father, absolutely nothing," he answered, somewhat consoled. There was nothing else to do.

"Fine, then why not get comfortable and let's see what is troubling you so." Father Reyes sensed his hesitation immediately. "Would you be more comfortable in the Confessional?"

The priest was good.

Father Romero and Wycheck always talked in the Confessional. There was something about the anonymity of the booth. In it, Wycheck thought out loud, confident that there was no one to betray those innermost thoughts.

"Yes, Father, I would," answered a relieved Wycheck.

He settled into the booth. Even after so much time, it was still familiar to him. Frank Wycheck was comfortable, at home. His hand reached up to feel the walls. They were worn smooth and there were new damaged areas. The booth's fragrance was mustier than he remembered. But it was the same.

Many hours were spent in this small closet. In other lifetimes, still, Wycheck was soothed and calmer than he had been in days.

"It's a rather long story," he sighed.

"My son, God is eternal, this church has been here for eighty-three years, and I have all night."

"I don't know where to start, Father. I'm a flawed, weak man, always having chosen the path of least resistance. A hedonistic, pleasure seeking fool, but I would never let my follies hurt anyone. I've always tried to do the right thing, to be a good man."

"Yes, my son, that is evident from your torment. God sees that."

"Yes, of course, God sees everything." Wycheck settled in. "My name is Frank Wycheck."

"Frank Wycheck, Wycheck..."

"Yes, Father, the writer."

"The one who wrote all those articles about the neighborhood." Wycheck nodded, though it was doubtful the priest saw it. "Oh yes, Frank Wycheck, I'm a very big fan. Used to read you every day, but I haven't seen anything for quite a while."

"Yes, Father, quite a while, almost two years. That's when it all started. No, it was before that. I suppose it started during the 'Jaws murders'."

The words suddenly ceased to flow. Frank Wycheck's thoughts raced far ahead of them and only silence was left in the wake. So many thoughts of so many events passed.

"Frank?"

"What? What's that?" Wycheck stammered.

"You were saying how it all started during those horrible Jaws murders."

"The Jaws murders, yes, no, I don't know. That's one of the things I've been racking my brain about. There was absolutely no connection that I could think of. But there had to be one. There had to be. Those murders and the subsequent trial are what set him off."

"Set him off?"

"It was a game to him, Father. You understand? A game! It was always a damn game." Wycheck was losing control as the full weight of his problem again pressed down on him.

"That's all right, Frank," said Father Reyes soothingly. "Relax. Take your time. Let it all out."

"Yes, Father, of course. It was a game to him. His Grand Game, where he was the player and we were all pawns. And, Father, the pawns were sacrificed freely."

1

John Hightower was taking some time off from likely the most stressful job in the world. He returned to southern California, his former home before he lived exclusively in hotel rooms and carried his life around in a suitcase. Hightower had just completed the Maldanado case in Atlanta, a nasty little affair that saw eight children die. Tired and anxious to relax, he had come to do a little sailing.

On his second day out on Santa Monica Bay, Hightower was already getting bored. His cell phone had been silent, though usually it was attached to his ear, feeding him information while he barked orders into it. Relaxation was tolerable only for so long, John Hightower was feeling the itch to put the harness back on.

By the third day, he was ready to tear the wallpaper off his hotel room walls with his teeth. As Hightower thought about it, a new record had been set.

The fourth day the cell phone mercifully rang, and the sound of the annoying little song sent his adrenalin rushing.

"Hightower!" he answered, short and brusque as always.

"John? This is Kevin Fitzpatrick."

Kevin Fitzpatrick, head of the L.A. office, as pompous a bureaucratic ass as existed in the FBI, Hightower had worked for him early in his career, and with him on a number of occasions since. Fitz was FBI Regional Director and harbored hopes of rising higher. The two men were complete opposites and clashed constantly.

"Yes, Kevin, what can I do for you?" Hightower could tell from the conciliatory tone that Fitz wanted something.

"Listen, John, I know you're here on vacation, but…"

Fitzpatrick never liked John Hightower. He was a prima Donna, a loose cannon, and an insubordinate son of a bitch. However, Kevin Fitzpatrick did know how to butter his bread. Unsolved cases made for very bad politics, and John Hightower solved cases.

"Yes, yes, Kevin," Hightower cut him off. "What's on your mind?"

"Have you heard about the Jaws case we have here in L.A.?"

"Yes, of course. It's all over the news. Those media fellows just love the bizarre ones, don't they?"

"Yes, and they're crucifying us. Anyway, John, I was wondering if you might take a look. Tell us what you think."

Jaws, first assumed to be a wild animal, then when the killings exhibited too regular a pattern, they were thought to be cult ritualistic murders using dogs as the weapons. Local authorities were stumped. With the third victim, the FBI was called in. There had been two more killings since.

"This one isn't exactly up my alley, Kevin." Hightower was scheduled to leave for Detroit in three days. "And besides, how hard can it be to track these dogs down?"

"We haven't found a thing, and we have five bodies." Fitzpatrick sounded more distressed than Hightower had ever heard him. "Just take a look, John."

"Sure, Fitz, why not?"

2

Special Agent Mark Berlanger drowsily shut off the alarm next to his bed. He awoke unaided every morning about ten minutes be fore the alarm went off, yet he religiously set it every night. His clothes were laid out and waiting for him. His suit, matching tie, socks and shoes sat at the ready. Mark Berlanger was a precise man, a careful man.

A disturbing telephone call woke Agent Berlanger this morning. A jogger had found another victim. Berlanger was told to expect a gruesome scene, similar to the others. No mystery, it was Jaws for sure.

He jumped out of bed and into the shower. Three minutes would have to do, instead of the full fifteen-minute soaking he preferred. Mark Berlanger viciously rubbed the water into his eyes, trying to exorcise his sleepiness. He dried himself quickly and chaotically then threw on his clothes. There was not even enough time to make a proper knot in his tie. Berlanger drove off in his six-year old Toyota without taking time to warm the vehicle up adequately.

It was still dark, not quite six o'clock, as he arrived at the sixth Jaws crime scene. Mark Berlanger was tired, but what else was new these days? Phil Hardy, his junior partner, and John Hightower were already at the scene. Berlanger was disappointed. With John Hightower there, he was no longer in charge.

The press was already encamped and pushing against the barriers, their cameras and microphones pointed inward, straining for just a slightly better view or a few overheard words. The media often beat Berlanger to crime scenes. Jaws had put them in a frenzy. The biggest story in years, it was just the kind they prayed for, bizarre, gory, and frightening.

The news vultures, sitting at their word processors; killing time with their police scanners turned on, waiting for the next call. With luck, they'll get some really R-rated stuff for the evening broadcast.

Berlanger tried unsuccessfully to avoid the cameras. The newshounds had learned to look for his white Toyota. They were on him immediately and he had to fight through the jungle of microphones, cameras and questions. Berlanger steeled himself and simply repeated, "No comment," as he passed through the gauntlet.

"Well?" he asked Hardy, who was coming toward him.

"Tough crowd, huh?"

"Never mind them," Berlanger snapped back. "Hello, John," directed at Hightower. "How are you?" John Hightower was the legend whom Berlanger had worked for years before. When Assistant Director Dawson pulled Hightower from L.A. and made him national, Berlanger inherited the slot. He was intent to appear in control. "Talk to me," he snarled at Hardy.

"Same as the others, sir. This one is a male."

"His tastes don't seem to go by sex. That makes three females and three males." Berlanger threw an inquisitive look at Agent Hardy.

"Yup," Hardy replied. "The genitals were bitten off, just like the others."

"Hmmm," grunted Berlanger as he paced toward the yellow tape. Hardy and Hightower followed behind.

Special Agent Berlanger paused before entering the cordoned off area. "Who's been in here to fuck up the crime scene?" He was anxious to impress the master.

"Two Uni's, but they were careful. This scene is much better than the first few."

Mark Berlanger ran his investigations strictly by the book. He disdained *inspirational* investigations. Feelings, hunches, deductive intuition, he left the instinctive methods to those who had the instincts. Not everyone was a John Hightower.

Berlanger was, instead, a stickler for procedure. "Next to high priced shysters, carelessness lets more criminals go free than anything else." It was a favorite saying of his. With it he killed two pet peeves with one phrase, very efficient.

The body was located behind some bushes, no more than ten feet from the jogging path. Not a shred of clothing was on the victim. Torn pieces of a dark gray suit were lying near by. Eventually, as with the other victims, they would find the rest of his clothing and belongings.

"They don't like the taste of the clothes," Berlanger mumbled to himself. The victims were always stripped; even watches and rings were removed then discarded, never stolen.

"Do you think they eat the genitals, sir?" asked Hardy. "We haven't been able to find any of the missing parts."

"How the hell should I know?" Berlanger growled.

Judging by the amount of blood, the man was killed on the spot, bitten to death. The forensic team was taking pictures of the bite marks.

Like the other murders, there were no witnesses. The bites were virtually on every square inch of the body, the number depending on the size of the victim, usually ranging between one hundred fifty and two hundred.

Mark Berlanger and John Hightower each hunched over the victim. He was at least two hundred fifty pounds.

"Judging by the size of this guy, Jaws may have set a new record," said Special Agent Berlanger sarcastically. "Even in poor shape, he should have put up a credible struggle. Six murders, how could this be done, even at night, without anyone noticing? And, how could the killers go around with a pack of wild dogs and be unnoticed?"

"No animal committed these murders," stated Hightower calmly and quietly. He was hunched over the body inspecting the wounds. "The bite marks are evenly spaced, much too regular. How did you come to the conclusion this was a cult, that animals were involved? One man did this."

"But the teeth marks, the canines," protested Berlanger. "They're not human."

"Not human, not animal, given the choice, I pick highly unusual human. These are ritualistic murders, granted. But, what you have here, Mark, is a lone serial killer."

3

An investigation is like a giant jigsaw puzzle, with thousands of disjointed pieces of information that have to be evaluated and fit together. To that end, thank God for computers.
The computer is the single most important investigative tool ever invented. Next to the pencil, that is.

- Into the Mind of a Killer, John Hightower

We're scanning in the records of every dentist's office, starting in L.A. and spiraling out. The computers' optical recognition software is comparing every bite with those we got off the bodies. We're past Riverside and still haven't got a match. Is it possible, John, Jaws has never been to a dentist?"

"What's that, Mark?"

John Hightower's attention was fixed on Fitz's office. Through the glass walls, he saw the fat Irishman talking to the District Attorney, Janet Bultaco.

Hightower knew her for years. They met nearly twenty years before, when she was a junior prosecutor and he started with the Bureau. Hightower testified on the Hectman case, a man who killed his wife and two children. They had their first lunch to go over his testimony, and the attraction was immediate. Both married, they were both safe.

They worked together on four more cases over the years. Each looked forward to the other's company; neither would think to make a move. Their relationship was completely platonic, with enormous overtones of "what if."

By the Rubinstein case, Hightower was working nationally and Bultaco had become Assistant District Attorney. Janet had divorced her husband, an obnoxious prosecutor Hightower never liked, and his wife, rest her soul, was dead from cancer nearly three years. Rubinstein dictated that they work closely together for more than a week. John Hightower wanted to make a move but let the moment pass. He regretted it ever since.

"John?"

"Yes, yes, Mark," stammered Hightower. "You checked the bite marks?"

"Uh, that's right, no match."

"Really?"

Janet was as attractive as ever. Prim and proper, businesslike as always, but with a natural beauty that few took the trouble to notice. The District Attorney glanced out through the glass wall. Their eyes met, locked onto each other, and the magnetism floated back and forth across the room.

Quiet, shy John Hightower had always been afraid to utter a forward pushing word. Dignified, correct, and unapproachable, Janet Bultaco would never dream to presume. There had always been plenty of fuel between them, but never a spark to ignite the flame.

John Hightower was determined. This day, he would change all that.

"I'm not surprised," Hightower continued, though his attention remained diverted. "That was not a human bite pattern."

"What do you mean, John? You were the first to discount the animal bite idea."

"I didn't say it was from an animal. I said it wasn't human."

Mark Berlanger was perplexed.

"Think man!" Hightower coaxed Berlanger. "What is unusual about the bite pattern?"

Since the day Mark Berlanger left the Academy, John Hightower asked him questions. He was always teaching. Hightower felt it his duty to help produce good cops. "The teeth, particularly the canines. They're long and sharp, like an animal's," answered Berlanger dutifully.

"The killer's killing teeth, like an animal. Now tell me, Mark, do you think Jaws was born with those canines?" Hightower did not wait for an answer. "No, of course not! No one is born with teeth like that. Jaws had to modify them, file them sharp. Or, he may have built them up somehow. And therefore…?"

"And that's why we're not getting a match."

"Exactly! Try the bite patterns again. Exclude the sharpened teeth. You already know you aren't going to find them. Look for the other teeth."

"Yes, of course," exclaimed Berlanger.

"Go for the molars, smaller groupings, go for individual teeth, build his bite up backwards."

In three days, they had Jaws.

4

An agent's life is rarely lost due to an overabundance of caution. The same cannot be said for complacency.

- Into the Mind of a Killer, John Hightower

Mark Berlanger took stock of the terrain around the small farm, while John Hightower stood by silently. The little wooden house with adjoining shed lay in a clearing hacked away from the surrounding woods. Thick shrubs lined the front of the house and the windows were covered with sheets and blankets. An eerie quiet gave no clue that the house was inhabited, and if it was, by how many.

In the woods there were no less than a hundred agents, all in black, all with the giant FBI letters on their backs. They wore bulletproof vests and their weapons carried live ammunition.

"This is the FBI. Come out with your hands up," shouted Special Agent Berlanger into a megaphone. He waited. There was no movement in the house, although a dog began to bark in the shed.

"Come out, and no one will get hurt," he shouted again.

Still nothing except the dog.

That they discovered Jaws at all was a stroke of luck. Mark Berlanger quoted John Hightower in his mind. *Never underestimate the importance of luck.* Twenty-three years before, a boy was brought to a clinic where a badly infected tooth was pulled. The teeth patterns scored the highest correlations with Jaws. Even the pulled tooth matched.

Amazingly, the dental technicians were found and interviewed.

They clearly remembered the "strange people" and estimated the boy's age at twelve or thirteen.

Agent Berlanger screamed into the megaphone once more. "There's no reason for anyone to get hurt. Come out. No one is going to harm you."

There was no response from the house. Special Agent Berlanger gave some hand signals and agents began to draw closer.

"This is your last chance. Come out!"

Berlanger gave the signal.

The agents stormed the house. They crashed through the windows, and scanned the interior with their assault rifles. Other agents broke in the door and entered with their weapons sweeping left and right. After a few seconds, they stepped back out through the doorway, rifles lowered.

"No one here," one of them yelled.

"Someone shut up that dog," bellowed Berlanger.

Berlanger and Hightower entered the one room house. It appeared empty and unlived in. "Now what?" asked Berlanger rhetorically.

"Sir," one of the agents interrupted. "You've got to come see this."

They went to the small shed at the side of the house. An agent pushed the small door open carefully with the butt of his rifle. Special Agent Mark Berlanger got on his knees to look inside.

Cowered in a corner, alternately barking and snarling, unkempt, dirty, fingernails thick and sharp, but most glaring of all, those teeth. Spikes, sharpened to a fine point and the long canines that flashed their terrifying warning. Death here!

THE GAME IS ON

5

Father, I remember that night as clearly as the night I was married. Or the night Jenny was born. Or the night I sat right here with Father Romero and gave up the bottle.

It was the night of April 7, my anniversary, and I was driving to my ex-wife's house. Yeah, Jane finally divorced me. Good Lord, I gave her no choice, but we still stayed in touch, and there was the unspoken understanding, if I ever got my act completely together, then, maybe.

Professionally, I had fought my way back from drunken oblivion with stories from the underbelly of society. Stories about drunks, the homeless, prostitutes, nothing earth shaking, but the work was unique. I was developing a small readership and I was making a living, Father.

The big break came with the Jaws murders. Two of the victims, a prostitute and a homeless man, were killed on my beat. Murders in South Central were common enough. The death of a prostitute or homeless person never commanded much interest. It was the horrific and bizarre nature of the Jaws murders that made them news.

What is there to say? I was in the right place at the right time. I knew the prostitute and Lord I knew the life of the homeless. That gave me the edge over every other reporter. My victims were real people. I wrote about their lives and their lifestyles. My readers were presented with the stark reality of the killings, not just the gory details. With each story my popularity grew.

The Paper's circulation almost tripled, primarily because of me. My salary was doubled, then doubled again when the Paper learned, through a rumor I started, that the Times was courting me. Free enterprise, Father, you gotta love it.

After Jaws was captured, I continued with the personal approach I had become known for. I studied the killer's background, did research on the effects of extreme deprivation and abuse, and tried to climb into Jaws' head. Then I wrote my stories from that perspective.

He was born and raised in Hell. Surprising, or maybe not surprising, you would know better than me, Father, the most loathsome killer in recent history, was himself a most unfortunate victim.

For three months, the Jaws trial was the biggest media circus since O.J. I was given court priority covering the trial, a real coup.

The extreme circumstances surrounding that poor man didn't diminish even slightly the thirst for his blood. We were getting close to the elections. The politicians were all anxious to polish up their crime fighting credentials. They were in a hanging mood.

Janet Bultaco tried the case herself. They called her "Bulldog" and "Madam Prosecutor" when she tried a case and I could see why. She was relentless.

The big issue at trial was not if Jaws was guilty. There were trainloads of evidence against him. The point of contention was if he was competent to stand trial.

"Madam Prosecutor" dispensed with that issue quickly. The experts on both sides cancelled each other out. Bultaco cast doubt on the insanity plea. The killer could easily be faking to avoid the needle. His barking routine was an insult to our intelligence. Such heinous crimes had to be punished. The victims were crying out from their graves.

That line sent Jaws to his death, Father. "The victims are crying out from their graves. Please, for the love of God, give us justice." Talk about drama!

Funny, Father, I always thought that doubt went to the side of the defendant. I stand corrected. The trial was a slam-dunk and Jaws sat in a cell on death row, snarling at everyone who passed by.

I had just left the District Attorney's office where I interviewed Janet Bultaco on the quickly approaching execution. I was big time, could get any interview, just like Larry King. And with the elections coming up, can you believe it, her office actually called me!

I was on my way home in my new red Porsche. Sports cars should always be red. Don't you agree, Father? It was raining, the first time for the Porsche. I remember watching the drops bead up and run down its smooth sleek lines, such a beautiful machine, when my cell rang.

I was sure it was Christine calling. I didn't give the number to many people, not even to Jane or Jenny. Christine and the Paper were essentially it. Christine knew it was my anniversary, and I always spent the night with Jane, so I assumed she wanted to make plans for another day.

"Wycheck!" I always answered that way. It made me seem businesslike and busy.

"On your way home to the ex wifey, WIH..A..CHEE..YOOK..HUH?"

I had never heard my name said in such a weird combination of sounds, screeches, and changes of pitch and tone. It was painful to listen to and I pushed the cell away from my ear.

That pronunciation could not have been an accident, and was by no means easily accomplished. I have since tried many times to duplicate those sounds and have never done it successfully.

"Who is this?" I asked. *And how did you get this number?* That was the real question of the moment.

"Always the good reporter. Ask your questions. But, you are asking the wrong question."

The voice on the other end was electronically distorted, and my guess was, by expensive equipment. Though disguised, the voice did not conceal a condescending tone.

I was irritated though curious. "And what question should I ask?"

"Don't ask who. You will never learn who. But what, where, when, and why, those you might have a chance with."

It sounded like a male, but even that could have been altered. I thought of the caller as the "Voice." I was more curious.

"Very fine coverage of Jaws," the Voice continued. "You are the only one who tried to understand him."

"Thank you," I said. At the moment I was more interested in the caller.

"Tell me, Frankie, Jaws was presented as a serial killer, wasn't he?"

"Technically yes, but I wouldn't classify him as such."

"So, you are an expert on serial killers. Excellent! Tell me then, who was the most successful serial killer?"

I actually knew very little about serial killers. I had done a small amount of research as background for the Jaws articles. Not much was needed though. I taxed my brain to answer the Voice's question. "Bundy,

DeSalvo, John Wayne Gacy, that guy in Russia?"

"Chicatilo! Fifty-two plus, a good guess, but wrong. You are thinking in the box Frankie," chided the Voice. "It's a trick question though the answer should be obvious."

"Ok. I give up." I was duly annoyed.

"You will never know! The successful killers never get discovered or caught. We never know who they are. I can tell you for a fact, there are men out there who have killed hundreds."

"And how do you know that?" I was really getting aggravated.

"Because WIH..A..CHEE..YOOK..HUH, I am such a man!"

The answer surprised me. Was it possible? Unlikely, but what if it was? It seemed far-fetched. Still, if a man like that were to call a reporter, I would be a logical choice.

The Porsche had nearly driven me to my old home. I pulled over to the side of the road and parked. The Voice had me hooked pretty good at this point. "Are you saying that you are a serial killer?"

"One to be most feared. But I'm not a killer, technically yes, however, I take no joy in it. The deaths are a necessity. If you want to be accurate you could call me a thief, though I am entitled to what I take."

"A thief? And what do you steal?"

"People, Frankie, people. Mostly women. Actually, almost exclusively women."

"And you have killed, hundreds?"

"Yes, of course. I can't let them go now, can I?"

"And you, you have done this all in secret, unknown, and successful, as you say."

"Yes."

"Then, why, enlighten me, why are you telling me all of this?"

"Very good, Frankie. A good question at last, I will answer all of your questions in good time. For now, let me just say that I have entered a new phase.

They're going to execute Jaws soon." The Voice was changing the subject. I didn't try to stop it. "What do you think about that, Frankie?"

"I don't know. He did kill those people and in a most horrible way."

"He lived locked up by his parents. He was abused every day. They beat him and treated him like a dog, worse than a dog. When he finally escaped them, the system got him. He attacked those people and bit them to death. Horribly, yes, but how could he be responsible? He acted out of rage, like the animal he was made into."

"Yes, yes, but…"

"He filed his teeth sharp with rocks! He ate genitals! They had to put a muzzle on him! Yet, they proved him sane and competent to stand trial. Why was that do you think, Frankie?"

I didn't want to answer. I already had my opinions. "Tell me," I said.

"To find him guilty and to kill him. Why? For profit, Frankie! For their fame, for their careers, for their pocketbooks; they used his life to pay for all that."

I didn't want to agree with him so I didn't respond. There was a pause. What was the Voice thinking, I wondered?

"Tell me, Frankie, who is more to be feared? The wild man, like your Jaws, who slaughters a few viciously, unpredictably, randomly, or the anonymous man who kills many but does so quietly?

He chooses his victims and makes his plans, carefully and deliberately. Then he executes the plan and takes his prey with nothing left to chance.

Who is more to be feared?"

"Well, uhhh…"

"Once chosen, the prey is doomed, nothing can be done to prevent it. If a man wrongs him, he says nothing, then steals the man's wife one night.

Who is more to be feared, Frankie?"

"I don't know. They are both killers. Are you like that?"

"Yes, I am."

"I see." I was almost positive that the Voice was a fraud. "And what do you want of me?" I played along but I was really trying to figure out who the Voice was.

"Excellent question. I wish to play a game, and you are part of it, but only if you choose to be. Would you like to know more?"

"Yes," I said impatiently. *Who are you really?*

"I sense your skepticism. But then, a good reporter does have to follow his leads. Come to the Bluebird Motel, room sixteen, one week from today at noon. You know the place. Been there recently, haven't you?"

I suddenly froze. Sure, I'd been to the Bluebird, but no one could have known that, or so I thought.

About a month before, Christine and I had played out a sexual fantasy. She dressed as a hooker and I picked her up like a john. I could remember her that night. She was magnificent in her long shaggy blonde wig, tight sweater, short leather skirt, black stockings and garters and those six-inch stiletto heels. Man!

Christine was the queen of the street when I picked her up in the Porsche. We went to the Bluebird, the hookers' motel. We stayed in room sixteen, and made love like animals, some of the best we ever had.

How could the Voice have known about that?

My mind raced. Just maybe, the Voice was as advertised and I really was talking to a calculating killer. The prospect frightened me. I remembered, "Who is more to be feared?" and "I wish to play a game, and you are part of it." I sat in awkward silence.

"What's the matter, Frankie? Are you worried? You have nothing to fear from me. I'm strictly a ladies man."

The Voice had read the fear in my mind. "That's comforting," I said. I was happy to get anything out of my mouth.

"Your participation in my game isn't mandatory. There is always another day. And always another reporter who will play."

"If you're legit, I'll play," I shot back with bravado usually only exhibited when loaded.

"Fine. Enjoy your dinner with your ex-wifey. The cake is a nice touch."

I froze again.

"Speak to no one. Remember, I'll be watching you."

I didn't have time to respond. The Voice hung up. I was left with a head full of question marks.

6

I sat in the Porsche reviewing the call from the Voice, then finally decided what I needed to do most was to get myself in order. The Voice could wait. I considered doing a small line, then decided against it. To spend an evening with Jane, I would be better off on the down slope.

Jane was my high school sweetheart. Even in those days, there was no doubt that she would be the woman in my life. We were two kids, in love, doing stupid things and acting crazy. Teenagers, what else need be said? We got married and Jane grew up. I never did.

Jane was the best part of me then, and always will be. She was supportive when I took a notion to be a writer and spent my early years failing at the attempt. There was never a negative word from her, and I will never forget that. Jane stayed at my side as I started my slow descent into the bottle. She remained loyal when I took a two-year sabbatical from the human race, and was there for me when I finally returned.

Playing Frank Wycheck's wife, Father, was an impossible role. Jane did it with dignity, kindness, and love. I often wondered why. For the life of me, I still can't figure it out. Perhaps, she did it for Jenny. Maybe in those dark days Jane sacrificed herself so that Jenny could still have a father.

But, eventually I made it impossible and she did what she had to do. It's been up to me to straighten out ever since.

I drove to the house and couldn't stop thinking about the Voice though I had vowed to do otherwise. Jane was still getting ready. It would be another twenty minutes; the wait nearly drove me crazy. God, I wanted a hit.

We had dinner at Chasson's. A corsage was waiting for Jane as we entered. I had preordered Chateaubriand, and a bottle of fine Cabernet recommended by the house. Dinner was as good as Sam Poline, the Paper's food editor, had promised me it would be. I drank one glass of wine even though I knew it pained Jane to see me do so.

For dessert we had a rum cake baked especially for us by Chasson's. The chocolate icing on top read, "I Still Love You."

When the cake arrived, a shiver ran through me. The comment about it had been the Voice's last little parting shot. The Voice, whoever he was, whatever he was, had been watching me carefully, and for some time. I couldn't stop thinking about it.

We sat over our coffees silently. There was so much to be said and, yet, I had nothing to say. Frank Wycheck was still a work in progress and far from worthy of another chance.

And, my mind, as it often was, was elsewhere.

7

He called himself Simon though that was not his given name. He needed nothing given to him; he would take what he wanted. The single name Simon suited him well enough. No further identification was needed. He was one of a kind.

The "Freezer" was a six-foot by six-foot special purpose room. Simon walked in to check if the carcass was fully frozen. He knew it was, having performed the chore hundreds of times, but his personality dictated that he check anyway. The carcass was hoisted over his shoulder. *One hundred forty five pounds,* he estimated, *a substantial one.* Simon had no difficulty handling it.

The Jaws case was in his mind, as it always was. *A dirty game they played there.* Simon followed the coverage closely, of the wild man who came down from the woods to gnaw city people to death. The whole world was mesmerized. Unlike the others, Simon viewed it from a different perspective.

For months, he observed his future adversaries gloating. *They bask in fame and fortune derived from victory over a lesser opponent. Their smug faces are pasted on magazine covers. Their pompous personalities ooze constantly from television screens.*

Their fortunes are about to change. The Grand Game is yet to be played.

Simon carried the frozen carcass to the room called "Processing." He entered and turned on the dim red light. The carcass rode easily on his shoulder, requiring little of his effort. Simon had always been strong.

Pausing at the scale, he weighed himself and the carcass. Three hundred thirty four and a half pounds less his one hundred and eighty six made the carcass one forty eight and a half. *Three and a half pounds off, 2.4% error, acceptable, but I should do better.*

The carcass was placed on the main cutting table. A wry smirk dominated Simon's face as he positioned it in front of the band saw. The processing room had been built to exacting standards and was crammed full of equipment. Simon took a moment to admire his design. "You can get anything for money, no questions asked," he murmured as he began to saw the limbs.

The carcass was frozen to allow nice clean cuts and to avoid the messy gush of blood and other fluids. *One learns with time and experience.* Simon worked quickly, expertly, first cutting off the main limbs, and then cutting those into smaller more manageable pieces.

He threw the carcass around angrily, recalling the many newspaper articles. That media given name, Jaws, irritated him doubly. His mind replayed visions of the trial's news footage. *They made a circus clown out of you.* An angry scowl erased the earlier smile. His mood, which had drifted toward anger, suddenly erupted in rage. Violently, Simon forced the last few chunks through the saw until the carcass was completely dismembered.

Each piece, no larger than a shoebox, was taken to the grinder, a heavy-duty piece of machinery that could crush rocks into dust instantly. One by one the cold hunks were tossed in.

Zodiac is the only Master of the Game. He was the last of my kind to precede me. Now, I too will play the Grand Game. I too will be a Master. I will take my place next to Zodiac. I shall rise above Zodiac!

Zodiac chose his victims at random and had no use for them. I choose more discriminatingly. Zodiac gave the opponent eight tries. I will go one better. We shall play nine, my FBI friends. Nine innings – like baseball.

The carcass was completely ground to frozen sand that spit out the back of the grinder and was collected in a large stainless steel pot. Simon carefully carried the pot to the sink and washed the contents down the drain.

Dust from the cutting and grinding was everywhere. Much of it had melted, messy but unavoidable. Simon hosed down the equipment, the walls and floor. All of the liquid funneled into a large drain in the middle of the floor.

Processing had to be left spotless, as it had been when Simon entered. He was a fastidious man, compulsively so, compulsive as he was in all things. It was boring, tedious work, but there could be no employees or accomplices. *Rule Number Five, Trust No One.*

Despite her size, Simon had liked Diana very much. Were it not for the Game, he would have kept her longer. Simon hated wasting prey. It was simply a question of logistics. The Castle had limited space and rooms were required for the Grand Game's future guests.

Every minute detail of the future endeavor was planned, as one does in chess, as Simon did in all things. Over and over, the permutations, the possibilities turned in his mind. Constantly, relentlessly, it never stopped.

Every game follows its own course, every one determined by circumstance and subject to the actions of the opponent. With each move the planning begins anew, the strategy modified, the tactics changed.

Diane Fletcher was an eighteen year old high school senior. She vanished on a Thursday afternoon. Her parents reported her missing to the Fullerton Police Department the following day.

Simon watched the last trickle of water and Diane Fletcher flow down the drain. He rinsed the stainless steel equipment one last time, then dried it to a shiny new. *Goodbye my dear; goodbye my lovely Diana.*

Diane Fletcher had disappeared without a trace. Now, five months and fourteen days later, every last trace of her disappeared. That was how it ended for all of Simon's "guests." R*ule Number Two, Leave No Bodies.*

The Rules, the sacred doctrine, that had protected him a lifetime from detection and penalty would have to be set aside. To date, Simon had played his little games by the hundreds, games like Diane Fletcher, in the safest of all camouflaged obscurities, absolute anonymity.

The Grand Game will not tolerate such timidity. Simon would have to be courageous and outrageously bold. The Game required that he risk and put up his life as stakes.

But the opponent too would have to ante up.

They will all pay that profited most from their counterfeit victories. They will become players in my game and they will pay.

There is always another day. And tomorrow, we commence our play.

THE EARLY INNINGS

A FEW SMALL PLAYS

8

In our business you throw away the clock. There is no such thing as tomorrow or later. No tolerance for half commitment, lack of effort or a thing undone. Forget nights, weekends and vacations. You must give everything.
Procrastination costs lives.

- Into the Mind of a Killer, John Hightower

Special Agent Mark Berlanger drove to the office in his new white Jeep Grand Cherokee. A far cry from the old Toyota, it was unbelievable to him that he had put up with that piece of junk for so long. Berlanger held the steering wheel loosely, caressing it lovingly with his fingers. He adjusted the mirrors and seats and reset the controls on the dash constantly.

Mark Berlanger rode through traffic relaxed. He was not hurried, not like the old days, when the Jaws case was going badly. Berlanger was comfortable in his new bucket seats. He looked down on the road from the Cherokee's new height as he now looked at life from his new level. He was no longer a grunt, a mere serf of the almighty clock. After the successful Jaws capture, he was given a promotion, and with it came several pay grades increase in income.

The stereo surrounded Berlanger in glorious sound from six strategically placed speakers. The morning talk shows were still captivated by Jaws, only now the vitriol was replaced by the sweet sound of praise. The Bureau had triumphed. He had triumphed. Jaws had been captured and tried. The listening had become easy.

Agent Berlanger walked up the steps to the Federal Building. There was a different feel to the place now. "Hello, Mr. Berlanger," the guard said to him politely, as he passed by the station. The elevator was filled with people who looked at him with respect. He was ten minutes late, his new habit, and a fitting time for a man of his stature to arrive.

Pausing slightly at the Receptionist's station, Mark Berlanger exchanged discreet knowing glances with Cindy. He would see Cindy after work. They met two, sometimes three, times a week, most often Tuesdays and Thursdays. A man at his level and prominence should have an outside interest.

Mark Berlanger stepped into his new office. Undeniably a very small room, actually more an alcove, but he was no longer on the floor with the peons. Berlanger sat down behind the small metal desk to notice a single sheet of paper, something out of place. Mark Berlanger always left his desk clean and tidy before leaving.

He picked up the interloping piece of paper, a fax.

MY DEAR FURBANGER,

SUCH CELEBRATION AND FOR WHAT CAUSE?
NOT FOR THE CAPTURE OF THAT POOR DEVIL JAWS.

MINOR LEAGUE BALL YOU PLAY AT BEST.
THE MAJORS WILL BE A BETTER TEST.

NINE INNINGS WE SHALL PLAY.
INNING ONE, WHERE IS MARY SPLITORF TODAY?

S.

"Hardy!" Berlanger shouted as he stormed out of his office. "What kind of joke is this?"

"It's not a joke, sir. We received it this morning. I thought you should be the first to see it."

"Good thinking, Hardy."

Phil Hardy was a good man. Just nine months out of the Academy and he already had a good appreciation for protocol. Hardy was eager to learn, could take orders, followed procedures, and he knew the regulations, to the letter.

Hardy was a small man, appearing smaller even than his five feet six inches and he was well shy of a hundred forty pounds. That lack of stature cost him on Academy training fields but he overcame the handicap with the determination of a terrier. He was a crack shot, noting that a well-placed bullet would even out a lot of weight disparity. Hardy was bright and with a near photographic memory, had graduated at the top of his class.

Mark Berlanger liked Hardy. Hardy called him sir from day one. Hardy too would rise. "Have you checked this out, Phil?"

"The Riverside Police have a Missing Persons Report on a Mary Splitorf, a college student at USC. She was seen leaving with another student. They were described as being romantically inclined. Neither of them showed up again."

"So she's a runaway?"

"That's what Riverside thinks. They're probably in Vegas, by now, getting married."

"Fine," said Agent Berlanger as he started to crumple the fax.

"Sir!" reminded Hardy.

"Yes, of course, procedure." Berlanger handed the document to Agent Hardy. "Start a file."

9

I registered at the Bluebird Motel as the Voice had instructed me and parked the Porsche in front of room sixteen. I didn't want to leave it too far away. In that neighborhood, you never knew what you might find missing, maybe even the whole damn car.

Sixteen was a downstairs room near the back, convenient yet discretely out of street view. It was one of the better rooms the Bluebird could offer. Not particularly clean or well kept, that was standard for motels in that part of town, but it had a chair that was still standing and most important a queen size bed that I knew was quite serviceable.

I opened the drapes so that I could keep an eye on the Porsche, then sat down in the chair to wait. I checked the Rolex; four minutes to three, I was early. That was my practice, to be early, to insure that I didn't miss a source that may have gotten cold feet and changed his mind. But not too early, I never wanted to seem too eager. I often had to pay my sources. There was no sense encouraging them to get greedy.

I wondered if the Voice would show up. In my business you get many false leads and often follow them to hell and back. That, unfortunately, is part of the job. The time passed; the first minutes were always critical. I scanned the Rolex, twelve past three. The next time I checked, it had become eighteen past. I began to have my doubts.

I rarely waited that long for a blind lead, but the Voice was different. He had taken too much trouble, done too much research and knew too much about me for an idle prank. I had to wait it out. There was nothing else on my schedule anyway.

I did a small line to help in the waiting. Almost immediately, I was more relaxed, the chair became more comfortable, the Porsche a little brighter red. I recalled my last visit to room sixteen. Just the thought of that day made me horny. *If this turns out to be a no show, I'm going directly to Christine's.* I was feeling good, powerful.

I checked the time again. It was three thirty five. *Fuck the Voice! He had his chance!* I decided to leave. *Next stop, Christine's.*

I was about to get up as the door flew open with a loud crash. There in the bright daylight, blocking my exit stood an Amazon. She was statuesque in the truest sense of the word. My jaw dropped as I took all of her in. The woman had to be at least six feet, though in her bulky red platform heels she stood closer to six foot six. I could tell because her head nearly touched the top of the door jam.

Now this was a whore, Father! She wore a short red plastic skirt with a bright yellow top. Both had to be two or three sizes too small. The skirt revealed all of her long legs while her ample breasts hung well out of the top.

I was stunned for the moment and simply gawked at her in the doorway. Not your everyday whore, this was a giant make-believe doll, Big Stacked Call Girl Barbi. I stared without speaking. *Strange though,* I thought at the time, I didn't know her but she seemed familiar. I attributed it to the Cocaine.

The whore remained blocking the doorway, then spread her legs slightly as she tugged on her short skirt exposing the little bit of thigh that was still covered.

"Hello, Sugar," she said in a deep sensual voice. It was the only voice that could possibly have gone with that body. The whole package was quite stimulating.

I was about ten feet away and could smell the heavy scent of her cheap perfume. High volume whores rarely take the time to shower between tricks. "French baths" they're called, they splash on the perfume to cover the odor of the sweat; the stronger the perfume the busier the whore. This one looked and smelled of Olympic caliber.

Now I'm no prude, Father. Raunchy turned me on. Under other circumstances, I would have bought the deluxe package from the whore. However, that was not the reason I came.

"I'm sorry," I said. "There must be some mistake." It was best to simply leave, take my losses and call it a day.

I moved toward the doorway to make my exit. The whore put her right hand in my chest. I hesitated then tried to push my way through. She shoved me backward like she was tossing a shot put, and I was sent sprawling across the room, not stopping until I had fallen over onto the bed. She was an Amazon all right, stronger.

"What's the matter Sugar? Don't like me as much as the last whore you brought here? Christina?"

I was angered by that characterization of Christine then realized I should have been more concerned about the whore.

"There is no mistake, WIH..A..CHEE..YOOK..HUH."

It was him, the Voice! Or was it her, this creature in the doorway? Worried, my hand dug into my coat pocket and wrapped itself around the Baretta. I carried a Baretta, James Bond's gun, for such situations. There was always danger on my beat.

"We have an appointment. Don't you remember?" continued the whore. She tugged again at her skirt. "Do you like my outfit?"

"Yes, I suppose so," I said. "Are you? I mean, are you?" I felt incredibly stupid.

"Why yes, of course, Frankie. Under the circumstances, certainly, you don't expect me to reveal myself to you, do you?"

"No, I suppose not."

"But tell me, Frankie, you don't mind me calling you Frankie, do you?"

Frankie, only Christine called me Frankie. Could the Voice have known that too? "Certainly," I said. Anything was better than that "Whaceekkoohh" thing, though it did serve to identify the whore as the Voice.

"Very good," she continued. "Then tell me, Frankie, how do you like my outfit? I call it my Venus outfit."

"Excellent disguise," I said. I was truly impressed. "Tell me, are you, I mean are you…"

Venus sat down in the chair and crossed her legs. "A woman?" she finished for me. "Well tell me, Frankie, how many women serial killers do you know of?"

"None. Serial killers are invariably white males."

"Then make your assumptions."

Venus uncrossed her legs slowly and suggestively and again tugged at her red skirt. She laughed when my attention was drawn to her crotch. I felt incredibly embarrassed. "Yes, well then, where shall we start, I have many questions…" I was stammering and I could swear she, he was enjoying it.

"All in due course, Frankie. First things first. Would you mind standing up?"

I complied. Venus got up and walked over to me. Now, I'm six feet, one eighty, not a small man, but in her huge platform heels Venus towered over me. I felt threatened as she moved closer, more so when she reached down and began to feel my body. Actually, I was being frisked and quite efficiently too.

Venus continued the search, eventually finding my recorder and the Baretta. She took them both off me. "This you can have, and anything else you like to keep notes," she said, turning on the recorder and handing it back to me.

The gun was thrown into the bathroom. "That you may not have. And if I catch you with another weapon, our relationship together will have ended and you might get hurt. Do you understand?"

I nodded and theorized what was meant by "relationship." I already understood the hurt part.

"Those are some of the rules of our little game," Venus went on. "If you decide to play, you may ask me any questions you like and I will answer. I will answer, but I will not necessarily tell the truth. That is for you to find out. I don't plan on giving you any information that can lead to my capture."

"I see. And to what purpose is this game?"

"Why that should be obvious, Frankie. I hope you didn't think I was interested in you for sex.

You are a writer and did such wonderful work on Jaws, did your homework, not the usual drivel. In fact, you were the one who first called him Jaws, weren't you?"

I nodded, impressed. I was not the only one that did homework. Obviously, my *friend* here did too. Not many people knew and fewer remembered that I had tagged the vicious killer with the name Jaws. They all ran with it, it was on every tongue, headlined every paper, but it started with me.

"An excellent name Frankie. I'm sure it helped sell a lot of papers. It also helped get him executed, don't you think?"

"I wouldn't think so. That was probably inevitable."

"An interesting speculation, though I'm sure your sensational coverage didn't hurt. But, enough of that, I'm in need of a good name also. Perhaps you will give me one."

"Perhaps. And perhaps you'll tell me why we are here."

The whore smiled. "Excellent, Frankie!" She waved her arms like a magician, though I wasn't sure why. "Tell me, who was the most successful serial killer?"

I answered snidely. "We already did that, and I'm not here fishing for compliments."

Venus laughed and ignored my sarcasm. "Indeed," she went on, "the ones we don't know about. But of the ones we do, those who choose not to remain anonymous, the ones who play the Game, Frankie, which of those?"

"Hell, I don't know."

"Tsk, tsk, such a lack of patience." She shook her finger at me like an old schoolmarm. "Well certainly, he would have to be one that got away. Isn't that right?"

"I suppose."

"Jack the Ripper comes immediately to mind, doesn't he? He has passed the test of time, that's for sure. But, I think not, Frankie. It was too easy for him. Law enforcement was rather crude in those days. Why they didn't even have fingerprints, let alone DNA.

No, my choice is Zodiac, Frankie. You know about Zodiac, everything I'm sure, great expert on serial killers."

I have to tell you Father, I was more than a little annoyed. He looked like the whore of the ages, but he was condescending and lecturing me like a college professor. And, I had had it with school decades ago. But, I didn't stop him either.

"Yeah, I remember him," I said and let Venus ramble on.

"On October 30, 1966, Cheri Jo Bates, an eighteen-year-old freshman at Riverside Community College, drove her green Volkswagon to the school library. Four hours later, she was found dead in the parking lot. Her throat had been slashed almost completely through.

Six months later, the local police, the Riverside Press Enterprise, and Joseph Bates, Cheri's father, received notes from the killer.

BATES HAD TO DIE
THERE WILL BE MORE
Z

There was real flair in that note, wouldn't you say, Frankie? Succinct, to the point, but also ominous. Brilliant!

February 27, 1969, Darlene Ferrin and Michael Mageau were shot while on a date, parked at the Blue Rock Springs Golf Course. Darlene died from the gunshot wounds.

The following morning, the Vallejo Police Department received an anonymous call claiming credit for the crime. The caller gave details only the killer would know. 'I also killed those kids last year,' he said before politely saying 'goodbye' and hanging up.

Very nice! Very nice, indeed!

The killer was referring to Betty Lou Jensen and David Faraday who had been shot and killed in their vehicle. All four victims were shot with the same gun.

September 27, 1969, Cecelia Shepard and Bryan Hartwell were attacked and stabbed by an unknown assailant wearing a black executioner's hood.

Now that's a little hokey for my taste, Frankie, but it proved effective with the public.

Cecelia died from the twenty-four stab wounds. Bryan survived, describing the killer as wearing a strange symbol on his chest. The symbol was later identified as a Zodiac.

He called himself Zodiac. An excellent name, wouldn't you agree, Frankie? You simply must come up with one like that for me.

Twenty-one taunting letters including details to the crimes, diagrams, and intricate codes were sent to the police and newspapers. There seemed a mathematical relationship to the attacks, although the clues provided by Zodiac have never been totally deciphered.

For eight years, he terrorized California, continuing his murderous spree, picking victims apparently at random, with no common modus operandi, and without apparent motive.

No motive that they could find, Frankie. There is always motive.

Zodiac was associated with up to forty-nine killings, though he kept his own score. On January 30, 1974, a San Francisco newspaper published the final note.

ME-37; SFPD-0

Thirty-seven is a respectable total, if not spectacular. I see no reason to doubt the accounting.

The authorities assumed the Zodiac was a maniac, driven by a wild bloodlust. The letters and notes were used to satisfy an insane obsession for publicity. They tried to figure him out, understand him. FBI profilers forced Zodiac into their clumsy, preconceived serial-killer constructs. The fools were, of course, wrong.

The deaths, the victims, were necessary though inconsequential. The murders were not a bloodfest; they were most notable for their utter lack of passion."

"Lack of passion?" I interrupted. "How can you say that? Wasn't that one girl stabbed twenty four times?"

"Ah yes, Frankie, that was Zodiac's genius. Illusion can create powerful realities. Nothing does it like the free flow of blood. An insane, blood thirsty killer sparks terror and creates good copy.

Illusion, Frankie, all illusion! The real gruesome madmen are always caught.

No, the deaths were merely Zodiac's ante in the Game. The publicity was needed to raise the stakes. The taunting added interest.

Zodiac was a player.

The Game, the most primeval of all games - glory to the winner, death and dishonor for the losers.

Zodiac was never captured. To this day, he remains the only Master of the Game.

Until now, Frankie. Until me!"

"And you want me to write about you?"

"Finally! You will chronicle everything. That is your part in my game. Want to play?" Venus did not wait for me to answer. "Don't decide now. But, these are the rules if you decide to play.

You will keep all of our meetings to yourself. You will keep all materials and information to yourself. If anything leaks, if you contact the authorities at any time, I will know, it ends, and you will be punished.

You will devote your full time to our effort. You will quit your job and write nothing else. You will have to give me your word, and if you do, you had best keep it. Do you understand, Frankie?"

"Yes, of course..." Venus cut me off by putting a finger over my lips.

"I know Sugar, It's a lot to ask without you knowing if I'm for real." She reached into her top and pulled out a folded piece of paper. God, Venus seemed real. If the Voice was a female impersonator, he was the best I'd ever seen.

"What shall I call you?" I asked. It no longer seemed appropriate to think of *him* as the Voice and Venus was only a disguise.

"Call me Simon." *Simon!* He handed me the paper.

"What's this?" I asked as I unfolded the paper. There were approximately two-dozen names and addresses, all women.

"That is my bona fides. Do some homework, Frankie. Check it out."

When I looked up from the paper, I was alone.

10

I folded up the paper Simon had given me and put it in my pocket. There was too much nervous energy in me. I got in the Porsche and sped off to Christine's place, a twenty-minute drive, even speeding. I punched up her number on the cell and found her shopping at Nordstrom.

"Meet me at your place," I said without saying hello. "And, Christine, get ready for a first class ram job." I always talked that way to Christine. She loved it. This time I really meant to deliver on the promise. I was high on adrenaline and residual cocaine and had some first class horns on.

I knew Christine would drop her shopping bags and race home. One of the things I most loved about her was that she was always ready to play. When I arrived, Christine would be waiting, wearing something sexy, and eager for the best I could deliver.

I was driving much too fast, which I knew was a big mistake. I couldn't stop thinking about Simon and the list. The women on it were his "bona fides," his references. "Do some homework. Check it out," he told me. I was anxious to get started. I pulled the list out of my pocket and dialed information. I was fifteen minutes from Christine's.

The phone company got me the number for the first name on the list, long distance. I let them rip me off and dial it. I always did. The Paper paid for it anyway.

No answer, damn! The second name on the list was Virginia Roth. The phone company connected me. I was in luck. A woman answered.

"Hello," I said. "Is Virginia Roth home?"

The Porsche is not the quietist car in the world and my cell never had the best reception, but I could swear I heard the woman gasp.

"Who is this? Are you with the police?"

"No maam," I said. "My name is Frank Wycheck. I'm a reporter. May I speak to Virginia, please?"

"Very funny, whoever you are! Go to hell!"

"Wait maam! I assure you this is not a joke," I interrupted her. "If I may just speak to her."

"Virginia has been missing for over a year!" She shouted, then hung up.

Suddenly my desire for sex was completely lost. The call took me down like the iceberg did the Titanic. My mind was locked onto Simon and the list.

I was five minutes from Christine's.

I felt stupid for not having anticipated what to expect from the "references." What else would provide "bona fides" for a self proclaimed serial killer?

I sat silent while the Porsche sped on. There wasn't time for more calls. I was only a few minutes from Christine's.

Christine once told me that there were two things in life she loved more than anything. One was sex. The other we never got to. Christine was not the most understanding woman and non-performance was one thing she would positively not tolerate.

I had to get myself in order. I was coming down and my attention was focused elsewhere. Another dose was beyond my daily limit and I was well aware of the danger. But hell, I needed a boost.

I have always needed something, Father. The last few years I settled onto cocaine, getting by on a precarious balance, letting it satisfy my compulsion, but limiting it so that it didn't take over.

I was stepping over the line, but it didn't matter anyway. Christine would have a couple lines waiting for me. She liked to keep me loaded, said I wasn't any good to her straight. Christine was a woman who could never be satisfied and absolutely refused to be disappointed. I prepared a small line at a stoplight, and by the time the Porsche pulled up in front of Christine's building, I was Superman.

She met me at the door in a pale pink teddy, a cowboy hat and boots. That was the best thing about Christine. She took our lovemaking so damn seriously. I stood in the doorway and stared at her for a moment. The comparison with Venus inevitably flashed into my mind.

Christine was a doll, lovely, willing, sexy but still classy, the anti Venus. I had no problem at all getting into the swing of things.

Three hours later, I left for home. I was anxious to do my homework. Christine was on the bed, the way I liked to see her, wearing a big smile.

11

Recording B-3

"Rule Number Two   Leave No Bodies

No body, no crime.

Do you remember Jimmy Hoffa, Frankie?"

"Yes, of course."

"A very high profile guy, wouldn't you say? He disappeared one night. Made all the papers for months everyone knew he was murdered. No body, no crime, no case was ever filed. Compared to Hoffa, a simple bitch missing is a small matter."

I spent the next three days checking out the list. My first call was to Virginia Roth's mother. I apologized for my previous ignorance, and without offering her too much hope, explained that I was working on a lead that could develop some information about her daughter.

She told me that Virginia went to school one morning and never returned. She was a high school junior, blonde, blue eyed, and a cheerleader. Mrs. Roth faxed me several pictures of Virginia, including the most recent one in her cheerleader outfit.

Virginia was lovely. Wholesome and still innocent looking, she appeared to be the All-American girl. Based on the few inquiries I made, there was no reason to change that perception. Virginia Roth was described as being sensible and quite well adjusted.

The local authorities had Mrs. Roth wait three days before they would investigate. Until then, Virginia was not considered missing. No body had turned up. Mrs. Roth was asked about boyfriends and if

Virginia could possibly have been pregnant. How was her relationship with her daughter? Did they have a fight?

Disappearance is not evidence of a crime and with more than eight thousand runaways each year, after a few weeks the Roth matter was dropped.

I was able to contact another seventeen of the twenty-four "references." The story was similar for all of them. Missing daughters, missing wives, girlfriends, single women, white, black, Asian, Hispanic, tall, short, slender, mildly chubby, teens, twenties, thirties, one forty, and all of them disappeared without a trace.

In all cases, the investigations were shelved. It was understandable since each disappearance was an isolated incident and law enforcement is always overworked. Nothing tied the cases together. Nothing except the piece of paper Simon had given me. With all the disappearances considered as a group, the conclusion was horrifying.

Bona fides accepted, Simon. Now what?

12

> We are zealous in our search for evidence, always seeking additional clues with which to view the killer. It is a conflicted effort, since the information is usually bought with lives.
>
> - Into the Mind of a Killer, John Hightower

They said in the Bureau, that when God made Kevin Fitzpatrick he named it Irishman. Kevin Fitzpatrick loved his dinners and a taste of the ale. He loved elegant desserts with delicate little ruffles of whipped cream. He loved the feel of a fine smoke in his mouth and a rich roasted coffee to relax with.

Kevin Fitzpatrick loved his position of prominence in the FBI and the power that came with it. He loved being arbitrary, curt, and making his staff grovel.

Kevin Fitzpatrick divorced his wife and married his secretary. It made him feel young and strong and virile.

He was a round-faced man with a body to match. Both were maintained through his healthy appetite and hearty appreciation of the ale. Fair of complexion with the exception of a pair of oversized, flushed cheeks and a cherry red nose, Fitzpatrick was topped off with a head of curly red hair, which fifty-four years had thinned considerably and interspersed with gray.

He was infamous for his raucous behavior at office parties and famous for his love of lunch. Kevin Fitzpatrick never missed one and usually let a subordinate take him. They competed fiercely to dote on him, and that, he loved most of all.

Lunch with the boss was highly prized among the staff. It was a good opportunity to pitch your stock, uninterrupted, and at a time when Fitz was always in a good mood.

For lunch, Fitz had salad, prime rib, baked potato with all the fixings, and two large glasses of stout ale. A healthy slice of strawberry cheesecake, dark coffee, and a big black cigar finished off a solid hour and a half of hard work. Berlanger had a Seafood Louis followed by a cup of coffee. He still had a lot to learn.

Mark Berlanger and Fitz returned from lunch heading toward their separate offices. The fortunes had been kind, yet Mark Berlanger remained mindful. *Had Jaws turned out differently, Fitz would have been the first to shovel the dirt on me.*

Agent Berlanger rounded the corner from the elevator proudly. Simply coming back from lunch with the boss, in full view of the bullpen, and being late to boot, added to his prestige.

He turned into his office to find Phil Hardy waiting for him. Hardy was holding a fax, which he immediately handed to Berlanger.

FEDERAL BUREAU OF INCOMPETENCE

I HAVE ONE, BUT YOU HAVE NOT YET LOST

INNING 2 – WHERE IS KATHLEEN HARPER?

S

"Another one?" asked Berlanger.

"Yes, sir."

"We ought to catch this obnoxious bastard just to kick his ass." Special Agent Berlanger snickered. "Anything to it?" he asked.

"Another Missing Person, a wife this time, twenty-six, last seen shopping at the Glendale Galleria. Her car was left at the mall. There were no signs of foul play."

"Have we heard anything?" asked Berlanger. His tone suggested that he was hoping for a no. Mark Berlanger did not believe in looking for trouble.

"The Glendale Police are handling it."

"Good."

"I think we should bounce the notes off Fitz though," said Hardy.

"Agreed," said Berlanger.

It was always good practice to cover one's ass. They turned toward Fitz's office. Francine was not at her desk and Fitz's door was closed. The two agents looked at each other.

"Dictation!" said Berlanger. "Just file it."

13

I waited for Simon to contact me again and played the tape of my meeting with Venus over and over. Simon wanted me to write a book. He was a careful man and a clever man. Why on earth would he take such a chance?

No guns, no leaks, no cops, those were basically the rules. I decided, if he was willing to take risks, so was I.

"You will devote your full time to our effort." I was prepared to do that, anxious actually.

I waited and organized my notes from the homework. The cell rang and I ran to pick it up. It was Christine. She was wondering where I had been for the last few days. Three days without for Christine, she was probably humping the furniture, or at least thinking about alternative playmates.

I explained that I was working on something big, that I hadn't spent five minutes on anything else. "I'll try and break away soon," I told her, hoping that would do, but knowing it wouldn't. Christine and I had an understanding, if either of us became dissatisfied, no hard feelings.

It was more Christine's understanding than mine. I was petrified of losing her. Christine was the most exciting woman I had ever met, and I was completely infatuated with her. "I'll be over in an hour," I finally said, afraid to say anything else.

The next morning, five days after meeting Simon, I listened to the tapes again and decided to transcribe them. I wanted everything to be in writing so that I could see it in front of me.

Father, I was never any good at waiting. CNN was cycling the same news for the fifth time. A hopelessly messy man, my notes and desk were in impeccable order. I was sick of surfing the internet too.

For some reason, nervous energy probably, I checked for messages on my cell. I seldom did that. Not many people had the number and the phone was almost always at my side. I punched up voice mail. One message, it was him!

HELLO WIH..A..CHEE..YOOK..HUH.

I wished Simon had some other way of identifying himself. He was using the Voice again. Who else would I think it was? I held the phone away from my ear till he was finished with my "name."

HAVE YOU DECIDED TO PLAY?
I THOUGHT YOU MIGHT.
YOUR FIRST INTERVIEW IS FRIDAY AT TEN AM.
THE CIVIC CENTER, THE BENCH IN FRONT OF THE COUNTY COURT HOUSE.
DON'T BE LATE.
REMEMBER THE RULES!

I played the message over and over while transcribing it. It was recorded at four p.m. and I realized that Simon had left the message during my afternooner with Christine. *He followed me!* Why was I surprised?

I had left the phone in the Porsche to avoid any interruptions. Other than those few hours, it was always with me. Simon could have called me anytime. He preferred to leave the message. He was sending me a message within the message. That I couldn't hide from him.

Simon had obviously been tailing me for some time. *How long,* I wondered? *How much does Simon know about me, and more important, is his purpose as advertised or is there something else?*

One thing was for sure. Simon knew a lot more about me than I knew about him.

14

Janet Bultaco woke up at five thirty a.m. as she had every workday for more than twenty years. It was a Tuesday like all other Tues days, but also a day like no other before it.

They called her "Madam Prosecutor" and "the Bulldog," titles she wore proudly. In her absence, they called her many other things. Those names she found inconsequential. What did it matter what the spineless people thought?

Janet Bultaco competed in a man's world and she was committed to the contest. Her sole ambition in life had been to rise in the bureaucracy, and she meant to win whatever the cost.

Bultaco was devoid of hobbies or leisurely pursuits. Nothing besides her career interested her. The office was Janet Bultaco's lair, the Courtroom her territory, and politics the hallowed ground. She went home only to sleep, shower and change clothes.

Janet Bultaco reached blindly into the drawer for a blouse. No choice was required; the blouses were all the same, white and long sleeved, and they were always worn buttoned at the neck. This day, she chose to leave the top button undone.

Her wardrobe was business conservative, drab and professional. Business suits were dark, fitted but never tight and hemlines were always modestly below the knee. Janet Bultaco's shoes lifted her exactly one inch off the ground.

An angular woman, she was quite slender, though not unpleasing to look at. Her hair was kept plain, lipstick slight, and no other make up. Her appearance did not concern her, other than it was professional - until recently. Janet Bultaco spent an extra few minutes in front of her mirror.

She entertained and was entertained only for direct gain. Her smiles were carefully dispensed, each measured against the benefit to be garnered. Wry smiles for the jury, a smirk for the judge, meaningful smiles for potential political benefactors, and full on smiles were reserved for the cameras. Last night, Janet Bultaco had fun and laughed harder than she could ever remember.

Her mother was dead, father estranged, and husband long divorced. She did not have friends, only workplace acquaintances. Janet Bultaco took no lovers. Men were simply not worth the effort. Aside from the production of offspring, which was never her intention, she saw sex as a completely valueless endeavor. Janet Bultaco now had cause to change that opinion.

Her life was exactly as she had crafted it. Bultaco had been completely alone and without outside diversion. She thought it was what she wanted. This Tuesday morning, Janet Bultaco considered she might have been wrong.

She glanced over to the bed, so many years her pristine chapel of solitude. Lying comfortably under the heavy blanket, face buried between two pillows, was John Hightower, a man she had admired for several decades, grown to like over a number of years, and fell in love with overnight.

Bultaco recalled the first time she met John, and how handsome she thought him. *We were so young then.* Tall and lean and dark, not that it mattered, she was already engaged to Jack Bultaco, a lead prosecutor and a good catch. *What an asshole Jack turned out to be!*

John Hightower was the star witness in her first case. A young FBI agent, even then his brilliance was clearly evident. *I made many mistakes that day, and John, in his testimony, helped cover them over. I thought it was so easy. How could I know then, that John Hightower was the best of them?*

Bultaco's gaze was fixed on the bed. John was still tall, lean and handsome, though now somewhat wrinkled and a good portion of his jet-black hair had turned a silvery gray. She smiled while making her final preparations to leave.

Their paths crossed every few years, careers intersecting on this case or that. Janet Bultaco sought him out as witness whenever possible, and they would go to lunch or dinner to discuss his testimony. For the case they said, when actually each looked forward to the other's company.

So much time wasted. Finally, during the Jaws case, John took a bold step forward. *He asked me to dinner – not business, to discuss testimony, or any other pretext.* It was a date.

He came to L.A. regularly after that, *to go sailing.* Janet Bultaco and John Hightower had become an item. *Last night, I did him one better. Didn't think I'd have the nerve.* Janet Bultaco asked John Hightower in. Never could she have dreamed it would come to this.

Ready to leave, Janet leaned over to kiss him on the cheek. He awoke with a start. John Hightower was a very light sleeper. The rich blue eyes opened and stared up at her.

"You're up mighty early," he said groggily. "It's still dark outside."

"After six, I'm late."

"To work already, Madam Prosecutor?"

"I know, first one in. But…I get to stay late." She gave him her best smile.

"I thought you're the boss now," he said yawning and rubbing his eyes.

"Actually, I've got the hardest boss in the world." Janet lifted up her middle finger jokingly. "She's a bulldog; won't let anything go. Besides, Mr. Big Shot, between cases with nothing to do, your reputation is well known. John Hightower doesn't eat, drink or sleep until he gets his man."

"But, I listen to music."

"Yeah, I heard that too. Beethoven solves the cases."

John Hightower was tempted to pull her down into the bed and convince her to spend the day with him. Janet Bultaco, a woman who he had known for so many years, but never really knew. Janet, who had stolen a heart he had comfortably locked away in loneliness. Were he younger, Janet would certainly be under him already. But it was too foolish, and foolishness was a right reserved only for the young.

"Gotta go!" Janet said with new urgency, remembering that she should already be on the freeway. "Don't get up. Stay and rest. You've earned it."

"Sure you don't want to rest with me, a little?"

"Can't."

Hightower made a sad face, which made her chuckle. "Then, how about I take you sailing Sunday?"

"Can't. Have to go in."

"Damn! That boss of yours is a bitch."

She leaned over, kissed him lightly on the cheek and whispered in his ear, "told you."

"But, I am taking you to lunch today, right?"

"Twelve noon. Don't be late or I'll have you arrested." They both grinned.

He stopped her from kissing him goodbye and leaving. "Didn't get a chance to tell you yesterday." The slightest look of concern appeared on her face. "I already talked to Dawson. I'm going to be moving back here permanently. Plan to spend the day looking for a place."

Janet Bultaco smiled. "I wouldn't be too hasty, Hightower. About getting a place, I mean. You look pretty at home right where you are."

15

I always called Cocaine by its correct name, sometimes Coke, affec tionate though still deferential. I studiously avoided familiar slang such as snort or blow. What kind of names are those anyway, stupid at best. Cocaine must be shown its proper respect. I was well aware of its power.

There was plenty of time to think before Friday, ten o'clock, and I decided to reduce my usage in order to keep my thinking straight. Simon was for real. The bona fides confirmed that to a certainty.

Up until Simon, the idea of writing a book was way back on the rear left burner for me. The earlier failures were still fresh in mind. That kind of embarrassing defeat does not leave you quickly or easily, Father.

I was lucky at the Paper. I had no illusions. Jaws was a random phenomenon and my success had to be considered the same. A great story fell into my lap and I capitalized on it. Familiarity with the gutter gave me some unique perspective and the public ate it up. That was a far cry from being a real writer.

Still, what greater stroke of luck than Simon could ever have presented itself? Here was a bona fide serial killer and he wanted me to be his biographer. *What fabulous material!* Hemingway I was not, but I could write well enough. A book was there for sure.

The more I thought about it, the more I liked the idea. And, the more I began to fear that Simon would change his mind. *Doubtful*, I comforted myself. *He has gone to too much trouble to pull out now.*

I got to the Civic Center at ten minutes to ten. I knew the bench that Simon specified; it was directly across from the courthouse steps. I used to sit on that bench often, for hours after the Jaws trial let out, organizing my notes and writing on my laptop as quickly as I could so as not to lose any ideas.

Did Simon watch me even then? Coincidence, or was this exact location picked for a purpose?

I approached the bench that was already occupied by a sleeping bum.

The irony of the Civic Center was something that always mystified me. The very symbol and seat of governmental authority was also the location for the largest congregation of vagrants and homeless in the city. They lived there in numbers, with their shopping carts and cardboard boxes, sleeping in their makeshift shelters, behind bushes, and on benches.

The high dollar lawyers and government officials walked past them as if they were part of the landscaping. No one knew what to do about it, so everyone pretended not to notice.

The old man looked like he had been on the bench for decades. He was gray and bent, and knotted up from too much weather and hard living. His long hair and beard were matted and tangled from years without attention. The hands were gnarled with the bones protruding; the knobby fingers were tipped with long, rough fingernails.

Here was a man beyond worry or caring. He reeked from booze, his clothes were wet from a recent urination, and from the smell of it, there was more than one load of crap in his pants. The man lay on the bench passed out drunk.

His brains were fried, Father. There was nothing to be done.

Even at the Civic Center, this kind was rare. This man no one touched. The police would absolutely refuse to handle him. Placing him in a patrol car was out of the question. No officer wanted shit in his vehicle. At best, a patrolman would prod the bum with his nightstick and herd him off.

I went to get a stick, something adequate for the job but still not too large. One had to be careful these days. No matter how far gone they were, modern bums still knew about lawyers. If I got too rough, I could be sleeping on the bench and this bum would be driving the Porsche.

It was the Civic Center, for God's sake, in front of the Courthouse. Lawyers came in and out all day. This was where the vultures lurked. I smiled as I imagined a shiny suited lawyer hidden behind some bushes, just waiting for me to present him with a new client and a retirement sized case.

Maybe counsel would clean him up and dress him up. "Crazed writer attacks ordinary citizen in the Civic Center." Or maybe he would leave the bum as is, au natural. "Greedy yuppie brutalizes homeless for the one thing he had left, his spot on a bench."

I got a small branch and broke it down to an appropriate size, then sat down on the small space at the end of the bench that was unoccupied.

"Hey fella, it's time to move on," I said.

No answer, no movement, I was not surprised. The stench of the booze was overpowering.

"Hey! You have got to leave!" I took the stick and discreetly yet very firmly poked at him.

"Grrrrr…Leave meh duh fuck ehlone!" he growled back. The voice was low and raspy. It was barely human anymore. How might he have sounded in a younger, better day, before all the booze and weather and abuse?

The bum was wearing several layers of clothes. My first poke was inadequate. I thrust the stick harder in the rib area; he needed to feel some pain.

"Out. Get out!" I insisted again, still not too loud.

"Grrrrr….Owww!" He thrust his leg out in response to my jab, kicking me in my thigh. *Very good, Frank*, I thought to myself. So far all I had to show was a muddy footprint on my three hundred-dollar slacks. "Leave meh duh fuck ehlone! Ah'll keell yeh, yuh motha fucka!"

I became angry and started jabbing at him like a Class A fencer. "Get the hell out of here, and now!" I shouted at him. I no longer cared about being discreet.

"Owww!… Owww! What yeh doin? Let meh be! What's the madder wi yuh? Yeh cock suckin, shit eatin, piss drinkin, cum faced, asshole, pig fucker!"

No doubt he had heard every profanity there was. To his credit, he did remember most of them. I couldn't help but notice how he spit out the words. Not "pig fucker" as you or I might say, but "Puhh-hig fuck-a-herrr'," the emphasis on the end with a raspy full expulsion of air. I had never been cursed at with so much feeling before.

He seemed to be picking up steam and was getting louder, which began to disturb me. I was sorry I started with him. Which way to the egress?

"Ok, Ok" I said trying to calm him down.

"Fuck yeh Ok! Yeh ass wipe, motha fuckin WIH..A..CHEE..YOOK..HUH!"

I became immediately paralyzed. "Simon, is that you?" I asked quietly.

"Who duh hell did yeh tink it were? Weh had an apperntment."

He sat up straight and reached over to frisk me. I was not armed. He smelled like a pig farm. In a minute, so did I. Purposefully, I was sure, in the process of searching me, Simon rubbed some of his shit all over me.

"Not goin tuh see yeh girlfriend after dis, heh Frankie?"

"No," I answered meekly.

"Yuh got time fur meh. Nuttin to do but smell dah fresh air. Hehh…hehh…hehh. Aint dat right, Frankie?"

"Actually, I have smelled fresher."

"Hehh…hehh…hehh. Yuh like meh outfit?"

I was amazed at how authentic everything was. The shit was real enough. And the clothes couldn't have been from some costume store; they had to be real. A dark thought crossed my mind. Did Simon kill some poor homeless just for his clothes?

"What, mit yuh bein an expurt on bums an all. Ah valur yeh opinin."

I ignored the insult and the dig at my past. "The clothes are real enough. How did you get them?" My tone did not hide my conjecture.

"Hehh…hehh…hehh. Di yuh tink ah keelled somewun fur em? Hehh, ah tole yeh, ah dunt like keelin!

"Then how?"

"Hehh…hehh…hehh. Yuh tink da bums dunt kner commerce? Ah got em fur some newur clothes an eh jug uh wine. Duh wine wer deh clincherr." Simon stroked his overcoat proudly letting some of the stuck on feces go flying. "Purdy good, ehhh Frankie?"

"Very good, just one thing." I was foolishly annoyed at Simon's arrogance. He had been trying to antagonize me, I knew that, and I steeled myself against it. Yet it was still working, a little.

"Ehh whut is dat, Frankie?"

"Where is your bottle? There is always a bottle."

"Meh boddle?"

Simon fumbled around, fighting with his clothes, searching for something hidden below, the way an old drunken derelict in his sixties would. As a serial killer, I assumed Simon was probably in his mid to late thirties. He was playing the part to perfection. After a few minutes, Simon produced from the deep recesses of his attire, a bottle of cheap wine about one third full.

"Kare fur ah drink?" He opened the bottle with difficulty and took a drink. Half was ingested and half poured down the side of his face.

"No thank you," I said, feeling stupid.

"Ah am uh purfeckshunist, Frankie. Yuh shud kner dat."

"I'll try to remember that." I reached for the recorder. Simon knew I had it; he had fingered it while searching me, and true to his word allowed me to keep it. I held it up and waited till Simon gave me a nod of approval.

"Shall we get started?"

"Shurr Frankie, ah dudn't buy dees nice clothes jus tuh sit on dis bench."

I complemented Simon on his fine accent then asked him to drop it. I had difficulty understanding him and the problem would be compounded when I listened to the tapes. He agreed though he kept the drunken old man's voice.

Then I informed him that what he had in mind would require that we spend numerous sessions of many hours together. He told me he understood and that he had no plans to abduct or kill anyone for the rest of the day.

"All right then, why now?" I asked. "You've been operating anonymously with your crimes never being detected. Why come out of the shadows now?"

"Because now I play the Game. And my victory must be documented."

"The Grand Game?"

"Yes, the Grand Game, the ultimate challenge for one like me. I play against a warped society and its self-serving system. I play against its rules keepers, the FBI and law enforcement. I shall impose my will. They will be humiliated and shown for the frauds they are."

I remembered my first conversation with Simon and then the one with Venus. Something about the Jaws case had infuriated him. Simon railed at the FBI, called them a pack of arrogant cocksuckers. Now, he was doing it again. I took a shot.

"What was it about the Jaws case?" I continued. "What special significance does it have for you?"

"None really. Jaws just came at a propitious time, showed the assholes for what they were. I intend to take them down, Frankie. They'll all pay, all that profited. But it's just part of the Game."

I wasn't sure I believed him. Simon seemed so intense about it. To this day, Father, I'm still wondering.

16

Recording B-9

"Society decides who is the criminal by first deciding what the crime is. I take bitches for my pleasure and they would hang me. For almost half of this country's years, men took slaves and they are called patriots."

The bum and I sat on that bench for six straight hours, with the time seeming to pass in an instant. Every word held me captive. I was oblivious to anything going on at the Courthouse or the square; didn't get hungry or thirsty. The Cocaine and its nagging call passed me by unnoticed. Even the stench of the shit and piss that covered both of us vanished.

I had taken half a dozen cassettes with me but ran short during the last hour. Simon chided me for my lack of preparation. I carried on, trusting to memory.

When we were finished, I sprinted to the Porsche where there were more cassettes. I quickly dictated everything I could remember. Fortunately, Father, I have a very good memory.

Simon had asked me if I had made my arrangements with my employer. He became angry when I told him that I had not.

"I told you that you would have to give your full attention to our effort. That means you will discontinue your employment and concentrate solely on this project. You do agree?"

I nodded and said Ok.

"You will publish nothing during our whole time together. You will want to very much and you will have a great deal to write about.

But you will do as I say. Clear?"

"Yes."

"We embark on a great adventure, you and I, Frankie. You must devote yourself fully. I hope you haven't wasted my time!"

"No," I said quickly. "I will make the arrangements."

I sat there wondering just how I was going to do that. I was making a very good salary at the Paper. My standard of living had risen dramatically. But I still hadn't saved a dime.

I had a family, bills of my own, and a costly habit to support. Which said nothing about Christine who was not at all cheap to play with. How was I going to quit my job?

For the moment, I put it out of my mind. I'd find a way. Simon was the opportunity of a lifetime. I had no intention of blowing it, not after what I had heard.

I continued my dictation. Simon's words rang in my head. I doubted I would ever forget them, but I still spoke into the recorder as quickly as I could.

I had asked Simon about what seemed an inconsistency to me. When I inquired about the names on the list, he told me that only the last three were still alive, and that they would soon "have to check out" also.

"By your own estimate, you have killed hundreds. In our first conversation you bragged how dangerous you were. Yet," I challenged him, "you consistently resist being called a killer."

"I'm not a killer!" he exclaimed emphatically. "I take no joy in killing. It is strictly housekeeping. Wasteful, but you see there simply is no choice."

"No choice? How can you possibly say you have no choice?"

"You are correct, of course, if you want to be literal. I have a choice.

Technically, I am a serial killer. By definition, I'm a serial killer. But I'm not one of those demented sociopaths, driven by an insane lust for blood. Poor twisted devils, raised monsters, delusional, schizophrenic, abused, cat torturing, pyromaniac, bed-wetting, pathetic mama's boys! They are cursed. They must perform their insane ritualistic sexual fantasy murders and bizarre mutilations.

I take women because I choose to. I take them for the pleasure they give me, as nature intended. But I take no joy in killing. It is a distasteful chore."

"So you catch them, and use them, then kill them. You kill them to keep from getting caught for the other crimes."

"Exactly! But is a crime really being committed? No, just a misguided society that thinks there is. I am acting no differently than our ancestors did for thousands of years."

"But if you have a choice, why take them at all? Pleasure can be derived by less extreme methods. What need is fulfilled?"

"It suits me. I need no further reason. I take them for pleasure, theirs and mine."

"Their pleasure? What possible pleasure could there be for them?"

"Pleasures beyond your wildest imaginings. Not all of them, it is their choice of course."

I said nothing. Simon had given me my first true glimpse of him. I had done quite a bit of research on serial killers since that first telephone call. Simon fit the pattern, anti social, intelligent, but not in touch with the real world. He understood the social order but considered it a fraud. Simon thought himself above it; there was a different set of rules for him. He maintained his own standard of right and wrong.

No guilt whatsoever, the women were completely expendable. Delusional, Simon thought he was doing his victims a favor. *Pleasures beyond my wildest imaginings,* he was giving his victims pleasures to die for. *Literally!*

Simon stared at me as my wheels were spinning wildly. He was a keen observer. I had once again given myself away.

"Ohhhhh, I see," he said. "And it is fortunate that this has come up. That is a very important point. You must see it from their point of view. You must know the pleasure. How else can you write about it?"

I became frightened and said nothing.

"Can you remember this," he asked, "since you do not have your tape recorder and have no notebook for backup?"

I ignored the dig and nodded.

"Fine. You have much to do, so let's give it a little time, say, two weeks. Is that sufficient for you?"

I nodded again.

"Good. Two weeks from today, that would be Friday, July 24, go to 422 Le Grande Street. Do you know the area?"

"Yes," I said. "Not much there, mainly warehouses."

"Not much is known to be there. Arrive at eleven p.m.! Knock on the steel door around back. You'll be expected."

I repeated the address back to Simon. He nodded approvingly.

"Wull, den dat shuld do er, Frankie."

Simon got up slowly, stumbling and falling in the effort. He was still perfectly in character. As he moved off, he paused to hand me copies of three faxes. He said that the first two were already received and the third would be sent to the FBI overnight.

"Dunt try tuh foller meh!"

I watched as he slowly dragged himself off. *Very authentic*, I thought to myself. Simon was a perfectionist. The bum was perfect.

The dictation was complete. I had seven full tapes to review, transcribe and organize. I would have to check out the information and try to figure out what was true and what wasn't. Simon's estimate of two weeks work seemed quite reasonable to me.

I remembered the faxes, which I had slipped into my pocket. I hastily pulled them out and read them. Simon had taken three women and was challenging the Bureau to try to capture him.

Apparently, the Grand Game was already on.

17

FITSFATPRICK AND FURBANGER
TWEEDLEDUMB AND TWEEDLEDUMBER

INNING 2 IS COME AND DONE

AND WHERE WERE YOU?
MY HUNCH, OUT TO LUNCH!

INNING 3 – WHERE IS MARY BENSON?

S

Mary Benson was reported missing to the Santa Monica Police by her fiancé, Jim Feingold. She was last seen leaving work with a coworker by the name of Mark Harris. Neither Harris nor Benson were seen since. There was no evidence of foul play. Despite Mr. Feingold's protestations, the Santa Monica Police assumed that the two ran off together. The case remained open.

Mark Berlanger took the latest fax received from S, and thanked Hardy for the information on Benson. The notes were turning into something of significance. Berlanger knew that this time, he had to take the matter up with Fitz.

"See what you can do to trace the source of the faxes," he ordered agent Hardy. Berlanger declined Hardy's offer to accompany him to see Fitz. No sense giving subordinates too much exposure with the boss.

The door to Fitz's office was closed and Francine was not at her desk. Berlanger understood the significance – early morning dictation. It seemed that Fitz was getting more and more prolific in his writing. Mark Berlanger knew better than to interrupt. He sat down and waited.

Francine was probably the only remaining secretary in the world who still took dictation. Although, it was commonly known in the Bureau that she gave much better than she took. Kevin Fitzpatrick's love affair with his secretary was the worst kept secret in all of government.

The two continued their immature behavior even after they were married. They were two peas in a pod, or more accurately, two Irish peas. If ever there was a matched pair, it was Kevin and Francine.

She was a round faced, pleasant woman who was liked by everyone. Francine was a consistently friendly person and always wore a warm and friendly smile. Her bubbly personality was judged to be one hundred percent authentic and the childish naiveté considered charming.

She was an attractive woman, though somewhat overweight, with flaming red hair and constantly flushed cheeks. She loved to eat, to drink and make merry, and she loved Kevin Fitzpatrick. Though separated by nearly twenty years, it was generally thought they made a perfect couple.

Mark Berlanger waited patiently outside the boss's office. He weighed how best to present S to Fitz, worried that the Irishman would be angry that the matter wasn't brought to him sooner. On the positive side, Berlanger was fairly confident that Fitz would be in good spirits.

When the door finally opened, Francine came out with her cheeks flushed as they usually were after dictation. She carried her steno pad close to her chest, and as always, nothing was written in it.

Mark Berlanger stepped into the open doorway and knocked lightly on the door. "Sir, something has come up that I think you should look at."

Fitz was sitting at his desk, trying his best to look busy. He tilted his head upward and motioned with the fingers of his left hand for Berlanger to enter. Special Agent Berlanger dropped the file on the desk, and waited while Fitz thumbed through the well-organized paperwork.

Fitz scanned over each fax, then Hardy's notes which were attached, then the faxes again more carefully.

"What the hell is this, a joke?" he bellowed.

"I don't think so, sir."

"This S, whoever he is, how does he know us? Are you sure this didn't originate within the Bureau? There is too much inside knowledge here. If this is a prank, someone is going to pay dearly!"

"I don't think so, sir. You and I have been on the tube a lot recently. And don't forget that article in Newsweek where we were the "Top Cops." Anyone could have picked up our names."

"You think someone is playing off the Jaws thing?"

"Quite possibly, and three women are missing."

Mark Berlanger could see Fitz's wheels turning. He knew how the Irishman thought, tried to think that way himself. Things were going well. They were still basking in the limelight created by the Jaws capture. Political appointments were being made as a result of successful elections. Higher positions were being freed up. The vacuum quite possible could suck Fitz upward. Why spoil things? Why go looking for trouble?

"Have any of these local agencies contacted us for help?" Fitz asked.

"No," answered Berlanger.

Fitz handed him back the file with some finality. "Let's wait until they do."

18

The day after my meeting with Simon in front of the Courthouse, I decided to go in to the Paper. I was scared, Father, I don't mind telling you that. So, I did a full line before leaving. The Cocaine was marvelous for cranking up my courage.

I had been avoiding work for weeks because of Simon. I didn't want to cross him but I wasn't ready to face unemployment either. In the interim, I wrote nothing and put the Paper off with obscure evasions. Finally, I returned one of Harry's many calls. Harry was my editor and one of the few people in the world I truly cared about. I couldn't keep ignoring him.

Some years before, Harry Coyle gave me a chance when no one else would. And Father, I mean absolutely no one else. Harry treated me like a wayward son returned. I was fresh off the drunk heap, inexperienced in journalism, and had nothing to show as a writer. To this day, I still can't figure out why he did it.

The early days were tough. Harry was patient as I learned on the job. My work was amateurish at best. Harry said there was soul in my writing. I joked back, that there was something there, but it certainly wasn't soul. Most of my coworkers agreed with me.

Harry gave my stories space they really didn't deserve. Many genuine reporters were angered. Harry never wavered. He shielded me from the deserved criticism and I was encouraged to persevere. "It takes time as well as talent," he told me.

Maybe more importantly, Harry protected me from the accountants, who considered me a non-performing asset and were anxious to trim the waste. I owed much to Harry Coyle. He was the only one, besides Jane, who ever had confidence in me.

"What the hell are you up to?" Harry yelled at me. I wasn't ready to explain so I simply told him that I had something important to discuss and that I wanted a meeting with Chub.

Melvin Timlin was the jefe at the Paper. We called him Chub because he weighed more than three hundred pounds. Chub ran the show, that is, he made all the business decisions. Chub left the daily operations pretty much in Harry's hands, his wisest decision ever. Chub couldn't pass grade school English.

The Porsche was eating up white lines. Fortunately, it still remembered the way to work. I was preoccupied, worried as to how I could present my requirements to Chub and still keep my job. A bold plan was formulating in my mind.

I decided to confront Chub, not like the child caught stealing candy, but as Patton! The only financial success the News had in years was due to my coverage of Jaws. I remembered how Chub panicked when faced with the rumor I started that I was leaving. That got me a raise then. Since my last article, circulation had again begun to slump. I was still hot stuff.

And I had Simon. Neither Chub nor the world knew it yet, but he was going to be a huge story.

Something that Simon had said stuck with me. I fumbled through the tapes to find what I was looking for.

I generally listened to music when in the Porsche, cranked up loud naturally, though I rarely heard it. The Porsche was an excellent place for me to think. Many of my best columns were composed in it.

No longer though, since the interview with Simon, the stereo was turned off permanently. I played the tapes instead.

I searched for the section of the interview I recalled.

"With the future determined by such capricious fate Frankie, how can life be anything but a game? Two ants scurry across a sidewalk. One is stepped on while the other continues on. Two young ladies stroll down a campus lane. One takes my fancy.

The world was made for the players Frankie. It is for them to play the Game. The rest are mere fodder.

And now I play the Grand Game!"

"The Grand Game is a competition? With law enforcement, the FBI, hence your communication with them?"

"Just the beginning, my friend. Just the beginning."

I stopped the tape. That was the phrase! I rewound the tape slightly and listened on.

"With law enforcement, the FBI, hence your communication with them?"

"Just the beginning, my friend. Just the beginning."

"Just the beginning?"

"We are playing a nine inning game. These were just the early innings. Hardly interesting yet, just a feeling out process. Soon the world will know of my greatness. The best is yet to come!"

I turned off the tape. "The best is yet to come!" Oh yes. Patton! I would take Chub like Grant took Vicksburg, the way Agamemnon conquered Troy, Wellington at Waterloo. Well, you get the idea, Father.

19

I walked into the newsroom with my head high and my chest out, the way Patton would enter a room. The mission was to dictate terms, not beg for clemency.

Harry was in his usual position behind his desk inside his glass cage off the floor. He was peering over his bifocals in classic Jason Robards' style. Across from him sat Jim Potter, a young recruit from Stanford. How many times I sat right where Potter was.

Watching the two men through the glass left me feeling oddly displaced, as if I had died and the world carried on just fine without me.

Harry Coyle was well into his seventies, though he still had every hair from his twenties. His face had become a prune and Harry weighed no more than his pencil. For years his hand shook uncontrollably from Parkinson's. Yet, that same hand could still flay open any poorly crafted story.

Despite a life immersed in words, Harry Coyle used them sparingly. His critique of a story was delivered simply by the way he glanced over his glasses. A slow lifting of the eyes meant he liked it. If his eyes rolled at all, it meant you had served Harry tripe for his breakfast.

Harry's eyes came up slowly. Potter had done well. I knocked on the door. Harry pretended to be surprised, but I knew he saw me when I first came on the floor. Nothing ever escaped Harry's view.

"Well," he said, drawing it out for at least five seconds. "Our esteemed superstar has graced us with a visit. To what do we owe this great honor?"

"Hello, Harry," I answered as if I hadn't missed a minute. "Is Chub available?" Harry winced. I looked down at Potter. "I mean Mr. Timlin."

"As a matter of fact, he is quite anxious to see you. Will you excuse me, Jim?" said Harry to Potter as he got up slowly.

We walked briskly toward the elevator. It always amazed me how such a slight diminutive man could have so much energy. More than thirty years his junior, I still had trouble keeping up with him.

"Been thinking of giving this one to Potter," Harry sniped as we passed my desk.

I shot back. "A new protégé for you. A collaboration perhaps, 'Harry and Potter and the Magic Quill'."

When we arrived at Chub's lair on the top floor, I had the distinct feeling that I was walking into a trap. None of the usual waiting outside the office, that obnoxious practice designed to emphasize our relative stations, we were shown right in.

From his expression, it was clear that Chub was not happy. Actually, he looked like he wanted to kill something and then swallow it whole.

Chub greeted me with, "Where have you been, Wycheck? You would already have been fired were it not for Coyle here."

Patton! I reminded myself.

Chub was lying. He didn't give a shit what Harry thought or said. If he wanted to fire me, he already would have. But then, he would have lost his most popular reporter. No, he wanted me to stay. With a pound of my flesh removed, of course.

So I still had a job. A good start, but that was not enough to satisfy my needs. What I required was a sabbatical with full pay. *Patton! Patton! Attack! Attack!*

"Funny, it was Harry who convinced me not to quit," I said smugly. "He feels that we might be able to work something out. I'm here only because of Harry."

I always remembered my debt to Harry and touted his stock at every opportunity. I never went around him, even when Chub wanted to talk to me directly. Harry attended every meeting. The fat ignorant man never showed Harry the respect he deserved. *Doesn't he know that his debt to Harry is far greater even than mine? Let him think that Harry is critical to our negotiation.*

"What's that?" Chub asked. *Great!* I had him off balance. The shocked look on Chub's face gave me confidence.

"Why yes, I have a lucrative book deal and I have to concentrate my full efforts on it."

"A book?" Chub looked like he had caught a sudden case of indigestion. "What kind of book?"

"I'm afraid I can't divulge that information. All I will say is that I have the inside track on a story greater than Jaws ever was. I'm here as a courtesy to Harry. He has loyalty to the Paper that quite frankly I don't share. But I do have loyalty to Harry."

"I see." Chub leaned forward over his desk. He was a big man. I resisted taking a step backward. "And you're here because you have some kind of proposal?" he asked.

Yes! He is hooked. Patton!

"Harry's idea, to give the Paper priority. The book is mine, non-negotiable! However, we could talk about exclusive rights to publish chapters on a daily basis as you see fit."

"I see. And what would we be getting and for how much?"

"We can negotiate later."

"Just a minute." Chub seemed panicked. *Wonderful!* You must give me some details on this book. What's it about? How long will it take? What's it going to cost? You must tell me something!"

"I can tell you nothing, except that it's big." I went to Chub's blackboard, which was actually a white board, picked up the chalk, which was actually a black marker, and drew a large letter S.

"What's that?" asked Chub. There was a quizzical expression on his face.

"You'll know shortly and you'll understand just how monumental this story is. We will negotiate then. In the meantime, I'll stay on under the current conditions, salary and expenses."

There was no objection. I won. *Thank you, Patton. Thank you, Cocaine.* "I will tell you this though." A long pause for effect, and I enjoyed every second of it. Chub was hanging on my words. Harry wore a puzzled look. "It's going to cost you plenty!" I said turning away.

Then, with a wink for Harry, I triumphantly walked out.

20

Recording B-1

"Tell me Simon, how have you managed not to be caught all these years, not even to be detected."

"Very simple really, by strict adherence to my Rules."

"Rules?"

"Yes, my Rules. Rule Number One - Take No Chances. Make a plan, one that is foolproof, then execute. If the slightest thing goes wrong, back off!"

"Sounds simple enough."

"Were it so, then Death Row would not be so crowded.

Rule Number Two - Leave No Bodies.

Rule Number Three - Leave No Crime Scene.

Rule Number Four - Leave No Credible Witnesses.

No body, no evidence, no witnesses, no crime.

Rule Number Five   Trust No One."

"Trust No One? Aren't you in a sense trusting me?"

"I play the Grand Game now, Frankie, and all the Rules must be set aside. I must give up the safety they provide if I am to become the most famous person on earth.

So yes, I break Rule Number Five with you. I trust you, Frankie. I trust you to keep your word and uphold our agreement.

And you, Frankie, you trust me as well. You do trust, don't you?"

I have to say, Father, I looked forward to March 22 with some trepi dation and more than a little anticipation. What kind of spectacle or demonstration did Simon have in store for me? He promised to show me how he pleasured the women that he kidnapped. That was going to be a job.

Was he going to have one of them there and demonstrate? Impossible, not even Simon was that insane, and he never presented himself as foolhardy. My speculations got out of hand so I decided not to theorize further.

I got to Le Grand Street at ten minutes to eleven, and drove around back as instructed. There were no cars in the lot. I parked the Porsche and walked up to the metal door.

A man, as big as a house, opened the door for me. *Is it Simon?* He was wearing black leather, and had chains over his entire body. His exposed arms were enormous and with the leather half mask on his head, believe me, he was frightening as hell.

"Good evening, Mr. Wycheck," he said in a deep rich Genie voice. "My name is George."

George showed me in. "I'm a little early," I said nervously.

"No, you are right on time. We were told to expect you ten minutes early."

George closed and locked the heavy metal door behind us. It was dark and very difficult to see. Ponderous, repetitive music, like nothing I had ever heard before, rumbled from the walls. George led me to a doorway that was covered with what appeared to be red velvet.

"Is anyone else coming tonight?" I asked George.

"No, Mr. Wycheck," he answered in his calm Genie voice. "Private party, just for you."

"Private party?"

"Yes, Mr. Wycheck. Your experience has been arranged, to the last detail."

My experience?

We walked under velvet arches, through a doorway and down some dimly lit hallways into another room that was completely dark. I couldn't see a thing, though the room felt large to me. George locked the door behind us.

"Mistress Pleasure will be with you shortly. Make yourself at home." I was left alone as George disappeared into the darkness.

Mistress Pleasure? What is Simon up to?

I refused to speculate further, opting instead to take a few blind baby steps forward. There was a thick rich carpet underfoot. That was all I could tell. In the pitch black, where did I think I was going? I decided to simply wait.

Suddenly, two red spotlights lit up either side of the doorway that George and I had entered. Each light illuminated a huge man, dressed exactly like George. I stared at them in awe. They made George look like their kid brother. Muscular, six feet seven, three fifty at least, for sure they were refugees from someone's defensive line. Both giants stood motionless and silent, arms crossed, guarding the doorway.

Additional spotlights began to turn on around the room, highlighting an extensive collection of bondage and torture equipment. Shackles of all sorts, crosses, tables, and hitching posts, as well as whips and chains in impressive numbers.

The room was quite large. It was supposed to look like a dungeon and, Father, it did. My eyes followed the lights around the room, heavy rock walls all around and all that stuff used for God knew what.

My view retraced its way back to the giants then back the other way again. It was quite a display. I was getting concerned.

"George?" I said nervously. There was no answer.

Four or five spotlights turned on at once, illuminating a large ornate four-poster bed on a raised pedestal at the far end of the room. Red velvet draped liberally from the canopy and down the heavy wooden posts. The bed itself was covered with red satin sheets, plush red pillows and a large voluptuous blonde.

I watched, mesmerized, as she slowly got up. She was statuesque, fully six feet, with an hourglass figure emphasized by a tight black leather corset. Her full breasts spilled liberally out over the top of the corset while a slim thong allowed her tight butt to be fully exposed.

Mistress Pleasure, I presume.

Walking toward me in stiletto heels, the small mask covering her eyes and her long flowing blonde hair gave her a majestic, mysterious look. She was quite stunning. I barely noticed the small whip in her right hand.

"You have brought me a slave for the evening's pleasure, George?" The voice was low and sultry, definitely feminine, and quite sexy.

This is the best one yet, Simon, I thought to myself. She walked forward while scanning me up and down, finally stopping only a few feet away. *This definitely is your best.*

"Yes, Mistress Pleasure, a slave," answered George. He was right behind me. I couldn't believe that I had misplaced him. I turned to look when I felt a sharp pain in my chest.

"You have no permission to look at us, slave!" I heard the order in between the stinging surges of pain. She was whipping me! "Cast your eyes downward! You have no permission." Another quick snap of her wrist and I felt more pain.

"Simon, you bastard!" I shouted instinctively.

Another quick snap of the wrist!

"Quiet slave! You have no permission to speak."

I held my throbbing chest and cast my eyes downward to the floor. *Simon,* I thought to myself, *what on earth are you up to?*

Wycheck, you dumber than dumb fuck. What have you gotten yourself into?

21

Recording B-5

"I have always enjoyed games. I played chess, and quite well I might add, starting at the age of five. Chess teaches discipline and preparation, an excellent game. But it wasn't until I got into analysis that I learned what fun real mind games could be.

Quite simple actually. I went from psychiatrist to psychiatrist. With each I researched a new condition, paranoia, schizophrenia, paranoid schizophrenia, and so on. Then I tried to give responses that would lead the 'doctor' to conclude my chosen malady. I did quite well, provided the psychiatrist was any good.

For the last game I tried something different. I was honest. What would the results be?

'Perfectly normal' was the conclusion. It was perfectly normal for a young adolescent male to have sexual fantasies, even strange ones. 'If he didn't have them, well that would be abnormal.' And as far as the rest of it, unusual yes, maybe even a little bizarre, but it also was quite within the bounds of normal.

So there you have it, Frankie. Whatever conclusions you may draw about me, I present you with this professional diagnosis. I am perfectly within the bounds of normal. One really can't hope to do better than that, can one? To be normal, that is."

George held me tightly in the vise of his muscle bound arms. I was not going anywhere. The whipping made me scream, which didn't appear to bother anyone. They acted as if shrieking from intense pain was a common occurrence. With no one seeming to care, I let loose with all the gusto in me.

"Silence slave!"

A small gesture of Mistress Pleasure's whip was all it took to shut me up completely. *Very convincing, as always Simon!* I waited for the Whyacheeyuka to come.

"This slave must be taught a lesson!" she said sternly. "Damon! Jarmon!"

The two gorillas from the doorway grabbed me and carried me to the bed. They were about as gentle as they would be with the opposing quarterback. I was bent over the edge of the bed with my face planted into a large pillow. In two seconds they had removed all of my clothing.

"Ok, that's about enough, Simon!" I shouted before getting two quick snaps of the whip across my butt.

"Silence slave!" ordered Mistress Pleasure. I shut up immediately. "Now let me check this slave out."

Mistress Pleasure hovered over me. I could feel her breath up and down my back as she inspected me. Her hands followed. I was uncomfortable, more so when she got to my crotch. I started to squirm.

"You have no permission to move!"

Another quick snap across my butt and I stopped moving. I would not move again. I would have to endure.

Mistress Pleasure spent a good ten minutes around my crotch alone. She fingered me liberally and massaged my genitals and not too gently. She was hurting me but I neither moved nor made a sound.

I was in a most unflattering and highly vulnerable position, angry and embarrassed, utterly helpless. She could do to me whatever she wanted. And she did. Or should I say Simon did! I was revolted and disgusted. What a sick fuck he really was.

"Bring me oil, George," ordered Mistress Pleasure.

She began to massage my neck, then my back, then my buttocks and legs, and ultimately my genitals again. It was hard to believe that someone who had been so crude and rough before could now be so gentle. I refused to take pleasure but I was happy not to be whipped.

"Very nice stuff on this slave, huh, George?" Mistress Pleasure said in her sultry voice. "Very nice ass!"

"Yes, Mistress," he answered obediently.

She spread extra oil on my buttocks, while slowly, methodically, kneading the flesh. "I think this slave needs to be fucked!"

Fear shot through me faster than a bullet. What was Simon going to do to me? Or worse, what were those three gorillas going to do? They were hung like horses! I started to twist and squirm. Mistress Pleasure did not swat me; she did laugh heartily. I had never felt such panic, as I feared what was about to happen. Did they mean to rape me prison style?

If this was Simon's idea of pleasure, he was more deranged than I gave him credit for. What a fool I had been. *How could I have trusted such a man? What did I expect, poetry?* Simon was a killer. He took his pleasure as a kidnapper and a rapist. People were fodder to him; women were merely bitches, to do with as he pleased. How could I have been so arrogant as to think that I would be treated differently?

The Cocaine did this to me! It clouded my thinking and made me feel I was invulnerable. Now I was another of Simon's bitches. He had told me as much, but in my hubris leaden, self indulgent, drug rotted brain, I wouldn't listen.

I kept staring at the Gorilla crotches, scared to death.

"Turn my bitch over, George," Mistress Pleasure said, when she was finished laughing.

I can't tell you, Father, how relieved I was to be on my back. They tied me spread eagle to the four posts of the bed. I didn't care. I was happy that my worst nightmares were not being realized.

Mistress Pleasure got on top of me. "More oil, George!" she ordered.

She massaged my neck, my chest, arms, legs, feet, fingers, toes, and then concentrated on my genitals. I closed my eyes and by the time she was finished, amazingly, I was as hard as a rock and ready to explode.

"Well," she said in an admiring tone, "I think my bitch is ready for me."

I didn't know what to expect and it showed on me immediately.

"Oh, shame," she said. "But no matter, we can get you ready again."

Mistress Pleasure began to undo her corset. *What is Simon up to?* She shook her head and her blonde hair spilled backward. Her breasts were as perfect as any I had ever seen.

She removed her corset completely. This was not Simon. This was Mistress Pleasure, and she was magnificent! Father, never had I seen such a woman, not in real life, not in stage shows, the movies, or anywhere.

I was at full erection when she mounted me. She rocked back and forth slowly and methodically while gently squeezing me. Her blonde hair cascaded over her shoulders onto her breasts. I was dying to touch those breasts. Restrained the way I was, that was not in the cards.

Mistress Pleasure continued rocking back and forth on top of me. Her pelvic muscles intensified their fabulous pulsation. She was working me toward a climax, and Father, it was an orgasm I will never forget! Ever!

I lay on the bed exhausted, but incredibly relaxed, and slept for I don't know how long. When I awoke, Mistress Pleasure was gone. The gorillas untied me and helped me get into my clothes. George walked me to the door.

I never saw any of them again.

22

Recording D-6

"In the end, Frankie, you must admit there are no absolutes. Nothing need be what it appears. The more certain you are of a thing, the more you may be deluded by it. That is the power of deception and misdirection."

I sat in the Porsche dazed, trying to figure out what had just hap pened to me. What had I learned from my experience? What was I supposed to learn? I was still tingling from one of the best orgasms of all time.

Was Simon trying to show me that his victims somehow enjoyed their plight? That was as delusional as it was absurd. Simon didn't strike me that way. Deranged yes, insane quite possibly, but devoid of all logic, no chance. Simon's mind worked like a computer. There were calculations at work for sure. My task was to try to figure them out.

What was Simon trying to accomplish? Did he mean to show me that fear and the associated heightened emotions could raise the level of sexual sensation? Or more accurately, the relief from such fear and panic could do so. That case was absolutely made.

Certainly though, he realized there was a difference between a woman, kidnapped and raped, and a loose, drug crazed, oversexed, horn dog like me. I would look back on the experience as one of the great excitements in my life. No woman would feel the same. More to the point, I was let go. Simon's bitches never survived their experiences.

I considered that Simon might be making a statement about the pleasures of sexual bondage? I have never been one to criticize any form of sexual pleasure, regardless how bizarre. I was always too occupied trying to find my own new ways to do it. My attitude had always been, if they took pleasure in it, God bless them. Excuse me for that, Father.

The cell's silly insistent ring interrupted my thinking. I fished it out of the glove box and answered.

"Wycheck."

"Well, well, well, and how did you enjoy your experience, WIH..A..."

"I know it's you, Simon!" I interrupted, wanting to spare myself from listening to him squeal my name as identification. "Who else could it be? Please don't." Simon was using the "Voice." "You're right though," I added. "It was an experience."

"I thought you might like it – gain some perspective."

"I'm still trying to figure out what that perspective is supposed to be. Tell me Simon, how does one arrange such a thing?" I asked, legitimately curious.

"You can buy anything for money. No questions asked."

"That couldn't have been cheap."

"Frankie, money is never a consideration.

It suddenly occurred to me that Simon scheduled my session with Mistress Pleasure for the same reason he did all things, his own satisfaction. He was showing off, demonstrating his power. It was just another mind fucking game. Like with the psychiatrists, I was the latest would be shrink led down the merry path. I consoled myself that I was not the psychiatrist but merely the biographer. Let the doctors figure him out. I was satisfied simply to write my book.

"Now, Frankie…" The Voice had suddenly turned serious. "Now for your warning."

"Warning?" I became scared as hell.

"That's an awfully nice little bitch you have. Christina."

23

Panic devoured my every cell. I worshipped Christine and worried what Simon might have done to her. I dialed Christine's num ber, and the phone just kept ringing and ringing, till I got her machine.

The Porsche flew down the Harbor Freeway, and in fifteen minutes I was racing up the stairs into the bedroom, fearing what I might find. Simon stole women. Would she simply be gone?

Christine! She was on the bed, naked, spread eagle with a red sash yanking each of her limbs away from her. *Be alive,* I prayed. I leaned over and kissed her uncontrollably. "Chrissy, my love! Be alive, please be alive!"

She was moving ever so slightly and was faintly murmuring. "Oh, Frank!" I was so relieved and couldn't stop kissing her. "Oh Frank, again?"

"What?" I answered, surprised.

"Oh, yes, do it again."

Christine was only semi conscious, but purring in a way I had only heard a few times before, one night at the Bluebird, and once at the Bonaventure.

"Oh, Frankie, this was the best ever."

"What? Yes. Tell me about it, Chrissy. Tell me everything."

"You know," she cooed.

"Yes, of course. But I want to know from you, everything."

"All right. Well, I came home, tired from work as usual, pissed that you hadn't come by or even called me in days. I had been stewing the whole day.

When I opened the door, it was dark inside. I reached for the light switch and you grabbed me from behind. Oh, Frankie, I never knew you were so strong! You lifted me off the ground like I was a rag doll.

You put a towel over my face and I was breathing in some kind of drug. The world was spinning and I was about to pass out when you pulled it away. I wasn't sleeping and I wasn't awake. It was dreamlike. What was that drug you used, Frankie?"

"Never mind that. Go on."

"You carried me to the bed. I could feel you, excited, behind me, and I got excited too. I couldn't resist, not that I would have when you tied me up. You really tied me up this time, not those silly make believes we did those other times. You did it like you meant it. Mmmm."

"Yes. Go on."

"Then you took me, over and over, like a savage. When I would start to wake up, you would give me the drug again. Just enough to get me back to dreamlike. And then you would take me again, hard. Mmmm, Frankie, you were never like that before."

Funny, Father, how your emotions can change so quickly. I felt a gnawing at the pit of my stomach. My mind drifted back to what Simon had said about giving pleasure to his captives and how insane I thought he was to believe it. *The joke is on you, Wycheck!*

"Is there more?" I asked.

"No that's it, and it couldn't have been better, darling. Thank you. Thank you so much. Do you want to give it to me one more time?"

"No, that was plenty for me. Let's get you untied and into the shower. It's time to get cleaned up and out of dreamland."

I began untying the red sashes when I noticed something written in red on Christine's lower abdomen.

YOUR ONLY WARNING!

I rubbed the lipstick off with my hand, realizing how lucky I had been, and how stupid. I had been treating this whole thing like so much fun and games. But the Game was only for Simon and only he intended to have fun.

This was a warning, thank God, not punishment, and the message was clear. Don't dare betray me! What was it that Simon once said? I had it on tape. "There are the players and all the rest, they were the played with." It suddenly occurred to me that perhaps I was not a player.

I put my arm around Christine and helped her up. “Come on, let’s get you in the shower.”

“In the shower? Do you want to do it in the shower?”

“No. I’ve had enough.”

“Ok, darling,” and she gave me a small kiss on my cheek. “But promise me you’ll do it all again.”

24

My son," interrupted Father Reyes.

"What, Father?" Wycheck was startled, even by the soft mellow tones of the Priest's voice. He had not said anything for some time. A check of Wycheck's Rolex verified that two hours had slipped by.

The young Priest was good to his word. Father Reyes was willing and able to devote the time necessary. Father Romero did not have such stamina. He would have long since excused himself politely, to rest and to continue another time.

Frank Wycheck was calmed by the two-hour catharsis, but he was also consumed by it. He paused to gather himself and get reoriented. His hands stroked the worn velvet of the booth. His eyes strained for a peek of the young priest through the grate.

"Shall we stop, Father?" Wycheck asked.

"No, of course not," answered Father Reyes. "But I am troubled. Simon was a mass murderer. You verified that. He abducted and killed many, and was continuing to do so during your contact with him. Then he raped your girl friend."

"Yes, Father, that is correct."

"And you did nothing? You didn't go to the authorities?"

"God forgive me, it's true."

"Why, my son?"

"I don't know. God help me, I don't know. Chrissy was all right. Hell, she loved it. I was too embarrassed or didn't have the guts to tell her that her wonderful experience, maybe the best in her life, was not provided by me.

Yeah, there was that.

But honestly, it was the story. The story, the story mesmerized me.

I was a reporter, a writer, and not a policeman. My job was the story. Somehow Simon was not a vicious killer; he was the protagonist of a book. There weren't crimes and atrocities committed; it was plot. The women, they were not lives lost; they were my characters.

"I see," said Father Reyes in a somber tone that was not interpreted as judgmental.

"Forgive me, Father."

"It's not for me to judge, my son."

25

I didn't hear from Simon for over two months. There was no surprise there. He had warned me, but I was dying from the anticipation. What was he up to, and when would I find out about it?

I was back to avoiding Chub and the Paper. Harry called me several times, under orders I'm sure, and I took each of his calls. He told me that Chub was getting antsy and wanted to know why didn't I write a story or two for the money he was paying me.

I responded by restating my requirements, which annoyed Harry. Harry Coyle remembered everything he was told and considered anything repeated an insult.

We left it at, "Tell that stupid fat son of a bitch that I'm working and making progress; he will see it all soon, and then it'll cost him plenty. And finally, if Chub doesn't want to pay me that's fine, but the deal is off!"

Patton, I told myself. My experience with Chub was that he was a coward. He would bark but was afraid to bite. Someone might just bite him back.

I spent my time going over facts and again contacting the parties on Simon's list. I visited as many as possible. Then I focused my attention on the three new victims that were in the Grand Game. Their loved ones were just as puzzled as those from the list, and they were just as angry and frustrated with the police.

I felt guilty not telling them what I knew, getting information from them, information not intended to help, but for use in my book.

All of the tapes had been transcribed. I listened to them and read them at the same time, over and over. I was hoping for an insight, the slightest glimpse into Simon that he had not intended me to have.

Simon was clever, there was no doubt of that, but with so much talking, something had to have slipped out.

I began spending more and more time with Christine, trying ever so hard to please her. But, I never seemed to be able to duplicate the great feat of that day, and she seemed to be losing patience. So, the Cocaine and I were becoming chummier. I would have done anything for that woman.

THE MIDDLE INNINGS

A SIGNIFICANT PLAY

26

The two girls sat chatting on the living room couch when the front door bell rang. A single ring, not the annoying flurried staccato that some of the solicitors used. Either way, if ignored they usually left quickly. Danielle hesitated only a moment then continued her discourse on the new shopping mall in Westchester.

Danielle Rickford and her friend and classmate Susan Benchly were going to be naughty. They had just returned from their eleven o'clock psychology class, and decided to ditch the rest of the day's sessions. For Danielle it was a boring History class, which she didn't like in the first place and resented doubly because of the inconvenient four-hour break. Besides, it wouldn't matter since she could ace History by studying the book and cramming before the exams.

Normally, Danielle came home on Tuesdays. She would make herself lunch or sometimes stop off and bring in junk food. Then, alone, she would kill the time, studying or doing homework, until she had to return to campus for History.

Danielle lived in a condominium purchased by her parents. Small, cozy according to the real estate broker, modern and new, possessing all of the important conveniences, and too expensive, Elaine Rickford, Danielle's mother, considered it to be appropriate under the circumstances.

The accommodations were well below Rickford standards. Another of the many compromises insisted upon by Danielle in her quest to fit in. Not many at Stanford realized she was the heiress to the vast Rickford fortune.

Danielle would have loved to share the second bedroom with someone like Susan. Yet, she lived alone. Her parents insisted on that much.

They did not want her to be distracted, and they wanted the other bedroom for their weekend visits. Henry Rickford never came, Elaine always.

The weekends shot, it was not difficult for Susan to convince Danielle to make this Tuesday afternoon a holiday. The rest of the day would be spent in a glorious frenzy of shopping. The only unresolved question was which mall to go to.

The doorbell rang again, another short delicate ring. Danielle paused. "Sometimes they don't go away," she said annoyed. "You have to tell them to leave." She made a face designed to be funny and pointed her index finger to her temple. "Duhhh…I'll go tell them to leave. Be right back."

Danielle walked toward the door. The doorbell rang again before she got there. She approached the door carefully, not having decided if she would confront the pest or simply wait him out. Danielle looked through the peephole.

Whoa, she thought to herself, *we don't have guys like that on campus.* Danielle peered through the peephole again, scanning the man, up and down and side-to-side, as best she could. He was extraordinarily good looking; she decided by far the best-looking man she had ever seen. Danielle could tell from his uniform that he was from the Cable Company.

Her mother had not yet completed making her paranoid, but Danielle did have a good appreciation of the dangers that lurked for an attractive young woman. She rarely opened the door to strangers. Danielle quietly went to a window that looked out at the street. Parked in front was the familiar Cable Company truck. She went back and opened the door.

His name was Jim. The name was monogrammed on his shirt. The peephole had not done Jim justice. He was tall, maybe six foot two or so, and gorgeous. Well-defined muscles stretched Jim's uniform taut. He had the physique and face of a Greek God.

"Hello, my name is Jim. I'm from the Cable Company." His voice was deep and rich.

"Uhh, yes I know," Danielle said sheepishly as she pointed to the name on his shirt. She felt awkward and childish.

Danielle was extremely attractive at five foot eight, a slender but shapely one hundred twenty two pounds, blonde this week, and blue eyed. She was popular, sought after on campus and carried an appropriately snooty attitude. The boys she knew were all immature dorks. Few, if any, were worth dating, and none, none could ever approach Jim.

Danielle giggled nervously.

"Yes, I suppose you do," Jim said looking down at his shirt. He laughed pleasantly with her. "And what's your name?" He scanned her blouse playfully, pretending to be looking for her name.

"It's Danielle." They were both laughing.

"Danny?" The voice was approaching from the other room. *Susan, of course!* How Danielle wished she wasn't there now. Susan was attractive in her own right, short, petite actually, but substantial in a way that turned men on. Susan was always worthy competition. *Damn*, Danielle thought, *not now*. At best, Susan's presence made it an awkward trio.

Susan turned the corner and could not prevent a double take when she saw the handsome Jim. "Well…" was all she could muster.

"I'm the Cable guy," said Jim brusquely, then he turned to Danielle and asked if he could check around the house and do his work. Some of the neighbors were having service problems and he was running behind schedule.

"Of course," said Danielle hardly able to conceal her disappointment.

"What a hunk!" said Susan after Jim had left. Danielle could tell that her friend had not taken a breath since that first glimpse.

"Tell me about it," she replied. The two began to sigh and giggle and gesture.

It was a hopeless fantasy, Danielle decided. Jim was well out of their league. He was something the two friends could talk about for days, *soooh* gorgeous, alas too gorgeous for them. He probably had an equally gorgeous goddess girlfriend tucked away. Still, Danielle wondered if Susan weren't there, what might have been?

The two returned to the couch with something new to talk about and there was still the matter of where to go. They would wait until Jim was done and gone. Then they would shop their brains out.

27

Jim walked down the stairs to the garage angrily. *Damn it,* he thought, *all of that work and preparation. That other little bitch was not supposed to be here. The Rickford girl was always home alone on Tuesdays. Why not today?*

He traced the cable lines, though he had no interest in them whatever. He remembered Rule Number One. *Take No Chances. There is always another day and there is always another way.* Rule Number One called for a retreat, but he never had to walk away from so much time and effort.

Three months had been spent on Inning 4, Danielle Rickford, one month in the selection alone. At this point in the Game, a high profile victim was required. Who could be better than Danielle Rickford, the heiress to the Rickford Empire?

He sought royalty but might have chosen Danielle anyway. She was easily attractive enough and with those bluer than blue eyes the bitch was nearly irresistible.

For over two months he had been studying Danielle Rickford, watching her, preparing to take her. The Cable man disguise, one of his best ever, was also one of the most difficult. Six hours he toiled just to put it on. Nor did the truck come easily, requiring another false identity and a good deal of creative artwork. He had put a lot of effort into Inning 4.

Jim thrust his tools on the stone floor. *Do I have to start over now?* The prospect infuriated him though he knew that Rule Number 1 required it.

The Rules had served him well, but that was before the Grand Game. The Game required boldness. *That is the point of the Game, win big, but also a chance to lose.* Still, old habits died hard.

He was a man who was dominated by perfection. The slightest flawed detail derailed his equilibrium, leaving him searching for a remedy. *Should I wait until the other bitch leaves?* It was unlikely that she would. *Should I leave and return again later?* There was of risk to that idea also. If a cover was reused there was always vulnerability. Prudence dictated that he write the whole thing off as a loss.

Jim mulled over his dilemma as he gathered his tools, dissatisfied and disgusted. Then it occurred to him. *Why not play innings 4 and 5 together? Why not take them both?* Now there was a bold stroke, worthy of a would be Master of the Game.

He had never taken two bitches at one time. It would be risky. The word foolhardy did come to mind. Such action went against his most basic doctrine. *Don't want to get caught? Rule Number One!*

But the Grand Game had its rules too. It required that he move forward. Three months had passed. *To start completely over, wouldn't that constitute an unwarranted delay of play?*

Besides, the Cable Man ruse was working perfectly. *Both of them would gladly spread their legs for the handsome Jim. Funny how easy it is for the good looking.*

He had spent countless hours fashioning the Jim disguise. A good-looking man was needed; he emulated Cary Grant. He was confident that the Rickford bitch would not notice the resemblance, *too young, too stupid.*

The loss of the time and effort seemed intolerable, and the thought of a double began to intrigue him. Jim dawdled in the garage tossing about the possibilities. He argued pros and cons, finally deciding he would go for them both, though cautiously. *I can do it. I can do anything.* Though the idea of the additional risk still did not sit well. A premium had always been placed on caution. Adrenaline rushed through his body.

I will proceed carefully, feel the way. If it goes well, I will continue; if not, I'll bolt, nothing lost.

Jim took his flashlight out of the tool kit and started upstairs. He quietly walked to the living room and meekly stuck his head in.

"Excuse me," he said sheepishly. His voice was deep and melodic. The two girls stopped their chatter immediately, looking up at him with longing eyes. No one had ever gazed at him that way before Jim.

"I need someone to move the car out of the garage."

"Of course," said Danielle jumping up immediately, while glowering at Susan, a look that said plainly – don't dare move! Susan took the indelicate hint and stayed on the couch quietly.

He was in luck. The fear was that they would go together.

"I'm happy to help," said Danielle.

I'll bet you are. "After you," Jim said politely while making a chivalrous gesture with his arm.

Danielle skipped forward lightly toward the stairs leading to the garage. Jim followed closely behind. Her lean body moved gracefully, swaying slightly back and forth. Practiced, he figured, but the desired effect was achieved.

He was already quite familiar with Danielle's smooth, flowing gait and the classy lines of her body. He had been watching her for months. She was chosen only partially because she came from a prominent family.

Danielle backed her Toyota out of the garage and parked it in front of the condominium. It was not an expensive car and certainly not flashy, but practical and reliable, a wholly proper and discreet vehicle. Danielle and Elaine had shopped for it prior to Danielle's leaving for Stanford.

She returned through the garage and headed upstairs while leaving a smile behind for Jim.

"Oh, Daniella." Jim called to her, warmly, teasingly, invitingly.

She froze in place. Her hopes rose through the ceiling. "Yes, Jimmy," she cooed trying to match his playful tone.

"I could use your help for a minute," he said. "To hold the light for me."

Jim handed the flashlight to Danielle. "I really appreciate this," he said pointing to a box high on the garage wall, an electric box having nothing to do with the cable. He assumed correctly that she would not know the difference. "It's a little hard to get to and hard to see inside."

He showed her where to point the flashlight, high over her head. Danielle stretched both arms upward holding the flashlight. She rose up on her toes to get the light as close to the box as she could.

Jim stepped back to admire her. She had the long slender legs of a fashion model. Her calves were bulging from standing tiptoe and her tight little skirt was raised up from stretching her arms. How helplessly inviting she was.

"Just a little higher please," Jim said. He couldn't resist.

The muscles in her butt went taut underneath her skirt as it rose another inch. Jim could clearly see their outline through the material. Danielle's shapely legs strained fully, the calves became even tighter. There was not a loose ounce on her.

Jim visualized Danielle Rickford on her back with those long, shapely legs well spread and the bluer than blue eyes looking up longingly at him. He was getting excited.

"Is that all right?" she asked.

"Perfect," Jim answered. "Couldn't be better." He drew up close behind her, breathing in the aroma of her perfume. Too much of an expensive brand, overpowering; he would have much preferred her natural fragrance. *She is too young to have learned subtlety.*

The blonde hair hung down over Danielle's shoulders as she strained to keep the flashlight up. Not the perfect style or length for her long lean body, and looking down on it he could see the brownish roots. Too bad, he had hoped the golden hair was natural.

Jim reached into his bag and prepared his handkerchief. Danielle was still holding up the flashlight. She was getting tired but fought bravely to maintain her position. He came up behind her, very close, touching her with his body.

No objection; he knew she felt him there. *She wants it, and she will not be disappointed.* However, this was not the time for such diversions. Jim quickly and firmly placed her in a chokehold and covered her mouth and nose with the handkerchief. She struggled for only a few seconds, then slumped to the floor.

Sleep well, Daniella, my angel.

28

Jim climbed up the stairs from the garage. He was hot and his makeup might have run. Sweating, he feared that his strap on physique would slip. *Will the other bitch notice anything?* It wouldn't matter if she did; he would overpower her anyway. It was more a question of style.

Susan was still sitting on the couch, doing her nails to while away the time. She stopped immediately when she saw Jim, embarrassed that he caught her in such a mundane activity. By the way she stared at him, Jim knew that he was still grand.

"Excuse me," he said politely, "Danielle has cut her hand. Do you have any band aids?"

Susan jumped off the couch. "I don't live here, but I'm sure she does. Probably in the medicine cabinet."

There was not the slightest hint of suspicion in her. His story was weak, a hasty contrivance. He was sure she would question why Danielle hadn't come up herself. *Young and stupid, always a matched pair.*

He had not paid much attention to this one up until now. She was really quite attractive. Jim admired her round little ass as he followed her up the stairs. In her tight cut off jeans with the deliberate hole just where her leg ended, *the little bitch knows exactly what she is doing.*

He wanted to reach out and grab her right there, but didn't, knowing that he had to act quickly. The handkerchief in his pocket was almost dry, the ether almost dissipated. Jim wondered why she didn't smell it. He did.

Susan opened the medicine cabinet as he stood closely behind her. She was tiny, five feet, no more. He knew she sensed him behind her. No objection. *What fantasies is she entertaining?*

Jim reached into his pocket for his handkerchief and clamped it tightly over her face. He would have liked the ether to be more potent; fortunately she was small. The dosage was sufficient. Susan went quickly.

How easy it had been, his first twosome. Some new excitement had been added to the Game. He decided he would have to do it again.

Jim backed the Cable van into the garage, and loaded his cargo. A little extra ether was given each of them for the trip, just to make sure they didn't wake up. He drove off, closing the garage door for the last time.

Jim drove slowly and carefully, and thought of the accommodations at the Castle. He had only planned on one guest. Just one room was available. That was never a problem. Another guest could always check out.

I have a better idea. They can share the master, the room with two tables. Jim visualized the two girls in the room. Danielle, on her back with her arms and legs well spread. And the other, she would be face down, with that juicy round butt sticking up in the air.

Jim breathed in and out deeply. The hunt was over and the quarry captured. He had played well and scored. His anticipation grew. The Grand Game was getting interesting and the best was yet to come.

Innings four and five, in the book.

29

I found out about the Rickford kidnapping like everyone else did. On CNN and in the morning papers! You have no idea how much that pissed me off. I was supposed to be on the inside track. Another fax was sent to the FBI.

FINE BUNCH OF IMBECILES

THREE INNINGS PLAYED AND YOU REFUSE TO BAT.
PRAY TELL, WHY IS THAT?

INNING 4 – WHERE IS SUSAN BENCHLY?
INNING 5 – WHERE IS DANIELLE RICKFORD?

S

Copies of all four communications to the FBI were sent to the Los Angeles Times and San Francisco Chronicle as well as the New York Times, the Chicago Tribune, the Washington Post, and USA Today. Also sent, was a copy of a note that went directly to Henry Rickford.

LORD RICHFUCK,

I HAVE YOUR DANIELLA.
SHE LIVES FOR MY PLEASHAH.

SIMON

News of the kidnapping of Danielle Rickford spread through the country with the suddenness and ferocity of a tornado. The Rickfords were an institution, titans of industry for over a century, fifth generation money, as close to royalty as the American public would allow.

The story was up there with Lindbergh and OJ. But I don't have to tell you, Father. Everyone remembers that.

Chub finally knew the significance of the big "S" I drew for him. He was in heat for me. I ignored him for the moment. I was concerned that I had somehow lost "S."

Finally, after three days, Simon called me. He wanted to meet at the Santa Ana Public Library of all places. Whatever, wherever, as long as I got my information!

I had no idea what I had stepped into with Simon. How could I have? He had promised big things, but who could have thought. Simon said he laid a trap for the FBI, and boy did he ever. He bragged they would no longer be able to ignore him, and man was he right about that too.

The press was in a feeding frenzy. It was the notes more than anything that set the news dogs biting. Why were the notes swept under the rug? If not impressed with the first, then there was the second and then the third. Did the FBI think that, Simon would go away if they ignored him? Was wishful thinking the official FBI policy? If the FBI only took the information handed to them, perhaps Daniel Rickford could have been spared.

Please don't ask me the question that's in your mind, Father. I know. I know.

30

Janet Bultaco unlocked the door to her Marina Del Rey condominium. It was ten p.m. as usual, and she was tired. Bultaco flipped on the light and was startled by the smiling face of John Hightower. He had left on a case two weeks before and, as it was unsolved, she didn't expect him back. John was holding a serving spoon in one hand and a take out box in the other.

"Care for some Chinese food?" he asked cheerfully, as if he had never left. "I know you're hungry. You never eat enough."

"John? When did you get in?" Janet dropped her heavy briefcase and threw her arms around him. "I thought you were in the middle of a case in Minnesota. Did you catch the guy already?"

"Yes and no, yes, I was on the case and no, I didn't get the guy. I've been pulled. Dawson yanked me, threw me on a Lear Jet, and here I am. Seems there's this little Rickford matter."

"God yes!"

"Anyway, come and eat my little bulldog." John led her to the dining room, the table filled with no less than two-dozen to go boxes. "I trust I have your preferences covered."

"John, are you nuts?" Janet seemed baffled. "We can never eat all this."

"Now, you see, my dear," he said while sitting her down. "You're single, but you're not a bachelor. This isn't dinner. What I bought was a week's worth of leftovers. Shall we start with soup? Wonton or shark's fin?"

"I'm really not that hungry."

"Wanton or shark's fin?" he repeated sternly.

Janet rolled her eyes. "Wonton."

He filled her bowl. “Excellent choice, madam.”

“So, you're going after this Simon. How much do you think he's going to try to get? Henry Rickford is one of the richest men in the country.”

“You think it's a kidnapping too. That seems to be the consensus. They're all set up, waiting for the demand.”

“Why do you say that, John?” Janet asked as she played with her soup. “This is an obvious kidnapping case, the biggest one since Lindbergh.”

“Why is it so obvious? Was there a ransom demand?”

“No. Not yet.”

“Then why is it so obviously a kidnapping case?”

She was confused. “What else could it be?”

John finished chewing, then answered. “Simon sent notes. He told us what he was doing. Why not believe him? These people don't like it when you don't take them seriously.”

Janet remained puzzled. “If it's not for the money, why take Henry Rickford's daughter?”

John smiled. “If for the money, why take the other women?”

“True,” she answered, deep in thought. “But, the Benchly girl, they think, was just in the wrong place at the wrong time. She was taken along with Rickford.”

“Reasonable deduction,” commented John through some Mongolian beef. “What about the first three?” There was no answer. “Kidnapping for ransom is possible. I haven't had a chance to really review the case. But, it just doesn't smell right to me.

Some kung pao chicken, fried rice, sweet thing?”

Janet Bultaco was tired from another long hard day. She was happy that John was home and didn't want to waste any more energy on Simon speculation. She had had enough of it at the office. “Actually, John,” she said in her most seductive way. “You've been gone for more than two weeks. I wouldn't mind having a little taste of you.”

“Gee,” he teased, “and I bought all this food. Has it been two weeks? I barely noticed. Oh, and I've been on a plane for five hours and haven't had much sleep lately. God, I'm tired.”

Janet grabbed him by the arm and yanked him toward the bedroom. “If you think you've got jet lag now, wait till I'm done with you.”

31

The door was opened only slightly. A small stream of light from the barely lit hallway darted into the room. Simon was comfort able in the dark and the dim. Bright light made him uncomfortable. He refused to face it without protective guise. The condition dated back to when Peter Simmons was trapped by a burning timber and perished in a fire that was set too soon.

Peter Simmons struck his father on the head twelve times with a 30 oz. Louisville Slugger. The first blow killed him instantly. Peter returned to the house where he repeatedly and viciously raped his mother. "Your perfect little bitch has come to repay you in kind, Queen Bitch!" he shouted at her. Peter was certain that his mother was pleased and proud of him for the very first time. Afterward, he killed her as well.

Peter carefully laid his parents on the cabin floor. A space large enough for him was left between them. Then the fire was set.

Simon pushed the door slowly, no wider than needed to slip his narrow frame inside. The door closed silently behind him. Simon made not a sound, his custom, as he turned on a red light of low wattage. Slowly he walked across the room to his workbench.

It was a large room, a workroom with no windows and no door other than the one he had entered. Multitudes of faces and torsos lined the walls. An assortment of garb hung from clothing racks in its center. The room was cold, the way he liked it. Simon hated anything hot. Heat brought back painful memories.

It was time to put on the Gomer disguise, this time for real. Gomer had been a particular challenge. For weeks Simon had practiced getting used to the way it constricted his movement.

Simon sat down at the workbench, lit by two candles, and glanced at his own face one last time. He began adding the many layers of the sticky slime that would fill out his gaunt skull to become the round cherub faced Gomer. Simon worked slowly, efficiently, with a steady hand and an unerring eye. Facial stubble was painstakingly added to the cheeks. New teeth were inserted over the mangled snarl that was his. A false scalp was placed over a bald skull. Half of Simon's head could no longer grow hair, the rest he kept clean-shaven.

The Gomer hair was arranged carefully. Nine hundred power contact lenses were placed into his eyes to counteract the nine hundred power Gomer glasses. No fake glasses were allowed.

For more than two hours Simon toiled with the Gomer face before making his final inspection. Acceptable only, nothing ever surpassed acceptable. Simon added a wart to the upper lip as a final touch.

He was ready to put on the body, a reverse from the usual order. The faces were usually applied last. Gomer's extreme requirements made the change necessary. Simon strapped himself into the harness, which fit him tightly around the knees, crotch and shoulders. He gave the first tug, which bent him over and curled his spine. Exactly two minutes were allowed to accommodate the discomfort before the next tug. It was a contraption similar to the one Lon Chaney used to contort into the Hunchback role.

Chaney could shorten himself by over a foot. The best Simon could muster was seven and a half inches, a fact that initially drove him into a fit of self-derision and rage. Whenever Simon became angry, one or more of his guests usually paid a price.

He would not give the final tugs to the harness until fully dressed and ready to leave. Four and a half hours were required in the Gomer disguise, several in cautious travel and three, at least, with Wycheck. Gomer was a painful and dangerous identity, fraught with possibilities of dislocation or other injury.

Pain was not an issue. Simon scoffed at pain, knew it well, welcomed it, often pursued it. Pain was his constant companion during the "lost" time, when his flesh was charred and his sinew torn. He had known pain so great that only the melting of the nerve fiber released him from its long and lingering kiss.

Simon disdainfully held his left hand over one of the candles. Already scarred and gnarled he did not remove it until the flesh seared.

Pain far less than that experienced by a seventeen-year old boy in a hospital bed, tormented by countless plastic surgeries, each designed to make him less hideous.

Peter Simmons watched the old movies from beneath his bandages - James Stewart, Cary Grant, Jimmy Cagney, and Lon Chaney. Chaney inspired him, an ordinary man who transformed himself into the most horrible monsters. A plan formulated in the boy's mind. Through illusion, he, a horrible creature, would do the reverse.

Simon stuffed mounds of fake spongy material into place. His body was but a skeleton, barely covered with flesh; Gomer was a heavy man. Simon carefully put on the Gomer clothes and cinched up the belt just so.

He reviewed himself one last time in the mirror and made a few last adjustments required only by his discerning eye. *Acceptable*, he was ready to leave. Simon gave the harness its final tugs.

Every detail of the disguise had been planned to perfection. *Would the fool reporter appreciate the trouble I have gone to? Doubtful, do any of them ever? It matters not.* Simon's own harsh critique was the only one that counted.

The door was opened slowly, just wide enough for him to squeeze out. Simon turned out the light and silently closed the door. The room was again still and dark. A skeleton of a man had slipped in.

A Gomer had gone out.

32

Recording C-5

"I started, as we all did, with prostitutes. They are the easiest prey. Prostitutes are not suspicious of strangers; they seek them out. They do not question being spirited off; that is expected. Prostitutes do not object if they are handled strangely or restrained; that is what was contracted for.

When a prostitute disappears, no one reports her missing. And should the bitch turn up dead, no one cares.

In a truly decent society, the concern for a prostitute would be no different than that for Princess Daniella. Tell me, Frankie. In our perfect society, is that the case?"

I arrived at the Santa Ana Public Library five minutes late even though it bothered me to do so. A small concession to my pride, I was still pissed at Simon for making me wait those three days. It was also my wish that my tardiness would reestablish some control while not making him angry. Rationalizations, Father, the Cocaine made me late.

I looked around hoping to spot him, some outrageous looking whore or bum or the like. The place was full of students, nerds, and other library types. I was a reporter for a newspaper and was writing a book. I made my living off words. A library should have been like a second home. But honestly, I felt totally out of place.

I waited awkwardly for a few minutes then sat down at an empty table at the far end of the room. I took my cell phone and recorder out of my pockets and placed them neatly on the table. They were my companions in the waiting. I checked my Rolex; it was eight minutes past the scheduled time.

Waiting always made me uncomfortable. It made every addict antsy and fidgety; came with the territory. There was some solace in knowing that Venus had also kept me waiting. Simon would show. He was probably already there, watching me.

Simon would keep me waiting purposefully. He liked to annoy me and he needed to maintain his power over me. That was what it was about for him, power and domination.

Simon took his bitches, he claimed, strictly for sexual gratification. Though judging from my "experience," he could easily have afforded any sexual fantasy for himself. Actually, Simon kidnapped women because he needed to. His uncontrollable urge was to dominate them, impose his will upon them, and ultimately decide life and death for them.

I was determined to look relaxed, and fought off the temptation to check the Rolex every ten seconds. What a fool I was for not taking a stack of magazines to the table with me. I could feel Simon watching. My discomfort would give him pleasure. I resolved to minimize that and wait him out.

After about twenty more minutes, a short, fat, balding man carrying a stack of books sat down at my table. He was most likely in his thirties, although he was so out of shape, he could have easily been younger.

His hair was straight, too long, and unkempt. Ultra thick glasses made the side of his round face jut in as you looked at him. He had a double chin and a double belly and a huge wart on his upper lip that you couldn't take your eyes off. I would have bet the world it was Simon were the man not at least eight inches too short.

"Do you mind," he said. "If I sit here, that is?" He had a nasal voice that suggested allergies, and his words whistled through a chasm located between two large buckteeth.

Not waiting for me to respond, he sat down two chairs away from me. The large stack of books was cast down on the table. One, a dictionary, slid into the Nokia, causing it to fall off the edge of the table.

We each dove for it, with the result our foreheads crashing and the Nokia landing untouched on the floor.

"I'm terribly sorry," he snorted. "I hope it's not broken."

The words and some liquid were propelled at me through the hole in his teeth.

"No, that's Ok," I said, picking up the Nokia and placing it on the table a safe distance away.

Were it not for the anxiety of waiting for Simon, I would have gotten a kick out of the whole incident. The absolute king of the nerds was sitting right next to me. It would have made a good story for Christine over dinner. I was always looking for material to make Christine laugh. I loved it when she laughed.

"Really, I mean it. Let me pay you if it's broken. Try it out. I insist." The words came in a stream, or should I say, with a stream.

"No, that's Ok," I repeated.

"Try it out. I insist WIH..A..CHEE..YOOK..HUH!"

"Simon?" *Impossible!* He was far too short.

"That's Gomer, Frankie."

"Gomer?" Now I didn't even know how tall he was, six foot two or five foot six?

"Yes, Gomer. I would say Gomer is appropriate, wouldn't you?"

"Now that you mention it, Gomer is perfect."

"Let's not waste time, Frainkie. We have much to catch up on." He reached over and turned the Sony on for me.

Simon, or should I say Gomer, proceeded to tell me every detail of the taking of Danielle Rickford and her friend Susan Benchly. I listened and recorded for over two hours without interrupting. Not a single question, Father, I just sat there with my jaw hanging down.

Simon spoke in an emotionless monotone as if he were describing mowing the lawn or how to make a soufflé. He stopped only for me to change tapes and once to push my mouth shut.

"They can't ignore this, can they, Frankie?" Simon said when he had concluded.

I didn't answer. I was mesmerized.

"We are finished," Simon announced suddenly. "Stay here for another ten minutes."

I wiped my face as I watched him leave. Bright checked shirt, half tucked in, half out, baggy tan trousers pulled tight below his overhanging belly with at least a foot and a half of extra belt trailing down, and red canvas tennis shoes with dirty laces dragging behind. It was quite a sight.

33

It was the story of a lifetime and Chub, no fool, wanted to lock me in. I visualized him drooling at his desk with his fat stubby fingers on his checkbook. And I was more than ready to let him write that check.

Just in case, I did a small line. I wanted Patton on my side.

"Done any writing lately?" Harry asked me as we headed toward Chub's office. He waited to dig into me until we passed my old desk, occupied by Jim Potter. It seemed like Potter was there for months. Nothing personal, Jim Potter was a nice young man and talented, too. It just bothered me to see my desk lost, another lifeline cut.

"Gathering data and organizing mostly," I said as if I didn't notice.

We didn't talk again till we got to Chub's office. Chub was poised behind his desk like a pit bull ready to pounce on a piece of meat he'd been eyeing for hours.

"Hello, Melvin," I said politely. It was no longer boss, sir, or Mr. Timlin between us, but for Harry's sake, it wasn't Chub either.

"Wycheck," he acknowledged. Chub was physically restraining himself, trying not to seem too anxious.

"Let's get on with it. My schedule is tight," I said curtly.

Chub was clearly relieved. He was eager to get on with it. Had I realized that, I could have dragged the process out instead of cutting it short to act tough. I so liked to annoy Chub.

"You have a line on this S, this Simon?" he asked meekly.

"That should be obvious!" I turned to Harry. "You did tell him that everything has to be kept totally secret. I cannot compromise my situation!"

"Yes, yes," said Chub. "Ok, here it is." He slid a contract in front of me. "One million dollars for the exclusive rights to serialize the book prior to publication."

One million dollars! Holy shit! I never dreamed Chub would make such a lucrative offer, especially not first thing out of the chute.

"One million dollars!" I turned again to Harry. "Is he trying to insult me?"

"No, no..." stammered Chub. "What did you have in mind?"

"Two million, half now, half when you get the manuscript, for the exclusive rights to serialize the book concurrent with publication."

"Concurrent? You know it's worth much less concurrent."

"Of course I do. That is why I'm giving it to you so cheap."

"Cheap?"

"Yes, cheap! What do you think the Times would give me?"

"The Times, The Times, do you know what resources they have?"

"Yes, I do, Melvin. If you want to play with the big boys, you have to ante up. So, what's it going to be?" I looked at the Rolex impatiently, just for effect.

"All right, all right. But I can't go more than five hundred thousand down, the rest prorated as we get the manuscript."

I looked at Harry and gave him a wink Chub couldn't see. "If it wasn't for this man, I wouldn't let you rape me like this, Melvin. You have a deal. Cut me a check and you can send over the contracts when you like."

Ten minutes later I was in the parking lot, sitting in the Porsche, admiring my check.

Was I fucking fabulous or what!

34

Recording B-9

"Most of my brethren lead dual lives. One life within society as they try to fit in. They need to earn livings; they have jobs, neighbors, and even families. Then there is the other life, the secret one.
Their crimes are acts of desperation. They are part timers, amateurs. They invariably get caught.
I have no such weaknesses. My pleasure is my profession. There is no other life, and money is never a consideration.
My games are luxury items, Frankie. It's nice to be able to afford them."

I fucked up plenty in my life. And I was about as careful with money as the federal government. So, I stayed off the Cocaine for a few days and did the right thing, paying off Jane's house, our house, and setting up a trust fund for Jenny's college. I owed them that much, at least.

The rest was deposited in that temporary bastion for spending, my checking account. The addictive personality never looks too far ahead. Spend it while you have it, and right then I had it. What the heck, life was short and God made it to be enjoyed. So I enjoyed. What was wrong with that? And I was being a good American too, doing my part for the economy, spending more than I should have.

I loved the Porsche, but a new more expensive version was on order. Lavish gifts preceded me everywhere I went. Christine and I no longer ate dinner at a small Italian restaurant after which we retired to her apartment. It was banquet night every night and a room at the Ritz Carlton.

Gomer had told me that the next inning and subsequent innings were going to be more challenging and would require more time and planning. "Be patient and wait," he told me. "Be a playboy," he advised me. It seemed like a jolly good idea.

I called my travel agent and booked a long weekend in the Bahamas for Christine and me. I was losing ground with her and was desperate to put some new zest in our relationship. I told her to pack an evening gown, a cocktail dress, a bikini, and to fill the rest of her suitcase with negligees. She giggled like a schoolgirl.

God I loved that woman.

35

Mark Berlanger drove his White Jeep Cherokee into work with that same wonderful feeling he had just before Jaws was cap tured. *I have got him, this greedy Simon.* When it was all over, the world would look on this investigation as one of the finest ever conducted by the FBI. And he, Mark Berlanger was in charge.

Berlanger had acted quickly and decisively. Agents were immediately placed in the Rickford home. Wiretaps were set, waiting for Simon's ransom call. Both Henry and Elaine Rickford were instructed how to respond to the inevitable demand for money. Both were given twenty-four hour protection.

Kidnappers were usually caught when they tried to pick up the money, the big failing of the crime. *It is one thing to steal wives and children, quite another to collect the ransom. The relatives are always willing and anxious to pay large sums. But try and get it.* Mark Berlanger would not allow Simon to get away with it.

The taunting son of a bitch, sure he had gotten Danielle Rickford and thereby committed the crime of the century. *But he was more lucky than clever.* Several of the neighbors saw the Cable truck and its driver. Agents had obtained good descriptions of each.

In half an hour the FBI knew the truck was not from the Cable Company. No such call was scheduled, and Cable trucks were never pulled into a garage as was reported by several neighbors. The perpetrator posed as a Cable man to gain entry. Simon pulled the van into the garage to load and transport the kidnap victims.

FBI computers checked for all late model white vans rented or purchased within the last six months. Each instance was investigated and cross-referenced with the description they had for the driver. A big job, but FBI computer power was monstrous for those who knew how to use it, and manpower was not an issue on this case. Every request received top priority.

In a few days they had him, Jim Barker. Barker had rented a white Ford Econoline van two months previous to the Rickford kidnapping. A female attendant remembered him well. Barker was an extraordinarily good-looking man. She identified him from the artist's drawing. *The fool paid with a credit card.*

The credit card had also been used to buy art supplies. A female clerk at an Aaron Brothers recognized Barker immediately.

Visa was able to supply vital information such as Social Security Number, California Driver's License and, most helpful, banking relationships. The address listed on Barker's application, not unexpectedly, turned out to be false.

Barker had a checking account and small savings account with Wells Fargo. He had opted for the bank to hold his checks for him. *How stupid could the guy be?* With the bank's cooperation, the checks were obtained. The signatures on the checks matched those on Visa.

Checks were individually reviewed and payees contacted. Barker had written two sizable checks to Debra Bishop, an elderly retired woman. Mrs. Bishop identified Barker as the man who had recently rented her former home in Silverado Canyon.

The house was a secluded two bedroom, deep in the woods. A small dirt road was the only access. The house was placed under immediate surveillance. A white van was parked outside. One of the residents down the hill reported that she had last seen the van pass by over a week before and had not seen it leave since.

A female clerk at the local market recognized Barker as a customer who bought three hundred dollars of groceries the week before. She reported watching the man all the way into the parking lot where he loaded the groceries into a white van.

Mark Berlanger had reason to believe that Barker was in Mrs. Bishop's house and that he was holding Rickford and the other women there. The property was quietly surrounded. Barker would be apprehended. The main cause for concern was the safety of the Rickford girl.

With his agents around him, Mark Berlanger went over the details of the assault. The house and surrounding terrain lent themselves nicely to the quick strike that was called for. *There should be no difficulty, textbook all the way.* The book called for a predawn raid.

A nice bit of police work all around.

36

They ravage our daughters and brutalize our sons. They torture and kill our sisters and brothers, wives and husbands, some never to be seen again. Others are left for us to find, defiled and disfigured, mangled and mutilated, and always crudely displayed.
My colleagues, as much as experience anesthetizes you to the horror, you will never be prepared for it all.
Though an open mind and creative thinking are important, it is often a strong stomach that you will need most.

- Into the Mind of a Killer, John Hightower

John Hightower was filled with misgivings about the assault on Mrs. Bishop's home. It was all too pat, too easy. Jim Barker had left too many clues behind, the trail too easy to follow.

Hightower stood by as Mark Berlanger directed the men. Everything was eerily familiar. The small wooden house stood in a clearing surrounded by woods. Thick shrubbery lined the outside walls and heavy drapes covered the windows. It was as if they had all been there before.

For days, there had not been a sound or any sign of life. High-powered binoculars did not detect any signs of movement, and state of the art listening devices heard no sound inside.

Mark Berlanger began to wonder if they would find anyone alive. *Could Jim Barker be some whacked out cultist, bent on suicide, who decided to take the Rickford heiress with him? Was that why he was so careless and easy to track?*

They waited till five a.m. It was still dark, though no longer pitch black. The men readied their weapons. They put on their night scopes and moved in. In a few minutes they were in position and ready. The only sounds heard were the subtle noises of the woods. Mark Berlanger took a deep breath, then gave the signal.

The calm quiet buzz of night insects was shattered by the sound of breaking glass and smashed doorways. After that, the night was filled with stark silence. No gunfire, no struggle, Berlanger was not sure if that was a good or bad sign.

The men secured the building, then backed off. They had been well trained not to contaminate a crime scene. John Hightower and Special Agent Mark Berlanger entered the house slowly, Berlanger using his flashlight to guide the way. He shone the light toward the kitchen. Four bags of unpacked groceries were on the table.

"It's upstairs, back bedroom," said agent Pierce. "You won't fucking believe it."

Berlanger and Hightower marched up the stairs, carefully staying only on the edges of the steps. If there was evidence on the carpet, they did not want to contaminate it. Berlanger waved his flashlight back and forth in front of them, checking for anything obvious. The house looked completely unlived in.

Berlanger pushed open the door to the back master bedroom with his elbow. Any agent who needlessly touched a door handle was incompetent. The two stepped into the room, carefully avoiding the direct pathway. The flashlight lit the way into the room then settled on the large bed at the far wall.

Special Agent Berlanger froze. A chill coursed through his body. John Hightower stopped breathing. The air was trapped within him and his stomach knotted up. Involuntary gasps escaped from deep within each of them. The flashlight and both their eyes were transfixed on the headboard.

"Holy Mary, mother of God," exclaimed Berlanger.

FBI agents for many years, they had each seen many things. The recent Jaws victims were not pretty sights to behold. Yet, as God fearing men, some things could never be accepted.

They were the faces of wooden angels staring down from the church walls! Their accusatory gazes were pleading, "Where were you when we were being butchered? Their mournful cries wailed to them, "Where will we find peace now?"

On the headboard, neatly arranged and close together, their lives stolen, their futures silenced, their souls shrieking for salvation, like three members of a choir, were the heads of Mary Splitorf, Kathleen Harper, and Mary Benson.

"They were slaughtered mercilessly and senselessly," groaned Berlanger.

"Mercilessly but not senselessly," commented a somber John Hightower. "There is purpose here." He prayed the girls were again with God.

On the mirror above the headboard was written in blood –

THREE INNINGS WASTED

THREE BITCHES WASTED

SIMON

37

Father, if the authorities planned to keep any part of the discovery in the little canyon house a secret, Simon dashed those hopes. He sent graphic pictures of the bedroom scene to the newspapers and to CNN. The Grand Game was a high visibility contest. Simon would not give the opponent any relief.

He also sent another note intended for Henry Rickford.

LORD RICHFUCK,

YOUR LINEUP IS WEAK

TIME TO APPEAL TO A HIGHERPOWER

SIMON

I needed Simon to explain the meaning of that note to me. I also wondered if there was anything personal with regard to Henry Rickford. Simon had led me to believe that Danielle Rickford was just another bitch to him, special only in that her taking would garner the kind of publicity he sought. Was Simon simply milking the situation or was there more?

I was driving on the 405 Freeway when the cell rang. It was the "Voice," as if on cue.

"Yes, Simon, I know it is you."

"Nice car, Frankie."

I had the new Porsche for only three days. Shiny new, a little flashier looking, slightly more powerful than the old Porsche, interior quite similar, handling identical, I had difficulty telling the difference. Certainly nothing that could justify doubling my payments. I loved the old Porsche, which was actually only about a year old, and couldn't see how this one could serve me better, but what the heck. A man in my position deserved a new car.

"Very nice. It's really very nice," I answered. "But let's not talk about that."

"You have questions?"

"A few." I tried to be cool.

"Good. I only have time for a few. You have no idea how busy the Game can keep you. Ten minutes!"

So much for being cool, I knew if Simon said ten minutes, I would get ten minutes, not a second more.

"Tell me, why the heads? Rule Number Two, Leave No Bodies." I was frantic to get my questions in, and set the alarm on the Rolex to ten minutes.

"Rule Number Two, all the rules are suspended. And you are quite right, Frankie, the heads were a disgusting, ostentatious display. But necessary! It takes blood to get their attention and respect. The more abhorrent, the more respect they pay. Tell me, Frankie, who really are the sick ones?"

"Why just the heads?"

"Well I couldn't give them the bodies, could I? There is a gallon of my DNA in each of them!"

"The bodies will never be found?"

"Never!

I would keep the Game a battle of wits, like chess. But they will not allow that. They need the gore. The heads were required; they needed to see the blood. They can't write this off as runaways now, can they, Frankie?"

"And Rickford?"

"What about Richfuck?"

"There is nothing special about him or his daughter?"

"Richfuck is just another rich fuck. But Daniella, she is special. As fine a bitch as I have ever entertained."

"And the note? Is there a special meaning for Rickford in the note? Was it a threat? He should pray for his daughter's life. What?"

"None of the above. A Master of the Game must play against the best. Richfuck is a powerful man. He will make sure that I have my worthy competition."

"I don't understand?"

"You will. Now, tell me, Frankie, are you ready for your little holiday?"

"That is another question. Maybe I shouldn't be away for four days."

"Nonsense, Frankie. You won't miss a thing. That's a pretty sweet little bitch you have there, Christina. And I ought to know. Enjoy yourself."

I cringed when Simon mentioned Christine. I knew that was his intention and tried not to let it affect me. I failed.

"I have sent you a package of materials for the book," he continued. "Pictures of the heads and some other stuff, things I didn't send to the papers. Look for it.

Oh my, where does the time go?"

"Simon, wait!" I had so many more questions. He hung up. I checked the Rolex. Ten seconds left, my error, no doubt.

38

The travel agent booked us for four days, three glorious nights at Sandals. I had every confidence that Sandals would be outstand ing, as it was outrageously expensive.

Christine and I pretended to be on our honeymoon. We told lots of people, on many occasions, that we were either just married or celebrating our anniversary. It made it easier for them to accept our childish behavior together.

The trip was everything I had hoped for, great weather, great view, great room, great food and service and, of course, great sex. Being with Christine was like taking a time out from reality. With her I could put everything else out of mind.

Not that I needed that. The recent events and excitement were hardly burdensome. Quite the contrary, I was more alive and vital than I had ever been in my life. The book was coming together nicely, money concerns were completely eliminated, and, without deadlines, I even had time on my hands. Things were about as good as they could get.

Christine and I lay on the beach and swam all day. We danced and drank ourselves silly all night. We made love when we woke up and before we went to sleep and once sometime during the day. I was in heaven, yet Christine seemed dissatisfied. It wasn't until dinner of our last night that Christine dropped the bomb on Luxembourg, me being Luxembourg.

She was wearing my favorite dress, tight, black with sequins, short and low cut. Christine saved it for special occasions and great sex always accompanied the dress. Like Pavlov's dog, every time she wore it I got extra excited.

The evening went pretty much by script until halfway through the lobster, when Christine asked me, "Frank?"

"Yes," I answered, my head still spinning as it had been all weekend long.

"Frank, do you remember when I told you there were only two things in the world that I loved more than anything?"

"Yes, Chrissy." I rarely called her that – only when I was in the deepest throes of infatuation. "One was sex. You never told me the other."

"I'm going to tell you now."

"Yesss," I said, as interested as a full bottle of wine and worn out pecker could make me.

"You. You are the other thing. I love you, Frank, more than anything."

Father, it was the sweetest music my ears could ever imagine they heard.

Christine was the pure goddess of sex, high priestess of casual lovemaking, and the Joan of Arc of non-commitment. Christine, who always said, "If you are in love, there is a sense of security, and soon no need to try hard, and then the sex becomes ordinary. A relationship like ours, Frank, is a thousand times more difficult to find than love."

"Honey." It was all I could say. I was so happy.

"What about you, Frank?"

"I love you too, Chrissy. More than anything in the world."

We finished our meal in an eerie silence. I could tell Christine was anxious to get back to our room. I was anxious too, damned anxious.

"Then promise me one thing, Frank," she finally said. "Give it to me like you did that day, and even worse. Be rough with me, hurt me, love me."

A deep sense of foreboding was in me as we walked back to the room. I had been trying all along. And, I had felt guilty over that day, what happened to Christine, and, at the very least, my not being honest with her. I was ashamed, but even worse, I felt inadequate.

I waited on the bed, my stomach churning, while Christine readied herself in the bathroom. She stepped out and posed in her red negligee, my favorite. It finally sunk in that Christine had planned this evening for a long time, maybe for months.

Christine walked toward the bed, her slinky walk that always drove me nuts. She paused at the nightstand where she deposited a handful of powder.

"What's that?" I asked knowing full well what it was.

"Why Coke, darling. Have some."

I tried so many times to quit, and Christine was always there with more. Don't get me wrong, Father, I'm not blaming her. It never took much to get me to indulge. I'd regret it but I'd take it, every time. And this time, I sure as hell needed some.

"Christine? Where did you get it? I hope you didn't smuggle it in."

"Of course not silly," she answered with a devilish little smile. "I bought it in town during your nap yesterday. You were exhausted. Remember? Well, I went shopping."

I drew in the Cocaine like a tornado sucked up a farmhouse. After three days without and with what Christine had laid on me, I really needed it. Christine joined me. She breathed in the precious powder delicately, ladylike.

I was with Christine for four years and was still madly infatuated with her, eight times the normal six month maximum. She was all woman - beautiful, intelligent, and best of all, exciting. Christine was my goddess.

Lord knows I tried that night. I tied Christine up and slapped her silly. I was rough and crude and nearly choked her to death. She screamed in pain and delight and writhed in pleasure.

But in the end, it was clear that I had fallen short, left her unsatisfied. I did not measure up and Christine never used the word love again.

39

Serial killers are most often captured due to their own blunders. Their eyes are on the prize and not on the process. They are careless. Many killers have a subconscious need to be caught. They are compelled to leave evidence.
All of that is good, because it keeps our apprehension statistics tolerable.
But what about the clever killer, the one who doesn't want or need to get caught, how do we handle him?

- Into the Mind of a Killer, John Hightower

Special Agent Mark Berlanger had composite drawings of the sus pect widely circulated and published in the newspapers. Cops up and down California and in neighboring states were pounding the pavements searching for Jim Barker. Finally, someone pointed out that the great manhunt was looking for Cary Grant.

Jim Barker was the only suspect and a once hot lead quickly turned to ice. Every conceivable database was searched. Barker applied for credit cards seven months before and used them liberally, however, nothing prior to that. DMV had no record of a California Driver's License, although the rental company had a photocopy of one used by Barker to rent the van. No Social Security Number was on record, although one was shown. No birth certificate existed anywhere.

John Hightower was right. Jim Barker was much too easy. Simon was either an accomplished forger or he had access to one. Jim Barker was a disguise. That was consistent with the traces of makeup found at the Rickford condo. Analysis showed that the makeup was not a commercial brand, the kind that would have been used by Danielle Rickford, but rather a theatrical type.

Special Agent Berlanger considered the crime a kidnapping for ransom. Though Hightower had his doubts, Kevin Fitzpatrick supported the theory. *What other motive could there be?*

The FBI wired the Rickford mansion and everyone waited for the inevitable call demanding money. It had been several weeks and Simon had not yet made contact. Henry Rickford was a very wealthy man, an important man with many strings to pull. He was also an impatient man.

The mounting tension weighed on Mark Berlanger as he headed home. He rolled down the Cherokee's window for some fresh air. The cool night air was a small compensation for the late hours; missing the traffic was the only other one. Berlanger noted how dirty the vehicle had become and tried to remember when it was last washed. *It's a crime to allow a quality vehicle to look like this,* he thought. Mark Berlanger made a mental note to get it cleaned no matter what.

He was running a flawless investigation. *For all the credit I'm getting!* He had to admit Simon was smarter than he thought. *But sooner or later he will want his money. They always do.* Berlanger was sure that the three women killed and gruesomely displayed were meant solely to frighten the Rickfords into paying without questioning. The extra waiting was no doubt for effect also. *Let them stew, that's the idea, huh, Simon.*

Just ask for the money, Simon. Ask and then I'll have you.

The cool wind rushed over Mark Berlanger's face and through his hair. He turned up the CD player to compensate for the wind noise. Alabama was playing loudly in his ears while visions of Simon's apprehension played in his mind.

Mark Berlanger was finally beginning to relax. The days were long, hard and frustrating. The tension wound his muscles tight from early morning on, and, unnoticed, the knots were tied taut throughout the day. Only now, in the cool night air, did they begin to loosen slightly.

The Cherokee passed through the gate of Berlanger's tract. He drove slowly before pulling into his driveway. The garage door opened smoothly, but a little too noisily he thought. Berlanger made a mental note to oil it first chance he got. He hoped it wouldn't wake Maureen or the girls.

Special Agent Mark Berlanger was now officially off duty, determined he would think no more about the case. He walked up the stairs quietly and checked his daughters' rooms as he always did. Suzy and Heather were both asleep. They slept like angels, always had, since they were babies.

A shiver sliced through Berlanger's abdomen as he recalled the angels he had seen on the headboard. They were not sleeping so serenely. *God help them.*

40

They stormed in like the Khan's army looking for heads. Public pressure was mounting exponentially, fueled in large part by Simon's humiliating and taunting notes. The people were incensed and worried. Women did not feel safe and the authorities seemed impotent. The press was never satisfied and would not be mollified. Each day their reporting became more caustic and derisive.

A determined Henry Rickford marched vigorously toward Kevin Fitzpatrick's office. Senator John Lawton, Mayor Steven Plank, and Lieutenant Governor Raul Sanchez trailed closely behind the kingmaker. On Rickford's left arm hung political hopeful, district attorney Janet Bultaco. Beside her was Tim Dawson, Assistant Director of the Bureau.

The lovely Elaine Rickford held Rickford's right arm as she always did when accompanying her husband. Her face showed the strain of weeks of worry.

Of the group, Elaine Rickford was the only one Mark Berlanger liked. Elaine Rickford spoke sparingly. Berlanger thought it gave her an air of regal dignity. He had admired her often as she accompanied her obnoxious husband.

Supposedly the story of Pretty Woman was inspired by the Rickford's courtship. Elaine was the beautiful actress/waitress and Henry the filthy rich tycoon. While Elaine was clearly as beautiful as Julia Roberts ever was, Henry was no Richard Gere. *All men are attractive when viewed through an eight-carat diamond,* concluded Berlanger. To him, it was an otherwise impossible coupling.

Berlanger watched through the glass walls as Kevin Fitzpatrick nervously waited for the invading hoard. John Hightower was with him, but could never be counted on for support. Hightower was sent by Dawson to figure things out, but so far, he had only been skeptical and critical.

Fitz was a political animal with constant political aspirations. Under other circumstances, such contact, with such dignitaries, particularly Henry Rickford, the king maker, would have been a great windfall. Perhaps soon it would be, when Simon was apprehended, but, for now, Fitz's play had to be strictly defensive.

The party squeezed into the small office like sardines fighting to enter the can. They would want to know what progress had been made. Then they would question why it was so little. *These people don't understand how investigations work. Rickford thinks you can get instant updates, like watching the ticker on a stock.*

Berlanger knew how Kevin Fitzpatrick worked. He was Fitz's man but he could also be his fall guy. Fitz would step to the fore only when Simon was captured and there were rewards to reap. It would be Fitz's success then.

In the meantime, he would remain in background mode, pushing Berlanger out front. It was Berlanger's investigation, Berlanger's progress, Berlanger's questions to answer, and, if it came to it, Berlanger's failure.

Mark Berlanger knew that he only had minutes to prepare himself before he would be called in. There were those moments that defined careers. Berlanger gathered his files and his wits, then sucked in as much oxygen as he could. A good presentation was mandatory.

Special Agent Mark Berlanger had to be impressive.

Through the glass wall of Fitz's office he could see the boss signaling him to come. *Showtime!*

41

"Come in, Mark," said Fitz. *Welcome to the bear trap,* thought Berlanger. "I think you know everyone here, even if you haven't actually met them before.

Gentlemen, Mrs. Rickford, Ms. Bultaco, this is Special Agent Berlanger, who is in charge of the investigation. I am sure he can answer your questions."

"Thank you, Mr. Fitzpatrick is it?" asked Senator Lawton.

"Yes, Senator," said the boss meekly. Mark Berlanger realized just how far down the ladder he was.

"Well then, Mr. Boulangier," continued Senator Lawton, "tell us. What is the progress?"

"Yes, Senator. Our investigation is proceeding with all diligence. We have literally thousands of agents on the case. Forensics has uncovered some important evidence at the crime scene. There is a suspect and we are pursuing all avenues to locate him."

John Hightower fought to keep from rolling his eyes. He could see the skepticism, then anger brewing in his Janet's eyes. The District Attorney had very little patience for bullshit. He wondered how long it would take for her to erupt.

"I am certain that very shortly…" Berlanger went on as if reading from a script.

"Blah! Blah! Blah!" interrupted the District Attorney. "Don't waste our time! You have nothing. Isn't that right, agent Berlanger?"

Mark Berlanger had always had a fine professional relationship with Janet Bultaco. He testified for her often and was an important witness in the Jaws case. She was an excellent prosecutor. Berlanger admired her. Janet Bultaco had always treated him with respect. That was when he was the competent detective, who captured Jaws, with evidence to present and not horse manure. Mark Berlanger stood awkwardly silent, searching in vain for the words to respond.

The boss came to the rescue, stepping into the void to break the silence. "You are right, Ms. Bultaco," picked up Fiztpatrick, "in that we have little to go on for now. With kidnappers, the best chance to capture them is with the ransom."

"And you expect to get Danielle back? And safe?" asked Mayor Plank.

"Very soon, Mayor, I am sure," lied Berlanger. He hoped Janet Bultaco would not challenge him again. Fitz had put him on firmer ground. A kidnapping case was something Berlanger could talk competently about and he spoke up quickly to preempt the District Attorney. "I expect that the kidnapper will contact the family soon. We have…"

"It's been weeks and there has been no contact!" interrupted Henry Rickford angrily.

"Yes, sir, I am aware of that. The delay is intended to build up the tension, to get everybody worried, to build up the pot. The kidnapper is going to ask for a lot of money."

"Let him ask already, God dammit! I'll pay."

"I'm sure he is counting on that, Mr. Rickford." Mark Berlanger loathed the man. He understood that Henry Rickford was tortured by the loss of his daughter and that he was under great strain. What father wouldn't be? But what other victim's father was given such license?

Rickford's wealth and power bought him that. Politics runs government, and money runs politics. Everyone in the room understood that. When Henry Rickford spoke, the political tones were deafening.

"Please keep in mind. Mr. Rickford," continued Berlanger, carefully. "As difficult as it is, we must stay calm. We have to play Simon's game for now. It is unlikely he will hurt Danielle as long she is worth so much money to him."

"What about the note?" pressed Rickford. "She lives for my pleasure, what about that?"

"Again, intended to make you agonize."

"What about the heads?" screamed Elaine Rickford, no longer able to contain herself. She had been quietly crying. "What about the heads?" she sobbed.

It was a question meticulously avoided. The prospect of a dead Danielle Rickford was unthinkable, though all knew it to be a real possibility.

"I believe," answered Berlanger, "the other women were abducted and killed for the same purpose. Simon wants to show you he means business. Those poor girls died just to frighten you more. It's all about the money."

"Son of a bitch!" yelled Rickford. "He'll get his money. I want my daughter back unharmed. That is the first priority. Even if the bastard gets away with it, I want nothing done that might jeopardize her safety!" The silence around the room confirmed the order was received and understood. "Then, after Danielle is home and safe, I want this asshole caught and hung!" Rickford shouted sternly.

He peered around the room pausing to stare at each occupant. Henry Rickford's stares issued strings of orders. "That prick," he went on, "telling me to pray, telling me to appeal to the higher power. I'll send him to the higher power!"

"Actually, Mr. Rickford," interrupted Assistant Director Dawson quietly, "I think he is referring to John, here, John Hightower, our best."

"John Hightower? What the hell is going on here?"

"Actually," Hightower began to speak, "Mr. Rickford, I think what Simon seeks is competition, not money."

"You don't think this is a kidnapping?" pressed Rickford, his stare aimed directly into Hightower's eyes.

"No sir, I don't." Kevin Fitzpatrick and Mark Berlanger were both stunned. Hightower simply was not a team player.

"However," continued Hightower, "we should not rule it out. It is possible."

"The best possibility we have," interjected Fitz quickly. "We should proceed as we have."

"God damn it!" shouted Rickford as his scowl circled the room. "You, God damned better do something!"

42

I read the articles in the papers every day. My own paper, the Daily News, was doing a piss poor job covering the story of the century. Simon snubbed the Paper. His messages went only to the big boys, understandable and probably intentional.

Sure, the Paper was at a disadvantage. As Chub so often pointed out, they had inferior resources. So what else was new? In my opinion, the reporting was far less than inspired. The little guy needs to be different, grab a new angle, and be more creative. You simply had to be better to compete. And let me not be humble, Father, without me, the Daily News had become at best ordinary.

I talked to Harry a few times and kidded him about getting my desk back. He asked me what I needed a desk for. What was I doing to earn the paychecks I was getting? It's hard to win with Harry.

Chub's patience was dwindling along with circulation. Though I didn't care for him much, I didn't want his "welfare." It would have been fine with me to keep working, except for Simon's dictates. Chub would have to stay patient, I told Harry. Simon was playing a nine-inning game, and my book wouldn't be finished till he was.

I hadn't heard from Simon in some time, although he warned me that would be the case. He was busy planning inning six. What could he possibly have had in mind? There was nothing to do but wait along with everyone else.

I was desperate to win back Christine's love and was using more cocaine to try to do it. Everything seemed so much in flux. I almost forgot Jenny's birthday. My little girl was eighteen. I couldn't believe it. A nice saleslady at Saks helped me pick out a gift and I rushed home to give it to her.

"She's not here, Frank," Jane told me coldly.

"Where is she?" I wanted to know.

"If you were here at all, if you spent any time with her, if you cared even a little bit, you would know she is at Berkeley."

"Berkeley?" I asked.

"Yes, Frank. She's going to college next year. She's at Berkeley for orientation."

"Berkeley. My Jenny at Berkeley!"

"Yes, Frank, Berkeley. Jenny has turned out quite well. Even without a father."

Jane was a saint, but she knew how to plant a dagger with the best of them. She cut me deeply with guilt as I realized again how much, over the years, I neglected my family. Jenny was a senior in high school. She was going to Berkeley, and that was the first I knew about it. I felt so ashamed.

"Will you give this to Jenny." I handed Jane the box. "I'm so very sorry, Jane."

My heart was about to explode.

I was at hell's doorstep when Father Romero turned me around. He saved my life for sure. But it was Jane who escorted me from the darkness back into the light of day. And she did that little trick more than once. Jane was better to me than any other human being ever would be.

I resolved to change, to do better. How many times did that make?

43

I left the house depressed. Why did I always feel depressed with Jane?

I drove a few streets away from the house and parked under a big tree on a dimly lit street. It occurred to me that I had been there often. It was a favorite spot for me to load up. We are all creatures of habit, Father, regardless of circumstance. I sat and pondered the depths of that thought as I snorted up a nice little line.

Because of seeing Jane, I held off all morning, so the Cocaine seemed to pack an extra punch. There's nothing like a little bit of abstinence to make a thing more appreciated. I could feel the rush pulse through my veins, exorcising the guilt and depression out of me like the devils that they were. I was back!

The Porsche's tires squealed as it raced away. I wanted out of that neighborhood and fast. We got on the freeway and began gobbling up white lines. The cell called Christine for me.

"Chrissy, I'm coming over!" I shouted over the music. "Oh and Chrissy, don't make any plans for tomorrow. You aren't going to be able to walk."

She just giggled, loved it when I talked like that, liked it even better when I delivered. I was damn well going to try.

Without traffic, and at the speed I was going, I was no more than fifteen minutes from Christine's house. She would spend the time getting ready, getting sexy for me and getting herself excited. By the time I got there Christine would be an animal in heat.

I pushed down on the accelerator a little extra. The Porsche lurched forward. God, I loved that car. An excellent bit of German engineering, it flew down the freeway hardly even trying. There was a finely tuned piece of high performance machinery. Just like me.

Unfortunately, soon, I was stammering, talking as fast as I could. "With no one else on the road, it was difficult to gauge my speed. Heavy metal was blasting on the radio, so I couldn't hear the siren. The lights were flashing, but I simply didn't notice them right away."

The cop was not impressed with my explanations. He had to chase me for nearly ten miles at well over a hundred miles an hour. The officer was also not impressed that I was Frank Wycheck, the famous reporter. My attempted bribe didn't go over well either.

Mental note, Patton useless with cops.

They booked me for driving under the influence, speeding, and reckless driving. The cop ignored my bribe attempt, so they didn't charge me for that. I guess I should have been grateful.

They threw me in with the drunks for the night. The poor bastards! As always, they were dirty, smelled like hell, and most of them were not sure what planet they were on. That's how they rehabilitate well to do Porsche drivers. Indulge too much, act a little childish on the streets, get locked in with the drunks!

Don't get me wrong, Father; I've been in the drunk tank many times before. But that was different. I belonged with the drunks then. I was a drunk. I was a derelict. I was disorderly. So, fine! Lock me up.

This time, it just felt unfair to me. I was above all that now. I was a prominent citizen and deserved more respect. It was a gross miscarriage of justice. You couldn't convince me otherwise.

What a damn fool I was.

44

It was a beautiful sunny morning, as it usually was, in southern California. As John Hightower drove in to the office, he knew he wouldn't enjoy the fine weather, or much of anything else, for some time. When Hightower was on a case, he immersed himself completely. He was well rested and ready.

Fitz spotted Hightower as he came onto the floor and waved for him from behind his glass wall. He and Mark Berlanger were having, what appeared to be, a very animated discussion.

"What's up?" Hightower asked on entering.

"It's Rickford," said Berlanger. "He's getting impatient, planning to go on the offensive, on TV, newspapers, everything. He's going to offer Simon a ransom for his daughter."

"I would highly recommend against that," said Hightower firmly.

"I know your feelings, John," Fitz responded, looking confused. "And I think that kind of move is premature. However, Mark feels otherwise."

"It would be a gigantic mistake," Hightower pressed. He had resolved to avoid one of their famous shouting matches, but a girl's life was at stake. "Kevin, it's all about control. Henry Rickford is a hard driving businessman. He's used to being in control, frustrated if he isn't. But trying to take charge of Simon would be catastrophic.

You are dealing with a very delicate psyche, nothing that works in a normal fashion. Simon is in a fantasy where he is the main player. He has to feel that he's in charge.

We have to play this carefully, strictly by Simon's rules. If it turns out to be a kidnapping, although I still doubt that's what it is, we always have the leverage of the payment.

Let Simon call the shots for now. Do nothing to disturb or anger him. He has to feel powerful or the chances of getting the girl back alive will diminish greatly. This is not about money, gentlemen. An offer of payment could insult Simon. Infuriate him and he might blow immediately. We could see the Rickford girl's head next."

"My God!" gasped Fitzpatrick. "Mark, get back to Rickford. Talk him out of it."

Mark Berlanger's face turned sour. For once he had agreed with Henry Rickford. "Fat chance, with that arrogant bastard," he complained.

"Do it!" ordered Fitz.

John Hightower waited for the walls to stop shaking then added quietly, "Oh, and Fitz, you know how I like to work. Have a copy of everything sent to the house."

"Sure, John," agreed Fitz, with a snide look on his face. "That would be the District Attorney's address?"

"Yup. For the rest of my life, if I'm lucky."

45

They shock. They anger, disgust, sicken, and frighten. To the world they are madmen, beasts, degenerate and abhorrent. They are deviates, horrific creatures, vile aberrations of nature; they are anything but human.Their crimes are committed without conscience or guilt. They are driven by tortured minds with dark passions they do not understand and cannot control. Their logic suits their needs. They have their own morality. They have their own reality.

They cannot stop. They will not stop.

The world goes about its business despite the horrors. We cannot afford ourselves such a luxury, for we have to stop the killing. And to do so we must understand the serial killer. We must view things as he sees them, feel as he feels, and think as he thinks.

In short, my colleagues, we must journey into the mind of a killer.

- Into the Mind of a Killer, John Hightower

John Hightower's eyes were irresistibly drawn to the coffee table where the manila case files sat. Five female victims now resided in those cardboard folders and they beckoned him, *help us, find the killer, find him for us, and for others to come*. Hightower walked past the coffee table several times. How many times could he pass by without touching the files?

It was a standard ritual, diving into a case was an all out commitment. Once underwater, John Hightower would not come up for air until it was solved.

He opened the CD changer, choosing Brahms for this occasion.

Serious business required serious music. All four symphonies and the two piano concertos, *yes,* he thought. *A piano concerto first, just to phase in, one must not rush.*

He reviewed his meeting with Fitz and Berlanger as he loaded the music. *What had Simon called them, Tweedledumb and Tweedledumber? Crude, but actually, couldn't have put it better myself.*

Brahms' first piano concerto, first movement, *very lyrical, very smooth, very much instrumental at first, hard to tell it's really a concerto.* He stood and listened to the music, concentrating on it for the moment. John Hightower knew that he would shortly not hear the music at all.

Music set him in the proper mood, relaxed and receptive. It opened his mind and then withdrew. He would become immersed in the evidence, be transported to the crime scenes, and begin to see things through the killer's eyes.

A final breath, and a final appreciation of the precious notes, John Hightower opened the first file. He was ready to organize the evidence.

Typical Fitz, he thought as he pulled out the one large Rickford folder and four other smaller files. *When the Rickford girl was kidnapped, he focused all his resources on her, and ignored the early victims and the early notes. Politics!*

That should be corrected. As much evidence as possible, from all the crimes, has to be compiled. It is the common elements, the patterns of behavior, the little habits and idiosyncrasies that might lead to Simon's apprehension.

More killings make the commonalities more evident. Gruesome business we are in that we often need more deaths in order to catch the sick sons of bitches.

Investigators should never make preconceived judgments on the evidence, what is important and what is not. That is Fitz to the letter; mind closed and already made up!

And, Berlanger is not man enough or cop enough to stand up to him.

Hightower laid out the papers on the floor, starting with the killer's notes. *The killer speaks and we must listen.* Below the notes he laid the pictures of the abducted women, arranged in order. In a separate area he placed the pictures of the crime scene where the three heads were found. *They also speak and we must listen.* The lab results and other data were put in their respective places.

The evidence grid was complete. The living room floor was covered with the data from five serial abductions and three serial killings. *So far!*

He challenges us to a game. Nine innings and we have played five so far. Is he a baseball fan, a sports fanatic? How important are games to him? Is it all a game? Catch me if you can. I give you nine tries.

John Hightower began by reading Simon's notes. After two hours, he was still reading them. Hightower was reminded of the old Chinese tale of the fish, a favorite of his. He used it in his book and always when training new agents.

Inning one, Simon defines the game and taunts us to play. He makes reference to Jaws. Is there a connection? Check it out!

Inning two, another kidnapping and another taunt.

Inning three, more of the same.

Then Rickford and Benchly.

Berlanger is probably right; Benchly was unfortunate, a throw in. Rickford was the target! Simon wanted a high profile target, aristocracy, a Lord's daughter.

Only then did you go public. Why? Were you frustrated and angry at being ignored the first three innings? Most likely, but I think it is more than that. You planned it to go that way. A very calculating man, aren't you, Simon?

You could have taken Rickford right away, and you would have gotten the attention you needed right away. But, you didn't. You took your time, step by step, by design all the way. You wanted to twist the knife just a little extra.

And you know about the Bureau. You know about Fitz and Berlanger and about me, Higherpower. Coincidence? I think not.

Were you one of ours, Simon, disgruntled, turned, whatever? Do you hold a grudge? You must! Were you convicted, a relative convicted, someone killed, someone wronged, Waco, Ruby Ridge, something else?

You know too much about the Bureau. We will have to check that out!

The very real and disturbing possibility that Simon once belonged to the Bureau gave Hightower pause. He lifted himself up off the floor, out of the evidence, for some air. The stereo had moved on to Brahms' first symphony.

Beethoven's tenth they called it. It was said that Brahms was consumed and intimidated by Beethoven, who preceded him. That first great symphony liberated Brahms from the master's long shadow. Finally, he was able to step out into the light and cast his own.

Are you also troubled by a long shadow, Simon?

Hightower went to the kitchen for a glass of iced tea, the only nourishment he took time for, as he again concentrated on the music. Brahms was his personal favorite. He knew every note by heart, often played Brahms to himself in his mind, out in the field, out at the crime scenes.

LORD RICHFUCK,

I HAVE YOUR DANIELLA.

SHE LIVES FOR MY PLEASHAH.

SIMON

"LORD RICHFUCK, not Richfuck, or rich fuck, but Lord Richfuck. Is there some delusion there? The good Lord, unlikely, Rickford is the evil Lord. And who are you Simon, a champion to battle the evil lord?

Is there a grievance against Rickford? They have been checking that and have found nothing. Still, it's a possibility.

I HAVE YOUR DANIELLA, very personal, not I have your daughter or I have your little bitch. I HAVE YOUR DANIELLA.

SHE LIVES FOR MY PLEASHAH. Not she lives by my pleasure. Not she lives till you pay! Or, she dies unless you pay! Not a note designed for a ransom.

"SHE LIVES FOR MY PLEASHAH. God help us, we must believe you. She lives for your pleasure - what ghastly pleasure? And what, when you are finished? And what if Rickford goes public?

A chill came over John Hightower. He went to retrieve his master to do list, on which he always wrote the highest priority items. He scribbled on the bottom of the list, Stop Rickford!

Reviewing the list, there were now four entries, get milk and toilet paper, need new tires, call plumber, Stop Rickford. Hightower looked at the list as a wry smirk crossed his face. *Fill the refrigerator, get a leak fixed, oh, and if you are not too busy, save a girl's life.*

46

From the beginning John Hightower had a bad feeling about this case. He sat back on the couch with those misgivings very much reinforced. Brahms was into the third movement of his second symphony the second time around. So, by rough calculation, Hightower had been at it a little over seven hours.

Janet had come home from the office about two hours before, though he did not notice. She knew better than to interrupt him, understood perfectly. They each did. The work was that important, and they each required the time and space to complete it. Janet loved John, but went to bed alone.

Her pristine little home was becoming a sty for pigs, and she would indefinitely be forced to walk around stacks of paper. John would not have time to give her a nod, and she would be neglected for as long as it took. And, Janet Bultaco would not utter a word of complaint.

The Second Symphony, first movement, one of Hightower's favorites, had slipped by unnoticed. He considered replaying it, then decided against, could catch it the next time around. Hightower was just getting started.

He leaned back, closed his eyes, and recalled teaching at the Academy, a case study, of one who got away. That man, too, was a high profile killer who also challenged the authorities. He also sent notes and played a game. He too, taunted law enforcement and the victims' relatives. John Hightower thought back to the days of Zodiac.

BATES HAD TO DIE
THERE WILL BE MORE
Z

BATES HAD TO DIE – taking credit. THERE WILL BE MORE – the challenge. Z for Zodiac. S for Simon. Too much similarity for coincidence.

Are you a fan of the Zodiac, or simply a student of the art? You are not a copycat; you are too much the individual. Yet there are similarities that cannot be ignored. Is there a connection, Simon?

John Hightower opened his eyes, climbed down from the couch and got back on his hands and knees. The dearth of evidence from the first three kidnappings annoyed him anew. First time through the evidence he always preferred to proceed in order. *Not possible when there is nothing to look at.* He reviewed the scant data then turned again to the Rickford information.

One thing is common, sure enough. Everything is well planned. And it is well executed.

The Splitorf girl supposedly ran off with a fellow student. You sat in class with her for weeks, didn't you? Harper disappeared from a shopping mall, unnoticed. No struggle! Was she with a friend, someone she knew for a while? You? Mary Benson disappeared with a coworker, also no sign of foul play. You again?

Why didn't Berlanger check those people out?

Hightower made a fifth notation on his master to do list – Do the homework.

My guess, Simon, is that you are compulsive, a thinker, a brooder, an intense planner. Now, there's a difference from the Zodiac. He didn't seem to plan anything.

There was no sign of a struggle at the Rickford condo. How could you have abducted both of them without a struggle?

Did you kill one first, or both of them? No, that would not be consistent. SHE LIVES FOR MY PLEASHAH.

My guess, you took all the victims alive. Besides, in killing, you risked leaving evidence. And that is definitely not your style. Yes, you take them alive. Kill them when it is your pleashah. They all live and die for your pleashah, don't they?"

You drugged them! That would make sense. Chloroform perhaps, neat, clean, and effective.

Jim Barker had Cary Grant good looks. Hah, you must have been laughing when you saw the Cary Grant composites in the newspapers. Tweedledumb and Tweedledumber!

Cary Grant, two young girls, I can see how you maneuvered them quite easily. You separated them somehow, then drugged them individually.

The neighbors said that Danielle moved her car. Maybe that's how it was done. You drugged the friend when she was gone. Then you got Danielle when she came back. Moved the van into the garage, loaded them up, end of story.

Hightower turned his attention to the pictures of the three heads. He grimaced at the thought of Berlanger leading the cavalry into the small house. *We were obviously expected. And the house, so very familiar, I wonder.*

The display was made for effect. Why? To show us you were serious? Yes, I think so, not for Rickford but for us. But, it's more. Kidnapping Danielle Rickford made you serious enough! You didn't need to leave the heads to get attention. You already had it.

Why then? Why take the additional and unnecessary risk? Why leave us our first piece of real evidence?

To raise the status of the game! It's not a game of kidnapping. You're playing the ultimate game for the ultimate stakes. Your game is a game of death.

John Hightower took out his master to do list. He drew a star in front of the entry Stop Rickford!

He turned his attention to the lab reports on the heads. They were severed cleanly. Skin, tissue, bone were cut as one. According to the pathology report, the bodies were frozen at the time of the beheadings.

The job was probably performed with a high-powered saw. *Could you be some kind of craftsman, used to working with power tools?*

The heads were likely transported frozen. They were posed on the bed while frozen. *Only as they sat on the bedposts and thawed out did the blood drain from them. That's why there was so much blood. I couldn't understand it at first. Did you freeze the heads just to preserve the blood for us?*

Hightower took a deep breath before he turned his attention to the message on the mirror.

THREE INNINGS WASTED
THREE BITCHES WASTED
S

He studied the pictures. The message was neatly printed in blood.

The lab results indicated it was Mary Splitorf's blood and only her blood.

Neat lettering, that is consistent. Not a drop wasted! Why only Splitorf's blood? Everyone assumes you're a bloodthirsty ghoul. That you perform bizarre rituals with the victims, devil worship, black magic, unimaginable things.

Just the opposite is true, isn't it? This wasn't the scene of a wild blood orgy. You hate the blood; go out of your way to avoid it. Blood is too messy for you. The blood was for us!

That's why the heads were frozen. No chance of soiling your hands or your carpet. And the blood for the mirror was probably extracted from Splitorf neatly with a syringe while she was still alive. Took only what you needed from her, no need to take from the others.

So, it was just a necessary chore, huh? You needed the blood for show.

No frenzied activity for you, Simon. You went about the task as an accountant tallies a column of numbers or a bricklayer fashions his next row. No emotion, you were just doing a day's work in the prescribed manner. As another man, a generation before, calmly sliced a girl's throat in a parking lot, then just as calmly walked away.

BATES HAD TO DIE
SPLITORF, HARPER, AND BENSON HAD TO DIE

The first piano concerto again, how many times did that make? Hightower had seen enough. *You will not be easy to catch.* He thought back over his studies and more than twenty years of experience. Was there ever one such as this? *Just the one, Zodiac, and we never caught him.*

Some serial killers subconsciously need to get caught and leave clues until they are. Nine out of ten who are caught are captured because they are careless or don't care. Only a few are captured because of good police work and most of those still require some bit of luck.

You do not intend to get caught. You are not stupid or careless. Quite the opposite, so far you've played your dangerous game flawlessly. You have been masterful in your planning, meticulous in the execution, and remarkably patient.

You are going to be very hard to catch.

John Hightower was tired, had been at it twenty-six hours straight. He turned off the stereo, quietly said "Good night, Johannes," was headed upstairs, when something in the timeline troubled him. Back on the living room, on his hands and knees, Hightower groped for the necessary papers.

Barker rented the house months before. He bought the groceries the day before. There were many witnesses. You planned it.

You planted the heads the day before the Rickford kidnapping!

Confident bastard! How could you be so sure of yourself? You programmed all of it. Had it all timed – the groceries, the heads, the kidnapping, Berlanger, everything!

No wasted motion. No chance of error or delay. Synchronized perfectly, like a fine Swiss watch.

God damned! It's worse than I thought.

How many levels of planning are you capable of, Simon? How many years have you been preparing for this game of yours? How much have you practiced? How many hours have you studied the fish?

47

They had trouble putting on the makeup. Henry Rickford was on his cell phone constantly. *So what! Do they think I'm a novice?* Henry Rickford had made commercials before and was interviewed frequently on the CNBC business shows. His time was what mattered. *They can wait.*

Henry Rickford was an important man and *didn't get that way waiting for opportunity to come to me.* True, he inherited. His father handed the Rickford Empire over to Henry some twenty-four years before. *But, it is eight times the size now.*

Elaine Rickford, dutiful wife and loving mother, sat by his side. She would not speak. Elaine was there for show. Every great man needed a beautiful woman hanging from his arm.

The family never liked Elaine. They deplored the marriage. She could never be a Rickford they said. "Play with her, set her up, make her wealthy, but for God's sake don't marry her," his father told him.

The family didn't understand their young Henry. What he couldn't have was what he had to have. Henry Rickford was as headstrong then as he was now.

The FBI warned him that his idea was risky. *Weak minds, only through risk can success ever be attained.* How many times through the years had Henry been told not to do this or that. It was best to wait, the FBI counseled him. Let the matter play itself out. Waiting gave Henry Rickford indigestion.

He was a bold man, not afraid to stick his chin out. Henry Rickford made up his own mind. He imposed his will on others. *I am not a follower; others follow me.* He was a persistent man. His father often called him a mule. Success through the years only hardened his resolve.

"Two minutes, Mr. and Mrs. Rickford."

The voice came from somewhere in the darkness. All that could be seen were the tips of the cameras. Henry Rickford continued talking on his cell phone. Two minutes was an eternity of time for a busy man.

They can shoot and reshoot as often as necessary. I am, after all, paying for it.

Elaine was visibly pale even through the makeup. She was nervous and becoming more so.

The family was right. She was not made of the tough stuff. *So what! That is not her function. She only needs to be a wife and mother. And you shall be again, my dear, when Danielle is returned. I swear!*

Unlike Elaine, the family loved Danielle. She had her mother's good looks and her father's intelligence; her mother's charming smile and her father's drive; her mother's deep blue eyes and her father's strength. Danielle was majestic grace and beauty combined with the perfection of pedigreed intellect. She was every inch a Rickford.

"Ten seconds!"

Danielle had also inherited her father's granite skull. She demanded a *normal* existence. She wanted to go to college and be like everyone else. *She wanted to be a coed, join a sorority, and go out with just anyone.* Despite her wealth of superior qualities, despite the careful nurturing, Danielle was still a teenager. *What was there to do?*

Henry calmly put the cell phone down. His message would be brief. He had rehearsed many times. Henry Rickford often did that before important business meetings though he would never let anyone know it. The Rickford armor was always worn. *Image is important.*

"And three, and two, and one!"

"Hello." Henry began calmly.

"My name is Henry Rickford. This is my wife, Elaine.

I am here to talk to the kidnapper of our daughter, Danielle. To the man who calls himself Simon."

A slight pause.

"I am prepared to pay one hundred million dollars for the safe return of my daughter."

Another slight pause.

"That is right. One...hundred...million...dollars.

I will pay you ten million up front, in any manner you say, to show my good faith. There will be no police interference.

Then I will pay you the balance, ninety…million…dollars, when we have Danielle safely returned. Again, in any way you specify."

Another short pause as Rickford looked directly into the camera.

"I swear to you, I will pay, and there will be no attempt to capture you on the transfer.

One…hundred…million…dollars."

A longer pause, then Rickford turned stern.

"However, I warn you, Simon, if my daughter is hurt in any way, then you get nothing. And I will spend the full hundred million and more toward your capture and execution.

If you harm Danielle, I will see you hanged!"

Another short pause. He stared into the camera, the famous Rickford stare.

"The choice is yours, Simon. Rich or dead!

We await your decision."

Henry Rickford gave the camera a long hard stare.

"Cut! Outstanding, Mr. Rickford." They could hear clapping from the dark.

The spot would run on every major television station every hour of the day until further notice. A full-page reprint of the text would appear daily in each of the major newspapers that Simon had contacted.

"Was I forceful enough, do you think?" Rickford asked.

"It was perfect, sir."

"Let me see." He reviewed the tape. "I don't think so," he said. "I need to project more. Look him in the eye.

Let's run it again!"

48

An average lawyer can make you wealthy when you trip over the neighbor's curb. A good lawyer can get you off for drug possession. A great lawyer can help you get away with murder. But let me tell you, Father, no lawyer, no matter how fantastic, can do you a damn bit of good in traffic court.

Jimmy Bryant was a fantastic lawyer. He made his living, a good one at that, getting small and mid sized drug dealers off. Occasionally, he did DUI's, reluctantly, only as favors for good clients. I was not a client, but Jimmy did owe me a few favors. I covered some of his cases, and a little good press never hurt anyone's practice.

We waited our turn in court. Jimmy and I always got along well together, though we were not friends and never saw each other socially. He worked hard but he also knew how to enjoy himself. We talked about our Porsches, and I think I convinced him that he needed a new one.

When it was our turn, Jimmy was his usual brilliant self. Arms waving, presentation dramatic and flamboyant, Jimmy made a strong case for me. There were important mitigating circumstances that the arresting officer did not take into account. I was a substantial member of society and had done much good for the community. I had learned my lesson and everyone, especially fine citizens like me, deserved a second chance.

The judge was a woman, which had to be a plus. Jimmy was a very attractive man in his early forties. He was liked by the ladies and always fared well with the women judges.

Judge Eve Powers was duly impressed, specifically commenting on Jimmy's dynamic and persuasive presentation. She knew me and said that she read me religiously during the Jaws case and that I was an excellent reporter. Judge Powers then proceeded to throw the book at me.

"Mr. Wycheck," she stated calmly, "you have no business and no right driving down the freeway at one hundred miles an hour while intoxicated."

I got a thousand dollar fine, six months in jail, which she reduced to one week, fifty hours of community service and one year's probation. I also had to attend traffic school and an alcohol rehabilitation program. I didn't tell Judge Eve that I'd been to enough of those drunk classes to teach them.

Jimmy said that I was lucky to still have my license. He advised me not to let it happen again, at least to be more careful about getting caught. We had drinks and lunch at a nearby watering hole. Turns out I had a lot more in common with Jimmy than I thought.

You would think, Father, that would have been enough excitement for one day. It wasn't.

I was driving home after lunch with Jimmy, at the speed limit. Set the cruise control to ensure it. No way was I going to get another ticket. The music was on, loud as usual. No cocaine for me, even though Jimmy had offered, swore off it for the umpteenth time.

The cell phone sang its annoying little song from inside the glove box. I fished it out and answered.

"Wycheck."

"The god damned son of a bitch! The mother fucking asshole! Who does he think he is fooling with?"

It was the "Voice." I hadn't heard from Simon in months. He was screaming, seemingly out of control, furious. I held the Nokia arms length away from my ear, wishing I knew the way to turn the volume down.

"Simon," I said, "please, tell me, what's going on?"

"What is going on? Don't you watch TV or read the fucking papers?"

"Rickford?"

"Yes Richfuck! Haven't you been listening to him? Rich or dead! Rich or dead!"

"Why yes, of course. That's quite a bit of money he's offering."

"Try not to be an asshole yourself, WIH..A..CHEE..YOOK..HUH.

You know. the Grand Game is not about money! The Game is a test of wits and will. It's not commerce!"

"Simon. Simon." I tried to calm him, but didn't even slow him down.

"Rich or dead! Richfuck scorns me. He would cheapen the Game. Rich or dead! Richfuck trifles with me. Rich or dead! Well, for that he must pay a special penalty."

"A special penalty?" I asked.

Simon fell silent for the moment, as if he were thinking to himself. After a few seconds he went on, much calmer, actually, totally calm. The change was amazing, as if a switch had been thrown. "Yes..." The voice tailed off. I could envision him thinking, planning who knew what. "Not in the original plan, more work for me, as if there isn't already enough to do."

"What kind of penalty, Simon?" I asked again.

"You shall see. It will be another chapter for our book. Rich or dead, perhaps, I'll take his little wifey, the fair Elaina. I could do that you know. I can take anyone!"

"Simon," I gasped. "He's just a concerned father, who wants his daughter back."

"He has insulted me. And, for that he must pay."

"Simon!"

"Enough, Frankie! It is decided. By the way, how was Court?"

"Pain in the ass," I answered without thinking. My mind was definitely elsewhere.

"You must tell me about it someday. I have never been to Court myself. Never got a speeding ticket. Just have too much respect for the law."

A NECESSARY SIDE PLAY

49

When Linda Symes first began working at Tiffany's, her friends thought it was so cool. On Rodeo Drive and around all that neat stuff, what could have been better? And the pay was good, too. "You're so lucky," her friends told her.

Linda did consider herself fortunate to get the position, being so young and inexperienced and all. After work each night, she told her friends about the jewelry, how gorgeous it was and, more importantly, how very expensive. The wrinkled old ladies came in to pick out the jewelry. Then the husbands would follow within a few days to buy it.

That was over a year ago, more than enough time for the novelty to fade. Linda no longer talked about her job. Now, the jewelry all looked the same and she had long since been anesthetized to the prices. The customers were nothing but spoiled rich assholes with nothing to do. Linda smiled at them and acted as if they were gods because she had to.

There was nothing at all glamorous about her position. Each day, Linda dressed in clothes designed for her mother. She had to look refined. *Blah!* Linda came to elegant Rodeo Drive, to legendary Tiffany's, and stood around all day listening to *blah* music. Most of the time Linda wiped down the glass counters waiting for a customer.

And none of those customers was ever the handsome young rich executive Linda dreamed would come in, fall madly in love with her, and sweep her off her feet. Alas, no Cinderella, she. The customers were all so old. They, more than anything, were *blah!*

Linda was bored and disgusted with her job. She was meant for better things. Tiffany's was a job, *a job, a job!* If she could find a better one, she'd be gone in a New York second. But, for now, Linda needed the money.

Tuesday's were slow days; lowest in the pecking order, Linda always worked Tuesdays. It was ten minutes after eleven and not a single customer, until an elderly gentleman walked in. He looked remarkably like James Stewart at the end of his career, though at her tender age, Linda did not notice.

The man was tall and thin, with a graceful gait, and a head of distinguished thinning gray hair that was neatly combed back. Handsome, ancient to Linda, he walked around the floor like most of the old men, timid and lost. Linda gave him a few minutes, then approached quietly, unthreateningly. She hoped for a quick and easy sale.

"Can I help you, sir?" *You old fart.*

"Well, I certainly hope so," stammered the man.

He already didn't like her, having detected a slight pique in her tone. He was not a man from whom the slightest insincere inflection could be hidden.

"I need a pair of earrings for my wife. It's our fortieth wedding anniversary."

"That's wonderful," Linda said blandly.

"Yes, thank you very much." *Not very sympathetic, I must be interrupting something important.* "My wife is a large woman, good-sized head with a lot of hair. I think I need large ones, wouldn't you say?"

"Large what, sir?"

"Why earrings, of course." He made a circle with his thumb and index finger. "About this size?"

"That big?" *Nice taste, Bozo!*

"Why yes, a large woman, with a large head and a lot of hair would need large ear rings. Wouldn't you think so?"

"Why yes, certainly, sir." *Whatever!*

"You agree, excellent!"

She was beginning to anger him. *Sales clerk, lowly hired help, forgetting her proper place, acting superior, condescending, irritating, demeaning, and all this from a mere bitch.* He had known many like her.

"What's your name," the man quietly asked her.

"Linda." She had been taught to get personal with the clients. It helped make sales. Be friendly; get on a first name basis. Spend time establishing the proper rapport. Get them to like you and you will own them. Remember people buy the salesperson not the item.

The old fool, he was doing her job for her. Still, reluctantly, "and your name, sir?" *Like I care!*

"Max. Max Schmelling. Nice of you to ask." *I know how busy you are.* "Can you show me what you have?"

"Nice to meet you Max *Shithead*. Yes, we have some very nice things. Is there a price range, Max?"

"I only brought ten thousand dollars. Don't want to break the retirement fund. Do you have anything?"

Only ten thousand, you rich asshole? How long would it take Linda to earn $10,000? "I don't blame you, Max. It's better to be rich than dead."

The phrase was being used by everyone, and he tried to hide his irritation, wondering if she noticed his increasing hostility toward her.

"I'm sure we can find something suitable. I have a very nice pair over here for $8,500, diamonds and rubies."

Snide, irritating bitch! He picked up the sarcasm in her tone, so slight, so carefully concealed, never noticed by Linda's other customers.

"They are Ok."

"They're not right. What don't you like about them, Max?"

"They are a little smaller than I care for, *like your tits.*"

"How about these for $9,200. *Are they large enough, you fuck?* Would they be more suitable?"

"These are better." He held one up and compared it to the circle his hand made. "Maybe something just a little bigger."

"All right, how about these *ugly pieces of shit* over here? They are about the largest we have and they are quite nice at $9,000, don't you agree? I'm sure they would look quite nice on your wife."

And I am sure you would look quite nice with your ankles at your ears, Leendah! He was not sure how much longer he could tolerate this bitch. She had done more than enough to be a Castle candidate. Linda would not be the first young obnoxious saleslady he had taken. And few of them raised his ire as she had.

Were it not for the Game, he would return for her. He would study this Leendah, follow her, learn her habits and preferences, where she lived, where she ate, what she did in her off hours, the type of men she cared for, what diversions she craved, what she feared. He would study her until he knew everything she did. He would view the world as Linda Symes did. He would journey into the mind of an obnoxious sales bitch.

And then, dear Leendah, I would make you disappear from the world. And you would reappear in mine, where you would learn humility and your proper place.

Irritate me? Your station extends no further than my pleasure.

The Game was tightening its grip around him, restraining his freedom of action. The side play and this little exercise at Tiffany's was already outside the original plan. He could not afford further distraction.

He would not play with this little bitch any further. *Were it not for the Game, Leendah, I would certainly see you again.*

"Yes, they are perfect. I'll take them," he said calmly. "Now show me your boxes, your special Tiffany boxes."

See… nile! "All our gifts come in boxes. These earrings come in this box."

"Too small! Have you one larger? Presentation is very important. Forty-five years in business taught me that much."

Linda reached under the counter and retrieved all of the velvet boxes she could find.

"Here you are, Max, *moron*. These are all of our boxes. Why don't you choose one?" She tossed the boxes down on the counter in front of him.

Bitch! Don't toy with me! Or, I swear, I will make time for you. The rage welled up in him as it always did.

Linda watched as the tall gentleman tried out several of the boxes. His hands were shaking. *Take any fucking box you want.* The sale was what mattered. Linda did not comment as a box much too large for the earrings was picked.

"Presentation, Linda. Presentation is very important." He fought to stay calm.

"Shall I wrap them for you?"

"No, I think I'll wrap this gift myself. How much do I owe you?"

After a short calculation, "$9,675."

Slowly he reached into his pocket, pulled out a thick envelope and handed it to Linda. "That's ten thousand dollars. Don't like writing checks. Keep the extra for yourself."

"Why thank you, sir!"

He waited while Linda counted out one hundred Benjamins. *Remarkable change in attitude,* he noted as he passed the time inspecting her line. The slightly tapered waist, hips too full, breasts smallish, calves lacking in shapeliness, face pleasant to plain, Linda was at best ordinary. Not nearly attractive enough for him, but her personality begged for attitude adjustment. Simon envisioned Linda in one of his Castle chambers in some of his favorite positions.

"It all seems to be here," she said finally. "And again, thank you!"

"Consider this the luckiest day of your life, Leendah," the gentleman said to her quietly. *That there is no time for you,* he thought to himself as he left Tiffany's.

Simon walked slowly, in character, toward his car parked several streets away. *No time! Distractions must be avoided. Keep your eye on the ball, as dear old Dad used to say. Kept my eye on your noggin, didn't I Dad, eh?*

No time! Around the corner was Bellagio's, where he worked each day. In the evenings, there was the fitness center. He also had to monitor Wycheck, the FBI and the rest of them. *No time!*

Simon struggled, as always, to maintain control; his reservoir of rage was still full. The anger could be managed if he forced himself to concentrate on future strategy. That was the trick; the offender started to pay with the first thought.

This intolerable Leendah will not be punished. Damn the Game! No matter, there is always another day and perhaps then, Leendah, we shall play.

Simon focused his attention on the remaining plans for his little side play. E*nergy must be conserved. It must be preserved, used wisely.* The anger had to be harnessed and channeled; it was constructive, kept him sharp, provided more energy, but only if tightly controlled.

His thoughts turned to Henry Rickford and again his heart started pounding wildly. The breath raced into and out of his lungs. *That is what this is about, not the stupid little sales bitch. Rich or Dead! Rich or Dead! Rich or Dead! You will have your answer soon enough, Lord Richfuck!*

Simon envisioned the adversary after his mighty blow was delivered. It helped to calm him. He walked slowly, perfectly in character, toward his car. Soon the Jimmy Stewart disguise would vanish forever. At the next corner was a trash receptacle. Simon opened the velvet Tiffany box to scrutinize the just purchased earrings. *Decadent mani-*

festations of a truly misguided society! And the same for Richfuck's money!

He scooped the earrings from their box. Simon's hands moved deftly, smoothly and with the slightest motion of his arm the box was deposited in his pocket and the earrings in the trashcan. *Disappeared, worthless baubles.*

Enough time wasted! Wanda still has to work out tonight.

50

Recording C-8

Tell me, Simon, where do you take them."

"To my Castle of Pleasure."

"Castle or dungeon?"

"Now, that might depend on your point of view. However, every self respecting Castle must also have its dungeon."

Simon pulled into the warehouse he had made his Castle of Plea sure. Inside, more than two dozen different vehicles were parked, all acquired for use in the Grand Game.

His building was the first to be built on a sea of empty pads. Overoptimistic expectations had caused the developer to overreach. There would be no other buyers for years. The pads would remain empty.

Guaranteed seclusion was exactly what Simon required. He had scoured Riverside County for just such a location. The developer was anxious to build the special purpose building, a lucrative job to help forestall the inevitable bankruptcy.

The building was large, some sixteen thousand square feet, much larger than Simon required. Most of it would never be used; Simon always kept a reserve. There were no windows and only one entrance, the large steel door.

The warehouse was a concrete box, nothing could get in and, more importantly, nothing could get out. Hidden in the unused office was a two-inch thick steel door, entry to the Castle. Simon entered the combination and proceeded down the concrete stairs that led to the five thousand feet of special purpose construction.

He walked along the long corridor lit only by pale red lights, passing Processing. *Shame, tomorrow the room has to be used again.* Next on the left was the room he called the Freezer. *Later today*, Simon thought to himself. The prospect troubled him. This was not a good day. He hated wasting bitches, and today one of his best ever would be lost.

The Game and that ass Richfuck make it necessary!

Simon paused at the first chamber door and looked through the heavy glass window at Susan Blakely. *Would that it was her instead.* Alas, no one cared about Susan Blakely. She could live.

Rich or Dead! Rich or Dead! Arrogant Richfuck! How could such a complete asshole have spawned such an angelic bitch? I see nothing of him in her. She takes after her mother only, the lovely Elaina.

Simon thought about Elaine Rickford. She, too, had been studied closely. He envisioned her in one of his chambers. *Now that would really show Richfuck. And what pleasures might the fair Elaina bring with her?*

The next three chambers once housed Mary Splitorf, Kathleen Harper, and Mary Benson. They too were lost prematurely, pawns sacrificed to keep the Game moving. Simon liked the Splitorf bitch best of the three. Harper and Benson were not great losses. *Splitorf was an enjoyable bitch. Like Daniella, although hardly in the same league.*

There was now a shortage. The Castle's chambers were always full before the Game. *The Game! The Game! Daniella made up for the losses though. Her quality compensated for the lack of quantity.*

The task for this day had been put off several times. *Three times, at least, I have made excuses for delay. How long would Daniella have been kept, were it not for Richfuck?* Simon could not foresee the day when he tired of her. Could she have become the one bitch that might eventually have been trusted? He longed for a soul mate, though he knew it likely impossible. *Is she worthy enough? Perhaps, but we shall never know. Damn you Richfuck!*

Simon stared at Daniella through her chamber door. She was lying asleep on her cushioned table. Long and slim, Daniella was the way he liked them. Her waist was small yet long; the diminutive breasts were perfectly shaped; thin arms and legs, stretched and accentuated by the restraints, fit her slender line.

A beautiful sight! Daniella excited him, called to him. *I want you. I want you, again and again. Please, come and take me.*

Simon opened the heavy metal door. A bitch could never escape. Even if she got past him, if he died suddenly, anything, she would eventually die entombed in the Castle. Rule Number One, take no chances. *They live only for my pleasure. Period!*

The door opened with a loud creaking noise. All the chamber doors were noisy. They were kept that way on purpose. A *nice authentic touch.* Simon entered the room.

Danielle's blonde hair made the first impression. He was initially disappointed with the artificial coloring. But after having washed out the crude dye, Simon was pleasantly surprised by Danielle's natural blond color. *The new style fits her well also, quite lovely, actually.* He smelled the pleasant fragrance of Danielle's new perfume. *Heavenly!* Simon now applied her makeup for her. *Much more tasteful, elegant.* Daniella wore a green negligee chosen just for her. Each day she was dressed in a new one. *Exquisite!*

Danielle awoke from the sound of the door. Simon stood in front of her without disguise and without clothing. Only his bitches saw the real Simon. He gave them that honor. They had the right to see their one true lover.

"Daniella, open your eyes."

Simon gazed down onto the angelic face. He waited as she came to consciousness. This was the moment he enjoyed most, when her eyes opened and looked up into his. Dazzling, mesmerizing, intoxicating, this one most enchanting quality, that which first drew him irresistibly to his Daniella.

The bluer than blue eyes!

51

Recording E-3

"You cannot inflict pain on your enemy without experiencing some of your own. There are always casualties and losses. Some losses hurt more than others."

Simon's Daniella looked up at him with those expressive eyes. All of her emotions could be read in them. Early fear, then hatred, *yes, that is understandable, it always starts like that, then,* eventually, resignation, and after that, *well, that hasn't happened yet.*

Daniella has learned how best to handle her situation. She accepted her station; she lives for my pleasure.

He had prepared a special meal for their last supper together. Daniella did not speak. *Intelligent girl,* she learned early that bitches were not kept for conversation. Daniella ate less than half of what he had prepared. She was a light eater. *Good for the figure!*

He replaced her gag. No resistance, *Daniella understands.*

Danielle Rickford was fully aware of her situation. After her kidnapping she awoke on Simon's table, alone, naked, and bound. She hadn't been off it since. This brute of a man, grotesque and hideous, raped her every day at least once. He defiled her in ways she never knew possible. Tied up like an animal, she was turned and taken in every conceivable way.

He was grisly ugly. The putrefied flesh of his body revolted her. Every touch strongly induced her to puke. Instead, Danielle closed her eyes and grit her teeth. She was dejected and degraded, and had learned it best to let him have his way.

God help me! What diseases will he give me? What if I become pregnant with his child?

Simon cleared the dishes then climbed on top of his Daniella. She was comfortable and fit him well. Danielle tried to think of other things, of better times. He inserted himself into her. She tried to set her mind blank. *There is no sensation. My body belongs to someone else.* Simon began to pump furiously. Danielle swayed back and forth slowly, trying to increase his pleasure, hoping to get it over sooner.

Afterwards, he lay on top of her, stroking the golden hair and breathing in her perfume. His weight was heavy on her as she lay under him, repulsed by the smell of his sweat. Simon fell into a peaceful sleep. Danielle dared not move, afraid to disturb him.

I am spoiled forever. The monster has ruined love for all time. I am no longer pure, no longer innocent. I am turned to stained filthy flesh.

Daddy! Daddy! Please come and find me! Please find me! You must find me!

Simon woke after an hour's nap. He was rested and satisfied, but behind schedule. Tonight he worked at Bellagio's. Simon detested having to rush and compromise was never an option. Felix had to be perfect. *The Game! The Game!*

He got up abruptly. Danielle was relieved to see him go, only to have him return shortly. He had a syringe with him and stuck it quickly in her arm to withdraw some blood. Simon could see the fear gathering in her eyes.

"Fear not, Daniella, my darling, there will be no pain."

He watched as the panic grew in her eyes, heard it in the frenzied sounds she made through her gag. "Why, why are you killing me? I love you. I'll do anything for you." He was certain that was what she was trying to say.

"I have no choice, my dear Daniella. The Game and your foolish father leave me no choice!"

The blue eyes were open wider than he had ever seen. Worried noises pushed their way through her gag.

"I know, I know my dear, and I care for you, too. You are the best bitch I have ever had."

For a moment he was tempted to remove the gag. He wanted to hear the words he imagined her saying. *Nothing to be gained from that. Best to make it quick and clean.*

Simon reached for a second syringe, this one with a pale blue liquid in it. He was tempted, just for an instant, to delay one more time. *One more day, one more time for making love? Impossible! What must be done, will be done!*

The syringe pierced her skin and settled into her thigh. Danielle became desperate. The blue eyes welled up with tears and horror and the sounds from under the gag became frantic.

Simon had seen it before, heard it before, hundreds of times.

Here it all is again. The terrified pleading stare that begs, let me live, please, just let me live. The gagged rueful noises, the mournful laments that recognize the end is near. The last minute wailing, the final imploring gasps, that look of understanding, it is always the same.

He pushed down on the syringe. A sigh came out of each of them as they watched the liquid enter Danielle's thigh. She fell silent, recognition that it was hopeless. Daddy was not coming, only death.

They both knew it was over. Danielle stared up at him one last time, with revulsion and hatred, with disgust and loathing. Her only last wish, her final prayer that she could somehow see him die before her. *Is there no God to strike him dead?*

She had experienced nothing of life. Where was the time, so plentiful she gave it no thought? Never to walk a beach with her true love in hand, no grand wedding or blissful honeymoon, no career or experiencing the world. Never a daughter of her own to raise and nurture. Never to grow old gracefully with grandchildren to spoil.

A life barely begun would go no further.

"Sleep well, my angel. Sleep well, my Daniella."

52

Sally Phillips and Paula Spenser decided radical action was required to lift their friend Elaine out of the deep depression she was trapped in. Shopping, they found, could satisfy the need created by any emotion. Boredom required stimulation, happiness expression, apprehension comfort, creativity outlet, and sadness consolation. Shopping would set Elaine right.

Sally and Paula understood what it was to worry. They too had children. Anyone could put themselves in Elaine's shoes. They probably would react exactly the same way if faced with such an unthinkable situation. But enough was enough. Month after month, Elaine was not doing anyone any good and she was killing herself. Serious treatment, they decided, was called for.

Good healthy shopping was the antidote for what ailed Elaine. Bellagio's therapeutic powers would brighten her outlook and pull Elaine out of her funk. Well, at least it would take her mind off her troubles for a while.

As her best friends, that was the least expected from Sally and Paula. Hadn't Elaine herself done the same for each of them? Certainly! It was Elaine who helped Paula redecorate her house. And it was Elaine who comforted Sally when husband Dan was having an affair.

"It's their nature to wander," Elaine told Sally. "And when they do, it's the wife's responsibility to shop them to death." And with that, they buried Dan Phillips at the Beverly Hills Mall.

The three were a natural combination, best friends. Their relationship was based on common interests and mutual envy. Elaine and Sally envied each other; Paula envied them both.

Sally, years back, had been an attractive starlet with a few small parts in mostly B movies. After many headlong rushes at the brass ring, and with her physical freshness diminishing, Sally recognized that her window of opportunity was closing fast. She modified her objectives and, in short order, Sally was married to producer Dan Phillips.

Whereas Sally had done well, Elaine had hit the jackpot. Elaine was not simply wealthy; she was part of royalty. Dan Phillips had money, but he was hardly in Henry Rickford's league. While Sally often shopped at Bellagio's, she purchased sparingly. Elaine never looked at a price tag.

Elaine in turn was envious of Sally. Sally had been in films, not a star, but immortalized in celluloid nevertheless. Elaine was a waitress/actress, one in a long line of midwestern farm girls. She was strikingly beautiful, graceful and vivacious and was offered several screen tests. Alas, the young blonde beauty froze in front of the camera's fearsome eye and was barely able to squeak through her lines. After each test, Elaine became less actress and more waitress.

Both women were still quite attractive and the quest to remain beautiful was a common bond. They talked constantly about their losing battle with time and gravity. Each had made numerous boat payments for Doctor Frank Castle, plastic surgeon to the stars.

"We are going to Bellagio's, Elaine," said Paula proudly. "You are going to meet Felix, or should I say Mr. Felix." Paula and Sally giggled to each other. Elaine had no idea why.

"Then we are going to Truffeau's for lunch. After that, our afternoon is open. We can do whatever you like."

Paula was a Jewish girl from Brooklyn who got her Beverly Hills address through the hard work of her husband Sam, a down in the gutter plumbing contractor. She had two wishes, that her children were brought up right and that she fit in. On one count she was successful. The Spenser daughters went to the best private schools and were becoming two properly spoiled obnoxious little brats.

Paula was the hanger on. She went along. What Elaine and Sally did, Paula also did. What they wore she wore. What they ate, and so on. If Elaine and Sally bought Dr. Castle a boat, Paula certainly paid for his new Cessna. With every procedure known to modern cosmetology performed, the improvement in Paula's appearance was great, though the end result could at best be rated as plain.

The two women took Elaine by the arms. Paula drove while Sally sat in the back seat with Elaine. It was a well-executed mission. Elaine was a reluctant companion; she was going, but her mind remained tortured and at home.

"You simply must cheer up Lainey," ordered Sally

"Felix will cheer her up," came the comment from the back seat.

"And who is this Mr. Felix?" asked Elaine. Her answer was a new round of giggles.

"Well?"

"He is the new salesperson at Bellagio's," answered Paula.

"A man?"

"Well, not exactly," answered Sally with a quick downward flick of her wrist. She and Paula giggled some more.

"But he has taste like nobody's business," added Paula.

"That's true, Lainey. Felix can take a knapsack and make it look fabulous on you. You should see what he did for Paula last week." There was no comment from Paula.

"And he is quite entertaining. He always has me in stitches. Bellagio's now has a floorshow."

Paula and Sally giggled some more. The car sped toward Rodeo Drive and their therapy session at Bellagio's.

53

Oh, It iss my besst leetle thweetie piess!"

He could be clearly heard all over the store. Bellagio's was the crème de la crème of Rodeo Drive. All designer all the time, the prices and haughty snobbish air dictated who the clientele could be. And who the salespeople could be as well, at least up until Felix.

By any standard, Felix did not belong, except that sales more than doubled from the moment he was hired and the clients absolutely adored him.

Felix came tripping down the dramatic stairs located in the middle of the store. He wore an unbuttoned ruffled white shirt with bright yellow slacks, flared slightly at the bottom, covering pure white boots. A clown suit for anyone else, on Felix it was avant-garde stylish.

"Oh my darlingss! My beautiful Thally and the gorgeouss Paula. Come! Come! Come!"

Felix sounded like Liberace but with a decided Latin accent. He was six foot one or two, and well built, slim, excellent for clothes. Felix had a way of singing the words and his voice went up at the end of each sentence. He was either utterly outrageous or completely charming. The clientele of Bellagio's chose charming.

"Oh my darlingss, I have misssed you!"

Felix reached the trio of women before they had barely entered. He gave a big hug to Paula and then to Sally.

"And who, Thally, iss thiss lovely creature with you?" Felix asked as he was finished with her hug.

"This is our friend, Elaine. She used to shop here with us before you started working here."

"Thiss iss not work Thilly Thally! Elaine? *Elaina!* What a lovely name."

Felix hugged Elaine quickly and naturally, no time for her to think, let alone resist. He released her just as quickly. The hug meant nothing. It was no more than a meaningless embrace between women. Felix did continue to hold her right hand as he stepped back to inspect her. His eyes viewed her up and down. They were a woman's eyes, a critical viewing.

"Oh thweetie, with material like thiss, I could work miracless. You know Misster Felix will be famouss thomeday."

They all giggled, all four of them. Felix was one of them, just one of the girls.

"We need you to do something special for her, Felix," said Paula seriously.

"For her? No problemo, thweetie! Come!" He escorted them into the store. "You girlss come at a good time. We have thome fabulouss new Italian goodiess."

They went upstairs, away from the browsers, to the private rooms, where the real clients shopped. This was where the exclusive merchandise was shown and fitted.

"I hope your husband hass plenty o de monneh, Elaine."

"Are you kidding," blurted out Paula. "This is Elaine Rickford!"

"Oh, I thee. Well, thay no more. Let me take your coats, and let'ss get thtarted."

Paula and Sally sat down. Elaine stepped up on the pedestal surrounded on three sides by mirrors. She had stood there many times in better days, a wonderful place. Felix came back with a long black evening gown.

This was Bellagio's. One did not come in to shop for a pair of jeans or a blouse. Bellagio's showed you what you should be wearing, that one of a kind dress for a formal dinner party, or the Oscars, that one creation that even Sharon Stone would envy.

"Here, thweetie. Put thiss on."

He tried to look busy and not notice her disrobe. *What is it that makes women so comfortable with gay men?* Felix kept his back turned, straightening up some cushions as she slipped into the long slinky gown. He viewed her ever so secretly in the mirrors. *Magnificent!*

"You look great!" said Sally and meant it.

"You look fabulous, Lainey. I wish I could look like that," said Paula and also meant it.

"Yess, very nice, Elaine, but we are mithing thomething. Yesss I am thure of it."

Felix walked back and forth behind Elaine while looking into the mirrors. Paula wished she could walk exactly the way Felix was. He stopped to put his hands on Elaine's waist pulling in the material slightly.

"Yess, that'ss a little better, but no!" He let go of the material like he was angry at it.

Felix paced back and forth behind Elaine studiously peering into the mirrors. Sally and Paula held their breath. Elaine stood like a statue, not moving a muscle, as if waiting for the lightening bolt to strike. The master was at work. They were suspended in hushed anticipation, afraid to disturb his concentration, waiting for something wildly creative to happen.

Felix stepped closer to Elaine. His hands were on her waist again. "What iss it? Thomething!"

The hands moved down the length of Elaine's body and then up towards her breasts, down, then up again. He pushed on her breasts, forcing them closer together, pushing them up slightly out of the gown.

Precautions had been taken for such an eventuality. There was danger for him if betrayed by his lower half. He had strapped down his penis, which now strained against its bonds. He was close to his Elaina, touching her with his hands and his body.

On an earlier day, he had done the same with the daughter, Daniella, in her garage. He drew in Elaina's perfume. *The very same one*, more appropriate and better worn on the more mature woman.

"Very nice, thweetie. These are very, very nice. Doctor Casstle?"

They all laughed except Elaine.

"He doess the very besst work. I would get mine done too, if I could I mean."

They all laughed.

"What do you theenk Thally?"

He pushed on the breasts again, harder. *An unnecessary surgery judging from the daughter.* He was a man thoroughly familiar with plastic surgeries. *The nose was done, too. Beautiful was insufficient, perfect was required. The chin, probably, and perhaps some work around the eyes. The ass, something extra there? I wish I could investigate.* Elaine's nipples were getting hard against his fingers. He could feel himself getting hard against his leg.

"She looks great!" "Too good. I'm getting jealous," said Sally and meant it.

"Yess, we are going to take theess in a little here." His hands went downward. He pulled in the material from behind her. "A leettle back here, what do you theenk Thally!"

He pulled a little tighter and pushed his hand gently forward into the crease of her buttocks.

"Yes, Felix."

"And what do you theenk thweetie?" Felix asked Elaine. He pushed just slightly harder. It all felt real enough, no telling for sure though. How he hated fakeness, especially in a bitch that was naturally so attractive. Felix pushed just the slightest bit harder before letting go.

"It's ok," said Elaine viewing herself in the mirrors.

"Ok?" shouted Paula. "Lainie, you look fabulous!"

"You do, Lainie," added Sally.

"Girlss, leave her alone," said Felix sternly. "We all know, the world knowss the presssure Elaine eess under."

Felix let his grip go, stepped around her, and hugged Elaine firmly. He whispered in her ear, "I am praying for you." Then he stepped away.

"Rich or Dead, Rich or Dead, and all theess time no answer. You are tho thtrong Elaine! I am thure you weel have your answer thoon, and it weel be the right one. I weesh I could comfort you, but I am praying for you, thweetie."

"Thank you so much, Felix!" She hugged him and kissed him on the cheek. They were all crying.

"What shall I do weeth the dresss?"

"Oh, I'll take it, I guess."

"Want to thee another?"

"No, thank you."

"That's fine. "I'll have it feexed perfect for you, thweetie. Peeck it up anytime after tomorrow. Let me get your coatss."

They wore coats they didn't need. In Los Angeles, who needed a coat? A great disadvantage, no seasons, but they did their best to stay in fashion.

Felix helped them on with their coats and escorted them to the door. "Thtay beautiful thweetiess. Thay thtrong Elaine. Come back thoon. I love you."

Felix watched the bitches walk down Rodeo Drive arm in arm bundled up in their long coats on a fine balmy day. *Lovely Elaina*, the scent of her perfume still floated through his nostrils. The shape of her breasts remained imprinted on his hands and the thought of her round buttocks pressing up against him was ingrained in his memory.

In a different world, he would have taken Elaina. She would be spirited off to his Castle. They would have made love over and over. *Elaina and Daniella, each would have had their turns.*

Damn waste of bitches. But for you, Richfuck!

He had left a present for his adversary, deep in the large pockets of Elaine's coat. Given in the way of a Master of the Game, an answer for an arrogant foe who would challenge him.

Take your answer, Richfuck. Take it to hell. And toy with me no more, or I swear, Game or no Game, I will take your Elaina.

54

The coat went into the closet and would not come out for eight days. Elaine did not see her friends since that day at Bellagio's and she did not pick up her gown. It had been a nice change of scenery for her, a needed break, but Danielle was still missing and Elaine was in agony.

Not a word from Simon, that was the most excruciating part, the not knowing. Henry was also frustrated, and with nothing else to do, the ads continued. *Rich or Dead, Rich or Dead, the phrase is on everyone's tongue.*

The wild speculations about Simon continued. Women of all ages became suspicious of their fellow students, coworkers, and neighbors. *Who can blame them? No woman in her right mind can feel safe.*

Elaine had lost eighteen pounds since Danielle's kidnapping. She could not eat. Her stomach churned at the first bite. With the second she felt like throwing up.

"It's the grief diet," she joked wryly to Sally. "Most effective diet ever created." Elaine spoke to Sally sparingly on the phone and refused to see her. Sally wanted her to climb out of her funk, out of her room, to get out of the house. Elaine was too exhausted to argue and she simply didn't want to hear it. Her guilt wouldn't allow her to take any solace.

Why did we allow Danielle to live by herself? Why God, why?

Elaine knew she was driving herself crazy. *That is obvious. So what?* Hour after hour she remained fixated on the telephone. With harpoon eyes, she willed it to ring. *He has to call! Any minute now the phone will ring and Henry will receive his instructions. Take the money, Simon! Take it, and give us back our Danielle.*

They were to take the call in a room specially wired by the FBI, who would listen in and record downstairs. Elaine kept herself prisoner in the room. The furniture, everything else, had vanished. She was alone with the telephone, transfixed by it, mesmerized, hypnotized. Day in, day out, Elaine stared at the telephone. Nothing else existed. *Call you bastard, call!*

Elaine took the long coat out of her closet. She simply had to pry herself out of that room. The walls were closing in around her. Another minute and surely she would crack.

I'll go for a night drive. The SL with the top down, and the windows, too. The wind will chill me and breathe new life into my body. It will blow my hair in my face and leave it in snarls. Maybe I can forget, just for a short while.

Elaine put on the long tan coat and cinched it up with the belt. With conviction, she drove her hands down into the deep pockets, her left hand touching the box. Elaine pulled it out of her pocket and began to meticulously unwrap it.

Elaine delicately removed the bow and ribbon as she speculated on the gift. A habit shared by most women, to carefully open a gift so as not to tear the paper, to save the wrapping for another day, all the time knowing it would never be used again. It was from Henry. *Who else could it be from?*

She had assumed that their anniversary the week before had passed forgotten. Henry was never a sentimental man; the occasion gifts usually came from a secretary. With the pressure they were both under, the oversight was understandable and certainly forgiven. *Sometimes, Henry can surprise you.*

Elaine carefully undid the bright silver paper. The familiar Tiffany's box!

It is Henry, bless his heart. It's his way of trying to make me feel better.

Birthdays and anniversaries, Elaine always received something from Tiffany's. Occasionally, she got an unexpected little box, amends for an occasional dalliance.

Elaine worked harder than most to stay attractive for her husband but she understood. *High-powered men need their excitements and their conquests. Henry is actually quite good in that regard and, fortunately, far more drawn to mergers and acquisitions than to tits and ass. He is certainly a damn site better than that Dan Phillips Sally has to put up with.*

Elaine recalled her many lectures to Danielle on the subject. "Men are only as loyal as their opportunities. If the options are there they will wander. They only think with what is between their legs and they think only about what is between yours." It was advice Danielle did not need to hear. *Any man lucky enough to land Danielle would never be so stupid as to risk losing her.*

The thoughts of Danielle sent Elaine's stomach quivering anew. She took the box to her night table, wanting to view her gift under the light. It didn't matter what it was. Just knowing that Henry thought about her in this difficult time, that he cared, that he loved her, was enough.

Elaine sat down on the bed and held the Tifanny's box under the light. *Bless his heart. He is a headstrong, difficult man, but all things considered, not a bad one.* She opened the box.

They heard Elaine Rickford screaming everywhere in the house. Men and women in FBI jackets raced to the room with their guns drawn. Elaine was sitting on her bed shrieking uncontrollably, her eyes bulging wildly out of her face. Mucus ran down her nose and saliva dripped from her mouth.

Two female agents jumped to her side, each grabbing an arm. A handful of her long blond hair was in each fist. Hair lay all over the bed and floor. The agents tried to comfort Elaine.

"It's all right. It's all right, Mrs. Rickford. Whatever it is. It's all right," said one of the women to her.

"What is it, Mrs. Rickford? Tell us what it is," said the other female agent.

They could not get anything intelligible out of her. She was wailing wildly, screeching as liquid gurgled from her mouth. Elaine Rickford seemed to have finally snapped. The agents were aware of her long running depression. When, not if, Elaine Rickford would go over the edge was a common topic of discussion.

It was the third agent, standing in the room looking on helplessly, agent Timothy Porter, who noticed the Tiffany's box on the nightstand. He went to investigate and picked up the opened box.

Neatly set in the velvet, glazed, shiny clean, and looking out at agent Porter was a pair of bluer than blue eyes.

Above, in the satiny material of the box's upper lid, printed in red, blood agent Porter surmised, was the inscription

I CHOOSE DEAD!

IT GETS PERSONAL

55

We have all used the expression thinking outside "the box." The fact is, each of us is a captive in our own box and our thinking is constrained by its individual set of principles, morals, ethics, and values. That is how we view the world.
The serial killer has his own box and it is filled with things incomprehensible and unimaginable to us.
That is the task, to understand the incomprehensible and unimaginable.

- Into the Mind of a Killer, John Hightower

Janet Bultaco was worried about her man. A change of tactics was clearly called for. Janet would no longer allow John to commit suicide by self-neglect. She tried to make sure that he ate at least once a day, and insisted that he get a few hours sleep each night.

At her behest, John took an hour off and they went to dinner.

"I told him not to challenge Simon," John said more to himself than to Janet, while driving to their favorite French restaurant.

"Yes, John, I know. I was there."

Rickford, you insisted on an answer and now you have it. Your daughter has paid the bill for your arrogance. You pushed Simon to choose. And he has chosen in a way you cannot and will never understand. "I should have been more insistent."

"Trust me," said a knowing District Attorney, "it wouldn't have made any difference. Henry Rickford doesn't listen to anyone."

I should have been more insistent.

"Berlanger has completed a secret in depth check of all Bureau employees, past and present. Anyone with access to the Bureau or its employees was also screened. Half a dozen names sifted through. I put my money on Amanda Grove."

"Eat your salad," ordered Janet.

A secretary for approximately six months, who quit abruptly, and now couldn't be found. Her application and background check had seemed in order, but on more careful review were found to be falsified, and quite expertly at that.

"There's no history of Amanda Grove. She appeared, then disappeared." *The same way that Jim Barker, Danielle Rickford's kidnapper, did. And David Telsor, Mary Splitorf's classmate; Susan Felcher, known to have gone shopping with Kathleen Harper; and finally Mark Harris, Mary Benson's coworker. They all simply vanished.*

You wanted inside information before you started your game. Who was Amanda Grove, Simon?

"Berlanger also went back and did the homework on the earlier kidnappings." *Modus operandus was always the same. Painstaking preparation, no random actions, you stalk your victims then get close to them. They trust you.*

"He's beguiling, maybe even more so than Bundy was. But he's not careless like Bundy." *Bundy was arrogant. He didn't think he could get caught, and if he were captured, he could ever be held.*

You, Simon, you know you can get caught.

"The salad, darling," reminded Janet.

Disguised as three men and a woman, not counting Amanda Grove. You are certainly a master. Jim Barker was more than enough evidence of that. But to be a secretary at the FBI for six months and have no one notice?

Could there be a Mrs. Simon?

John Hightower played with his salad. "The public hopes it is over. It's not." *Time hangs heavy for you, Simon. The inactivity does not spell relief but rather preparation. The longer the wait, the more precise the planning, the greater your objective will be.*

The waiter brought their meals. Hightower pushed his salad aside and his fork began to massage the mashed potatoes.

"Eat, John." It was always the same. Janet considered it a victory if he ate anything at all.

Emotions crescendo in men like you. You will have to outdo yourself, always something new and something even more outrageous.

What will the next move be, Simon? Who will be inning six?

"John, please!"

"Sorry honey. It's just that I'm missing something. What's the connection between the victims? They're all young and beautiful. Yes, yes, but there's more. There has to be." *What is it?*

56

"Are you still there, Father?"

Checking his watch, Frank Wycheck realized that he had been talking for more than six hours.

"Why of course, my son."

Wycheck could not detect the slightest hint of fatigue in the young priest's voice. Father Romero would have excused himself at least three times. And he would have probably dozed off many times as well.

Wycheck thought back on the times he confessed to Father Romero. It never mattered what Father Romero listened to and what he slept through.

It was the same now. The catharsis was in the verbalizing. Frank Wycheck was a man of words. He respected words, made his living with them. Words were the outlet for his emotions. They had been trapped inside him. Their sharp edges lacerated his abdomen and stimulated the juices of anxiety. Expelled finally, the words took some of the stress with them.

"Are you weary?" asked Father Reyes. *The young priest is resilient.* "Would you like to stop?" he queried. *He is not tired. This was not a disguised wish, would you please stop, or a suggestion, we could stop, but rather a simple question from a concerned and compassionate man.*

"No, my choice would be to continue. But, I'm imposing now. You have other things to do."

"No, my son. You have come to God for your answers. And I am his servant. I have no other things to do. Perhaps a break then?"

"Yes, Father. It would be nice to stretch a little."

"Then do so. I will be here when you are ready to continue."

Wycheck was stiff in most of his joints. His back was sore and his shoulders ached from sitting hunched over. It was difficult but a relief to get up and walk around.

A new day was about to begin. The light from a bright sun was already shining in. The inhabitants of the night had departed for their daytime lives. The dirty man and Wycheck's Molly were gone, leaving only their body odors behind.

Frank Wycheck took in a deep breath of the foul musty air. It felt good to him. The best air he had consumed since he gave up cocaine over a week before. He stretched his torso forward then back, flexed his knees and arms, and rolled his head three hundred and sixty degrees. For the first time in some time it seemed worthwhile to be alive.

Though it was barely as spacious as a closet, the small confessional had given Frank Wycheck more comfort than any other place on earth could have. He felt a strong kinship with the young priest. He wished they could talk face-to-face, even if only for a few minutes. They could discuss other things, not just his terrifying dilemma. *How long have you been a Priest, Father Reyes? How long have you been here at St. Matthews? And are you happy?*

The sunlight shone in brightly through the part stained glass, part paper, part boarded up windows. Wycheck cast his gaze around the crumbling structure, the walls with their sagging plaster and peeling paint, pews bearing the etchings of a thousand messages, and the statues of the Saints, missing fingers, arms and noses. *What a waste it would be to lose the old church,* he thought.

Still, the daylight was proof there would be at least one more day. A priest, who Wycheck also did not know, was readying things for the morning mass. A chore Father Romero always excused himself for. *How many will attend mass today?* Frank Wycheck never did, probably never would. St. Matthews was his place for refuge, not prayer. *Three years since Father Romero died. And where was I?*

He slowly retraced his steps to the Confessional. Wycheck was anxious to return. His symptoms were treated but the disease still flourished. He opened the door to his sanctuary and his consciousness flowed naturally back into the booth while his body automatically reassumed the familiar position.

"Are you refreshed, my son?" asked Father Reyes.

"Yes, Father, I am. I saw another priest."

"Father Samuel. He is charged with the morning duties."

"Then your duties must be completed. You must have other things…"

"No, my son. Servants of God do not have shifts. Tell me. Have you found the answers that you seek?"

"No. I have not."

"Then we must continue until you do."

57

Recording B-9

"If a law is bad, it will be ignored. Prohibition was a law. People drank anyway. Why? Because it was a stupid law! But you already know all about that, don't you, Frankie? Cocaine is an illegal drug, is it not?"

You would think, Father, that drugs would be hard to get in prison, wouldn't you. And you would be wrong, dead wrong. There is more cocaine available in jail than on any South Central street corner.

I'm not a fool, Father. I, knew cocaine's insidious nature. I also knew how to keep it in check; Frank Wycheck was in control. All addicts know the danger, and they're all in control.

But, what was there to do in jail but wait? And what better ally could there be to fight the boredom? I found myself using more of the stuff in the joint than ever. Frank Wycheck took off when he arrived and he was flying all week long.

Two visitors did come to see me. After the first two days Christine came and told me how much she missed me. Missed me, I knew what she missed. But, Christine announced that she still cared and promised to faithfully wait for me the full week. I wondered.

My other visitor was completely unexpected, Jenny. Jenny was already attending Berkeley and came down just to see me. I was embarrassed that she had to come to jail to see her father and I was fearful that she would notice how loaded I was.

Jenny said that she and her mother were well and that they both still cared about me. You would think that Jenny just threw in that last part about Jane caring and you would be wrong. I knew it was true. That was Jane, always loving, always forgiving.

Never on the face of God's earth was there a better woman, and I fully intended to win her back, someday. But, to the weak, a woman like Jane could be a burden. I never quite measured up, and every time I fell short more guilt was thrown on the pile. For the time being, a simpler life with a less complex woman, like Christine, seemed to fit better.

Jenny had a lot of her mother in her. Except when I was with Jenny, I only felt love, no guilt. Jane always shielded her from the pain I caused. She made up excuses for me. Jane was the porter in the family. She carried my baggage for me. Because of Jane, I was for Jenny always, just Daddy.

I regretted the circumstances, but was extremely happy to see Jenny. She was studying journalism and said she wanted to be a reporter, a writer just like me.

I counseled Jenny in my most serious tone to study hard. Be a writer if she wanted and be a good one. Journalism was a very rewarding profession. But please, please, not be like me.

Tell me, Father. If I was a good writer, and I was sure I was. If things were going well for me financially, and I knew they were. If I was happy with my life, and I thought I was. Why would I tell her that?

58

Christine Taylor threw a lamp against the wall. She was frustrated and angry. *How could he do this to me?* She had given that snivel ing shit Wycheck everything and he had fucked up again. *A week without*, how did he expect her to do that?

Since losing her virginity at the age of nine to her step father and his two sons, Christine's relationship with men was, to say the least, unusual. She prepared a double dose of cocaine on her dressing table and hastily sucked it in. "I did just fine before I met you, asshole," Christine screamed while staring into her mirror. "Any man would kill to have me. Any man!"

She put on her makeup extra heavy, like she did when playing hooker. Her closet was filled with seductive clothing. Christine chose black leather, short and tight, for the evening. She slipped into her matching thigh high boots and marched out of her apartment, a woman on a mission.

Christine climbed into her lime green Mustang and squealed the tires as she drove off. "Where shall I go?" she asked herself. "Cariola's?" A good pickup bar, Christine had been there often. It wouldn't take her long to find an appropriate stud, or two. *Or three?* She was feeling extra horny.

Naah! She'd done the bars so often and the men were all pretty much the same. That's how she wound up with Frank in the first place. Besides, tonight Christine wanted it raunchy.

She was always searching for more excitement, had been ever since she could remember. And, never finding it, her life was a constant quest for that elusive something.

Christine sped down the five freeway, careening off at the Grand

Ave. exit. She changed the music to a Disco station. "Can only stand so much of that hip hop stuff," she shouted to herself, laughing wildly and full of anticipation. She was in Santa Ana, a bad part of town, and at Front Street, Christine jammed on the brakes and made a sudden right. The Mustang drove down the small dirt road to a dead end abutting railroad tracks.

Christine got out, leaving the Mustang behind and crossed the tracks to a small clearing on the other side. She was carrying a case of Budweiser in one hand and a super large jug of Thunderbird in the other.

"Hello gentlemen," said Christine cheerfully to the congregation of vagrants and bums. She was eyed with apprehension and concern until they spotted her cargo. Then, Christine immediately was everyone's best friend.

They were harmless enough, though filthy beyond description. Christine opened the case of beer and handed around the jug of Thunderbird. "Let's party. Anyone thirsty?"

Some talked to themselves, some sang, some rocked, but all were interested in the new booze. They drank until every drop was gone.

Christine lay back and spread her legs. "Now boys, who's going to be first?"

Only one taker, the rest were long gone. And, he performed badly. Christine was furious. She picked up a piece of broken glass and sliced him nicely for his inadequacy.

"Damn fuck! I guess it's Cariola's after all."

And yet, the ruby red blood dripping from the man was oddly enticing. Christine had to admire it and gave him another few cuts before leaving. She felt so strangely exhilarated.

59

The long thin one moved at a reasonable pace but carried little weight. The middle sized one made only stubborn, impercep tible progress. The short stocky one was intransigent, refusing to move at all. All three conspired in a sinister synchronous harmony, determined to impose their patient tempo on the world as they held it hostage.

Francine Fizpatrick stared at the hands of her wristwatch. She wished for a way to speed them along. The feeble progress tortured her. For eight hours every day, occasionally more, Francine sat at her desk outside Fitz's door.

Married life had failed to live up to its promise. Work had again become work, and the fun and excitement were decidedly gone. No more surreptitious touching, no morning or afternoon dictation and never a "nooner" *lunch* with Kevin behind closed doors. *These days anyone can walk into the Bureau at any time and they often do.* The District Director refused to live that dangerously.

He usually worked late and came home exhausted. They only went out to dinner occasionally and even then, Kevin would be preoccupied. No case, in all Francine's time at the Bureau, affected him so badly. *Small wonder, with hardheaded Henry, dandy Tim Dawson, bitch Bultaco, the Mayor, the Senator, and God knows who else constantly on him. All they do is stir his gastric juices and upset him.*

Though Kevin was much older than Francine, he did promise they would have children. That subject was no longer to be discussed. His career was Kevin's baby and the baby was ill. There was too much politics at the Bureau. "The conditions are wrong. Things are fine for the moment. This is not the time to take on additional responsibility.

But in the future," *he promised.* Francine resolved to be patient, confident that when the Simon case was over, everything would be perfect.

As it stood, she was on call. Nothing regular, things were too hectic for that. When he could, when he wanted, Kevin let her know. Otherwise, Francine was on her own.

She had begun spending her off nights at 24 Hour Fitness. Francine maintained her membership although she never attended more than a couple of weeks straight. Exercise and diet required discipline. Exertion was never Francine's thing, and she was Irish for God's sake. To eat, drink, and be merry was in her blood.

Besides, gym attire was not flattering to chubby women. Voluptuous in clothes at the office, Francine was blatantly fat at the gym. She was easily discouraged.

That was, of course, before Francine had so much time on her hands and before she met Wanda.

The day was passing slowly, uneventfully. Kevin and Mark had one of their two-hour update lunches. With so little progress on the case, it was difficult to understand what they could talk about for so long. Kevin yearned for a breakthrough. He talked about it constantly with Francine. *Perhaps Kevin thinks that by asking Mark enough questions he can produce one.*

Even, John Hightower seemed unable to help. *Poor Kevin, so desperate he even is nice to John, although the man frustrates him so – keeping his own hours, coming and going as he pleases. God, how John Hightower could infuriate Kevin without even realizing it.*

Francine liked John Hightower, who had always been nice to her. He was a character out of a storybook, a white knight in shining armor. Hightower was Lancelot of King Arthur's court, loyal, honorable and always ready to come to a lady's defense. Alas, the Bureau was not Camelot. John Hightower was a relic, lost in a time warp, unwilling, but also unable, to win the political jousts.

He would never move forward as Kevin did. And yet, John managed quite well. How? For the same reason they need him now. John Hightower solves cases. Francine was rooting hard for him.

She stared again at her watch. Soon the hands would allow her to leave. One way or another she would partake of the ale tonight, if not with Kevin, then with Wanda.

What was it about Wanda that Francine found so appealing? Everything, nothing, Francine still wasn't sure. A better question was what was it about her that Wanda chose to like? That Francine could not figure out at all.

Damn! Francine's watch told her it was time to go. She left for the evening, disappointed, longing for the day when Kevin would be hers every night. Then she could truly show him how a wife treats her man. Then he would experience the peace and comfort he deserved. Only then would they both share the happiness Francine dreamed of.

Alas, it was the Gym tonight.

60

As Francine climbed up the stairs from the locker room to the gym floor she could see the Wanda effect already in full force. Her tall lanky friend went from machine to machine completing her prescribed workout, while a cadre of men quietly and surreptitiously followed her. They jostled and elbowed each other, as they might at a strip club, each vying for the best vantage point.

Wanda was an original. Tall and thin and in shape, she had not an ounce of fat on a slender frame that stretched well over six feet. Her muscles were well defined and developed. She would have appeared masculine were it not for two luxurious breasts and a substantial well protruding ass.

Have they ever seen her face? They never seem to look above her neck. Wanda did have a beautiful well-sculpted face, with clear perfect skin. *Not fair*, thought Francine.

Wanda was on the pull down machine, a particular favorite among the men. She raised her arms and then breathed in deeply before pulling the weight down hard. As her arms came down, the weight and her breasts went up. *Wanda is fully fortified, that's for sure!* No slouch in that area, Francine was known for her breasts. *But hers are on a perfect body.*

Wanda was wearing a tight yellow halter-top and short, short hot pants that accentuated her other assets. White combat looking boots on raised platforms with tennis shoe soles lifted her an additional three inches off the floor. Wanda towered over most of the men; the rest were intimidated anyway.

The irony was that Wanda had no use for men. "Take away their dicks and what use are they?" she would say. *That doesn't stop her from teasing them to death. What is it about men? Wanda has them transfixed. Their eyes blatantly dive down her top and climb up into her pants.*

Not that the women ignored her, with their disguised glances from across the room. Their eyes were also riveted on her. Dagger stares that traveled around corners and would have gladly killed if they could.

But does Wanda care? She has no use for women either. "Take away their cunts and there is nothing left." *Wanda does things her own way. Period!*

Francine got on the stationary bike, setting two, an easy level. She had caught a bad case of melancholia at the office. Besides, Francine had to save her energy. Wanda was only two thirds through her workout. It would be some twenty minutes till she joined her. Then Francine would have to raise the level to at least five. Wanda did not tolerate slacking.

Her mind drifted as she thumbed through the pages of Glamour. The gym seemed blurred, surreal, as she started to pump her bike.

I'm not like these other women, thin and in good shape. They look forward to their workouts, enjoy themselves, are committed, and take pride in their results.

The pages of Glamour were filled with skinny women in their bikinis and special clothes made only for the anorexic. Francine wished she were slender like that, like Wanda. To be confident and independent, to have men long for her, and to cast them aside like so much worthless junk. She would have women envy her and hate her for being too beautiful, too sexy, and she, too, would ignore them as if they didn't exist.

Still, Francine would trade all of that and never again give it a thought. *If, if only I could have Kevin all to myself.*

The stationary bike suddenly lurched as the pedals jammed. Francine did not notice that Wanda had completed her routine and was standing next to her. Wanda had changed the level on her bike to six.

"You forgot to adjust the setting before I got here," she said smiling.

Busted! Francine lowered the level to four and pushed hard to get the bike started again.

"Why come, if you're not going to do anything?" Wanda chided her.

"You know," said Francine.

"Of course I do. Who would have thought that I would be second fiddle to a big fat Irishman?"

"He is not that fat!"

"Poor Francina! You've got it bad. No, I am sure he's very good looking."

Francine was struggling. Wanda sat on the bike next to her easily pedaling at level nine. *The machine is humming for her, those strong legs driving up and down like powerful pistons. She's not even sweating.* The water dripped down Francine's face and body in a steady stream. Her flaming red hair was soaked to a medium brown. *How can she do all that and not even sweat?*

"Right," she answered with difficulty. "I do have it bad."

How can these women do this for two hours? Francine hoped she could last for two minutes, make it respectable at least. She concentrated on the bike's timer, wishing for a way to speed it along. *Two minutes! God damn it! I've got to do two minutes.*

"So, tough day?" asked Wanda effortlessly.

Francine fought to nod. *Two minutes!* It took all of her energy to keep the pedals moving. *How can she talk while doing this?*

"Me, too. I've had a miserable day. I can really use a drink. You?"

Francine nodded again, this time with a grunt. Her legs were burning, ready to explode. *I was crazy to come. Who invented this bike anyway, the Marquis de Sade? Two minutes!*

"How about Seidelberg's?" suggested Wanda cheerfully.

Francine could barely manage a nod or a grunt.

"Fine, you drive," Wanda decided. "I'm a little beat."

She's a little beat! Francine collapsed on her bike. *One minute fifty-three, close enough. Who did I think I was kidding anyway? Certainly not Wanda! No one fools Wanda.*

"I have a half hour left here." Wanda was barely breathing. "Is that enough time for you to get ready?"

"Uh huh," managed Francine. She was puffing heavily, trying to capture some of the oxygen the gym owed her. The sweat was pouring down onto the bike and floor. Francine wiped her face then staggered off the bike to clean the puddle she had created.

Do only fat people sweat like this? "I'll be ready," she said as she staggered toward the stairs leading down to the locker room. Francine looked back at Wanda. Every hair was still in place. Wanda was ready for the presidential ball and she looked like she had just come from a shipwreck.

She doesn't sweat, so she doesn't need to shower. Wanda never went to the locker room, telling Francine that she didn't like to deal with the women. *Surprising though, I would have guessed that she would just love parading around naked, sticking those perfect tits of hers in their faces.*

Francine nearly fell down the stairs. Walking was difficult; the legs were gone. But, she had to admit the quivering empty feeling in her gut was gone. She was too exhausted to fret about Kevin. *One should never underestimate the therapeutic power of pain.*

The hot shower felt good.

A few good belts will feel better.

61

She was too fatigued to think about it at the time, but Wanda's desire to return to Seidelberg's shocked Francine. No denying, Seidelberg's was a good place to have a drink after a long hard day. Lifer bartenders could make any drink and served a myriad of chilled beers. *And the food! Smoked eel, seafood cocktails, Westphalian ham sandwiches, and scrumptious desserts, especially the apple strudel.*

But Seidelberg's was a man's bar, had been since the fifties, and was reluctant to change. It was old style German with a long wooden bar and wooden booths. Moose, elk and deer heads stared down at you from the walls. Seidelberg's was one final male chauvinist protectorate. Women were not welcome.

They had stumbled in last time, and were treated badly to pay for their mistake. The bartender scowled at them as they walked past the long bar. The regulars crudely taunted them and they were all but ignored by the waiters.

Francine was uncomfortable at the time and hinted strongly that they go to another place. Wanda refused, apparently unimpressed by the poor treatment. She smiled politely at the men and grabbed the waiter physically. *Wanda does things her own way. Period!*

The men of Seidelberg's were clearly irritated when the "two dykes" returned. "Not amusing, your coming back." "You should have learned from your first mistake." "Seidelberg's is a man's place." "Why don't you go to a shopping mall?"

Wanda led Francine back to the same booth they occupied the last time. They had come to relax and unwind, to have a few beers, and to talk. Wanda's defiant attitude dictated that they do exactly that.

She looks quite different outside the gym, only wearing baggy black sweats, never anything provocative. Ironic, in clothes Wanda seems too lean and too tall. What goes in nicely on her blends in and what sticks out spectacularly gets covered up. Francine wondered if the men of Seidleberg's would have been as cold if they had seen Wanda an hour before.

They seemed more animated than last time, more angry. Francine and Wanda sat quietly at their table waiting for service. The regulars were riled, very loud and becoming unruly. Francine worried. Wanda seemed more concerned about getting their first beer.

The men fed off each other, until finally, the self appointed leader of the crude and the rude stumbled over to their table.

"Which one of you tarts wants to play with me?" he sputtered loudly.

They called him Bear because of his enormous girth and because of the way he growled his words. Bear was large and baggy with a huge potbelly hanging over his belt. His head was a big round melon, cherry red where not covered by a thick full beard. A foul smell and disposition accompanied Bear wherever he went.

He leaned over their table. "How about you, sweetheart?" Bear snorted while eyeing Francine and spattering on her.

"I wouldn't mind, big boy," said Wanda in a quiet and sultry voice. Francine was startled. She had never heard Wanda sound quite like that. Bear did a double take.

"What have you got for me? Anything big?" Wanda continued.

Francine could not believe what she was hearing from her friend. She was, however, extraordinarily relieved to have Bear's attention directed elsewhere. He was a totally obnoxious drunk. Not at all like Kevin, who only got sweeter and more lovable as the alcohol took over his veins.

"More than you can handle, sister," Bear growled at Wanda.

"Well let's see about that. Come sit down." She patted the space on the bench next to her. "Let's see what you've got."

Bear's large frame crashed down on the bench next to Wanda. His huge arm wrapped itself around her neck and pulled her toward him.

"All right, cowboy!" Wanda purred as if she was enjoying herself. It was then that Francine realized how little she really knew about her.

"Now let's see what you brought for me."

Wanda reached down into Bear's crotch and began stroking it. An experienced hand, it knew its way around a man's body. The long slender fingers moved skillfully, feeling their way, touching, raising a libido that had been drowned by several quarts of brew.

"All right, baby," Bear chortled, spattering used beer into Wanda's face. Francine was horrified. *How disgusting!* She would have run but was afraid of the gauntlet of men. They were all watching and cheering Bear on loudly.

He pulled Wanda's head toward his. She did not resist. *How could she anyway,* thought Francine. *Wanda is strong, but this man is a monster.*

Wanda did not seem to mind, apparently enjoying herself. *Does she even want to resist? Doesn't look like it. Wanda is different, even strange, but is she so far out as to like this crude gorilla?*

The long slender fingers traversed the landscape of Bear's crotch. Each movement was sensual; every touch aroused him further.

"Hmm, very nice, cowboy, very nice indeed," purred the sultry voice.

Bear's tongue was out of his mouth only inches from Wanda's face. She was in his headlock and his other hand was around her jaw, pushing down on her teeth, forcing her mouth open.

"Whoa honey, slow down," Wanda said calmly. "Patience." Bear stopped. He took a drink from Wanda's beer glass.

"All right, all right, just keep it up, baby!" he sputtered then pulled her close again.

Wanda forced her head to the side. Bear's large wet tongue landed on her left ear. *What is wrong with her?* thought a shocked Francine. *How can she like this?*

The skillful fingers continued their exploration, settling around Bear's testicles.

Bear was excited. He licked Wanda's ear like it was a dripping ice cream cone on a hot day. Saliva was running down Wanda's face yet she did not seem to mind. *How can she possibly?*

Wanda's hand calmly continued its play with Bear's testicles. The knowing fingers investigated them carefully, arranging them just so in her palm. Then the fingers obediently settled into place.

The bear was in heat. His hand released Wanda's jaw and fumbled over her heavy sweats to her left breast. He squeezed it hard, ruthlessly. Still Wanda did not object.

Instead, the obedient tentacles tightened their hold. All of those pull downs, bench presses, and curls, this was merely another exercise for Wanda, a grip exercise to strengthen her forearm. She breathed in and squeezed down hard.

"You are not a gentleman, sir," she said quietly as she continued to compress her hold. "You should learn some manners." The vise tightened more, then more again.

Moments later Bear was singing well above soprano in octaves only dogs could hear. He was caught in the nutcracker and finally realized it. Wanda pushed her arm away. Bear scrambled to follow. She twisted her wrist and Bear responded with a 9.9 flip onto his back. He was suspended in space by Wanda's grip. She pulled her arm back slightly and the bear squealed like a pig.

Wanda slid out from behind the booth with her arm thrust before her. Bear struggled to maintain his position with her hand. The hand moved up as Wanda got up from the bench and Bear raised up backwards. His tree-like legs and stubby arms frantically worked to lift his huge torso.

"My balls! My balls!" he shouted.

The pain shot through Bear's testicles like lightening bolts. Every muscle in his body fought to float his genitals weightless in her grip. Wanda moved out onto the floor. Bear slithered with her. Though upside down, he scurried and scampered, taking a thousand pathetic little steps, trying desperately to keep up. Wanda began to sing and wave her arm. There was a polka playing.

Wanda's hand went left, "Tee dum, dee dum, tee dum, dee dum," sang Wanda. Left, two, three, danced the bear, fighting to raise his genitals to the highest possible level.

The hand went right, "Tee dum, dee dum, tee dum, dee dum." Right, two, three, went the bear, suspended on raised tiptoes.

"Tee dum, tee dum, tee dum!" Left, two, three...right, two, three. The Bear was dancing the polka!

The men at the bar were now cheering for Wanda. Their laughter was uncontrollable. The moose, elk and deer peered down from their perches approvingly. They had seen many things in their five decades at Seidelberg's, but never anything like that.

"My balls! My balls!" screamed the Bear.

"Tee dum, tee dum, tee dum" sang Wanda. "My balls, my balls, I'm dancing, hanging from my balls," she continued in tune.

"My balls, my balls" came the chorus from the bar.

The bartender turned the music louder. The men laughed and cheered and made room for Wanda and her bear. "Tee dum, tee dum, tee dum! My balls, my balls" they all sang.

"Please let me go!" pleaded the Bear, barely being heard. No one cared. Bear had not made many friends. A bully is a bully indiscriminately. They all had their grievances. The high shrills of pain only heightened everyone's enjoyment.

Francine sat and watched in disbelief.

"Tee dum, tee dum, tee dum!" Left, two three...right two three, Wanda and the Bear, dancing the polka. The jubilant men encircled the dancing couple. They sang and clapped in time to the music.

"My balls! My balls!" went the chorus.

When the polka was over, Wanda held Bear suspended for a few last seconds before releasing her grip. He collapsed in a fetal heap, clutching himself, paralyzed in pain. "My balls. My balls," his last sorrowful lament, as he lay whimpering and sobbing in a pool of his own puked up beer.

"I give him back to you, boys," Wanda said before returning to the booth. "He is not my type."

"Not ours either!" she heard above the laughter and cheers as she walked back toward Francine.

Bear needed help to get to a hospital. The damage was described as significant and irreparable. He never returned to Seidelberg's and was not missed. No one liked Bear anyway.

Wanda sat down calmly at the booth. "Don't usually like dancing," she said to Francine with a smile. "Now, where were we?" Wanda seemed eager to renew their conversation. *As if nothing had happened!* Wanda did mention without a hint of guilt or remorse, that she had felt some of Bear's things pop.

"It's as I was telling you Francina. Men always follow their dicks." Wanda smiled coyly. "They are the most plentiful, most easily replaced, and most worthless things on the face of the earth."

Francine sat with her jaw in her lap. She was in awe of Wanda. Not the thin body, the great ass or the spectacular tits. Not that she dominated the attention of every man and could have any one she chose. It was her absolute independence, the perfection of her self-confidence, the security she had in her actions.

The waiter brought them their beers. "Anything else I can get you ladies?" he asked politely. "Compliments of the house. The boss says there will be no bill for you tonight."

62

They sat in Seidelberg's for hours. New beers appeared every time their mugs ran low. Francine wondered about her friend, this woman who didn't shower and never ate. What did she know about her? Virtually nothing, except that she could drink and she did listen. It seemed enough.

They talked of many things that night, the way women did, unreserved. Wanda was interested in everything in Francine's life. *Why? Surely her life is much more exciting. I should be listening.* Still the questions came in an unending torrent and Francine was several steins of beer past resisting and even further from deciding what she should say and what she should not.

They talked about the Bureau and its politics. Wanda was titillated by the gossip. She wanted to know everything, about Kevin and John Hightower, and was strangely curious about Mark Berlanger.

Wanda was interested in Henry Rickford and how he took Simon's response to the ultimatum.

"A fool, now there is a fool," Wanda concluded as she raised her glass.

She relished the details of Tim Dawson's visits and those of the higher ups. Wanda was particularly interested in "Madam Prosecutor," Janet Bultaco.

"Now there is a bitch, a Queen bitch!" Wanda clinked glasses with Francine and drank to Janet Bultaco. "Finally, a woman of consequence!"

They talked about the case. Were they making any progress finding the fiend Simon?

"None yet? They'll find the fuck, don't you worry." Wanda raised her glass again. "Catch the fuck!"

Francine talked about Kevin, as she eventually always did, and the stress he was under.

"He will always treat you badly, stress or no stress." Wanda was never very sympathetic toward Kevin. There was no toast for him.

She seemed to like John Hightower better. "A much more honorable man, your white knight, Francina, and he's the best hope of catching Simon. Hightower is the only one worthy of the challenge."

And with that Wanda emptied her glass. Francine followed suit as if challenged. *This is not the bench press. Drinking is my sport, Wanda baby.*

The gym, the conversation always turned to the gym and why Francine went so often and did not see results.

"Because you go to the gym, but you don't do anything. Except your hair, maybe." The next mug was raised.

They had each had six large mugs of beer and were well into the seventh, which always tended to cut through formalities and delicate conversation.

Why was Francine unable to lose weight no matter what she tried?

"Because sister, you have not yet tried eating less."

"I have to go pee," said Francine as the waiter brought them each an eighth mug. "Want to come?"

"Pass," said Wanda, breaking the cardinal rule that women always go to the bathroom together. There were more important things to do.

The fat, out of shape sow can drink forever. Wanda waited till Francine was gone. A slender hand reached into a pocket. *You need a little help.* Wanda's hand waved over Francine's mug. From the long fingers a light powder floated down into the beer, then disappeared.

When Francine returned, Wanda said to her.

"I'm sorry. I've been mean to you."

"You have?" asked Francine.

"Yes, I should not make fun. I know how hard it is for you to lose weight. Tell you what I'm going to do."

"Yes?" asked Francine, beaming in anticipation.

"I'm going to help you, if you like."

"Why yes, of course," said Francine eagerly.

"I am going to help you. And I guarantee, starting tomorrow, you are going to get skinny. What do you say?"

"I say yes."

"All right then." Wanda picked up her mug. "Then tonight we celebrate and tomorrow we get skinny."

A proper toast and Francine downed her mug enthusiastically.

"Go ahead, sister," said Wanda. "Have anything you want tonight. Tomorrow you diet in earnest."

The waiter brought two more mugs. The men at the bar were duly impressed. Francine ordered the strudel. Halfway through it, she became violently sick. Francine needed to throw up.

"This has never happened to me before," she protested. "I need to go to the bathroom!"

Francine felt as if someone was pulling her stomach out through her mouth. She never made it out of the booth. Vomit spewed everywhere as she wretched uncontrollably.

"Oh, oh," said Wanda. "I think we better go." She looked at the men and shrugged her shoulders then put Francine's arm over her shoulder and began walking her out.

"Thank you gentlemen for the lovely evening. We have to go now," she said smiling.

Two of the men helped Wanda load Francine into the passenger side of her car. They lowered the seatback so that Francine could recline and buckled her seat belt. Francine was unconscious. Wanda got the keys from her purse and drove off.

Several streets away, in the dark, Wanda placed the ether over Francine's face.

Sleep well, Francina, my plump princess. My inning number six.

63

A Master brings a fish to his student and instructs him to study it until he knows it fully. The student dutifully scrutinizes the fish for an hour then returns to the Master.

"Go back and study the fish," orders the Master without asking a single question. "You do not understand it yet."

The student inspects the fish for another ten hours and again returns to the Master, confident that he has learned everything possible.

"Go back," orders the Master again. "You still do not know the fish."

The student is angry. He again studies the fish, this time for one hundred hours.

He does not return to his Master. He has learned the lesson.

I have told this story to all of my classes and all of my agents and it is almost universally considered stupid. A lot of words used to say very little. That is because they have not learned the lesson. Those few who have, however, know the true essence of an investigation.

- Into the Mind of a Killer, John Hightower

The strings of Dvorak's Cello Concerto vibrated harmoniously in the background. For three days the CD's played on. John Hightower was not paying attention to the music. He was yanking on a file that he did not notice Janet was standing on.

For three days, Janet Bultaco came and went with nothing more than a grunt from him. John insisted that she leave him alone and that requirement was absolute. Janet respected the work ethic and she, above all, understood the importance of his work. But, she was worried.

John sustained himself exclusively on iced tea, leaving untouched the food brought for him. He slept only in short fits of involuntary unconsciousness and when dragged to bed for a few hours, he remained awake.

Janet forced him to go to dinner, and she got his body only. His mind remained on the case. It did not allow him to eat or rest, working incessantly, and nothing on earth could slow it down.

The evidence is here. Then, so, too, are the answers. They are here waiting to be found.

The living room floor was no longer visible. Accumulated notes, documents, reports, forensics, and pictures completely papered over the white carpeting. The evidence grew in thick piles upward like vegetation in a small tropical clearing. *A forest of evidence and still we are no closer to catching you, Simon!*

John wandered continually amidst the evidence, refusing to leave. His fingers waded through the files, while his mind sifted through the data and his intellect struggled to sort it all out.

Hightower continued to pull at the file. He became angry, noticing that Janet was on top of it. "Get off," he barked. "I need this." It was additional background on all the victims, information he had ordered Berlanger to get. "Please," he implored. "Get off!"

The Bulldog refused to move. "Three days solid, John, time to take a break." Her tone was insistent, determined, an army could not have budged her.

"I can't," he implored looking up at her with his puppy dog eyes.

"That's not going to work either. Take a break. Take me sailing. Then I'll let you go another three days."

He pulled at the file again. Janet was not going to move.

"What, not working this Sunday, counselor?" he snapped at her, clearly irritated.

"Took the day off. Simply have to be out on the water today. Well, what's it going to be, John?"

It was a calm, balmy afternoon on Santa Monica Bay. John Hightower went through the motions of controlling the small boat, but his mind was still on the case. The new information was very illuminating. Finally the answer was before him. *The connection between the victims, what I was searching for, what I missed!*

Francine Brady, hell, why do I still call her that? Francine Fitzpatrick was not nearly as attractive as the other victims. She would not be your choice – for your pleashah.

Why did it take Francine before I could see it?

Mary Splitorf's aunt was a secretary for the Bureau from l988 to 91. Kathleen Harper's grandfather was an agent. Killed in the line of duty. Mary Benson had a cousin in the Academy.

Susan Benchly no connection, but that makes sense. She was just unlucky, there, so you took her along with the Rickford girl. Just to keep from losing the opportunity and wasting time. Am I warm, Simon?

Danielle Rickford, now that was a puzzle. She didn't seem to fit at all. Except, last summer, when protection was provided the Rickford's at a two week conference in Washington D.C. Seems young Danielle developed a crush on a certain agent, Mike Barrow. They had plans to run off and get married, until Daddy stepped in. Pulled a lot of strings to keep that quiet. But I guess that little episode was enough to qualify Danielle.

Simon, how could you have learned about that? Amanda Grove?

So, there's the connection. They're all ours. Your grievance is with us, Simon. What is it?

Hightower's mind turned to the picture of Danielle's eyes in the Tifanny's box, and the message written on the lid. *I CHOOSE DEATH!*

I CHOOSE DEATH, written neatly, meticulously, and in the victim's own blood. All in character for you Simon. In a Tifanny's box. You knew Henry Rickford bought gifts there for his wife.

You have studied the fish Simon. How long did you study the Rickfords?

TIME TO APPEAL TO A HIGHERPOWER. And, Simon, how well do you know me?

The box was slipped into Elaine Rickford's coat. How? When? Where? We're still tracking her movements. The likely suspect, a salesman at Bellagio's, now missing. What a surprise!

I warned Rickford! His daughter might be alive today if he had listened. Is there a grievance against Rickford? No, your game is against us. He just infuriated you didn't he?

I told Rickford that you're not motivated by money. You're a rich fuck yourself, aren't you?

All the crimes were well financed, without regard to cost. The time for research, the assumption of identities, the vehicles, the van, the cabin. The Tifanny's box!

They questioned a saleslady, Linda Symes, who said an elderly gentleman purchased ten thousand-dollar earrings and insisted on that particular box. An unusual box, they rarely use it.

You disguised yourself and spent ten thousand dollars for a box, and that just to heighten the effect on the Rickfords. Money, you dare bribe me with money? Take that Lord Richfuck! Am I right, Simon?

Clearly, you have substantial financial resources, and that too will make you harder to catch. Most criminals don't have money. They reuse weapons, vehicles, false identities, even hideouts. They haven't the resources to do otherwise. Hell, some of them even have day jobs. No such weakness for you, huh, Simon. You have the cash to wage the battle any way you like.

So, Richfuck has had his lesson. Dare not challenge a man such as you.

They had been out on the water for two hours. Immersed in his thoughts, John Hightower did not notice Janet was missing. The sound of heavy upchucking could clearly be heard from below. John realized he had heard it for some time, but hadn't allowed it to register. He jumped below decks. "What's the matter, honey?" he asked, distressed.

"I'm seasick, you big oaf!" Janet fought to say, before heaving again. "Nice of you to notice."

"But how? It's such a calm day. We're hardly moving."

"Happens to me every time, without fail."

Never before had John Hightower felt like such a sap. Janet had drawn him away because she was worried about him. "*Take me sailing," because she thought it might help to entice me. She's sick as a dog now. And she did it for my sake.*

He wrapped his arms around her. Janet's face was sheet white. "Come let me take you home, my poor baby. I love you so much."

64

Recording E-5

"Guns and might are powerless against deception and misdirection. Technology is no match for illusion. Let them come after me with all they would. I have power to appear and disappear, to be anyone and no one."

What an absolute pain in the ass Community Service is! Most people are afraid of prison. Prison! "You're going to prison," the judge says, and you panic. You know you are going to be stabbed. Or worse, you visualize yourself being punked all week by the entire prison population.

Community Service, now that sounds so much better. No danger. At worst it's an inconvenience. Just from the sound of it, "Community Service," it's a good thing.

Bullshit!

First of all, they don't exactly send you to Alcatraz when you go to "Prison." You're in with the drunks and low-grade drug offenders, my kind of people. Forced relaxation is what prison was for me, one long cocaine bender. I swear if they let me take Christine, I would gladly have done a week in jail every month.

Community Service is, well, work, back breaking, tiring, demeaning, unending work that you wouldn't give a mule to do. Forget the illusion of handing out meals in soup kitchens or comforting cancer patients in hospitals. For two days they had me cleaning fucking toilets at the beach.

I wouldn't go into those bathrooms, even to pee, they smell so bad. But there I was all day with my nose in a urinal scrubbing away.

For the rest of my week, I was part of a modern day chain gang. Resplendent in my orange vest, with the sun glaring down and breathing in the exhaust fumes from every car in rush hour traffic, I pulled weeds all day on the San Diego Freeway.

And no cocaine! They watch you during Community Service. My morning dose had to last me all day, an utter impossibility. I thought there was supposed to be a law against cruel and inhuman punishment. I nominate Community Service.

Now, I'm not just venting, Father. I wouldn't tell you all this if it wasn't for Simon. Yes, believe it or not, the brash motherfucker visited me on my third 'ay of pulling weeds.

It was about ten thirty in the morning, getting hot, and I was beginning to go through early withdrawal symptoms. I started out each morning in a bad mood and it sank steadily from there. I wasn't interested in conversation.

We were chopping underbrush that day. The man next to me was swinging his scythe like a lumberjack in heat. He was a tall slim baldheaded man with lots of tattoos, who tried to engage me in conversation several times. I ignored him each time, hoping not to be insulting as he was clearly insane and was swinging a formidable weapon.

"Nice day to be working in the yard, hey man?"

I pretended not to hear. Again!

"The warm sun, the clean air, the plants, good exercise, what could be better?" he continued, not missing a stroke. He was strong. I'll give him that. His scythe was a blur as his muscles snapped back and forth like tight rubber bands and the vegetation flew in all directions.

"I love this kind of work, don't you?"

He was a persistent lunatic. "Uh huh," I answered grudgingly.

"I had to sneak in. Otherwise they wouldn't let me work."

"Huh?" I hated myself for involuntarily encouraging the conversation. The weeds kept flying.

"What's the matter, WIH..A..CHEE..YOOK..HUH, outdoor life not agree with you?"

"Simon?"

"Bartolo!"

"Yes, of course, Bartolo. But how did you, why did you..."

"Frankie, it's much easier sneaking into these things than sneaking out. It was safe enough. But I guess we have the rest of the day together. What shall we talk about?"

"I don't know where to start and I'm afraid I don't have my recorder with me. I never expected..."

"Will you never change? But fear not. I decided to save time and effort. I dictated tapes for you. Sent to the lovely Christina's."

"Francine Fitzpatrick, the FBI secretary?"

"Not just a secretary, Frankie, Fitzfatprick's secretary, and his wife. Yes, I've sent you the details, even stuff the cops will never figure out. Pictures, and a few sexy little tidbits, too. A little sex never hurt any book, huh, Frankie?"

"No."

"And there is quite a bit of stuff on Daniella, also. I guess Richfuck got his answer, huh, Frankie. Rich and dead, Lord Richfuck!"

The guard came over to remind me that I was there to work. The vegetation continued to spew from Bartolo's blade.

"Can't he work for the both of us?" I asked the guard. He gave me a look that said he wished he could whip me like they did in the old days. Something he must have seen in a movie.

"Keep it up dickhead and see what happens," he snarled at me. I almost felt sorry for him. A far cry from a cat of nine tails, a mere threat, the poor man had to settle so.

"Yes, sir, boss!" I shot back in my best slave impersonation. But I also took a few good whacks at the weeds.

"Frankie, Frankie, where is your respect for authority?" Bartolo asked me.

I shot back. "Losing it fast, and you?"

"The utmost. Remember I am here by choice. Now, where were we?"

"You have things for me."

"Yes, sent to you. Everything you need. You might say this is just a social call. Almost!"

I didn't like the tone in his voice. I had good reason.

"Yes?"

"You have been visiting your former employer."

Busted. "Yes, I have been meaning to talk to you about that."

And I was. The advance on the book was gone. Don't ask me how, but it was spent. I was supporting Jenny and Jane and living with Christine on my salary from the Paper.

The problem was, I wasn't doing anything to earn it and Chub had had enough. The contract for the book, he pointed out, did not include my salary. I disagreed, but even Patton couldn't help me. Chub was going to cut me off.

"And we can let the lawyers decide," the obnoxious fat fuck threatened snidely. No one had hold of my balls like that since Mistress Pleasure. And Chub was no Mistress Pleasure. Only bad things were about to happen.

So I made a deal. I promised to throw the Paper some unrelated stories, stuff like I used to do, and we would keep everything friendly. Chub accepted eagerly in hopes of getting some circulation back. My first series was going to be on prison, the next on Community Service.

I explained this all to Simon and hoped for the best. God I wished I had some cocaine!

"You should have managed your finances better, Frankie. Your new agreement with your employer breaks the rules we agreed to."

"No, not really. I have more than enough time to devote to our book. And besides these articles have nothing to do with you, nothing whatever."

"You are breaking the rules!"

"I can't help it. I have to eat." I was stammering wildly. "I'm not breaking the rules. I'm just making a small change, a minor alteration, a nuance. That's all.

"There is always another day, huh, Frankie? And always a new way to play."

"It's inconsequential to the book," I was talking as fast as I could, trying to explain before Simon finished his sentences.

"It increases the risk. It increases my risk! The more contact you have with them, the greater my risk."

"You know I will be discreet. It will not increase the risk, I swear. I have no choice, Simon, I need the money."

"Then, so it shall be. It's a little late for me to find a new writer."

"Then you're ok with it?"

"We all make our own choices, Frankie. And we must each live with them."

I didn't like the tone in his voice when he said that. It scared me. I knew Simon, could see his wheels spinning, plotting, already devising some punishment for me.

God I wanted to back down. But, there was no going back. I needed the money. Besides, the hard part was already done. I had told him.

"Tell me about the disguises and the false identities." I blurted out, anything to get his mind off my offense. "I've been curious about that for some time and have been meaning to ask you," I continued rapidly, nervously. "It's important for the book."

"The disguises and identities..." he repeated slowly as his voice tailed off. Simon knew I was trying to change the subject.

My attention shifted to his scythe. Bartolo had not missed a stroke. Long, heavy, powerful slashes, each one exacting a mighty toll from the weeds. Not at all comforting as I nervously waited for Simon's next move.

"Fine!" he finally said. I released the air that had been trapped in my lungs, relieved to have the matter behind us. Though inwardly I knew it wasn't.

"Let me start with disguises. Very simple, a little make up, a little role playing and shazam, Venus, your friend on the bench, Gomer, or this current one, Bartolo. I use them once and never again. They are relatively easy to create and the supply of them is limited only to imagination."

"And the one's like Jim or Felix or Wanda?"

"Those are a little more complicated. They are created especially for the Game. More time and effort goes into them. Every detail from their Driver's licenses to their high school transcripts has to be perfect. They require backgrounds, history.

I become each of them. I live their lives as they would if they were real. They are created and exist for a specific purpose and when that is fulfilled they disappear."

"Without a trace."

"That is correct, Frankie. They may search from now till doomsday and they will find nothing. All the identities vanish. The ability to appear and disappear."

"But what about your own identity, the real Simon?"

"The real Simon?

There are those identities we talked about, the ones devised as required by the Game, the intermediaries that do the dirty deeds and take the chances. They may be needed for weeks, maybe months, never more.

Then there are the long-term identities, which I have established over the course of years. Backgrounds, documentation, financial transactions and histories, hell, some of them run businesses. They own houses and make car payments. They are real people with real lives, although few have met them personally. Most of it is done by mail or telephone, and now internet. I maintain about a half a dozen at all times, different people, different lives, different cities.

"These long term identities, what are they for?"

"Refuge, Frankie, refuge. They do not participate in any of my games. I keep them hidden. And if, by chance, an identity is compromised, it disappears and I reappear in the next one. All of the identities also eventually lead nowhere."

"But what about the real Simon? Under it all, the disguises and identities, there is a real person. You must have a mother and a father. There has to be a real background, a real person. What if they find the real you?"

"Now you see, Frankie, that is exactly the point.

There is no real me."

65

John Hightower was back on the living room floor. Mercifully, Janet was working on a tough case and was busy herself. He would not be disturbed.

How could this have gotten so out of control? A shudder ran through him as he inspected the photograph that accompanied Simon's last note, received about a week after Francine's abduction.

It had become personal. Simon had penetrated the inner sanctum and taken someone close, one of their very own. Francine, *sweet, innocent Francine,* was the latest victim.

Hightower got up and moved away from the Rickford corner of the room toward Francine's area. *How many times have I traversed these stacks of evidence?* He could not recall and sat down next to the pile of forensic data. He had fallen asleep in that very spot, *how long ago was it? Ten hours, twelve, what does it matter?*

Hightower held the note in his hand. He knew it by heart, having read it more than forty times.

FITS-FAT-PRICK,

THE GAME YOU CANNOT PLAY
FIDDLE, DIDDLE, FIDDLE, DIDDLE
SO THE DAY YOU WILE AWAY
FIDDLE, DIDDLE, FIDDLE, DIDDLE

THE FAIR FRANCINA I DID TAKE
I HAVE HER FOR MY PLEASHAH'S SAKE

SEE YOUR CHUNKY LITTLE PRINCESSA
FOR ME SHE IS A LITTLE MORE SLIMA

SO NOW, YOU CAN ONLY FIDDLE, FIDDLE,
WHILE I DO DIDDLE, DIDDLE
A BIG IMPROVEMENT FOR FRANCINA I MAKE

SIMON

So much known about the Bureau, about Fitz and Francine. Amanda Grove. And how much new information have you drawn from Francine herself? She was last seen in the company of a tall slender woman. Tall and slender like Amanda Grove, although reportedly much more attractive.

They were in a bar talking for hours. Francine's companion made quite an impression on the bar's male clientele. There appears to be a tendency toward flamboyance in you, Simon. Does the flashiness come from arrogance? Arrogance is a weakness. It might just lead to a mistake.

The two women were also often seen together at Francine's gym. The woman was known as Wanda. Statuesque and very strong, never seen in the locker room, never seen without clothes on.

It was you. An accomplice does not fit your profile at all. You're a loner. You trust no one. There is no accomplice, Simon!

You were Amanda Grove. And you were Wanda. You fooled the Bureau and you fooled Francine, as you fooled Danielle Rickford and all the others. You are a first rate actor and impersonator, Simon!

We need to cycle through the actors and make-up artists again, recheck the sources of make-up, customer lists, go foreign as well. Simon, you must go through tons of the stuff. You have to get it somewhere.

And what about the identities? Gone, vanished into the thin air from which they sprang. Yes. Disposable, untraceable like the throwaway weapons utilized by professional killers.

How many identities have you stockpiled in preparation for your game, Simon?

That's where we are currently focusing the effort. A laborious job but it must be done. There is a flaw somewhere. There always is.

It pained Hightower to look at the picture that accompanied the note, Francine naked, spread eagled on a table, the kind used by bondage freaks. There were shackles on her wrists and ankles and one around her waist. A ball gag was clamped into her mouth.

We'll check every manufacturer of that disgusting trash. We'll check every sale. Every deranged weirdo will be investigated and questioned.

Francine was slimmer, at least twenty pounds by Hightower's estimate. The difference was unmistakable.

You're starving her! All that weight lost in only nine days.

Hightower studied the face in the picture. He saw much in that face, once so innocent and naïve, so trusting, and so foolish. The once happy expression was gone, replaced by that of a woman in complete terror. The anger welled up in him. Inappropriate for a good investigator, but how could he help himself? It had become personal. The fiend had Francine naked, gagged, and trussed up on his torture table. Hightower dared not imagine what she had already gone through. *Starvation, obviously. Torture, likely. Rape, certainly.*

Everyone loved Francine. She was authentic, pure and unspoiled. A trusting heart, Francine must have been easy prey, hardly a challenge for one who prepares as fully as you.

You study the fish carefully, Simon, and you play well. But, at least now, your game is clear, and so is your next play.

66

The Serial killer is a man devoid of conscience, to whom human life is of no consequence. He can commit any atrocity without a thought or the slightest guilt. For him, we are all raw material, existing solely to be at his disposal.
He is like Alexander, Hannibal, Hitler, but with his own worlds to conquer. And he need be no less clever or ruthless or determined.

- Into the Mind of a Killer, John Hightower

"John, you look terrible!"

Tim Dawson, Assistant Director, was John Hightower's boss, and having had others in the past, Hightower was thankful for it. Dawson was a straight shooter, relatively apolitical, and could be counted on to speak his mind truthfully. Hightower respected the man, though he wondered if it would last. Tim Dawson was a relative newcomer to the Bureau. *A fast riser because of his competence, an exception. How long before the politics swallow him, too?*

For the moment, at least, Tim Dawson could be trusted.

"Thanks for the compliment, Tim," Hightower answered with a wry smirk. "You are looking well too. Come in."

"Are you ill, John?" Dawson's concern was real.

John Hightower had not thought about his appearance or his well being. He had not bothered eating and slept only as long as exhaustion forced him to.

"No, I'm fine," Hightower said brusquely. "Let's get on with it.

There's no time to waste."

"All right," answered Assistant Director Dawson hesitantly, while looking at the man's back. The tall, lean Hightower was already halfway to the living room. To Tim Dawson he appeared a walking clothes hanger with the clothes dangling limply from him. *How much weight has John lost?*

"Have you been eating, John?"

Hightower did not answer as he removed several handfuls of folders from his white couch and placed them on the floor. Tim Dawson made note of the respect with which the documents were treated. John Hightower motioned for the Assistant Director to sit. Tim Dawson complied.

"Eating? Can't remember," Hightower answering the question posed more than a minute before. "Would you like some iced tea, Tim?"

"No, thank you."

Hightower carefully lifted a stack of documents from the matching white easy chair and placed it gently on top of another stack on the floor. He sat in the small space created, perched on the very edge of the chair, not more than three feet from Dawson.

"Fine!" Hightower announced. "Enough of the small talk. What do you want?"

"I want you to take complete charge of the investigation. Fitz is a basket case. I'm putting him on medical leave. He would be too close to it anyway, what with the latest one."

"Francine. The latest one, Francine, we're all too close to it now. Anyway, Berlanger is in line. You know, chain of command."

"John, please, not now. You know Berlanger isn't up to this."

"No one is, Tim. Not Berlanger, not me, not anyone. Not with the way things are being handled."

"Tell me what you need, John. Anything, just name it."

"Ok, Tim. Ready?"

"Yessss?" Dawson drew the word out slowly indicating he realized Hightower was laying in wait for him and that he was about to hear an ultimatum.

"Why Assistant Director Dawson, you look as if you're expecting me to make you eat a bug."

"Are you?"

"Not yet." Hightower chuckled. Dawson joined him.

Fortunate, thought Dawson, some of the tension in John Hightower needed to be dissipated. He read it immediately on the man's face, felt it, and was in danger of becoming entangled in it.

John Hightower was a legend. He lectured to Dawson's class when Dawson was a recruit at the Academy. Hightower's book was required reading. John Hightower solved the Bureau's most difficult cases and did it for decades.

In his few short years in the Bureau, Tim Dawson watched in awe as the master worked his magic. *John Hightower was always calm, always in control. He was never like this.*

The man was on the razor's edge of his emotions. For over twenty years he could allow his intellect to immerse itself in a case, while keeping his emotions in check. That was impossible now. It had become personal.

"The biggest problem, Tim, is you people still don't know what you're up against. Right around the time you were born, there was another madman on the loose."

Hightower looked for hints of displeasure in Tim Dawson. He knew he was being condescending, treating Dawson like a junior agent, almost demeaning. He wanted to see how the man who actually sat several levels above him would react.

Hightower checked the body language for a sign of discomfort and the young face for the slightest grimace. He saw nothing other than a man who respected him, his abilities and his many accomplishments and wanted to hear what he had to say.

Excellent!

"That was Zodiac and we never caught him. This man, our Simon, is the son of Zodiac, or at least a very ardent student.

In the beginning, I saw the similarities, which were many, and I assumed that Simon was a copycat. Some of the original notes could have been written by Zodiac himself.

But I was wrong. Simon is Zodiac plus, plus a lot. Zodiac was angry and acted brashly. I always thought he was lucky not to get caught. Simon does not need luck. He is smart and calculating, every move measured. He pays attention to details, plans ahead, miles ahead. Then he executes."

"Yes, we are all duly impressed by him, but..."

"But?" interrupted Hightower. "But? But nothing! Make no mistake Tim, Simon has been toying with us."

"Now tell me something I don't know, John."

Hightower felt he had more groundwork to do. A brash, unconventional gambit had come into his mind, a plan that normal FBI procedure would never allow. He wanted to lay out his plan slowly. *Fuck it! But first...*

"Ok. We will never catch Simon with that three ring circus you're running!"

Hightower paused as the young face in front of him turned white.

"What do you mean, John?"

"Since when do we let the victims call the shots?"

"You mean Rickford? Henry Rickford is a very important man."

"In chemicals, not criminals. And since when is it Bureau policy to give hourly updates to mayors and senators or even the Holy Ghost?"

"This is a high profile case, John, maybe the highest in a century. There are a lot of important asses on the line."

"So, what's new? But we used to focus on catching the bad guys, not running a political convention. We put our energies to investigating, not into preparing press releases."

"Now that's a low blow, John. The public is worried. Women are moving out of California because they're afraid. They're scared that the person working next to them or the classmate in the next seat might be Simon.

You can see what's going on. There's a very real panic and we have to do something. We have to reassure the public that we are in control, that they're safe."

"They are safe."

"What's that?"

"Later! Let's get back on point. There is such a thing as public relations. I understand that. There is placating an important man like Henry Rickford, and even political babysitting. I see the importance of it. But then there is also catching a killer.

You guys are making it easy for him. Simon was right calling you minor leaguers."

"Another low blow, John. All right, I'm listening. What?"

"You want me to run things. Fine! But I want a chance at catching Simon and hopefully saving the victims that are still alive."

"Francine."

"Yes, Francine. Now for your bug."

Tim Dawson smiled involuntarily.

"I want a complete firewall between the investigation and everything else. Everything else! I want a task force with people of my own choosing. Those people will be fully dedicated and answer only to me."

"What about the others?"

"Ship them out. The task force will have the highest priority on all resources, no exceptions. There will be absolutely no interaction with the press or anyone else unless it serves our purposes. If we want something in the papers, fine, otherwise no.

I will report to no one, answer to no one, and take direction from no one."

"You have to answer to someone."

"No, I don't! That will be your job, to make sure I don't. I'll keep you informed but that's where it stops. Simon knows too much about us and what we're doing. Let's at least take that advantage away from him. It's more important now than ever."

"What do you mean?"

"Later! Do we have an agreement? Tell me now if there's a problem."

"What you ask will be difficult. You may have to compromise on a few things."

John Hightower said nothing for a few moments as he stared into the younger man's eyes.

"I'm too old and much too stubborn to compromise. Do we have an agreement?"

"Now John, you may have to compromise a little."

"Wrong! Tim, do we have an agreement?"

Dawson hesitated only a few seconds. "Yes, John, we do. It won't be easy but I'll run interference for you. Just get the prick."

"I'll certainly try. But we've played six innings already and we're far behind. And the competition plays a very good game."

"Well, thank you for that." Tim Dawson threw up his hands, like the car salesman who had offered his customer every incentive at his disposal and more, and still didn't make the sale. "I'm probably burying my career but at least I have your confidence to reassure me."

"You're very welcome, Tim."

"Now tell me John, when you said later, when you said the public was safe. What did you mean?"

"Yes, of course, let me go back. You remember when I said I first thought Simon was a Zodiac copycat. There were very pointed similarities, particularly in the early communications. But he's not another Zodiac, merely playing with us. Simon has grievances.

"Grievances?"

"You've got to understand Simon."

"Journey into his mind, John?"

"I've tried and I must try harder. Our Simon is a very complex man, more so than any I have dealt with so far. He's filled with hate, as most of them are. He could explode at any moment as many of them do. But he won't. He has learned to control his emotions. Simon vents his hate in well-calculated doses. There is always a plan for his retribution.

Simon's game is meant to punish."

"Who, John?"

"Us, Tim, the Bureau, law enforcement, the whole criminal justice system. I don't know why yet, but we are most certainly the targets for his hate.

So your average housewife, secretary, student, topless dancer, they're all safe now. It is the wives and mothers and daughters and women in government law enforcement whom we must protect."

"Francine?"

"All of them, although I didn't see it till Francine. All have an FBI connection. And, he's not done, Tim. There are three innings left. The crimes will build in importance and significance."

"My God! You mean… Who do you think he will go after next?"

"Could be anyone, but my money's on Berlanger's family. He has a wife and two young daughters. Remember Furbanger in the notes. He was singled out. Fitz and Berlanger were both singled out."

"And they've been in the news so much, and Newsweek's 'Top Cops.' You solved the case and they took the bows."

"And they're welcome to them.

Remember, Tim, Simon plans to dishonor and punish us in the worst possible way, the way it has been done for centuries. He means to take our women!"

Hightower paused to look into the younger man's eyes.

"Then all women in law enforcement, and all the female relatives must be protected. And, especially Berlanger's."

Dawson understood perfectly. Hightower was pleased with the progress made. He decided to push for the goal line.

"Now, here's the thing, Tim."

"Yessss?"

"We have a much better chance of catching Simon in the act than we do tracking him down. I'm positive he is going after Berlanger. We've got to get him when he tries."

"You want to use his family as bait?"

"They're already bait. We have to protect them, sure. But let's do it in a low profile way. Let's protect them and set a trap."

Dawson grimaced as if in pain. "I don't know, John."

"If you want to catch Simon."

"I'll have to talk to Berlanger. If he goes along, fine. Pretty risky, that's quite a bug you're feeding me."

"Bon appetite, Tim."

THE LATE INNINGS

67

Surveillance must be tailored to fit the objectives. If you want to stop crime on a street corner, put a uniform there. To catch a perpetrator in the act requires a little more stealth.

- Into the Mind of a Killer, John Hightower

Mark Berlanger drowsily shut off the alarm next to his bed. Twenty-five minutes early, the stress was beginning to upset his internal clock. He took a few moments to rub his eyes but he would not be truly awake until after his shower.

Long showers were the habit of a lifetime. The warm water was his first pleasure of the day, sometimes the only pleasure. Mark Berlanger deliberated well in the shower, his thoughts usually about the politics of the day or details of the most recent case. Lately, however, he reflected only on the cadre of FBI that was hidden all around his house. It had been eleven weeks to the day since the formulation of Hightower's little trap.

The atmosphere around the Bureau had changed and nowhere was it more evident than in John Hightower himself. Intensity without the familiar wit; assertiveness not tempered by a willingness to listen; preoccupation from which there was never a withdrawal.

They were playing a private little chess match, Hightower and Simon, or so it seemed to Mark Berlanger. He had often witnessed John seize a killer's psyche, *climb into his mind,* but never with such passion or desperation. *John often refers to himself as Higherpower. Fitz is*

Fitsfatprick and I am Furbanger. John has completely assumed the killer's mentality and sometimes he even speaks to us through his lips.

Mark Berlanger did not question John Hightower's intuition. If anyone on the planet could crawl into Simon's brain it was Hightower. If he suspected that Berlanger's wife or one of his daughters was the likely next target, that hunch had to be taken seriously.

Divergent emotions converged inside Mark Berlanger. He worried for his family's safety, but thought the plan to snare Simon was sound. He was angry about his de facto demotion, yet was happy not to be Fitz, who was put out to pasture. He missed the spotlight, however, was relieved to no longer be criticized.

The family was kept in the dark. They were not told that they were considered Simon's prime targets. Mark Berlanger agreed with Hightower; they would play their parts best if they were not acting. Maintaining routine was critical.

The strategy was to funnel Simon's attempt into their home where the trap was set. Pam and the girls were each heavily guarded whenever they left the house, usually by two well-trained female agents. They were escorted everywhere, even to the rest room, no exceptions. Anyone suspicious would be apprehended immediately. *Deterrent surveillance!*

Berlanger recalled the chapter of Hightower's book on stakeouts and surveillance. *What was it called? The Art of Surveillance.* How many times had Hightower recited that chapter for him over the years?

"It is not the punishment of boredom, Mark. It is the triumph of patience. Surveillance must be fitted to the requirements. Deterrence to stop a crime. Undercover to capture. But remember Mark, the more clever the criminal, the more exacting the subterfuge must be and the more patient we need be."

Mark Berlanger got into his Grand Cherokee. He turned on the CD player, volume down. It was too early, even for Johnny Cash. The window was rolled down while backing out of the garage. Mark Berlanger liked the cool morning air. As it rushed into his lungs, he began to feel truly awake.

John Hightower had devised a devious little plan. Initially, the standard surveillance package was employed - the white van, the parked cars, and the loitering agents trying to blend in.

"I will be expecting this," John said as if it were Simon speaking.

"I'll give credit to Higherpower for anticipating my move and I will wait."

It was Hightower's opening move. Simon would never be fooled, he reasoned, by basic surveillance. Slowly, over time, resources were pulled, as if from discouragement or budget considerations. Finally, only a single parked van remained.

At the same time the "Stealth Surveillance" was gradually put in place.

The garage door creaked closed as Berlanger glanced at the brand new truck parked in his neighbor's driveway. *How can it be that a plumber makes more than a mid-level FBI agent?* In about a half-hour, Hank Randolph would get in the Randolph's Plumbing truck for a day of fixing leaky faucets. At night the truck sat in his driveway with a cargo of FBI agents and their equipment.

Nothing new or unusual must be introduced into the neighborhood.

Agent Berlanger heard the sound of power mowers. Today was the day for the Taylor's gardeners. Berlanger recognized agent Diaz working diligently with the hedge trimmer. John Hightower insisted that Diaz did a full day's work. *Authenticity!* Tomorrow it would be the Timmon's yard and agent Maldano on the clippers.

The cable company, laying new lines, had an extra workman. The trash collectors also had an FBI presence. How long an agent was in the area was not as important as maintaining the routine. John Hightower wanted coverage, but not at the expense of authenticity.

Everything must be normal, everything perfectly routine. The art of surveillance Hightower style, with unlimited budget. Only in his dreams, 'til now.

Next door at the Thomas' residence, the "gas man" secretly installed listening equipment. Aimed directly at the Berlanger house, any loud or unusual noise would sound the alarm.

Two FBI agents posing as a young married couple rented a house around the corner, no more than thirty seconds away on the run. They lived normal commuter lives, going and coming from work each day. Half a dozen agents were stationed at the house at all times. Shift changes were concealed, replacements smuggled in and out in the couple's minivan. A second house was rented two streets away.

Mark Berlanger backed into the street. He took in some shallow breaths of the cool air. His arm hung from an open window that would not be closed till he was on the freeway. Berlanger took a last sideways peek at the Randolph's Plumbing van, gave the slightest discreet nod, and was off. He cast his attention on the heavily brushed hills surrounding his housing tract. *"Unusual luck having those hills," Hightower had said, "a great advantage."*

As the Cherokee pulled out of the tract, Berlanger tried unsuccessfully to detect the hidden spotters. *Good,* he thought, *they cannot be seen.* Their presence gave him comfort. From the high vantage points they watched every inch of his house day and night. *If an unauthorized gnat comes on my property, they'll see it and twenty agents will have it surrounded.*

The stealth surveillance had been in place for two months without the slightest nibble. John Hightower remained unperturbed, no less certain than he was eleven weeks before.

"He is a patient man, bold, but a very careful man. He will study the scene tirelessly, and will monitor our resolve. He'll focus on the remaining van and figure ways to defeat it.

You see, Mark, he must have his chosen victim. Simon is fixated on it. It is a challenge he cannot resist."

Mark Berlanger had often witnessed John Hightower in role-playing mode. Never before had he seen the man so immersed. He would not argue against the heavy security for his family; he was thankful for it. *Still, it's eerie to see John this way.*

It was no secret that John had taken Francine's kidnapping quite personally and blamed himself for not being smarter. *And Simon's taunts only aggravated him further.*

He's too personally involved. Mark Berlanger wondered if in his zeal to climb into Simon's mind, John Hightower had quite possibly lost his own.

68

Mark Berlanger looked forward to his evening of "working late." *Lack of rank also has its privileges,* he thought to himself smugly. He had again become a nine to five man, except for Tuesdays and Thursdays.

Each morning Berlanger came to the office passing Cindy, the receptionist, his secret playmate. They rarely spoke, instead exchanged only the smallest of knowing glances. Mark Berlanger knew how to be discreet.

Cindy was twenty-seven, more than ten years Berlanger's junior. She was a pleasant girl, though naïve and small of mind. However, she was compensated well, being large of breast. Cindy wore tight sweaters and too short tight skirts, and was very popular among the male agents.

Mark Berlanger prudently refrained from peeking over the counter. He could afford to, knowing that in fourteen, maybe sixteen, hours his face would be well planted in Cindy's soft flesh. He would expend himself fully with her young body and then sleep an hour or so on those most perfect pillows.

Cindy was on John Hightower's third tier of Bureau women employees, those considered least likely targets for Simon. *A low-level employee like Cindy does not warrant protection. She would move to the top of Hightower's hit parade, however, if he knew of my relationship with her.*

Cindy was given some basic training. She was told to be wary of people she didn't know and to report anyone she felt was suspicious. Berlanger had briefly considered confiding in Hightower, then quickly rejected the idea. There was too much to lose, politically.

Mark Berlanger made his political calculations daily. Though his

GS rating was untouched, he was clearly reduced several levels in stature. John Hightower was now fully in charge of the investigation and he had been put in charge of checking obscure details and other minutia. My family is the *bait for Hightower's little trap. He doesn't want me to be too closely involved.*

That's ok. If John is wrong, and there is no attempt, it's all on him. They will question his decisions. How could he have spent all that time, effort and money on a hunch? They will pick at him like vultures. And not at me!

And if John's intuition is right, that's even better. I pray Simon does make the try. Let him fall into John's trap. Because when we do capture Simon, I'll be on the cover of Newsweek again.

"Top Cop does it again!" "Top Cop Berlanger puts his family on the line to apprehend Serial Killer!" I will be famous, as with Jaws. Quiet John Hightower will seek his privacy and sink into the background as he always does. And there I'll be. No Hightower, no Fitz, just me!

69

Mark Berlanger left for the day content with the political calculus. His career, though turbulent, was nevertheless progressing in a proper direction. He had a loving wife and two fabulous daughters. And he had Cindy to provide that much needed extra little spice.

He buckled himself in, turned on the engine, and listened while his Cherokee roared to life. The mellow sounds of Hank Williams began to reverberate around the cabin interrupted only by the squeal of the oversized Goodyears as Berlanger corkscrewed up to street level from his underground parking space.

When safely out of the choking parking lot air, he rolled down the window. His elbow found its familiar spot on the window ledge and his lungs sucked in a deep breath of night air.

Berlanger drove briskly, though not excessively fast. Cindy would be waiting for him anxiously, usually with a drink in her hand and a sexy outfit on. He was an exciting and important man to her, an FBI agent and a "Top Cop."

Mark Berlanger settled back into the rich leather seats, making a conscious effort to expel everything of the last eight hours from his mind. His only remaining tasks were to relax and to enjoy himself.

Cindy lived in a small rented cottage house behind a row of single-family houses. A converted garage, she had made it quite homey. Berlanger pulled the Cherokee into the small curving driveway and parked in front of the cottage. *Very discreet, very off the street, very perfect for a very perfect little discreet affair.*

He climbed out of the Cherokee and knocked gently on the door. Adrenaline racing through him when it opened. Cindy was wearing his favorite red dress, short and tight with a plunging neckline. High heels made her pleasantly taller, and she had obviously spent considerable time in front of her mirror. Cindy was ravishing, far prettier than she ever was at work.

Mark Berlanger embraced her. They kissed passionately. The door closed behind them as they entered Cindy's cottage.

All the while, Mark Berlanger was unaware that someone was watching.

70

Ahh, the Art of Surveillance!

Simon watched Mark Berlanger entering the small cottage as he had done many times before. *The Triumph of Patience! One must study the fish, quite right, Higherpower.* Simon was pleased to see Berlanger's bitch in her red dress. The red dress meant that Berlanger would stay longer. *You will wine and dine her. You will go to a quiet little restaurant and have a nice little dinner. What will it be tonight Furbanger, Italian, Greek, French, or plain old American?*

Afterwards you'll take her home for a good fucking. Then rest. Sleep with the bitch, an hour at least. Recharging the batteries, eh Furbanger? So the rocking can begin anew. You'll fuck the bitch again before you leave. Got to get your money's worth before going home to the sleeping wifey.

What do you tell your Pamela, Furbanger? Working late on the case honey. Do you get much sympathy? Poor man! Slaving away all the time.

"Top Cop," so dedicated!

Cindy played country western music for her "Markey" though she did not like it herself. They usually spent about a half-hour or so getting comfortable before leaving for dinner. Occasionally they made love before leaving. *Sometimes you go for a triple, huh Furbanger? But not tonight!*

Simon followed the white Cherokee to a small Chinese restaurant. *Ah, Asian.* They had about four or five favorite restaurants from which to choose. Simon waited outside, hidden, while they dined.

Anywhere from one to two hours for the meal, we must enjoy the repast! Learned that from Fitsfatprick, didn't you? Never missed a meal that fat fuck. Nor his hefty bitch, Francina, either. You should see her now, Furbanger! Quite the svelte young lady, a fine bitch she has turned out to be.

It was nearly eleven o'clock when the couple returned to Cindy's place. Simon watched them as they walked to the front door. They were already kissing and hugging. Berlanger's hands stroked the breasts he had admired across the dinner table for hours and had thought about all day.

Eleven. Simon scrutinized the house for another half-hour or so. *I must go. My appointment is at one a.m. I think it safe to assume that you are well engaged for the evening, Furbanger.*

71

At 12:30 a.m., Simon arrived at the garage where he stored the white Cherokee. The vehicle was purchased only a month after Mark Berlanger bought his. An identical Cherokee, identically maintained, from the parking lot sticker pasted to the front windshield to the small dents and scratches Berlanger acquired. For months the Cherokee waited unused for this one night's business.

Fortunately, Furbanger's Jeep is clean today. As is mine. Nothing further need be done.

Simon took a few minutes to inspect his face, comparing the one in the mirror to a handful of pictures taken of Mark Berlanger. There were minor adjustments to be made. There always were. *All things considered, not bad. I could fool myself.*

The blue suit today. Simon reached into the back seat to pull out his blue suit. He had reproduced Mark Berlanger's entire work wardrobe. *Light blue shirt and the red tie with the small checks.* Simon dressed slowly, meticulously. The tie was loosened and the top button of the shirt opened, the way Mark Berlanger came home from work.

In the morning everything is in place, but coming home, and especially coming home from your little bitch, a little more casual.

The Cherokee roared with power when he turned it on. Simon put in an Alabama CD and cranked the volume up. *It is the sound of a cat being strangled. But Alabama is what you play most coming home from your bitch.*

He drove to the 405 Freeway and traced Berlanger's route home, driving as Mark Berlanger would, in the left lane, a steady five miles over the limit. It was fifteen minutes before one a.m. Simon had twenty more minutes on the freeway.

The plan turned over a hundred times in his mind as he considered the potential pitfalls. This would be the most risky taking, actually double taking, Simon would ever have attempted.

He was expected at the Berlangers. *Higherpower has foreseen my intent. I am walking into the enemy's lair to steal the treasure right from his trap. The Game is truly getting interesting.*

Simon exited on El Toro Road just as Mark Berlanger did each night. The window was rolled down and his arm perched on the ledge at exactly the correct angle. Simon was about four inches taller than Mark Berlanger so the bucket seat was lowered accordingly.

He entered the Berlanger tract slowing to twenty-eight miles an hour. Corners were taken at the exact same speed and arc as Burlanger did. The CD was turned down. *Very considerate at this hour of the night, Furbanger. Don't want to disturb the neighbors.* It was ten minutes after one. *Or maybe you are just trying to sneak in.*

Simon looked out toward the hills that surrounded the tract. *A recent development, Furbanger, you never had much interest in the hills before. Could there be spotters and sharpshooters hidden out there? Their night vision scopes watching you as you come home so late.*

The Cherokee arrived at Mark Berlanger's street. Simon tipped his head ever so slightly at the Randolph's Plumbing Truck. *A few little FBI friends in there, Furbanger?* He ignored the white van completely. *The deterrence presence, subterfuge, a nice play, Higherpower.*

You are wise enough not to insult my intelligence. Thank you for that.

You are beginning to understand the Game, Higherpower, and you are playing it credibly. The heavy security presence to begin with, then the pull back, meanwhile, you set your real trap and wait as long as necessary. The triumph of patience!

Simon rounded the corner of the driveway exactly as Mark Berlanger did each night. *The Cherokee is parked on the right side of the garage. The left side is reserved for Pamela's car. Susana's white Toyota, handed down to her by you, is parked on the street.*

Simon tensed up. It was time to confront the one variable over which he did not have full control. Thoughts of failure and doom rushed through his mind. This was a moment of dread, a time of risk, something he had never before willingly allowed.

He reached up to the passenger side visor and pushed the garage door controller. The code was stolen more than six months before initiating the Game, as were those of all the other key players. Simon held his breath awaiting the catastrophe that would ensue if the code was no longer operable. *I will back out, leave slowly, and hope they assume Furbanger forgot something.*

The garage door rocked back as it did each night when Mark Berlanger came home. Simon released his breath. The Cherokee drove to its spot in the garage. Simon climbed out in the exact way Mark Berlanger did after a long evening and a few drinks.

He pushed the garage door button, relieved to have the door close behind him. Simon was in the house. *How fortunate it is that no one in California ever changes their garage door code!*

72

The house was quiet and dark. Simon waited for his eyes to get acclimated. He moved slowly in the unfamiliar surroundings, wondering if his surveillance and one great assumption were correct.

The Berlanger's was a small suburban house. Had he realized at the time that Mark Berlanger was such a bit player, the Game might have proceeded differently. Berlanger was a "Top Cop" according to the media, the captor of Jaws. *But what a pathetic little whelp!*

The plans for the Game had been years in the making. These were the late innings and no changes could be made now. Besides, with John Hightower in the Game, the challenge was more than sufficient and the risks were already uncomfortably high.

Simon moved quietly up the stairs, confident that the FBI was listening. *But are they watching?*

There were no agents in the house. *Too crude a play for Higherpower,* but had they hidden small television cameras? Simon assumed not. Such an installation would be difficult to conceal. *You knew I was watching. Besides with three women in the house, such an invasion of privacy would be unwelcome and the bait might get suspicious. Can't have that now.*

There were three bedrooms in the small house. The far door was obviously the master bedroom. Simon would enter there last. Checking the other two bedrooms, he entered the room where the younger daughter was sleeping. *Young Heather, just turned nine, a little too immature for my taste.*

Simon prepared an ether handkerchief and placed it over her face. Not a move from the young girl; he leaned down and kissed her on the cheek. *We cannot have you waking up, Heather, and making noise, now can we?*

The second bedroom was the older daughter's. A teenage girl's room, the closets so crammed full of clothes that the doors were forced open and the excess clothing spilled out on the floor. The folded piles were clean; the rest were strewn randomly around the room, landing wherever they had fallen, waiting to be washed.

Simon's attention turned to the bed where a small face could barely be discerned from a mountain of stuffed animals. He clamped an ether soaked handkerchief over the face. Unlike her sister, Susan struggled, but only for a few moments.

Simon hesitated over the motionless sixteen-year-old. If the FBI was watching, they would be on top of him in seconds. Simon waited and strained his hearing for the slightest sound.

Nothing! Well then Susana, let us have a look at you. He peeled back the comforter. She was an average looking girl with an ordinary face. She was not heavy, not slender, not shapely, yet not unappealing. Simon placed his hand on her breast and squeezed it through the heavy pajamas. *Young and firm, you will do.* "Now wait right here, I'll be back for you soon," he whispered.

Simon entered the Master bedroom. *Impeccably neat! Not a speck of dust, not an item out of place, I expect no less from a compulsive Furbanger.*

There you are, Mrs. Furbanger. Do you know where Mr. Furbanger is tonight?

Well practiced in the art of late arrivals, aren't we now? Pam Berlanger lay soundly sleeping off to one side of the bed. The other side was still made and without a wrinkle, *waiting for a naughty husband to sneak in.*

Simon pulled up the covers and slipped into bed as he imagined Mark Berlanger did. Slowly, quietly, so as not to wake her; lightly, gently, guiltily, so as not to have to speak to her.

The room was draped in a pleasant fragrance. *Very nice!* Simon snuggled in closer behind the sleeping woman. He breathed in the perfume she had put on that morning. *Jasmine!* Simon had always preferred that fragrance. His arm went around Pam Berlanger's waist and he pulled her towards him.

He was aroused and rubbed himself against her buttocks while he grabbed her breasts and pulled her tighter towards him. Pam Berlanger awoke, startled. *Not the way Furbanger comes to bed, Pamela?* She began to struggle, realizing it was not her husband next to her, but could not scream. The handkerchief already smothered her mouth and nose. Pam Berlanger resisted for a few moments, then fell limp.

Simon lay in bed with her, stroking her, touching her, fondling her, toying with the notion of taking Furbanger's bitch immediately. *How would that be Furbanger, if I take your Pamela right now in your very own bed?* He pushed himself against her again and again. *Yes, how would that be? Huh, Furbanger! How?*

Discipline! Discipline! There is still great danger here. No noise and we must not leave evidence. No genetic material for you, Higherpower!

Pam, then Susan Berlanger, were carried down to the garage and loaded into the Cherokee. Luggage restraints held the bodies firmly in place. A plywood board and gray tarp identical to the one in Mark Berlanger's Cherokee covered them. They would be undetectable from any outside inspection.

The garage door opened slowly, its creaking disturbing the late night silence. The Cherokee backed out of the driveway. An arm was perched over the opened window while subdued sounds of Alabama played from the CD. Simon nodded ever so slightly at the Randolph's Plumbing truck; he ignored the white van and looked out at the dark hills while driving through the tract.

Everything done exactly as it was by Mark Berlanger each day. *With the exception of his leaving so late at night. The final assumption, you would not compromise your surveillance, Higherpower, to challenge Furbanger now. After all, Simon might be watching.*

Innings seven and eight! Your move Higherpower, my worthy adversary.

73

"AND FOR YOU GUYS
WHO ARE THINKING OF DIVORCING YOUR WIVES
A GOVERNMENT STUDY NOW SHOWS
THAT THE QUICKEST WAY TO GET RID OF A WIFE
IS TO LET THE FBI PROTECT HER"

- The Tonight Show

The late night shows were not kind to the Bureau. Tim Dawson sat in John Hightower's office hoping to reestablish some equi librium. Never had he dreamed that the buffer zone between Hightower and the rest of the world could be so uncomfortable. With the latest debacle, what had seemed a difficult situation to Dawson was quickly turning impossible.

The abduction of Mark Berlanger's wife and daughter was a complete disaster. "Simon Takes FBI's Own" was the headline in the Times. "Protected?" read the Register. Dawson hid from requests for comment. He had nothing to say.

The public outcry and resultant pressure on the Bureau was unprecedented. Everyone was under siege; every career in jeopardy; the outrage and abuse tumbled down from the top unabated until it crashed into the buffer.

"It didn't help, John, when you threw the Mayor out."

"He had no business here. You know that."

"Yes, I understand that. But having two agents escort him out arm in arm, you could have been a little more diplomatic."

"I have no time for diplomacy, Tim. That is your part of our deal."

Dawson shook his head like a coach whose quarterback had just thrown his fifth interception. "And a fine deal it has turned out to be for me!"

"You are still wearing your head."

"Funny, it doesn't feel like that. I could have sworn I saw it in the Times editorial this morning. The Director, himself, gave it to them. Better mine than his. Or is that my head on Mayor Plank's desk? Or maybe Senator Lawton is taking it to Washington for a show and tell. Then of course, it could be hanging from Janet Bultaco's rear view mirror. She likes nothing better than taking heads."

"That she does. But, I'll put in a good word for you."

"Thanks," Dawson responded with an air of hopelessness, still shaking his head.

"Tell me Tim, where is Mark Berlanger? Haven't seen him and I'm worried. Is he on medical leave?"

Dawson's face turned livid. "Legal leave!" he sneered angrily. "That son of a bitch is suing the Bureau. Didn't waste a minute. Blames you, blames me, blames the Bureau, god damn it, he was in the loop, part of the plan. Hell, he welcomed it."

"Tim, he did go home and find his wife and daughter missing."

"I don't want to hear it, John. Berlanger always played the angles, and now he's playing us to get rich. Fuck him!"

John Hightower had never heard Tim Dawson so angry. On second thought, he had never heard Dawson angry at all. "They're still alive, you know," he said quietly.

"What was that, John?"

"They are still alive, his wife and daughter. The whole point of Simon's Game is to humiliate us, to put us in our place, and to elevate him to his. He'll use them, kill them only when it suits him."

"If only he wouldn't send the damn notes to the papers! They are crucifying us out there, John. The public, the media, the administration, they are all turning on us; hell, they are even talking about Congressional hearings.

Do they think they can catch the fuck by talking? Make life difficult for the people on the firing line, that's all they do. I'm sorry, John, I didn't mean to rant, just a little release of frustration."

"We were close, you know. Very close, Tim, I could almost feel him."

"That's true and that's the only reason we are both still employed. I sit and listen and wait for the tirades to die down. How can I argue when they're right? It was a disaster. The Bureau has become the butt of every joke and we deserve it.

But eventually, they run out of steam and rebukes. Then I point out that despite the outcome, John Hightower did predict Simon's last move. You're a genius and they know it.

And then I ask them, who they would rather put in charge. That's when they fall silent. For what it's worth, we get to play this to the end. So, tell me, John, where do we stand now?"

"Eight innings played, and Simon is pitching a shutout."

John Hightower swiveled his chair around and stared at the poster-sized reproduction of Simon's latest note. Tim Dawson's eyes followed Hightower's.

MY DEAR HIGHERPOWER,

A NICE LITTLE TRAP YOU DID MAKE
THOUGH NOT MUCH GOOD FOR FURBANGER'S SAKE
WHILE WITH HIS CUNT ONE NIGHT HE DID PLAY
I TOOK HIS TWO LITTLE BITCHES AWAY

THE PRICE WAS HIGH, THOUGH PAY HE MUST
FOR IN HIGHERPOWER DID FURBANGER TRUST
INNINGS SEVEN AND EIGHT ARE DONE, GRIEVE NOT
WITH INNING NINE, THE QUEEN B, THE GAME CAN STILL BE WON

SIMON

Dawson began to shake his head again. "Actually, John, I was hoping for a little more positive assessment. I've already seen that. Unfortunately, so have the papers."

"He sent me this too, Tim."

The small evidence bag contained a few locks of hair, red hair, flaming red hair.

"Francine?" Dawson asked.

"Yes, DNA verified by the lab, some of it pubic."

"Why?"

"Why do they stick the bull before they kill it? To make him fight more fiercely!

"Is it really only a game, John?"

"That it is, Tim, nothing but a game, but driven by a fierce hatred. And, that, I haven't figured out yet. His grievance is the key. What is the source of Simon's hatred? And there is only one inning remaining."

"Then what?"

"Then the game is over. Zodiac never reappeared and was never found. Or maybe, Simon will decide he likes playing too much. Maybe he'll decide to play a doubleheader. One thing is certain. There will be another abduction. The Queen B! The Queen Bitch!"

"John, please tell me something positive."

"Simon feels invincible and is reveling in his own success. Each inning he grows bolder and more daring. Let's hope too daring.

Inning nine is to be his masterpiece.

Simon has chosen a woman of prominence. She is in government, or married to, or the daughter of, a high official. Someone in the public eye, someone whose taking will stun the world, a fitting crescendo for the symphony he has been playing for us."

"Any ideas?"

"I have to think. Whoever his target is, Simon will not relent. He'll be patient, he'll lurk in the shadows, he'll study us and he will wait for his opportunity.

Simon will take his Queen B or die trying."

SOME MUCH NEEDED DISCIPLINE

74

We immerse ourselves in science. We deluge ourselves with facts. We bury ourselves in work. But never underestimate the importance of luck. So often, that one little piece of quirky good fortune is all that allows the case to be solved.

- Into the Mind of a Killer, John Hightower

Agent Phil Hardy considered himself fortunate to be serving under the renowned John Hightower. He was learning from the master, as opposed to Mark Berlanger, who was simply the poor student teaching from the master's book.

This case had brought out everything in the legend. It appeared to Hardy that it was also putting him in his grave. The strain on John Hightower was clear. Obsessed with the capture of Simon, Phil Hardy questioned if the legend was still on top of his game.

The white Cherokee had been purchased by a young man in glasses, who the career car salesman described as a wealthy brat who made a fortune at some defunct internet company. "Just took out his pen and wrote a check!" The checking account proved to be a dead end.

Phil Hardy sat at his desk working the few remaining clues that were not yet fruitless. Hightower had not been very encouraging. "Follow your procedures. Check your leads. Investigate. They will likely lead you nowhere, but do the work.

"Every criminal makes mistakes. There are always clues to be found. Study the fish, Phil, study the fish."

Phil Hardy was dedicated and hard working. He believed in God and that God rewarded those worthy. It was fate and a watchful eye from above, not lucky circumstance that allowed Hardy to work the case of the century with John Hightower. And, it was heavenly fate that made the phone ring that day.

"Agent Hardy," he answered.

"Yes, I was told that you would help me, that you were working on the Simon case."

"How can I help you, sir?"

"Do you know how long I have been trying to reach you? How long I have been placed on hold?"

"No, sir, I don't."

"You deserve the reputation you have. FBI, Full Blown Idiots, quite correctly! Do you know how difficult you make it for a citizen to give you important information?"

"No, sir. I'm sorry. You can understand how busy we are. Now, what information do you have, Mr.?"

"I can't give you my name. All I can tell you is that I work for the Daily News."

"Yes, and your information?"

"We have a reporter, perhaps you know him, Frank Wycheck."

"The Jaws reporter?"

"Yes. I happen to know that Wycheck is in constant contact with this Simon. Simon wants to have his exploits documented and Wycheck is secretly writing a book. I don't think it's right for Wycheck to profit when women are dying!"

"Tell me more. What else do you know?"

"I have told you enough. I could lose my job."

The caller hung up abruptly, leaving Agent Hardy with a thousand unanswered questions. He remembered Wycheck's Jaws articles, had enjoyed reading them. And since then, virtually nothing, not a single article that Hardy could recall.

And the caller's tip would explain why!

How many times already, in his short time with John Hightower, had he heard it? "Despite the best and most intense investigating, it is often that one bit of luck that is required to solve a case." Had God brought Hardy this the piece of good fortune that would break the case?

At a payphone in the San Fernando Valley, dressed as a businessman on his lunch hour, Simon hung up the receiver. *Break the rules of our game, WIH..A..CHEE..YOOK..HUH, and you must suffer the consequences.*

75

Agent Hardy was anxious to deliver his news of a telephone call that could change everything. He drove quickly to the Berlanger residence where John Hightower was investigating the crime scene in his own unique style.

A feeling of surreal incomprehensibility overtook Hardy as he approached the front door. Mark Berlanger, his last boss, was now departed. And the home into which he had often been invited was taped off in yellow ribbon.

His new boss, John Hightower was communing with the evidence while it was still *fresh. He insists on being uninterrupted. Perhaps there are vibrations or some kind of karma that he taps into.* Hightower was walking through the house in an apparent trance, retracing the hypothesized footsteps of the perpetrator, of Simon.

Agent Hardy followed John Hightower, but did not interrupt. He stood in amazement as Hightower, fully dressed, climbed into the bed and began hugging a pillow and continued to talk to himself, oblivious to everything around him. Hardy waited as long as his patience would allow.

"Sir!" he interrupted more assertively than he thought he dared. "Sir!"

"Yes, Phil? He drugged the little girl to keep her quiet but left her, too young for his taste. He drugged the older daughter and took her. The odor of the ether is still fresh in both rooms. He got into bed with Pam Berlanger. There was a large residue of the makeup in this bed that wasn't in the others. He indulged himself though not enough to leave us any real clues. Do we have anything new on the makeup?"

"Sir, I received an anonymous call. I think it might be a breakthrough."

"Yes?"

"It was from someone at the Daily News. The caller said he knew one of the reporters was in contact with Simon, that he thought they were working on a book together."

John Hightower climbed out of the bed. They weaved their way carefully around forensic men at work and did not speak until they were safely alone in the Berlanger back yard.

"What's his name?" Hightower asked quietly.

"Who, sir?"

"The reporter."

"Frank Wycheck."

"Frank Wycheck, the man who writes from the gutter, yes I know him, a good choice. Of course!"

"I'll make arrangements to haul this Frank Wycheck in and then we'll learn what he knows."

"You will do nothing of the kind! Do you hear me?"

"What, sir?"

"When you received this call, were you asked for specifically? Who else knows about this?"

"No one I'm aware of. The call came in like so many others. It just got to me I guess."

"You spoke to no one?"

"No one. I came directly here."

"Understand, Phil, the operation here at the Berlanger house, they're calling it incompetence, a bungled job performed by amateurs. It was nothing of the sort. Simon should be in a cell right now. Why isn't he, Phil?"

"I can't say, sir."

"Because, once again we have underestimated him. We can't afford to do that again. Do you understand, Phil?"

"I'm afraid not, sir."

"All right. Let's say that your tip was correct, and it makes perfect sense to me that it is. Then Frank Wycheck has information that might be helpful. But let's not be so foolish as to think he has information with which we could capture Simon. Phil, we can pull Wycheck in any time."

"I think I get your drift, John. We tail him and wait for him to lead us to Simon."

"Exactly! But don't be hasty, Phil. Simon sniffed us out here, a very impressive feat. He would certainly spot a tail on Wycheck.

Don't go anywhere near the guy. That is imperative. Use all the people you have to, but only the people you have to. Tell them nothing. Confide in no one, no matter who they are.

Place bugs in Wycheck's house, in his car, and do it in the most unobtrusive way. That's it, no more. I'd rather miss Simon from too little surveillance than to overplay and lose him for good. We're going fishing, Phil, and we are going to use the thinnest line we can get. Understand?"

"Yes, sir! I'll get on it immediately."

"Remember, we're dealing with someone smarter than we are. So be careful."

John Hightower returned to the house to climb back into the Berlanger bed. Again he crawled under the covers to resume hugging the pillow.

Yes, Simon, you must be so eager to brag to your reporter of the latest victory, innings seven and eight. You cannot wait!

No risk is too great any longer, is it? You are invincible.

It's your turn to be overconfident. Underestimate me! Just once, Simon, underestimate Higherpower.

76

Cocaine is truly a sinister beast. I had seen its subtle, devilish, black magic act often. Many of my articles tracked the unsus pecting victims on their journeys first to the heights and then relentlessly, inevitably, down society's drain.

Poor bastards! Common in their denial, they never noticed their capabilities eroding or their contact with reality dissolving. Theirs was a headlong tumble into the abyss and they were completely unaware that anything had changed. On cocaine, emotions rule, not logic. Drugged rationalizations always trump reasoned arguments.

Yes, I knew cocaine well. I was the first hand expert on addictions. I thought we had reached an accommodation. A friend, cocaine helped wean me from the bottle, my one true enemy. Only with its help could I have a drink in safety. It allowed me to work again and to prosper. It gave me Patton. Hell, the cocaine was Patton!

Slowly but surely it was beginning to take control.

So I quit. Just like that, and I have to tell you, Father, I was damned proud of myself.

I kept my agreement with Chub and wrote my "from the mean streets to you" articles. But neither my heart nor my mind was in them, and honestly, they were trash. Harry refused to edit my stories and published them only under direct orders from Chub. "It is not only the worst shit I have ever seen you write, Frank," Harry told me, "it is the worst shit I have ever read, period."

The fact was Harry was disgusted with me as well as my work. He made no effort to spare my feelings. That was Harry's way. He refused to waste time. Usually, he simply sauntered off in his own ancient style and avoided me. It hurt, Harry, the greatest gentleman I ever knew, my mentor, my savior. But, my sights were on the bigger picture.

Chub was not writer enough to realize that my stories stank, but he was accountant enough to know that they weren't helping business. The public was only interested in Simon. The big guys were kicking the Paper's ass. Chub knew I had his answer, and he was getting impatient.

So I told him little things to hold him off, things I knew I shouldn't. But then what else was there to do? I couldn't let him cut me off, not with Jenny in college and my other bills clamoring to be paid.

I simply had to buy time. Simon had only one more inning to play. Then I could complete the book, publish, and my money worries would be over.

I was driving down the Harbor Freeway towards Chinatown where I was going to meet Christine for lunch. The music was loud as usual. The Porsche snarled down the road, my time in jail and on the chain gang barely a distant memory. Thank God for Christine.

I had just passed the Vine Street exit when the cell rang.

"Wycheck!" "WIH..A..CHEE..YOOK..HUH!"

"Simon?"

"Yes, Frankie. How did you like my play in innings seven and eight?"

"How in the world did you?"

"Shhh…not now. I will tell you everything you will need for our book and I have a package for you. Meet me tomorrow at noon in the Civic Center. Make sure you are not followed!"

"As always. Where? The Civic Center is big."

"On the Promenade, the bench across from the street musician."

"Right!"

I felt immediately exhilarated. It had been an eternity since I last talked to Simon. I pushed down on the accelerator and the Porsche lurched forward. "Come on baby, show me what you've got! To Chinatown!" I shouted above the music and at the top of my lungs. I was anxious to get to Christine, eat lunch, then drag her off to a motel and show her what I had.

"Frank Wycheck never gives up!"

77

The meeting with Simon was critical and I got to the Civic Center twenty minutes early. When you're straight it's possible. I quickly found the bench across from the street musician.

He was a tall pale man in old ragged clothes, playing a violin, and not too badly at that. Homeless probably, he looked like he had been at his post for at least a decade. His violin case contained only a few dollars in donations. Business was bad.

Is it Simon? I knew better than to approach. Simon or not, I sat down and made myself comfortable. I would be kept waiting, out of Simon's caution, or certainly because he felt like it.

The Promenade was busy during the lunch hour. Many people passed near enough the bench to arouse my scrutiny. Would Simon be a businessman in a suit, a woman, a young derelict, or perhaps the street musician himself? Anything was possible.

I checked the time frequently. My hand slipped into my jacket pocket to finger my recorder, confirming it had not mysteriously disappeared in the last two minutes. My legs crossed and uncrossed randomly and constantly. Honestly, what I really wanted was a hit.

My imagination was running amuck. *Where is he? Did I piss him off and now he's fucking with me? He might not show up at all.*

It was about twelve twenty; a millennium that was actually less than forty minutes had passed, when Simon finally made contact. The lunch hour was at its peak, foot traffic on the Promenade at its greatest.

He was a tall slender black man, a rather ordinary disguise by Simon's standards, a player right off a ghetto black top. He was wearing an expensive Kobe Bryant tank top that was several sizes too large, well-worn dark blue warm-up pants and Nike basketball shoes. Very much in shape, the man moved easily, gracefully, like an athlete, circling indirectly toward me through the crowd.

I tried to be cool, pretending not to watch. He was noticeably apprehensive, looking about frequently, as if unsure of himself, not simply careful, afraid. Not at all like the super self-confident Simon, that must have been the point. Simon was always trying to catch me off guard. That was how I knew it was him.

I continued to secretly observe Simon slowly weave through the crowd toward me. In a few minutes he was standing next to the bench and acting as if he were trying to be invisible. I played along and acted surprised.

"Frankie?" he asked in a low raspy voice.

He was gawking around nervously and twitching wildly. Telltale heroin tracks on both his arms were there to confuse me but instead confirmed my suspicions.

"Feigned paranoia and an excellent disguise as usual, Simon. My compliments."

"What, mutha fucka? Are you Frankie?"

"Yes," I answered.

All the games had to be played out. Each little charade was a game unto itself. Venus, Gomer, Bartolo and the others, for me, Jim for Danielle Rickford, Felix for Elaine, Wanda for Francine Fitzpatrick, and all the rest of them, they were all small little games within the big game.

The man pulled out a tan manila package from his sweat pants and threw it in my lap. "This is for you," he said, nervously jerking his head in all directions.

"Why don't you sit down so we can chat?" I continued, playing along.

"Fuck you, mutha fucka!" he spit at me. Then he suddenly ran off.

All hell broke loose after that. Father, it was as if the world collapsed in around me. In less than a second, I was on the ground with my face mashed into the concrete. My arms were unceremoniously pulled up behind me and handcuffs were clamped on my wrists. I was sure both my shoulders were dislocated.

I didn't see much from my new vantage point. Simon had run into the crowd. He was fast; I'll give him that. I have to guess at least a hundred people were chasing him. There was a great commotion and I heard "FBI, FBI" being shouted loudly from all angles. Above, I heard the sound of a helicopter that suddenly appeared and was flying low. No, correct that, it was several helicopters, certainly more than one.

They crushed me into the ground with half a dozen revolvers pointed in my face.

And, believe it or not Father, I was relieved. It was a dangerous game I was caught up in, people were dying, and I was happy to have it over. The thought of Simon being caught almost made me euphoric.

And, mea culpa, I thought about the book and how I was going to complete it.

After a few minutes, the cops pulled me off the floor and sat me back on the bench. They were rough with me and hurt my shoulders some more.

"Hey, take it easy!" I shouted. "I didn't do anything. Do you know who I am?"

On the bench next to me, one of the feds, rubber gloves on his hands, was carefully opening the manila envelope. He pulled out a plastic package filled with white powder.

"Sure, I know you," he said snidely to me. "You're Frankie! Now is this what I think it is, Frankie?"

78

In all his years in the Bureau, John Hightower had never ridden in a helicopter. He often refrained from a pursuit. John Hightower's expertise was thinking. He figured out where to find the vermin. Left to others, better physically suited and more interested in the chase, was the task of rooting them out.

Hightower rode in the second chopper. This case was different from all those that preceded it. It was personal.

The Promenade was not a preferred location, too open, with too many escape routes to guard. The time of day was wrong, midday, lunchtime, and consequently far too many people at the scene. Innocent bystanders always created a multitude of unwanted problems.

But then, you, Simon, did the choosing not the Bureau.

Don complained plenty that there was not enough time to make adequate arrangements. Unfortunately, that is how it usually goes.

You have gotten bold indeed, Simon! But foolish, doesn't seem quite right.

"Don, anything?" Hightower shouted into his mike.

"Nothing yet, John," came back the terse reply.

Don is a good man. I just hope I haven't hampered him too much.

Don Furlong was given less than twenty-four hours to prepare. Hightower insisted that the operation be handled far more cautiously than usual. "Keep your distance!" he had insisted. "Remember, Simon spotted us at the Berlanger residence," Furlong was reminded. "If he gets the slightest whiff of a trap, we'll have a problem."

How long has it been since the man in the bright yellow Kobe Bryant shirt ducked into the crowd?

"It should be easy to spot him!" Hightower shouted into the mike.

A colorful disguise for sure, so easily seen, are you so cocky now, Simon?

Simon was somewhere in the crowd on the Promenade. With any luck he would run into an agent. *They are that plentiful.* Hightower waited and hoped.

"Anybody seen him?"

"John, get off the air!" came back the sharp reply from Don Furlong. "Close off the Promenade. No one leaves without being checked out."

Don Furlong is the best. In over twenty years of doing the job to the best of his ability, and without consideration once for expediency or politics, John Hightower had learned who the good people were. Don Furlong was specifically chosen to run this operation. With not enough time, Furlong had coordinated with the LAPD, organized and deployed his agents on the Promenade and throughout the Civic Center, manned reserve positions and air support, and had done it all quietly.

And still, Simon sniffed us out and bolted before we could move in.

"I see Kobe! He's heading into the Music Center!"

"Identify!" barked Furlong.

"Foster, SWAT, on the roof of Water and Power."

"Maintain perimeter on Promenade. Repeat, maintain perimeter on Promenade!"

"We have a Kobe sighting going into the Music Center. Preston, move your men in and seal off the Music Center!"

Dan Preston, LAPD.

"Chopper three, move your position over to Hill Street. Crawford, take your agents into the Music Center!"

"Don't forget Don, he is a master of disguise. He could turn into anyone!" shouted Hightower into his mike.

"We know! We know, John! Get off the air!" screamed Furlong back.

"I've got Kobe at Hill and First!"

"What? Identify!"

"Johnson, LAPD."

"Units at Promenade and Music Center continue as ordered! Chopper two to Hill and First! LAPD, Johnson, can you apprehend?"

"Have two patrol units, request back up. That's affirmative! Will apprehend!"

"Furlong, have witness who saw Kobe heading for lower levels of Music Center!"

"What the fuck? Identify!"

"Martinez, FBI."

"Pursue, Martinez. All units maintain positions around Promenade. Button up the Music Center, Benson!"

"Yes, sir!"

"Johnson, this is Furlong. What have you got?"

"Have the suspect in custody."

"Kobe shirt? Dark sweats? Over six feet. Black man."

"Negative. Just the Kobe shirt! Hispanic. Maybe fourteen years old.

"Let him go! Get back in position, Johnson!"

A bad feeling came over John Hightower. He remembered seeing a movie once, The Thomas Crown Affair. The thief wore a distinctive suit, bowler hat, and carried a smart briefcase. Very easy to spot, the only problem was, the thief had hired fifty men to walk around wearing the exact same clothes and carrying identical briefcases. The police were inundated trying to sort it out while Thomas Crown walked out unnoticed.

Is that Simon's game? Multiple Kobes? It would be your style and I'm afraid it might work. Except for one thing.

You won't copy! At least, let's hope not.

"Martinez!"

"Nothing yet."

"I see him! He is headed toward the basement."

"Who is that? Identify!"

"Martinez here. That's Stanley, sir. He's with us! Suspect is in the basement. Do we take him down?"

"No! No! No!" shouted Hightower.

"Negative Martinez! You may shoot to wound! Slow him down whatever way possible. But your orders are to take him alive."

"Affirmative, sir. We should be able to corner him down here."

"Crawford, get some back up down there!"

"Remember, we need him alive!" yelled Hightower.

Is this the end? Hightower wondered. In a sense, it seemed anticlimactic. The most brilliant adversary of his career trapped in a basement, *cornered like the rat he is!* John Hightower waited for the words from the radio. *We've got him. We have the rat.*

"Martinez, report!"

"Nothing sir, we've got nothing so far."

"What do mean you've got nothing! Crawford, get some more men down there!"

"Yes, sir."

What's taking so long? What's gone wrong?

"We have Kobe on Grand!"

"Identify!"

"Watson, LAPD. Suspect matches description. He's running like a mother fucker!"

"Dan, this is Furlong. Can you apprehend?"

"Get his cell ready!"

"Martinez, anything?"

"Nothing, sir."

"Get those plans to the Music Center. I want to know where that fuck is! Watson, Dan, report!"

"Watson sir, he's hauling ass toward the Hollywood Freeway."

"Take me over there!" Hightower shouted at his pilot."

"Sir, orders," protested the pilot.

"I'm going over there, Don!" Hightower yelled into the mike. "Take me over there, now!" at the pilot.

"He's heading for the overpass!"

"That's it. He's fucked! This is Crawford. I want two units with back up to cut off the other side of the overpass."

The helicopter arrived in time for Hightower to see the black man in the Kobe shirt and dark sweat pants run onto the overpass. He was about half way across when he noticed the blockade on the other side. Police cars had cut off his retreat.

Trapped like a rat, Simon!

"Take me down!" Hightower screamed at the pilot. "Don't shoot anyone. We need him alive!" he yelled into the mike.

"He's going over the side!"

"Back off! Back off! We need him alive!" shouted Hightower. "Take me down!"

"Can't, sir. There is no place to land!"

"Get me close! Give me the megaphone!"

"Simon! Simon! This is Higherpower!"

The man stared up at the approaching helicopter, then at the barricades of police on each end of the overpass. Hightower could see him screaming but could hear nothing. The noise was deafening, below from the freeway and from the circling blades above. The man climbed up on the railing. Noontime traffic was speeding toward Hollywood.

What can he be thinking?

"Can he hear me?" Hightower shouted at the pilot.

"I think so, sir."

"Simon, this is Higherpower!" he screamed back into the megaphone. "Simon, let's talk!"

The man in the Kobe shirt raised his fist up defiantly, middle finger fully extended. Hightower could not hear the words but could clearly discern, "Fuck you!" being mouthed at him. The man straddled the railing and flashed his head around as if to check his options for the last time.

He can't. He can't think he can escape down there. Surely he knows it's certain death.

"Wait, Simon, wait!" Hightower shrieked in desperation.

The man peered up at him a last time. He reissued his gesture then clearly mouthed the word "Asshole."

"No!" Hightower gasped. "No!"

The man in the Kobe shirt jumped over the side as if charging into battle. John Hightower was reminded of the young World War I doughboys desperately leaping from their trenches toward their impending doom.

"No, Simon, no."

Hightower watched helplessly as Simon floated down toward the pavement. It was as if the world had gone into slow motion while Hightower's mind raced through the consequences at warp speed.

Simon would not hit the roadway below. A dodge Durango struck him mid air, propelling him at least one hundred fifty feet. Before the traffic could stop, the body was run over by several other vehicles including an eighteen-wheeler.

"No! No!" moaned Hightower. Simon was dead and with him in all likelihood his victims. *Now, how will I find Francine and Berlanger's wife and daughter? Will they quietly starve to death somewhere, never to be found?*

"Get me down there," Hightower told his pilot sternly. "As quickly as possible."

And what of the many questions left unanswered. How Simon, why Simon? Yes, especially why.

79

We are the champions, the protectors of society, the guardians of the law. So noble, that is why we chose our profession. But did we ever consider the disappointments, the frustration. On our job, the rewards are what is difficult to come by.

- Into the Mind of a Killer, John Hightower

It took John Hightower eighteen minutes to get from the Heliport on the Arco Towers back to the Hollywood Freeway. Traffic had been stopped in both directions by the Highway Patrol. He was doubly annoyed that every reporter in the city seemed to have beaten him to the scene.

Hightower climbed slowly and carefully down the ivy-covered embankment to the freeway surface. He wanted to personally examine Simon's remains. They were still trying to locate all of the pieces.

So, is this how it ends? With an uncharacteristically rash action and a suicide rather than getting caught. And what of the imprisoned women? Will we ever find them?

Hightower caught sight of Don Furlong attempting to keep things organized while at the same time trying to restrict the press. "What have we got, Don?" Hightower asked.

"A lot of serial killer pieces, John. I have never seen anything like it, even if he had been hit by a train."

"Let me see him."

"The head and part of the torso are over here."

They paced hastily toward a taped off area. At its center was a barely recognizable piece of carcass. Crushed, flattened, every bone pulverized, flesh mashed, blood drained, one could barely guess that it once was a human being.

"I see what you mean, Don. Are the lab guys coming?"

"Yes."

"Did you find any identification?"

"No. Just a small stash of heroin in the pants over there." Furlong pointed to a taped off section some hundred feet away.

"What? Heroin?"

"Yes. He wasn't committing suicide. The man thought he could fly."

"What is that, Don? Heroin?"

"Yes indeed. He was an addict. If you look carefully at the piece of arm you can see the tracks. They are clearer in the other arm over there." Furlong pointed to a taped off area of vegetation at the side of the roadway.

"Heroin. Impossible!"

Hightower inspected a small piece of neck area that still showed black skin. No make up. "This is a black man. Impossible!"

Impossible!

"Don, nothing to the media, nothing that this had anything to do with Simon. Make sure all the men are in line on this. Dawson is the only one who talks to the press. Understood? Any exceptions and it's a transfer to Siberia."

"Why, John?"

"We have to find out who this poor bastard is. One thing I can guarantee you, it's not Simon."

"What, how?"

"This doesn't make sense to me, Don. I don't get any of it. This has all been set up, but why?"

For what purpose Simon? I don't get it. Why?

80

Christine Taylor had a way with men, a talent refined over more than twenty years. Her foster parent, a nice pleasant man, was the first conquest, seduced shortly after puberty. The poor devil did time for child molestation and statutory rape. Unfair and unwarranted thought Christine, he was merely giving her what she wanted. But she wept no tears for him; actually, thought it was all kind of cool.

Christine had learned the immense power that a woman possessed between her legs. Subtle, suggestive persuasions, teasing and the giving of pleasures that could get men to do anything. Yet, while she seemed able to please any man, Christine was never satisfied herself.

Except, once.

She was tired coming home from work that Thursday night, but planned to go to the clubs anyway. She had been twice during the week, and was horribly disappointed each time. One man passed out on her, and the other was so sad she had to stick him with her nail file.

Where was Wycheck when Christine needed him? *In jail, the dumb fuck!* Arrested more than a week before on a drug charge, and it didn't appear he would be getting out any time soon, maybe not ever.

Not that Frank was ever the answer, but he was better than most. At least, he could be counted on for minimal performance, much better if loaded up properly.

Christine opened her front door and reached for the light switch. The light failed to go on, as it had once before. She was grabbed from behind and lifted off the ground by strong arms. Hot breath tickled her ear and throat. Christine's heart soared.

A handkerchief was clamped over her face and she began to breath in a familiar gas. Christine moaned with pleasure.

She would be in dreamland soon, but before leaving, Christine fought to say, "Oh my darling. I have waited so long for you to return."

81

The phone rang once, then again. After twenty-six straight hours, a worn out John Hightower had fallen asleep on the living room. The phone rang again, then again. Startled, Hightower awoke and his mind resumed its cycling. *Why did you plan that whole escapade with the black man? What was the point?*

To set yet another trap, to let us proclaim victory, and then make us look foolish again?

The concession to sleep was usually made unwillingly, always grudgingly. John Hightower habitually brushed the urge aside, subdued it with the incessant working of his mind, until the adrenaline was used up, and his exhausted body refused to function further.

Hightower began to drift again into unconsciousness.

The phone rang for the fifth and final time before the answering machine took over and recited it's terse message. "This is John Hightower. Leave a message if you like. I make no promises." He heard the message followed by the long loud beep only subliminally.

"Higher...Power. Higher...Power. Higher...Power! I know you are there. I know you can hear me."

The voice was electronically altered, garbled, raspy, and completely unidentifiable. Even in his semiconscious state, John Hightower knew who it was.

"You should know by now, I do not take insults well, Higherpower. Ask your friend Richfuck."

New adrenalin began to pump through John Hightower. His mind was back on line again as he struggled for muscular control.

"I will give you to the count of ten to answer. If you do not, Francina will be forfeit. That is how the Grand Game is played, Higherpower.

One…two"

Hightower scrambled spasmodically along the floor.

"Three…four. Hurry, Higherpower, hurry. The bitch's life hangs in the balance. Five."

Hightower got to his feet and moved as quickly as he dared on still unsteady legs. He breathed in and out rapidly, trying to force air into his lungs and oxygen into his muscles.

"Six…seven."

He was almost there. Hightower grabbed at the phone, which slipped through his fingers and onto the floor.

"Eight …nine."

"Hightower here! Stop counting!"

"You sound, may I say it, a little frantic? Do I call at a bad time, Higherpower? Are you tired from your big chase?"

"No, I'm not tired, Simon."

He knows where I live and called my unlisted telephone number. He's aware of my actions and activities. He has been watching me! As he studied Berlanger and all the victims! What a fool I've been. What a missed opportunity.

"Disappointed?" questioned the garbled voice. "You were expecting an important call?"

Hightower's mind was in lightening mode. "No! No, I'm not disappointed." The garbled voice, what did it want? *To rub it in, to taunt, to brag, naturally!* And a golden opportunity to glean some information from it, he was talking to the killer.

"Well Higherpower, congratulations are certainly in order. You killed a most dangerous criminal. Heroin use and trafficking are very serious crimes!"

"Who was that poor bastard on the freeway, Simon?"

"A nobody, a concoction of scum, heroin and a little PCP added on the side. Makes them so brave, although the tiniest bit reckless. Shame he had to die, wouldn't you say, Higherpower?"

"It will be you someday, Simon."

"Your prediction? The great Higherpower and all those policemen at your disposal, it would seem that you should be correct. But then, that's why we play the Game."

Hightower decided to challenge Simon, see how he would react. *Will he flinch?* "Enough, bastard!" he screamed. "Francine, and the

Berlangers, what have you done with them?"

"Why nothing, Higherpower." *Calm, unaffected.* "You know the Game. They are still in play."

Hightower immediately changed his tone to conciliatory. "They are safe, unharmed?"

"Let's say we are currently enjoying each other's company."

Prick! I must be clever now.

"So to what do I owe this pleasure? A social call?"

"Hardly, Higherpower. We have business to discuss."

"Yes?"

"You are holding my Frankie. I want him back in play."

"In play?"

"Yes. I insist!"

Why? He needs the writer. He wants his book finished. Excellent!

"I see. An exchange. All right, I'll put Wycheck back in play if you will release Francine and the Berlanger women."

"Unacceptable and against the rules. You know that, Higherpower. There is only one way to save them."

"I must win the Game."

"Exactly, to the victor go the spoils, and, alas, but one inning remaining. So now, our business, will you release my Frankie?"

"Why should I? You give me nothing in return."

"That is your move? It is your prerogative." The voice had become angry. "Well then, if Frankie is forfeit so will the bitches be. I will send you proof of their demise."

"No, wait Simon!

I wish the bitches to remain in play. I will release Wycheck. They will all remain in play. Do we have an agreement?"

"Always a pleasure doing business with the white knight."

He calls me white knight. Francine sometimes called me that.

82

Sure, I was in jail before. Drunk, drunk driving, but not this, not heavy drug possession, I was in deep, deep shit.

After being tackled, shackled, and packed into a patrol car, they took me downtown. The Feds said I was caught with a pound of pure heroin and that I would never again see the light of day. I was sure to become the prison bitch and likely would be stabbed to death before my next birthday. My only chance was to cooperate.

And fuck, I was innocent. It was all a setup, Simon's punishment. Bartolo probably thought it up in Community Service, while chopping weeds on the San Diego Freeway. God dammit! Pardon, Father.

I called the best drug lawyer I knew, Jimmy Bryant, and was comforted when he told me that the success rate for drug cases was far greater than for traffic offenses. After that, he told me that I was basically screwed. My story about having a pound of heroin dropped into my lap by a perfect stranger was the worst one he had ever heard.

"You're a writer, Frank," he said, "You're a creative, bright man. Can't you do better than that?"

"They were after Simon," I informed him. "He dropped the package when they started chasing him. Jimmy, they have been questioning me about Simon, not the drugs. That's all they are interested in. They're using the drugs to frighten me."

"Well, I must say Frank, that is more creative. How much of the coke have you been using lately."

"None! I swear, what I'm telling you is the truth."

"You're sure."

"Positive."

"Well as the donkey merchant told his customer, it's your ass now.

We can go with your story. And, we'll imply the FBI set you up to force your cooperation. You were entrapped. You are a reporter. You were led to believe you were meeting an informant, getting a story. Yes, I like it, Frank, the Simpson defense. Put them on trial."

I was beginning to have hope when Jimmy suddenly told me that I was still screwed. The problem was, although I was in LA and would have an LA jury, I wasn't OJ. Jimmy suggested that I cooperate instead.

A few hours later, John Hightower came to see me. "Higherpower," as Simon called him, was far different than what I expected. You see, Father, I only knew John Hightower as Simon described him. What I had pictured was a colossus, a fierce warrior, Dirty Harry.

Meeting him finally, John Hightower just seemed like a hell of a nice guy. He was quite reasonable actually, didn't try to intimidate or coerce me. He said he was sorry for not getting there sooner and apologized for any rough treatment I may have experienced.

I was feeling better and asked him. "You caught him, killed him?" I didn't know what happened on the Promenade.

"Uh no," answered Hightower as if embarrassed. "That man wasn't Simon." Then he turned and whispered to me, like it was a secret. "Frank, I know you have nothing to do with those drugs."

I was ready to kiss the man I was so relieved. "Yes, yes, it was Simon or whoever that man was. He planted the drugs on me."

Hightower kept whispering. "Yes, yes, I know. And, I also I know about you and Simon. Now, if you ever want to get out of here…"

That was all it took. I spilled my guts, and told Hightower everything. Probably would have anyway. I was carrying a ton of guilt keeping Simon's secrets while he was killing people. I had rationalized that I was a reporter not a cop, and the story had its own importance. My duty was to protect my sources, like you, Father. Fuck, it was wrong and I knew it.

Hightower called my information informative and helpful, but he was clearly disappointed. I'd met Simon on quite a few occasions and my description of him – height, well, could be anywhere from 5'8" to 6'3", build, wiry, I thought, weight, not sure, facial features, no idea, hair, neither, age, couldn't really say, anything that could help identify him, well, actually, no.

But, it felt damn good finally cooperating, and I offered to help in any way I could. Then I thought about what I was doing and became panic struck. Simon's standard punishment was to take your women. "What about my family, my ex wife, my daughter. And, what about Christine?"

"I'll make sure they're safe, Frank," Hightower said reassuring me. "They'll go into witness protection till this is over. No one can find them. Remember, we kept people safe from the Mafia. Simon will never get to them."

The guy was smart. He could see I wasn't convinced. "Didn't protect the Berlangers very well," I could have said but didn't have to.

"I know there is reason for you to be skeptical, Frank, but what choice is there? They're not safe now, that's for sure." Hightower was right. No woman was safe, not Jane, Jenny or Christine, not the Queen of England, not while Simon was on the loose. "Who do you want to trust," Hightower finally asked. "Simon or me?"

The choice, no choice, I told Hightower I'd do whatever he wanted.

83

They loaded me up with bugs, let me out, and told me to carry on as if nothing had happened. I was sure Hightower was wasting his time, that Simon was done with me and that I'd never hear from him again. Hightower disagreed. He was certain that, sooner or later, Simon would reestablish contact. I was hoping Hightower was wrong.

Ten minutes later, he was right.

I was on the Ten Freeway headed home, relieved but disappointed. I had called Christine and wanted to celebrate and got only her machine. What a let down, I could already feel her in my arms. I threw my cell into the glove box in disgust and its little song started playing before it landed.

How the emotions can change. I grabbed the cell, pushed the button and, excited, shouted into it. "Honey, guess what!"

"What, WIH..A..CHEE..YOOK..HUH?"

It was the Voice.

"Simon?"

"You have betrayed me, Frankie!"

"What? No! How?"

"You have broken the rules, and now, after I have arranged for your release, you plan to betray me again."

I didn't know what Simon was talking about, except, for the last part. But, that, I knew, he was only guessing at.

"No, Simon. You're wrong all the way around. I didn't…"

The voice cut me off. "You informed on me and they set a trap at the Civic Center."

"No, Simon! I didn't. I don't know how they found out about

that?" And, I didn't. It was one of the many things I wondered about during my time in jail. Just who did tip off the Feds?

"I know you, Frankie. You're a weak man, always taking the path of least resistance, the easy way out. Now tell me you didn't sell out to Higherpower."

I didn't answer. What was there to say? I girded myself for what was coming next.

"A fine bitch, your Christina, a very, very fine bitch."

Christine? It hadn't occurred to me till then, but Christine would certainly have come to see me in jail and she didn't. I cranked up the Porsche and sped towards Christine's apartment.

"And for you, Higherpower," the voice continued as if I wasn't there. Not that it mattered; I wasn't listening anyway. My mind was totally on Christine. "Don't be jealous. Francina and the Berlanger bitches are mighty fine too. And so will the Queen B be."

I dialed Christine's number over and over and still only got the machine. Don't ask me how fast I was going. I can tell you I wasn't going to stop for anyone, no matter what color lights they flashed at me.

It must have only taken me a few minutes, though it seemed hours. I burst through Christine's front door and searched the house for her. Nothing. Then I checked for some sign of her. Also nothing. Christine was gone.

84

A deep sigh passed through the grate toward Father Reyes. Frank Wycheck checked his Rolex to confirm that another four hours passed. Time well spent, the anxieties beaten back, he could breathe freely again. Though nothing was yet accomplished, the catharsis before the pleasant priest did give him comfort. Now, he wondered, with his soul fully bared, would young Father Reyes be able to help.

"So there you have it, Father. That's my story. I've been on the run ever since, walking the streets, hiding from the feds and Simon, trying to figure it out. What should I do? What can I do?

I lived in these gutters without shelter; I've not eaten except for scraps found in garbage cans. But the cocaine has been purged from my body. My mind is clear."

"I'm sorry, my son, I do not see your dilemma. You already were doing the right thing cooperating with the authorities."

The priest spoke calmly and quietly, though Wycheck wondered if Father Reyes had heard anything at all. "You don't understand, Father. You don't understand Simon. He is not human. He can't be stopped. Christine was punishment, sure, but also a warning. Jane and Jenny…"

"Frank, you must trust in the authorities to protect your family."

"Sure! Like they protected Pam and Susan Berlanger. He took them from right under their noses? Like they protected Christine… They can't protect anyone, not from him. If I defy him, I know he'll come for Jane and Jenny."

"Your fears are understandable, my son. But, also consider this. They will never be safe as long as the monster is free. Is that not so?"

"That's true, Father."

"Certainly. And, with your help, Simon might be apprehended. Only then will your loved ones, indeed all of us, be secure.

The authorities are experienced in these matters. You were wise to trust John Hightower and to put Jane and Jenny into witness protection."

"Yes, I know that's true."

"Where is the problem, Frank? Your course is clear. You must do what you can to help. And when Simon is finally captured you can all return to your normal lives."

"Yes. Of course!"

"You must pray to God for guidance."

"No, Father, you are correct. I see that now."

"Shall we pray?"

"No, Father. Not now! Maybe another day."

"There is always another day, my son. And always another reason to pray."

"What? What did you say?"

"I simply say, pray to God. Do not rely on me. Don't rely on any man. You must make your own decision in such an important matter."

"Yes, of course."

"Simon is not someone to be treated lightly. Choose wisely. WIH..A..CHEE..YOOK..HUH!" Frank Wycheck sunk slowly in the Confessional. "Your course is clear, Frankie. Put your trust in Higherpower! And, I welcome the challenge of finding Jana and Jenna."

"God, help me!" Wycheck moaned. "God, please help me."

The low, ominous voice drifted back through the screen. Gone were the lyrical trills, the comforting tone, and reassuring calm of Father Reyes. Instead, the words returned made of stone.

"He will not help you either, my Son."

85

So, now there is no one, no one at all. Save you, my friend, my last remaining friend, dear, loyal reader. I have only you to tell my story.

I drifted around aimlessly for another week, then went to see John Hightower. There really wasn't any other choice, was there?

The months passed and I agonized.

The world was suspended, anticipating, wondering what Simon was up to. Where would he strike, how, who would be the target? Or would he strike at all? Had he simply disappeared and left us all hanging?

I knew better than that.

John Hightower agreed. Simon would make a try for his Queen B, no question. And, he was not finished with me.

THE QUEEN B

86

Sometimes the obvious is the most difficult thing of all to see.

- Into the Mind of a Killer, John Hightower

Why didn't I see it sooner?

John Hightower was on the living room floor munching on some KFC that Janet had brought home for him. What a marvelous woman she was; the only one who ever really understood him or ever could. Not even his beloved Maggie, God rest her soul, could tolerate Hightower's extreme eccentricities. Janet came home, kissed him on the cheek, placed the box down, and went upstairs without saying a word.

At first I thought you singled out Burlanger and Fitzpatrick as a coincidence. They were the FBI "Top Cops," in the news at the time you were ready to play your Game. But it was more, wasn't it, Simon?

So, now I have the grievance, your motive. The Game started around the time of Jaws' execution.

Let me tell you, Simon, a tale of two brothers. Separated by twelve years, they grew up independently yet in the same household, and though not in contact since those early years, they each experienced the same horrors. The brothers shared a bond of unimaginable abuse.

At seventeen, Paul Simmons ran away from home before Peter was old enough to know him. Six years later, Paul was institutionalized, while Peter tried to reconcile what was being done to him each afternoon.

Paul remained in an asylum as Peter matured and harbored his anger while making plans for his own seventeenth birthday.

Fifteen years later, Paul Simmons was released as cured, soon after to be arrested as the infamous Jaws killer.

And what of Peter?

It was reported that Peter Simmons and his parents died in a fire that destroyed their home. Of course that wasn't it, was it?

We have done a little checking, Simon. Autopsies of the exhumed bodies revealed that the parents were bludgeoned to death. And, funny thing, DNA proved that the teenage boy that died with them was not Peter Simmons!

You are just about the age Peter Simmons would be today. Coincidence? I think not. You killed that boy and laid him between your parents to take your place. Up in a blaze, the Simmons family and your real identity, so that you would be completely free to operate as a shadow.

You are Peter Simmons!

That is the connection.

That is why you chose Berlanger and Fitzpatrick, because they were Jaws' captors. Your grievance is obvious.

And, so was the identity of the Queen B, and it made Hightower sick to consider it. *God help me, Janet is the Queen B.*

The Game had become more personal than John Hightower ever dreamed.

87

John slipped into bed, worried. Six a.m., a pair of embracing arms reached out for him and the love of his life pulled him close. Without a word, Janet snuggled into Hightower's chest, not pushing, but making clear she was ready to give him whatever he wanted. The thought had not crossed his mind. John had come to bed on a mission, the hardest he could possibly imagine.

"Janet, honey."

"Mmm, John," she purred while kissing his neck.

He pulled away. "No, honey, this is serious."

"What?" she asked, surprised and disappointed.

"I know his motive, the reason for his choice of victims." Janet sat up straight in bed and listened carefully. She was the District Attorney again. "Simon is Peter Simmons, Jaws' brother." John stared into her eyes, which appeared blank. Behind them Janet was busy, thinking, considering possibilities, figuring it all out. "Do you know what that means?" John asked.

"What?" she answered from a distance.

John shook her until Janet was again with him. "Honey, you're the Queen B!"

"Me?"

"Who else could it be? You were the prosecutor, Madam Prosecutor, the Bulldog, who did her job so well that Jaws died."

"He deserved to die."

"Opinions vary on that one, sweetie."

"What are you talking about?" The fires in Janet Bultaco flared up. The District Attorney was ready to argue the case again.

John embraced her, smothering her against his chest. "Not now, honey." He was clearly worried. "You're in danger. That's all that matters. I've made arrangements to get you protected and into hiding."

Janet Bultaco fought him off. "Are you crazy?" she protested. "I'm not going into hiding. I have a job, a life."

"Just until this is over, just until we catch him."

"The answer is no!" As she was prone to do, Janet Bultaco could change emotions quickly. That and her answer were what Hightower had expected.

"Janet, honey..."

"Don't Janet honey me!"

It was as he had feared, as he knew it would go. "I love you. I can't have anything happen to you."

"Then don't let it!" The closing argument, "I'm going to work like always. No son of a bitch, especially not Simon, is going to make me run and hide."

John sat on the bed dejected, without arguments, and trying to regain his bearings. There was no reasoning with her, and no one on the planet could have changed Janet Bultaco's mind.

"Now, here's what we're going to do, John." There was stern conviction in Janet's voice while John shuddered. "We're each going to do our jobs. I'm going to go to work every day as usual. And, you are going to use that and set a trap."

"No!"

"John! You said yourself Simon won't stop until he gets his Queen Bitch. Right?"

"Right."

"Then use that. Use me! He's going to come after me anyway, right?"

"Right. Risk is no longer a consideration for him. Win or die. It's a game of death, honey."

"Then win, my love. Use me. Catch the asshole." She kissed him on the cheek. "Now, get out of my way. I'm late for work."

88

John Hightower sat on the bed alone with his thoughts.

My brave, foolish darling.

We both knew she wouldn't run, didn't we, Simon? And, you must have her. Nothing can stop you and you can't stop yourself.

So, where will you make your play? Here at home? Doubtful, who would you impersonate? And, Janet isn't home regularly. You wouldn't like that either. You prefer schedules that you can count on.

Like at the office.

She's in her office working late every night. You'll go for her then, when everyone has gone home. You'll be an attorney or some member of the office staff who is working late, or, maybe someone who works the night shift, a guard or maintenance man. Brash, dangerous, take her right from the D.A.'s office, that will suit you. Extra bold for the final inning, am I getting warm?

Just in case, let me help you with your decision. Overwhelming deterrent surveillance at home and in transit!

You'll make your move in Janet's office, or, somewhere in the building. In an empty hallway or the elevator, the parking lot, it won't matter really. We'll be prepared! The men will be in place for whatever you may try, close, close enough, but not too close, if you know what I mean. You won't sniff them out this time, Simon. I promise you that!

And what of your greatest strength, your patience, you wait until everything is in order. Months, years, you've always picked your time. The luxury of time is too great an advantage. I've let you have it for months. Now, let's take it away from you.

In the morning I'll get Dawson to arrange fingerprint scans on everyone entering Government buildings. That would be a prudent precaution, wouldn't it? Check out against our databases or get detained!

You wouldn't mind that, would you, Simon?

The system will be in place, in say, three weeks. How's that for a deadline? How about a little time pressure, asshole?

Your strengths are turning to weaknesses, Simon. Your attention to detail and your compulsion, now work against you. You must have her! You will make the try. And, I'll be there.

89

"Come in, Mr. Purdy. You have something for me?"

Alexander Purdy entered Henry Rickford's large control room. Never had he seen so much god damned high tech stuff in one place before. This was Purdy's third meeting with Henry Rickford. Each visit made him more uneasy.

They called Henry Rickford eccentric because of his enormous wealth, but by every standard he had clearly gone mad. Alexander Purdy had interacted with many unusual people in his sixty-two years, thirty-five in law enforcement and the last eight as a private investigator. However, Rickford occupied his own category.

His hair and nails were grown long, neither cut since that fateful day. A lengthy straggly beard ran down from his face. The clothes that covered his now emaciated body were never changed. Nor, did he bother to bathe any longer.

Henry Rickford was a man forged intense by a lifetime of competition. He was accustomed to sacrificing and committing all that was necessary to appease his extreme need to win. In this latest and most important contest, as the months dragged on without favorable results, Henry Rickford ultimately sacrificed his sanity.

His Command Center, the hub of "the Enterprise" had become Henry Rickford's permanent home and would remain so until his mission had been accomplished.

"Come on, Purdy. And don't waste my time."

"Yes sir," said Purdy meekly as he approached. There was no chair to sit on, which suited him perfectly. Alexander Purdy did not have any desire to stay longer than necessary. The whole business made him uncomfortable.

"So, Purdy?"

Henry Rickford stared out from behind a huge desk, the dark stare that he had become famous for, the stare that could no longer be turned off.

"Well, sir, I have found out that they have some information on the background of this Simon. Important stuff."

"Why haven't we got it?" bellowed Rickford. "Is my budget too small? Aren't I paying all you cock suckers enough?"

"I wouldn't know about that, sir."

"And what's the source of your information, Purdy?"

"Someone in the DA's office. Very reliable, although, may I say, somewhat expensive."

"Somewhat expensive. All you fucks are somewhat expensive. So?"

"Just saying, sir."

"This information?"

"From what I'm told, very good stuff."

"Then get it, Purdy!"

"Not easy, sir. Expensive. Illegal. We're talking break in."

The Rickford stare entered Alexander Purdy's eyes and burned its way through to the back of his head. "Get it, Purdy! I don't care what it takes or what it costs!"

"Yes, sir. It can be done. However, there's a problem. They're installing fingerprint-checking equipment. That complicates things. My source recommends that we move three days before it becomes operational. They'll be most distracted then, getting the system workning and all."

"Yes, so?"

"That creates time pressure, you know. Increases the cost tremendously."

"I see, Purdy. How much?"

"I would say about two mil would cover."

"Fine, do it. But don't fail me Purdy. Or you might get some of what Simon's going to get. Now, get out!"

Alexander Purdy was relieved to be leaving.

Were it not for the money, well, it was all about the money. Purdy was satisfied that after a few hours work and some risk, he would earn more money than he had in all his years in law enforcement and as a private investigator.

Henry Rickford watched as one more of a thousand like employees left. What had he come to? *No matter. The Enterprise, the Enterprise is what's important – the capture and punishment of the fiend, Simon.*

Henry Rickford was captive to that single purpose. By day, he sat in his Command Center directing and monitoring the Enterprise's myriad efforts to locate Simon. By night, he dreamed of the exquisite tortures that would be visited on the vile creature.

An offer was made - a fair offer, a generous offer. Further negotiations were always possible.

You choose death, Simon? Fine, I'll give it to you.

But, not too quickly!

He must suffer – excruciatingly, interminably, psychologically as well as physically. He must be kept alive and lucid as long as possible. He mustn't be allowed to die prematurely. I must have the best doctors.

And, he must be aware every moment that I'm watching.

Now, let me see. The aborigines tied their victims to anthills, the Vikings to stakes in the tidelands for the crabs to eat. The Apache Indians skinned their enemies alive.

All so primitive – I like that!

90

It was just before eight p.m., Tuesday evening and Janet Bultaco was still in her office. The briefs and working papers on every desk save hers had long since been locked away.

For most of three months, FBI agents were at her side every minute of the day. Janet Bultaco had nearly forgotten why. They rotated in shifts, four in all.

John Hightower had selected her agents personally. They had to have the right personality and demeanor. To the world, Janet could be a world-class bitch, and the constant shadowing tended to irritate her. Though she understood the necessity, deep down she resented the protection. Janet Bultaco had always taken care of herself.

After two months, her protection was lowered from two to a single agent. She was thankful for the change. By design, John had never informed her of the dozens of additional agents that had been secretly smuggled into the office. Agents in the storerooms, in the air conditioning ducts and a few brought in as new hires.

Sarah Toms was the District Attorney's protector for the evening. She was a large, physically fit woman, one of the Bureau's most capable agents.

Agent Toms performed the duty admirably and implacably. Humorless, she suited Janet Bultaco, whose own wit at work extended no further than an occasional foray into scathing sarcasm. Toms accepted the barbs stoically and served the long hours forced upon her by an overtaxed Bureau without complaint. Quietly and happily she and her husband deposited the overtime checks in their "house of our own" account.

Just before eight-thirty p.m., Clarence rolled in with his cart. Janet Bultaco had become edgy waiting for him. She needed her nightly caffeine fix.

Clarence Thorpe was the night janitor and had been for over thirty years. He cleaned up after the lawyers and their staffs, picking up debris and emptying their wastebaskets. Clarence Thorpe and his familiar cart were an institution at the DA's office.

"No one can produce trash like a bunch of government lawyers," he liked to say, laughing his wicked little laugh before going about his business. Bultaco paid him little attention. She would never have even noticed Clarence, were it not for the coffee.

Each night, Clarence Thorpe brought them pastries and coffee. Cream with lots of sugar and a berry danish for agent Toms; while Ms. Bultaco preferred something plain with her two black coffees.

Toms devoured the Danish and drank her coffee usually in less than a minute. The District Attorney finished her first coffee quickly, then nursed the other the rest of the night. She rarely finished her pound cake.

Ten dollars was left on the edge of Janet Bultaco's desk for Clarence, giving him a profit of $3.90 for his effort. Before agent Toms arrived, he was given five dollars. Then Clarence cleared only $1.10.

The real Clarence Thorpe had been turned into sewage a month earlier.

91

Recording F-3

"I never said, Frankie, I didn't know how to kill. What I said was that I didn't enjoy it. That is the key difference. The killing comes only from necessity and not for pleasure. However, when the need arises, I am most proficient."

The old man had been carefully studied before he was taken and killed. *Quite obvious really, he was the right height and build, voice easy to copy, simple makeup, and uncomplicated mannerisms. Lived alone, no family, minimal acquaintances, no one to miss him, and he had ready access to the Queen B. Exactly the person I needed.*

Simon had taken Clarence Thorpe on a Friday afternoon to allow the full weekend for his interrogation.

"I need to know what you do on your job, every little detail. Tell me, Clarence, tell me now, and I might let you live.

Tell me what you do when you enter the building. What do you do first? And then? And then? So you get your cart and clean the lower floors first. What time, when? When do you take your break? To whom do you talk? What are the names? Tell me Clarence, tell me, and when it's over I might let you go.

Now tell me about the upper floor. Tell me about Janet Bultaco. I know she works late, how late? And her guard, tell me about her guard! Do you speak to them Clarence? Tell me about the office. Where is the Queen B's desk? Tell me Clarence, tell me, or you will not live out the weekend.

Tell me everything you know. Tell me things I should know but haven't asked you. Yes, tell me about the coffee and Danish. Those are the things I want to hear. Tell me Clarence, tell me everything, or you die now!"

By four Sunday afternoon Clarence Thorpe was in the Freezer. Simon knew everything he needed. Starting the next Monday and for almost a month Simon became Clarence Thorpe and no one noticed. Picking up the papers, sweeping the carpet and emptying trashcans, he pushed his cart from desk to desk as it had been done for thirty years.

When each shift was over Simon climbed into the old man's dodge-em Toyota, drove to the Burger King for a Whopper, fries and Coke, then to Clarence's small flat. Everything as it always had been. Interrupted only by the need to return to the Castle to service the bitches, Simon stayed in the flat, planning, visualizing, and practicing the moves he would need to make.

Where do I want the FBI sow? I must eliminate her quickly, without fuss. She is a large bitch, armed, and probably well trained. I cannot have the Queen B escaping while I play with that Beast Bitch.

Hour after hour, Simon memorized steps, turning as he would, from the door to the table, two steps to the left, turn, and then a violent wave of his arm. *There bitch, there,* as if he were slashing his sword at some mythical dragon. *Again, again, what have I forgotten?*

He had practiced enough times over the month for it to become automatic. *The triumph of patience, Higherpower!* In the small flat and in the Queen B's office, dry runs, visualizing, planning, measuring steps, calculating contingencies.

If everything went according to plan, tonight would be the night.

He brought them their danish and coffees. *Excellent! They are alone in the building, the Queen B at her desk with her nose in papers, and the Beast Bitch at the table near the door. As if by design, everything in its place, excellent!*

A ten-dollar bill was waiting for him at the edge of Janet Bultaco's desk. *Condescending bitch! You will get your money's worth this night.*

"Excuse me, ladies," Clarence said quietly, timidly, politely. The voice was perfect; no one could have perceived the slightest imperfection in pitch or tone.

"I brought you your coffees," he continued quietly while entering the room. Two steps and a turn, he placed the tray on the edge of the table. His left hand picked up the coffee with the cream and three sugars, while his right slid innocently into his trousers.

Simon recalled the first time he brought the "toothbrush" with him. It was displayed deliberately to the ground floor guard at the metal detector. "What's that for Clarence?" *the fool wanted to know.* A smile and a mouth full of pearly whites was the only answer required.

He had fashioned the toothbrush prison style to accept a sliver of metal. The filed down razor blade was too small to set off the detectors. The blade fit perfectly in the slot created for it in the toothbrush handle.

How many times had he tested the weapon? Only Clarence Thorpe's furniture and mattress had the answer.

Yes excellent! The big bitch is at the table near the door as she must be. The Queen B's retreat is cut off.

The time is now!

92

Simon's dance had begun. Two steps to the left toward agent Toms, her coffee was in his left hand while his right gripped the tooth brush in his pocket. Turn, Simon was about to offer Toms the coffee, when suddenly there was a great commotion in the darkness outside the Queen B's office.

Men appeared from places where no one should have been and, with guns drawn, came running. Simon heard the shouting outside and through agent Toms' police radio.

He froze and, for the first time that he could remember, was afraid. Subconsciously, Simon tried to make himself smaller, to disappear, if that were possible. *How can this be?*

Through agent Toms' police radio, he heard wild shouting and then distinctly, "We've got him now! We've got Simon!"

Fear in stinging jolts surged through his body. *Can't be! How could I have not known about them? How, Higherpower, how?* They would be on him in an instant. The Grand Game was over.

Simon loosened his grip on the toothbrush and groped hastily for the cyanide pill he kept with him at all times.

He had lost the Game and he would pay his wager. *But no more! No media circus. No grandstand prosecution for you, Queen Bitch. No spectacle of an execution.*

He found the pill and held it between his thumb and index finger. Slowly, it was raised up toward his mouth. Simon prepared to bite down hard on the pill, and then no force on earth could deny him his chosen ending.

"He is here, level three!" Simon heard someone shout in the radio.

Level three?

Only then did Simon notice that the men were not coming, but rather ran toward the stairs.

"There he is. Freeze, motherfucker!"

"We've got him!"

Who?

"What's happening?" he asked in his Clarence voice. Simon hoped the fear crackling its timbre did not give him away.

"They've got him. Simon," answered agent Toms. "We knew he would come and we waited for him. I guess he fell into our trap," she continued in her professional monotone way.

Well played, Higherpower!

You would certainly have had me. But, you don't! Someone else has drawn you out. A piece of good fortune! A diversion has been created for me, not by my plan, but most opportune. How do you say it, Higherpower, never minimize the importance of luck?

"Yeah, we got the son of a bitch!" yelled the radio.

Someone, they have someone. Who? Who knows, who cares? It's not me!

"Aren't you going to go see, agent Toms?" asked Clarence.

"No! I'm ordered to stay with Ms. Bultaco, no matter what."

"Well, I'm going to see!" shouted the District Attorney.

"No maam, you will stay here. Those are my orders."

Janet Bultaco had learned to read people. Agent Toms would never let her out the door. Dejected and angry, she sunk back into her chair.

"Someone is going to pay for this, Toms," she snarled at her bodyguard. Agent Toms was duly unimpressed.

The shouting continued from the radio.

Simon had time to regroup and to recalculate. Despite his anger at being outplayed by Higherpower, despite circumstances having evolved that were not of his design, despite the near miss, he now saw opportunity.

They're all gone. The misdirection was not of my making but it's real enough. The time is now!

"Well, in that case, care for your coffees?" asked Clarence. The pill restored to its special place, his fingers again tightened around the toothbrush.

Two steps to the left, he held out agent Toms' coffee. Toms straightened up. Turn, she reached for the coffee with her right hand. Their fingers touched lightly.

Before agent Toms could say thank you, her throat had been cut clean through. Lightening fast, Simon's arm a blur, the thousandth practiced movement, and the shiny little blade had found its mark. Blood spewed instantly from Toms' neck. The vocal chords cut, she could not utter a sound. Agent Toms had only seconds to live.

Clarence continued to hold the coffee as Toms slowly sunk to the floor. He turned toward Janet Bultaco who remained seated at her desk, frozen, shocked, mesmerized by the sound of blood gurgling from Toms' body and the sight of the expanding blood pool on the floor.

"Now, bitch!" sneered a different Clarence. "Would you like your coffee?"

93

It took only a moment for Janet Bultaco to regain her equilibrium and to comprehend the situation. Simon was not downstairs. Clarence was Simon. *How is it possible? Clarence has worked here for decades. No time for that now. Keep your wits! I'm the target, inning nine, the Queen B.* Janet Bultaco knew she was fighting for her life.

She saw agent Toms' body with its cut throat gushing blood on the floor. *No help there.*

Bultaco was calm, focused, as she always was. Across the room, Clarence slowly put down the coffee cup. He put his toothbrush back into his pocket while removing a pair of latex gloves. Slowly, deliberately, practiced like a surgeon, he put on the gloves.

"What to do, what to do, Janeta," he said to her.

Indeed, what to do. I cannot run. He is blocking the doorway. The phone, the phone is no good. He will be on me immediately.

"What to do," he continued to taunt. "Can't run. No one to call out for. They have all gone downstairs. No one to protect you," Simon sneered wryly, while glancing down at agent Toms. "And you don't have a gun."

Simon had done his homework. No weapon registered to Janet Bultaco.

No gun! Why didn't I listen to them? They all wanted me to carry a gun. Even agent Toms urged me to do so.

The second glove snapped into place.

No gun, but there is the mace! Given to her years before, it had become a relic in her purse. A woman's purse, the black hole for possessions, things go in but they never come out. *Yes, it's still there, on the bottom somewhere. I am sure of it. God, I hope it's still working.*

"What, nothing to say, Janeta? What to say, what to say."

Indeed, what do I say? For Janet Bultaco, a vitriolic tongue had always been the weapon of choice. *But what words now?*

There are no words, no logic, but perhaps I can distract him, buy time.

"I wonder if I might have one of those coffees, Clarence," she said calmly while she reached under her desk for her purse. "I could really use it."

Simon laughed, and with the time she had bought, Janet Bultaco quietly fumbled through her purse. *Where is it? Where is it?*

"Fraid not, maam. You might throw it in my face."

"I am not that kind of girl. Tell me, why did you kill agent Toms? Why not take her like all the others?"

"Not my type. But you are."

She continued to search for the small can of mace. *Why is there so much crap in here?*

Simon reached into his other pocket to remove a handkerchief and a small bottle. Slowly, deliberately, the bottle was opened and some liquid poured onto the handkerchief.

The ether! *Janet Bultaco knew the routine.*

"Are you going to clean my silver with that?"

Simon laughed again. "No, Janeta. This is to give you peaceful sleep."

There it is! Now, please God, let it still be working.

Simon walked to the desk, around the side, past the ten-dollar bill, the handkerchief in his left hand. Janet Bultaco got up to face him. Behind her, in her left hand, she held the mace. He moved slowly towards her as if savoring the moment. *Please God, please God, be working.* She waited till he was almost on top of her, knowing that there would only be one chance. *Please God, please!*

One last diversion! "Are you going to kiss me first?"

"No Janeta. There is plenty of time…"

She did not wait for him to finish the sentence. Janet Bultaco thrust the can of mace up into his face and squeezed the trigger for all she was worth.

"Try that, fucker," she screamed, pushing him away with more strength than she realized she had. *It worked! He's stunned. But it won't last long.*

Bultaco saw only two options for escape. One, run and hope to get away. Janet Bultaco was no athlete and she knew it. The heaviest thing she ever picked up was a pencil and the closest she got to aerobics was an occasional flight of stairs.

Or, Bultaco could go for agent Toms' gun. With the gun, she could capture the bastard. Or she could kill him. Either way suited her fine.

Bultaco raced to agent Toms' body as Simon came to his senses; she fumbled for the holster as he regained his equilibrium. The gun went into her hand as Simon came forward. The safety was released as Janet Bultaco had witnessed agent Toms' practice hundreds of times. Simon was getting close. She pointed the gun as he was almost on top of her.

"Stop, you fucker!" she shouted as the handkerchief smothered her face. The gun went off in a large roar. Janet Bultaco felt the full weight of the man fall against her. She was pushed down to the floor unable to move. *Have I hit him? Is he dead?*

Suddenly, her wrist ached as it was yanked away from her. The pain was intense and she thought she heard bones breaking. The gun dropped, hitting the floor with a thud.

She was being held tightly, the handkerchief compressed so hard against her face that the material scratched her nose and cheeks. Breathing became difficult as a cloud began to envelope her.

Janet Bultaco's head was pounding, thump, thump, louder, louder, faster and faster. All that she saw was spinning about her until none of it was recognizable any longer. Then only darkness and the thumping.

And then, nothing at all.

94

The bullet tore through the scar tissue of his left shoulder, past the bone and out. The pain was sharp, but only mildly reminis cent of the agony Peter Simmons had felt.

The Queen Bitch's bullet entered a spot where a burning timber fell and pinned Peter Simmons to the ground those many years ago. *I deserved to die that night, consumed by the flames I created. Death not caused by fire, but by stupidity!*

Peter Simmons felt contempt for himself that night. Similar feelings now tormented Simon.

The bitch has shot me! I have been careless again! And so, the Queen Bitch shot me. And again death would be a fitting reward for one so brainless!

Peter Simmons escaped the collapsing house and forevermore became Simon. Only distant memories remained, of running and of agony that could not be endured until finally it was. The pain of the Queen Bitch's small bullet hardly troubled him now.

Simon was bleeding profusely. The blood dripped down onto the floor, some of it mixing with agent Toms'. Simon stuffed Janet Bultaco's delicate lace handkerchief roughly into the bullet hole. New stinging surges of pain shot through his shoulder. *Good, good for you, worthless sot! Suffer for your ineptitude.* The bleeding slowed to a trickle.

They have the blood now!

Simon was inconsolably angry.

His adversary would have the blood and with it the tell tale DNA. They would have footprints, fibers, tissue samples, and much more. There wasn't time to clean up. It was all theirs.

Not that any of it will matter. They still have to catch me.

The prize was his, the Queen Bitch. But, she was not yet in the Castle. *The inning is still not played out and the fools may see their error and return.* Simon threw Janet Bultaco's limp body into the cart and covered it over with papers.

A few more unplanned minutes, were spent in the Queen Bitch's private bathroom. Simon had to tidy up and hide the bloodstains on his clothes. Hastily, he washed the blood off his hands and face and fixed his makeup as best he could.

Time to get back into character. Clarence Thorpe still has work to do. Simon wheeled the cart to the elevator and rode down to the parking garage, where Clarence Thorpe emptied his cart into the trash dumpsters each night. Simon was relieved that the commotion on the third floor had not reached the basement.

He pushed the cart past the closest dumpster and headed to the one at the far end of the parking lot, where it was most secluded, where he could transfer his cargo into the trunk of Clarence Thorpe's Toyota.

He would have to cross directly past the night parking lot attendant. Also planned for, Clarence had taken the same route several times a week in the past month. But Simon hadn't planned on the bloodstains on his shirt and pants.

Clarence rolled past the attendant, trying to look effortless as, with a weakened shoulder, he pushed the heavy cart. He kept his body turned so that his blood stained left side faced away. *Will he notice? Who is on tonight, George?*

"Hey Clarence," shouted George. He did not get up from his seat. Barely moved actually. "How's it hangin?"

"Have to go to the far dumpster again. The other one's full. Can you believe it? No one can produce trash like a bunch of government lawyers!"

95

MY DEAR HIGHERPOWER

AT NIGHT, JANETA ENTREATS THE HIGHERPOWER
TO SAVE HER FROM HER DAILY HORROR
FOR THE WHITE KNIGHT JANETA DOES PRAY
TO RIDE IN AND SAVE THE DAY

ALAS, NINE INNINGS ARE COME AND DONE
WITH THE QUEEN B, THIS GAME I HAVE WON
TIS PITY, SOON I'LL BE GONE
THOUGH I TRUST, NOT FORGOTTEN

SIMON

John Hightower held the note received three days before. The living room floor was lined with statistics and facts of young women already dead. John Hightower was not yet ready to place the note down on the floor with them.

He had read it dozens of times. Each time he was stunned anew.

AT NIGHT SHE ENTREATS THE HIGHERPOWER
TO SAVE HER FROM HER DAILY HORROR

Hightower was losing the battle with his emotions. The Janet he knew was probably already dead. Distress, fear, and panic had no doubt already supplanted the confident, self-assured woman that once was. *What are you doing to my Janet? What horrors?* Hightower tried to tell himself it didn't matter, as long as Janet survived.

Calm down, Hightower, calm down! You must keep control of your emotions, more so now than ever.

You took Janet in revenge, because she prosecuted your brother, Paul. But, you also took her to punish me. Better you had taken my life.

Would you make such a trade? No, never, you have your ways.

ALAS, NINE INNINGS ARE COME AND DONE
WITH THE QUEEN B, THIS GAME I HAVE WON

Proclaim your victory. Don't tell the world, Simon, how incredibly lucky you were. That a worthless, burned out derelict ex cop, for reasons unknown, broke into the DA's offices. Otherwise, you would be in a cell right now.

We shall have to have a nice long chat with Mr. Purdy. He was working for someone. Not you, though. You trust no one.

I have a feeling, by the time we finish with Mr. Purdy, we will find Henry Rickford's fingerprints on him. The mettlesome fool!

Ironic, isn't it? Tragic!

Hightower's thoughts turned to Henry Rickford. He now understood, in his gut, how Rickford and all the other victim's relatives felt. *Desperate and helpless!*

Tell me, Simon, if Rickford were not so arrogant, would his daughter have lived? Or would she just have survived a little longer. And, Janet, how long will she be kept alive?

TIS PITY, SOON I'LL BE GONE
THOUGH I TRUST, NOT FORGOTTEN

The Game over, the clear victor and "Soon I'll be gone." Just like Zodiac, your case study? Went on his killing spree, taunted the authorities, then disappeared, and certainly was not forgotten.

How could Janet be kept alive? That question, above all others, tortured John Hightower. A simple question, but it was the answer that so tormented him. The Game over, Janet, Francine, and the others were doomed. Hightower read the note again.

ALAS, NINE INNINGS ARE COME AND DONE

This game is done. Hightower's body quivered. *This game is done... Time to clean up and move on, the heads go on the mantle.*

I cannot allow it!

I am the adversary, the competition you need to validate the victory in your game. Well, your opponent is not yet vanquished, Simon!

This game is not ended. I refuse to let it end. Besides, how can it, when there is still the matter of the book? The great victory must be documented. The reporter is a loose end. You don't leave loose ends, do you, Simon?"

96

Recording F-8

"What you may not realize, Frankie, is how much trouble it is to keep the bitches. You have to feed them and bathe them. You must attend to their bodily functions and clean up after them. The bitches lose their sex appeal quite quickly. They have to try hard to earn their keep."

It must have started before his memory began, because for young Peter Simmons it was always so. In their time alone each day, Peter's mother dressed him in fancy little dresses. She fixed his long hair in various styles, and painted his face with lipstick, mascara and rouge. Peter was primped, and fussed with until he was his mother's perfect little bitch.

When he was ready, Karen Simmons played with the little doll she had created. Peter was tousled and touched, poked and prodded, and strange objects were put inside of him.

He was not tied down until he was older and began to resist. Resistance was futile and he was punished for it severely. Karen called him worthless bitch. How dare he resist. A bitch was only good for giving pleasure. *Well, a perfect bitch you turned out to be mother, a Queen Bitch.*

Simon came to Janet Bultaco seven times and on each occasion ether was required. He had not expected so much resistance. The Queen Bitch was no ordinary bitch. More forceful measures were required.

On this occasion Simon brought a riding crop.

"Hello, Janeta," he greeted her.

Bultaco was still woozy from being drugged. Nevertheless, Simon's Janeta welcomed him with dagger eyes. She was well aware of what ensued after she passed out. Janet Bultaco was in a constant state of fury and it hung heavy in the room.

Simon delighted in her seething anger. The hatred that blazed forth from those darkly recessed eyes made him smile. Janet snarled at him through clenched teeth. "I will see you dead. I will have you dead. I will make you dead." In his wildest dreams, Simon could not have hoped for more.

Incensed, enraged, furious, frantic and frenzied, it was all so glorious. Simon rejoiced in her wrath, and celebrated the desperation she felt.

Mary Splitorf, Mary Benson, and Kathleen Harper were ordinary bitches, sexually appealing, but quite ordinary. Danielle Rickford was a prominent bitch taken for the Game, and she was enchanting. Susan Benchly was thrown in with the Rickford bitch, and had her moments.

Francine was taken to raise the stakes and for Fitzfatprick. She was a corpulent sow who disgusted him, till he made her more desirable. Susan and Pam Berlanger were taken for "Top Cop," Furbanger. They were mildly amusing, though hardly worth the trouble.

Unlike the Game's other bitches, taken strictly as punishment, Janet Bultaco was taken to be punished. She was the Queen Bitch and the Queen Bitch had much to repay. He would break her, humble and humiliate her. That was the tantalizing new game.

"So my lovely Janeta, it is time to play again."

He had come to her three times each day since having taken her from her office. Janet Bultaco writhed at his touch, pulling away to the extent her restraints allowed. She cursed him, fought, and clenched herself shut. No entry, she was determined, *kill me first!*

"What wonderful sport, Janeta!" Simon exclaimed with glee as he cinched up one of the restraining ropes and her middle was pulled upward. "Let's see. How do I want you this time?"

Simon glanced up at the tracks in the ceiling with their attached loops, pulleys and ropes. He pulled two of the ropes and Janeta's left arm and leg were yanked upward.

"Yes, very good." *A fine piece of engineering, brilliant design. I do not have to grapple or even touch the bitches to get them the way I want them.*

Simon pulled at the rope that would move her to the side. *A little rough around the turn,* he noted as he planned the required modification.

"No ether this time for you Janeta. I must say avoiding the ether is usually enough to make the bitches come around. Why suffer, fighting against the inevitable? A logical deduction, wouldn't you say?"

Bultaco hissed and cursed him through her gag. She was suspended high above, naked, pulled apart by the ropes, helpless to his most minor whim. She had always been a woman in complete control. Now she was powerless, a slave. The bastard could do whatever he liked with her.

"But no, not you. You will never give in will you, Janeta? That is why you are a Queen Bitch."

But not the first Queen Bitch!

When their time together was over, Karen Simmons removed the makeup from her son's face, and combed his hair little boy style. The dresses were removed and replaced with jeans and T-shirts.

Each day Peter was sworn to silence or there would be punishment on the morrow. He could not protest. She was the stronger. He could not appeal to a father who had long since been emasculated. It was their little secret, his and the Queen B's.

Simon pulled at the ropes to move the pulleys across the tracks. His Janeta suddenly flipped over. She was now suspended facing downward with a full view of her tormentor. *He is not a man. Naked and revolting he is only half man. The rest is an abhorrent scarred creature made from leathery, rotted, and dried over flesh.*

At night when Sonny returned from work, Karen Simmons lodged her complaints about Peter. "The boy is disturbed, just like the doctors said." "He is sullen, uncooperative, and won't listen." "He is worthless, like you." "Take him out of my sight." "Take him out and play baseball with your foul offspring."

Simon released some ropes and pulled at others attached to the pulleys on the floor. Janeta slowly moved downward.

"Gently, gently. We don't want anything dislocated."

Janet Bultaco fought violently against her restraints though it was useless. She would not give in. She would never give him the satisfaction.

"I want you with your face down and your ass up in the air. We are going to try a new approach, Janeta."

In a few minutes, Janet Bultaco's face was pressed down against the table; her arms, legs, and knees were pulled apart and tied down. Her waist was yanked upward and a great tension was created in her body. It was painful to move, but still she struggled.

Peter Simmons hated both of his parents, his father for his weakness, his mother for the daily torment. The young boy could do nothing but endure the mistreatment, endure and remember every vile act. Peter Simmons turned inward, thinking, calculating, brooding, planning, waiting for the day when his power would be sufficient.

"Ah Janeta, Janeta. So very stubborn! But you will learn that resistance is futile, and painful."

Janet Bultaco felt the first searing sting as the riding crop flashed across her backside. Then another, and another, and another!

"Is my argument convincing yet, counselor?"

She could feel the Beast's hands touching her, smoothing over the welts he had created. Then gently the hands moved towards her private areas, *private no longer!*

"Errrrr," she grunted as she bit down heavily on the gag. *I can't stop you but I will never give in. Never, never, never!*

"Not ready yet? You insist on your cross-examination. Very well."

Simon swatted her again and again, without pity and without pause. He struck her hard with the hatred that had been harbored for more than thirty years. He was angry and with every stroke he shouted at her.

"Here Queen Bitch, you need no quarter, for you give none. Here, no compassion for you, for you have no compassion for others." The emotions welled up inside him. Each word emphasized with a staccato blow that was harder than the last. "Here, Queen Bitch, accept the punishment, for punishment is your stock in trade. Embrace the pain, for pain is the only gift you ever bestow. Give something of yourself, for it is everything that you take from others."

She was almost unconscious. The agony from the repeated blows was overwhelming, the pain so intense that it provided its own anesthesia. Janet Bultaco was beyond caring and well past resistance.

Simon approached her quivering body. He took her from behind as he would, frolicking as he rubbed himself against her crimson bottom. The Queen Bitch's blood was proudly worn on his abdomen. The Beast entered her crudely and abruptly then took his pleasure slowly, fully savoring his victory over her.

There was no strength in Janet Bultaco to try to stop him. The only defiance left was to go completely limp.

"There now, Janeta. That was a good start. But you must do better. You shall give your love willingly and thrillingly. That is our game, Janeta."

97

Janet Bultaco awoke from merciful unconsciousness. It was the only relief from the searing pain of the Beast's latest beating. She could not tell how long she had been passed out but knew that he had again done with her as he would.

The Beast was gone. But true to his practice, he did not leave before cleaning her. The blood had been washed off her body and her welts were treated with salve. Fresh makeup was on her face and she was dressed in a new negligee.

Fastidious bastard! Always leaves everything neat and clean.

The Beast kept her limbs pulled taut, always uncomfortable and usually painful. Bultaco squirmed, hoping for a better position. She also tried to angle herself for a look at the door. Twice before, the Beast had left, leaving it unlocked. Janet Bultaco had struggled with her bonds on those occasions to no avail. She was shackled too tightly.

Yes, it's open! There was new hope.

Bultaco checked her restraints for the slightest looseness, twisting and turning her wrists until even the padded straps rubbed her skin raw. It seemed no use.

Never a quitter, she continued to fight. Her wrists were burning, *but what else is there to do? Wait here quietly for him to return? I must keep going!*

The strap slipped ever so slightly down her left wrist.

Bultaco contorted her body back and forth as she violently thrashed about with new enthusiasm. Her joints ached, her muscles burned, and her left wrist was on fire.

It's moving. Yes! I can feel it.

The edge of the strap had worked its way up onto her hand. It was on her knuckles, but stuck there. She struggled for nearly fifteen minutes before her hand suddenly slipped free. Janet Bultaco's body fell backward.

She rested just a minute, afraid to make it more, then again began contorting. *I have to free my right hand, then my feet.* The muscles in her abdomen, back, and shoulders burned. *God, I wish I were in better shape.*

She had visions of herself going to the gym regularly, of being lean and mean and not simply lean and weak and mean. The daydreaming was welcomed. Janet Bultaco wanted her mind elsewhere as she continued to fight, somewhere, anywhere, anything to escape the pain.

Then, she visualized Simon shackled in her courtroom, and Janet Bultaco could have continued forever.

The exhilaration was building up in her as she worked herself loose. It took nearly an hour, but Janet Bultaco was sitting on the table, free.

She became frantic, despite knowing that time was likely not a concern. Sometimes the Beast left her alone for days. Bultaco gave herself only a moment to rub sore joints and aching muscles, fearing that in this one instance, the Beast would return quickly.

Now, you bastard, now you'll get yours!

98

The door was ajar only a few inches. Janet Bultaco carefully peered down the long, dimly lit hallway.

The Beast is not there.

Strangely, she hesitated, as a pang of anxiety went through her. Then she bolted into the hallway. Through the first window on the right, she saw Francine Fitzpatrick. The poor woman was barely recognizable from her pictures. Appearing to have lost fifty pounds, her face pale and gaunt, Francine Fitzpatrick looked sickly and weak.

The bastard!

The door was locked. Francine would have to wait until she came back with help. Pam and Susan Berlanger were in the next cell. They appeared less mistreated, neglected actually, but with the door also locked, they too would have to wait.

Bultaco quickly scanned the remaining cells. All the doors were locked except one. She raced down the hall and into the room.

The smell of ether, that disgustingly familiar odor, was in the air. Two women, both unknown to her, lay on separate tables. One was unconscious and the other peered up at her with hopeful eyes.

"Who are you?" Bultaco asked. "Wake up! Wake up!" she shouted.

The women were both elegantly dressed in long red satin gowns and their makeup was impeccably applied.

He doesn't dress them up like cheap whores. Nor are they viciously hung and yanked apart by ropes. But then, they're not the Queen Bitch!

"Wake up! Wake up! We have to get out of here!" she shouted at the now conscious but still groggy woman. Bultaco left her for the moment to release the other woman. "Who are you?" she asked again.

"Christine Taylor. Her name is Samantha."

"Well come on, Christine, help me with her. We've got to get out of here."

Samantha was still groggy, but coming to. "What? Who are you?" They helped her up.

"We have to get out of here," they coaxed while holding her up.

"All right." Samantha's speech was slurred; she was only semi conscious, and struggling. "But, who are you?"

"I'm Janet Bultaco, the District Attorney. But, never mind that now. Come on. You have got to walk!"

"Ok, ok." The woman tried to get to her feet but failed and all three women slumped to the floor.

"Just a minute please. Just a minute," complained Samantha.

"We don't have time Samantha!" urged Bultaco and they yanked Samantha to her feet. "Everything's going to be fine. Stay calm, but we have to get out of here. Now!"

"No, wait. Wait. Wait!"

The first two were imploring pleas, the last "wait" was insistent. Samantha was fighting them. Janet Bultaco became furious. She was about to hit Samantha in earnest.

"What's the matter with you? Come on!"

"No, wait. His keys."

Keys? "Keys? What keys?"

"I was just going under his gas. I think I saw him put down his keys. Look! He has dressed me up again, put make up on, while I was unconscious. He is going to rape me again!"

"Forget that now, Samantha!" urged Bultaco. "What about the keys?"

"All of a sudden, I don't know why, he ran out of the room."

"The keys! The keys, Samantha!"

"Over there?" Samantha pointed to the chair.

There was a chair in Janet Bultaco's chamber also. Sometimes the Beast sat in it for hours, watching her hanging with her arms and legs pulled apart, talking to her, taunting her.

"Yes!" The keys were there, left on the arm of the chair.

Bultaco quickly retrieved the keys while Christine stayed with Samantha. Slowly, the three women left the room, proceeding down the dimly lit hallway until they reached a large, heavy metal door.

It was dark. Janet Bultaco could barely see. Her hands swept across the door searching for the keyhole. “There it is.” She tried the first of a half dozen keys.

“No.”

“Hurry!” screamed Christine frantically.

The second, “no.”

“Hurry!”

“Shut up! I’m trying.”

The third key, “no.”

The fourth key slid into the lock and turned easily. All three women sighed as the door clanked open almost by itself.

“It worked! Are we going to get out of here, Ms. Bultaco?” asked Samantha.

“Yes we are!” answered the District Attorney.

99

Is he going to pay, Ms. Bultaco?"

"Yes, Samantha, he is going to pay. In spades, I'll make sure of that myself. But, now we must hurry."

They began to climb the unlit stairway.

"You can't imagine what he has done to me, Ms. Bultaco."

"And to me too," added Christine.

"Oh yes I can. And he will die for it, I assure you both of that."

"Tell me, Ms. Bultaco. Tell me, what you'll do to him. I want to see him die."

"You will, Samantha. But now we must hurry. We have to get help quickly, before he returns, to save the other women. We have to get the police so they're here to capture him when he comes back."

"I want to see him die, Ms. Bultaco. I have to see him die. You must promise me."

"Yes, Samantha, I promise. But, now, we must hurry."

They stumbled twice climbing the stairs before reaching the next metal door. It was completely dark. Janet Bultaco's left hand clenched the keys firmly while her right felt the door for the keyhole.

"Hurry, find it," encouraged Christine.

"Yes, I will."

Bultaco's hand slid back and forth over the cold metal, but was unable to find the lock.

"Keep looking," implored Christine.

"Yes! Yes! I am."

"Can't you find the hole?" asked Samantha

"I'm trying!"

Janet Bultaco's hand slid frantically back and forth.

"I never have any trouble finding the hole, bitch."

"What? Shut up, Samantha!" Janet Bultaco was distracted. She pounded on the door desperately.

"It's only the second safety," she heard from behind her.

"What?" gasped Janet Bultaco as she turned.

Samantha struck her hard across the face. The heavy blow sent Janet Bultaco careening down the stairs.

"There is no hole. It's a cipher lock. Janeta, Janeta, have you learned nothing about me? There is no escape for your victims, is there, Queen Bitch? Well, there's none for mine, either."

"Simon! Why? Why?"

"Why indeed? It's a game, Queen Bitch. A not so funny game for you, as your games are not so much fun for your victims. Remember the bloodthirsty Jaws? 'The victims are crying out from their graves. Please, for the love of God, give us justice.' And now, you have it, Madam Prosecutor."

He dragged her by the hair back to her cell.

"Are you having fun, Queen Bitch? It is fun is it not, my lovely Christina?"

"Oh yes, Simon! The most fun."

He spoke again to Bultaco, still using the Samantha voice.

"Tell me, Ms. Bultaco. Tell me, what you'll do to him. I want to watch him die. Promise me, promise me, Ms. Bultaco, you'll let me watch him die." Then, in a voice that could have been Bultaco's own, "Yes, Samantha, I promise."

"Yes, Samantha, I promise," mimicked Christine.

"Very good, my sweet," complimented Simon. "Excellent for a first time. Try it from further back in the throat and make your mouth a little rounder."

"Yes, Samantha, I promise," Christine tried again.

"Better. Yes, Samantha, I promise," he repeated, perfectly in Bultaco's voice.

Then Simon spoke for himself.

"But, our little game is not over yet, Janeta. The best part is still to come. Tell me, what shall it be this time, blood or no blood?"

Christine Taylor giggled as she answered for Janet Bultaco. "Blood, for sure! Please, darling, please."

THE LOOSE END

100

We drive ourselves for a glimpse into the killer's mind. We struggle for the slightest clue to build our profile. A hint of his physical being, insight into his background or character, a tendency, a motive, anything that can assist in his capture.

And if we can provide anything at all, however minor, our effort is considered successful.

But, occasionally there is more. A bonus. We get to play offense.

-Into the Mind of a Killer, John Hightower

The game must continue, if Janet and the other victims are to remain alive.

Kirsty Dunn was the new anchor for the KCAL Local News. Though dedicated and hard working, her choice over several more experienced and senior reporters surprised some. The word was Kirsty was chosen for her looks.

A good appearance never hurt anyone, especially on TV. Kirsty was pleasant, pretty and had a charming smile.

She was surprised when the FBI contacted her and offered an interview with John Hightower, the reclusive, unapproachable head of the Simon investigation. Why, she wondered, had he chosen her?

I'll not give my interview to a large newspaper or TV news organization, but to a small local station. Slip it to you subtly, Simon. I cannot overplay, and a smaller station means less stature for you. It will irritate you even more.

KCAL was a local TV station. Located in Los Angeles, it was in the eye of the Simon hurricane. The news that night consisted of two killings, an horrific traffic accident involving four fatalities and, of course, the latest on Simon. Kirsty was not complaining. She was delighted with her promotion. Yet, she yearned to someday anchor for a real news organization, perhaps CNN, perhaps network. With this interview, that goal seemed far less remote.

"Are you ready, Mr. Hightower?" Kirsty asked, flashing her best smile. She still couldn't believe it was real.

"Yes, of course, Miss Dunn."

"We're not live, Mr. Hightower. We're taping. So, we'll simply have a discussion and edit later as per agreement. You'll be able to review everything. All right?"

"Certainly."

"All right then, let's roll. Mr. Hightower, thank you for coming and thank you for granting this interview."

"My pleasure, Miss Dunn."

"May I ask you why? Why after all of this time of complete silence? Why do you wish to speak now?"

"It is really quite simple, Miss Dunn. This Simon character has people worried. He would make himself into some kind of ghost or super being that can strike at will. He would have us believe that he is invincible.

Actually, Miss Dunn, nothing is further from the truth. Simon is really rather ordinary."

"Ordinary?"

"When I say ordinary, Miss Dunn, I do not mean it relative to normal people, but rather to other lunatics like Simon. I have hunted serial killers for over twenty years. They always have their common characteristics."

"Can you tell us something about that?"

"Of course. Simon was most certainly a pathetic mistreated boy. He was likely a bed wetter and probably still is. Insecure and likely impotent, he preys on women to cover his inadequacies. He also chooses them because they are physically weak and, therefore, easier victims.

Above all, Simon is a coward."

"Not at all the picture I've had of him."

"No, it's not, is it? Actually, of all the serial killers I have pursued and studied, I would say that Simon ranks in the bottom third. He's not particularly talented or clever. What he has been is extraordinarily lucky."

That should do it, Simon. I refuse to let you leave a winner!

Your play.

101

"I know what you are doing, Higherpower!" screamed Simon as he threw the television set across the room.

You are goading me!

"Ordinary!"

Notwithstanding one well-played inning, you know you have been shut out. No hit is actually more accurate.

"That's not what you call ordinary!"

Not particularly talented or clever, extraordinarily lucky? Tell me, Higherpower, who else has bested you so?

Simon stormed to the other side of the room, picked up the offending television set and flung it again.

"Bottom third!" *Best of all time and you know it!* Simon retraced his steps, then kicked the broken set. "Coward!" *I have been bold and brave. I snatched Berlanger's bitches right from under your nose. And even after your trap with the Queen Bitch was sprung, your dozens of agents running around like fools, I still took her. Killed your Beast bitch in the process, too. I would hardly call that timid.*

"Why don't you show me the respect I deserve, Higherpower?"

Your Janeta will pay for your insults!

"Bed wetter! Impotent!"

Simon could barely contain the fury that had risen in him. Boiling, ready to explode, as always, but, he had learned to control it, to harness and channel it. And, he would again.

"All right Higherpower! You shall have one more play. I will give you your last licks."

102

Recording B-3

"Have you ever played baseball, Frankie? A marvelous game of symmetry and timelessness, it is never over until the final out. You can be outclassed the entire game and still win at the end.
Even at your very last at bat, your last licks, you can still be the hero."

Eight-year old Peter Simmons gripped the plastic yellow bat tightly. There were two outs in the bottom of the ninth inning. His father wound up to throw the white ball towards the wall. Peter swung mightily.

"Strike one!" shouted Sonny at the young boy. "The bases are loaded with two outs. The crowd is buzzing, with the Dodgers down to their last licks. Their only hope is Peter Simmons at the plate."

The pitcher bore down again and with a determined heave, threw the ball into the wall. Peter concentrated and swung at the white blur. The pitch was much too fast for an eight-year old.

"Strike two!" shouted Sonny again. "Peter Simmons is down to his last strike. It is still not too late. With a homer, Peter can still be a hero. That's the wonderful thing about baseball, ladies and gentlemen. The game is never over until the final out. Even at your very last at bat, your last licks, you can still be the hero." Sonny went into his wind up. "What will it be this day for Peter Simmons, hero or goat?"

Sonny heaved the next pitch at the wall, the fastest yet. Peter swung at it meekly. "Strike three! And the game is over. Peter Simmons has struck out!"

Peter always struck out. He was never permitted to hit the ball in the bottom of the ninth. He was always the goat.

Peter despised his father, a weak, *small* man. Sonny took out his frustrations where he could. They played baseball every night before supper. Sonny played for his own escape, to gain one small victory for himself.

You lacked testosterone, dad. Why didn't you stand up to the Queen B? Where was a father when his young son needed him? Both of his sons!

Instead you pretended not to know. Sonny Simmons went to work each morning ignoring the obvious. *You left me to the Queen Bitch.* At night Sonny came home hoping only to avoid abuse.

Sonny put his arm around his son as they returned to the house.

"That's all right, son. Don't take it too hard. There is always another day. And always another game to play."

103

They yanked me out of bed and quietly took me to John Hightower's office. Completely unnecessary, all he had to do was call; I was more than willing to help in any way. "The need for secrecy," was the way Hightower explained it, so who was I to question? Hightower was right about Simon every time, though it didn't seem to help in catching him.

Hightower and Simon, oddly they were the two smartest people I had ever met. Simon was a demented genius and John Hightower tracked his thinking perfectly. That fact alone should have scared the shit out of me.

They fitted me with an elaborate set of bugs and told me that I was protected night and day. Translation, they wouldn't let me out of their sight. Hightower told me that, sooner or later, Simon would contact me and would want to meet. I should play along and do everything he wanted from me. That idea I found ridiculous, but I was willing, if it would help.

What was there to lose? My life? No big thing. But first, I told Hightower, he had to protect Jane and Jenny. The next day, they were spirited away into witness protection, their location a total secret, even from me. That's the way I wanted it. I'm certainly no superman, and under the influence, I was always vulnerable. Whatever happened, whatever Simon might do, they were going to be safe. That's all that mattered.

Well, not really.

There was Christine. God, I missed her. Simon took Christine from me, and I knew the terrible things he was doing to her. And that was the good news. When he tired of her, he'd kill her.

I wanted Simon dead so bad, but I wasn't the first for that, was I? So, Hightower didn't have to convince, coax, or coerce me. I was plenty motivated, and ready to do anything.

Two days later I was driving on the 605 Freeway when the cell rang.

"Wycheck!" I answered.

"WIH..A..CHEE..YOOK..HUH, hello. And to you, too, Higherpower, hello, and my compliments for keeping him in play."

My compliments for keeping him in play?

Well, so much for Hightower's "The need for secrecy." Simon saw through that and was actually talking to Hightower through my bugs.

My compliments for keeping him in play.

A small flicker of logic finally penetrated my Rock of Gibraltar head. *Of course, another of Simon's games!* They were playing a little game with me. Cat and mouse, and I was the cheese.

"Frankie, we have unfinished business. I assume you still want the last installment," Simon continued, now talking to me. He was using the Voice. Naturally, no sense giving Hightower anything he could use.

"Yes," I answered, trying to play my part properly.

"And surely you must know that Higherpower is watching you."

"Yes." I wasn't sure I should have said that. My briefing didn't cover this eventuality. I suppose that's the way Hightower wanted it, the cheese was just bait.

"And you must be aware that you are bugged. Not just you, your car, your cell phone, the clothes in your closet, everything."

"Well, uhh."

"Frankie, please. Don't insult me. If we are to meet, you must come alone. You must lose your friends, and go to the place of our first meeting, at the same time, and on the next day that is the same day of the week. Do you understand?"

"Yes," I said quietly. Simon knew everything.

"What was that, Frankie? They may not have heard you."

Fuck you, Simon! "Yes!" I shouted at the top of my lungs.

"Remember, Frankie, fail or betray me and I will know. And that will be the end of it for you. You do understand me."

"Yes." I sure as hell did.

"And as for you, Higherpower, this will conclude our business together. But first, let's see how you do with this 'ordinary' citizen. These are your last licks, Higherpower. You have not scored in any inning, but you can still hit a home run and win the game.

What will it be for you this day, Higherpower? Hero or goat?"

104

John Hightower didn't know about the Bluebird Motel. Was I supposed to try and tell him? No, I decided. Simon would know and as he put it, "And that will be the end of it for you." The phrase stuck in my mind, as did another from Father Reyes, "I welcome the challenge of finding Jana and Jenna."

Were they really safe? From him? Who could be safe from Simon? It suddenly occurred to me that I might have been betting on the wrong Titan. Susan and Pam Berlanger were bait too. And, the District Attorney, God, how she must have been "protected."

I was having big time misgivings and once again Frank Wycheck didn't know what to do. I drove around endlessly while trying to figure it out. After about two hundred miles, I decided not to put my trust and my family's lives in Hightower's plan. It just seemed that he was going to try the same things that failed at least twice before. And, that wasn't good enough, not with Jane and Jenny's lives on the line.

I formulated a plan of my own. I was straight, hadn't had cocaine in weeks, so, it wasn't drugs doing the thinking. I would throw them both a curve, Simon and Hightower, and resolve the matter myself.

But, I needed Patton's help.

I can almost see you rolling your eyes, my friend, but let me explain something to you. We all know about cocaine. On it you're always just about to solve all your problems. You can visualize the solution, see it clearly, it's right there, but always, it's tantalizingly just out of reach. With each near miss comes frustration and only more cocaine can dispel it. Then the answer is even more plain to seen.

That's if you're on the stuff. I wasn't. Sure, cocaine plants you in the gutter, but eventually, not immediately. And, if you control it, it can put you to the top of your game, at least for a while. And, that's all I needed, to be Patton for just a little while.

I received Simon's call on Monday. That meant, since I first met him at the Bluebird on a Thursday, there were slightly less than three days for me to lose the FBI.

"You must think clearly now, Wycheck!"

"Yes, Patton!"

I had to lose the Porsche, my cell, my clothes, everything that belonged to me, and ultimately myself. A wave of excitement rushed through me and I liked it. For so long I had been hiding and scared.

The plan was simple. Lose the FBI. Meet Simon. Meet him with the Baretta. Wait for him to show up, capture him or blow his ass away.

Now that was a final chapter to our book that really turned me on.

"The cheese eats the mouse! Make us one of the played with? I don't think so, Simon!"

"Right, Patton! Then I'll call the FBI. Sure, Hightower will be pissed, but what can he do to me when I was the one who finally stopped Simon? Prosecute me on some trumped up drug charge?"

I recalled my experiences with Simon, and visualized the new chapters. Venus, Mistress Pleasure, Gomer, Bartolo, the adventure at the Promenade, Jail, and now this. Sentences, paragraphs and chapters floated through my head. I liked the way it read.

"Stop day dreaming, Wycheck! We must get busy."

"Yes, yes, Patton. I know."

The rest of Monday and Tuesday were spent planning. Wednesday was D-Day, Patton's name for it. We left about ten in the morning. Patton did the driving and he liked it fast. We careened around the streets, into and out of traffic, like Popeye Doyle. *Let's see who's following us.*

A black and white did. The red lights flashed as he chased us. Then suddenly the lights and siren disappeared and the black and white pulled off to the side.

"They got to him, Wycheck, Hightower got him off our ass. This cheese was meant for someone else."

"Right, Patton. But Simon was right too. They have me under surveillance with or without a tail."

"Hah, they think we are stupid, Wycheck!"

Call it inspiration, call it sheer stupidity, but I made a sharp u turn in the middle of the street. Yes sir, right over the center divider, almost took out the Porsche's suspension with that one.

"Follow me now fuckers," Patton yelled.

I was a man liberated. It was going to be Simon or me. If I failed, if I got killed, no great loss, and Jane and Jenny were no worse off. But, if I was successful, then the whole nightmare would be over for everyone.

We continued driving around wildly, slaloming through traffic, great fun actually, then finally pulled into an Enterprise car rental. *Good-bye Porsche!* The Nokia and Rolex were left in the glove box even though I felt naked without them. *So much for those bugs!*

I rented a white Toyota Camry and the next few hours were spent driving around with me at the wheel. Patton's frenetic driving style would no longer do. I took funny little routes and parked often. I wasn't attempting to lose anyone yet, simply trying to identify who might be following.

About one in the afternoon, I drove to South Coast Plaza and parked the Toyota for the last time. At Robinsons, I bought several changes of clothing, paid cash, and left my old clothes in the dressing room. If Simon was right, my clothes probably were bugged too.

South Coast Plaza was a good place to get lost. I mingled in the crowd and plunged into stores while constantly checking behind me. Who did I recognize? Who had I seen more than once? On two separate occasions I ducked into rest rooms to change clothes.

By that time, Patton was already sure we lost the Feds. But I knew better. My good moves were still in reserve. We were just warming up!

When it was dark, I stole a Ford Taurus that was parked in a lot on the far side from the Toyota. Yeah, I knew how to steal a car, took a few in my teenage years.

I drove downtown to the Arco Towers and parked on level four. We played the elevator game, riding up and down, getting off on random floors. The FBI couldn't possibly have had enough new people to accompany us on all of our trips. It tickled me to imagine them trying.

On two occasions, I waited to ride an elevator alone. After getting in, I pushed all the buttons. *Hah, let them scramble to cover all of the floors!* I got off randomly, sending the elevator on its way alone. *Follow me now! No bugs, no helicopter surveillance, no satellites, and where are your people?*

That still wasn't my big move. I just wanted the Feds to think it was. Hightower expected me to make it look good, made it clear that I was "protected" no matter what. *Well, we'll see about that, huh Patton?* I couldn't have the FBI blowing everything up before I met Simon at the Bluebird.

I was taking a page out of Simon's book. Deception and misdirection; the power to appear and disappear! Quietly and mixed in with a crowd of people, I walked to the Bonaventure Hotel. Our room was on the eighteenth floor. Everything was right on schedule. I saw Kenny the Goat across the lobby and made eye contact. My plan was smooth as butter.

Kenny the Goat was good people, though I never knew his real name. Everyone called him Kenny the Goat, either because he would eat or sniff anything or, more likely, due to his stupid little Billy goat beard. Kenny didn't care. The name suited him fine.

The Bonaventure was a favorite hangout for Christine and me. The thought of her made me doubly angry and doubly determined. We had indulged ourselves fully and often, in food, drink, and fantasies. Kenny provided, prostitutes, drugs, whatever. As Simon correctly said, "You can get anything for money. No questions asked."

I ordered a couple of seven course meals from hotel room service, to be delivered in an hour. Kenny would bring them. I ordered two male and two female prostitutes off Kenny's room service menu. They would arrive at the same time. Smooth as butter.

In what was a really nice bathroom, I shaved my head and most of my beard, leaving only a goat-like remnant similar to Kenny's. A few minutes with red hair coloring and I marveled at how much I resembled Kenny. I must say, I had very mixed emotions about that. With his carrot red hair, all shaved except for the few ridiculous tufts on his chin, Kenny's appearance had always been a source of amusement for Christine and me.

My plan was elegantly simple. If the FBI were still on me, they would naturally conclude that I had done my best to elude them and failed. *Hah!* They would assume the room at the Bonaventure was the meeting place. They would lay back and wait.

The prostitutes were the diversion. The FBI would scramble to check everyone out. They might assume one of them was Simon. Kenny was a regular employee at the hotel. He would check out nicely. The FBI would not pay him much attention. Yeah, butter!

Kenny had been remarkably easy to enlist. He was in at "It's a surprise for Christine and if you like you can stay." Kenny had been to one of Christine and my sessions. End of story, Kenny was on board, no questions asked. Christine was that kind of woman.

The meals were wheeled in right on time, between the arrival of prostitutes three and four. The party was on. In minutes, Kenny the Goat was butt naked, sprawled on the king-size bed with a turkey leg in one hand and a nice blonde whore in the other. He was set for the night.

His uniform was a little tight on me but fit well enough. I checked myself out in the mirror before leaving. I really did look like Kenny! Trying my best to be calm, I wheeled the serving cart out and got on the elevator. We rode it to the kitchen. A beautiful plan, and as a bonus, I was also able to conceal a bag clothes and other goodies inside the cart.

I ducked into a rest room to change clothes and was out the door hidden within a group of people. Simple, elegant deception and misdirection, *how am I doing, Simon?*

105

So it was for revenge, Simon, revenge for a brother you never knew. Why didn't you visit him? Why didn't you try to help him? We all have our ways, don't we?

But, let me not be so simpleminded! You've been at it for some time. Sure, it was for revenge. But, the Game would have been played anyway, for sport, for fame, to be the best ever.

And the reporter is my "Last Licks."

John Hightower knew what the term "Last Licks" meant. He was from a time when baseball truly was the national pastime. Hightower remembered playing as a boy in the street with his neighborhood friends. There were no youth programs in those days. Sure they played football, in the winter. Some of them even played basketball for a few months. But baseball was played all the time. Nine innings usually, seven sometimes and occasionally fewer, but always the game came to the "Last Licks."

"Last Licks" were for the team that was behind, and although baseball's genius was in the possibility of always being able to win the game, "Last Licks" was usually synonymous with last rites.

I was worried about Wycheck. Could he play his part? The bizarre stunts in traffic were troubling. Much too stupid and amateurish! You would never accept that, Simon, would you? You simply wouldn't show up for the meeting.

Wycheck did better when he ditched the Porsche and his other personal belongings. Rented a car, gave us a nice little chase through the mall, very good. Stole a car, now that wasn't really part of the plan, then gave us fits at the Arco Towers. Excellent!

More than three hundred plain-clothes agents were allocated to the surveillance. An agent could be spotted only once, then was retired. Every entrance of the Arco Towers was watched for Wycheck's eventual exit. If he did not leave, more than enough personnel were available to keep track of him in the building.

However, the meeting wasn't to be in the Arco Towers. Wycheck, you have done a much better job than I could have hoped for. A trained undercover agent couldn't have done better. Were it not for the unlimited resources thrown at you, you would have certainly gotten away.

Slipped into the Bonaventure, rented a room under a false name and paid cash. That is the meeting place. Not what I expected though, the Bonaventure isn't creative enough for you, Simon. We can cover it too easily. You are trapped with no good opportunities to escape.

Phil Hardy was standing quietly, patiently in the office doorway. John Hightower had become annoyed at Hardy's timidity and reluctance to disturb his thinking.

"Dammit Hardy! How long have you been standing there this time?" Hightower did not like the long look on Hardy's face. "If it's important enough to bring you here, then spit it out."

"We lost him, sir."

"What?"

"We lost him."

Doubt grew into worry and it showed clearly on John Hightower's face. Several things had bothered him so far. *Why, Wycheck, did you remove all the bugs? Even the ones I told you Simon could never know about. And the Bonaventure, that was all wrong.* "How? How could you lose him, Hardy?"

"They must have pulled a switch."

"Who?" Hightower's mind was miles ahead.

"A waiter and Wycheck. He brought Wycheck room service last night. We checked him out before he went to the room. Kenneth DeFarge, a waiter for eight years, everything was in order.

We figured that the meeting would be today, that Wycheck was settling in for the night. They brought in whores, male and female. We focused on the whores. One of them might have been Simon. Or perhaps they were there to flush us out. So we laid back. No one was going to get away anyway.

When the prostitutes came out one after the other we snatched them up. We still have them. But I think what you see is what we got.

In the morning, we sent in a plain-clothes agent dressed as the chambermaid. She found him."

"Who?" *What is Wycheck up to?*

"DeFarge, he was on the floor, passed out, drugged and drunk to the hilt. He must have had quite an evening for himself. Wycheck was gone. They pulled the switch and we didn't catch it."

"What does this DeFarge know?" asked Hightower, reflexively. "Have you questioned him?"

"We are, but I don't think he knows anything."

"Probably not. Why would he?" John Hightower was clearly upset. "Listen to me, Hardy, we have to find Wycheck immediately! Fuck the stealth and secrecy. Call in the locals and the news. Get the bodies on the streets. Question everyone. We have to find Wycheck!

And we have to find him before Simon gets to him."

It was the worst of the possibilities. John Hightower reasoned that as long as Wycheck was on a string there was the potential of catching Simon. If Simon got wise and stayed away, well at least their little game was still on. Perhaps there would be another opportunity.

"But sir?" asked Hardy tentatively.

"Then Simon wins his game!" snapped Hightower. He could not verbalize the other conclusion.

Forgive me, my love!

106

I skulked into the Bluebird around one a.m. Skulking in was normal; everyone did. What was unusual was the time. People who went to the Bluebird were finished long before one a.m., home to their wives and families. "Had a tough time working late honey, so tired, have to get up early"; they slink into bed hoping that the smell of the evening is not too strong on them.

One a.m., naturally the rental office was empty. I pounded the bell mercilessly until the night manager showed up. He was a disheveled old coot, on drugs my guess, although he could have just been groggy from being awakened. Either way, I could care less. I wasn't there to write a story about him.

"Room sixteen please," I said brusquely and shoved a twenty across the counter. $19.95 was what the Bluebird charged for a room. A bargain until you saw what you got for your money.

I spent the rest of the night trying unsuccessfully to sleep. Never had a chance. The cocaine adrenaline cocktail makes quite an effective upper. I lay on the bed wide-awake and thinking.

All four legs of the bed were collapsed, a change from my previous visits. Only two were a problem when Christine and I used the room. I remembered propping them up twice during that day. Some other patron probably lacked my forbearance. I visualized an impatient john kicking the remaining legs out angrily. Well at least the bed was out of its misery.

Funny the things you think about.

"Pay attention, weak suck," bellowed Patton. *"This is serious business. You must be sharp!"*

"Yes, yes, I know." I took the rest of my stash and drew up six lines

on the nightstand next to the bed. Soldiers in the fight, there to provide reinforcements of energy and courage, lined up at attention, ready at a moment's notice to be sucked into the fray.

"Remember, Wycheck, you must act quickly, boldly. Do not hesitate. Be decisive. Don't let him distract you. Don't let him near you! Remember how easily he overpowered you last time."

"Yes, Patton, yes."

I checked my little Baretta. It was the only thing of mine that I still had. A tiny little gun the Baretta, a far cry from the pearl handled beauties that Patton preferred, but it suited my purpose. Easily concealed and potent enough, I could fire it quickly and often.

Simon had become too confident of his control over me. He disarmed me easily that first time and frisked me at each of our subsequent meetings. But the last few he did not. Simon thought I was hooked on his information as surely as I was on cocaine. I was no threat.

"Well he's wrong all the way around."

"Damned right, Wycheck! We're going to write the final chapter on Simon. He never leaves this room."

"I'll take him alive, if he lets me. I'm not a murderer."

"Sure, Sure, Wycheck, that's what we want. But let's be clear; take no chances with him. Stay on the bed. Keep him on the other side of the room. Don't let him get close. Blow him away if he makes a move."

"Yes, yes."

"Remember, Wycheck. He can kill you!"

"Yes I know. I must be careful. And I can't allow him to get away. Dead is as good as alive."

"Maybe better, Wycheck. No trials, no lawyers, no insane asylums, no worrying about Jane and Jenny for the rest of your life. But, if he gets away, then you're really fucked."

"He won't!"

Tomorrow was going to be the big day. Tomorrow I would make my move. Simon would pay for his sins and the whole world would be better for it.

107

I don't remember falling asleep, but a sharp persistent rapping on the door woke me up. No Rolex, but I knew it had to be pretty close to three o'clock.

"Who's there?" I uttered groggily.

I was stalling, knowing it was Simon, dressed up as who knew what, and there I was, completely unprepared.

"It's your birthday present, Sugar," came the voice through the door.

I leaned over the nightstand and did two quick lines. "Oh all right, just a second." The cocaine hit me immediately. *Yes, that's it.* My head was cleared of cobwebs, the blood was flowing through my veins, and my limbs were coming to life.

The knocking began again, this time quieter and slower, expressing impatience. It was asking "You going to keep me out here forever?"

I quickly drew in another two lines. The final two soldiers would be held in reserve. My mind began moving at light speed.

Patton was back and he was ready for battle. I put my hand into my pants pocket and found the Baretta. "All right," I said. "Come on in. It's open."

I sat back on the bed as planned, with my back against the wall. The hand in my pocket was holding the Baretta firmly. The door opened slowly.

Simon entered, dressed again as a prostitute. Not Venus, a much smaller version, but still good sized and quite nicely endowed. Short skirt, high heels, long slender legs, tight halter-top, protruding soft breasts, too much lipstick, too much makeup, and long black hair poorly dyed blonde.

"Hey baby, you Frankie?" Her voice was squeaky and childlike, a little singsongy, quite different than Venus.

"What's the surprise, Wycheck? He never uses the same disguise twice and anything is possible. You know that."

"Yes. Yes."

"Hello, Simon," I answered, trying to be calm. "Come on in."

"Ok, Sugar. But the name is Simone. The accent is on the end. Its French you know."

Simone, accent on the end, came into the room and closed the door behind her.

"That's excellent, Wycheck. He has closed off his own retreat. Careful! Careful now, don't let him get too close."

"Sure, Simone. Whatever you say."

"No, Sugar. It's whatever you say. I'm here for you! For as long as you like and whatever you like."

God, Simon was good. I played along. "Well, you know what I would like."

"No, Sugar, I don't. I'm paid for but you have to tell me what you want." *"Careful, Wycheck! Stay alert."* "How about a nice blowjob to start?" Simone licked her lips and rubbed her breasts so as to push them further out of her top. "How about that?"

"Didn't he do that the first time? Yes, I'm sure of it. He used the same move as Venus!"

"No, he didn't. I'm not sure, Patton. Doesn't matter anyway."

"Simon?" I was hoping for some confirmation.

"Simone, honey," he corrected me.

"Simone! You have to bring me up to date."

"Sure, Sugar. And I'll lube and oil you, too. Have any music?" She was already dancing. The music must have been playing in her head.

"Excellent disguise, *Simone*." My hand tightened around the Baretta. I was very confused. "Now, please can we get down to business?"

"Absolutely!" she exclaimed while gyrating wildly. "That's what I'm here to do!"

Simone was dancing like an old fashioned go go girl. Her breasts were nearly out of her top. Were this truly a whore, she would have made some pimp a fortune.

"What if it's not Simon? The guy on the Promenade wasn't him. He

hasn't yet identified himself. WIH..A..CHEE..YOOK..HUH, where's the WIH..A..CHEE..YOOK..HUH?"

"Shut up, you fool!" Patton chastised. *"Keep your wits about you."*

"Tell me about the Queen B." I had to get him to reveal himself somehow. I hoped the quivering of my voice didn't give me away. My hand on the Baretta was quivering too.

"Sure baby," answered Simone, licking her lips. "I'll give you some honey."

"Tell me about how you kidnapped her," I yelled. "What did you do with her?"

"Oh, Sugar, you are kinky. I'm getting so excited." Simone began to move closer to the bed.

"Stop! Stop him, Wycheck!"

I pulled the Baretta out of my pocket and pointed it directly at her.

"Now, motherfucker, let's cut the crap!" I screamed.

"All right, Wycheck! That's the ticket."

Simone stopped dancing immediately and stood frozen. She looked like a naïve schoolgirl runaway. That was what most of the young whores were anyway, under all the makeup and in previous lives. *Very good, Simon!*

"Please fella, I'll do anything you say. You can hurt me if you want to. Just please don't kill me."

Whores lead dangerous lives. They die every day, and it was obvious that Simone knew it. Simon was playing the part perfectly.

"Wycheck, get a hold!"

"Please, please!" Simone fell down to the ground whimpering, crying and pleading.

"He's an accomplished actor. You know that, Wycheck."

"All right, no more of this shit, Simon. Put your hands up now! Or, I'll kill you and not give it a second thought. I'll call the cops and the world will make me a hero."

Simone raised her arms and a big smile stretched across her face. "Ooh Frank," she purred. "I didn't know you had it in you."

The voice had changed. It was a familiar voice, one I never thought I'd hear again.

"Pay attention, Wycheck! Now, you know it's him."

"Frank, honey, you're scaring me now. Don't you know me?" Simone pulled off the blonde wig and rubbed away some of the makeup.

"Christine? Is it you?"

"Off course, it's not her! You know he can impersonate anyone. Shoot now, Wycheck."

"Don't you know me Frank? Remember the last we were here? Broke the legs off that stupid bed and it didn't even slow us down."

"Shoot Wycheck! He's coming at you!"

"No, it's Christine. Only she could know that."

"Frank, honey, please put the gun away. I can explain everything."

"Christine, is it really you?"

She wiped the rest of the makeup. It was really her, without a doubt. I threw the baretta across the room and jumped off the bed to embrace her. "Oh Christine, I never thought I'd see you again."

My friend, I'll never forget the devilish smile that took over her face. Not the playful little one I loved so much, but pure evil. Christine raised up some kind of stun gun, and the last thing I remembered seeing were the wires flying towards me.

The last thing I remembered hearing was Patton, *"You dumb, stupid, mother fucker!"*

THE END PLAY

108

For months, Janet Bultaco lay shackled on Simon's table. She had spent a lifetime living by the rules. Now, in the Beast's chamber, there were new rules and during her many solitary hours, Bultaco reasoned how best to play by them.

She was never a quitter, always having to swim upstream. That was the way it was for a woman in a man's world. Janet Bultaco never quibbled. She would defeat the current. *And, I will defeat the Beast.*

Simon fed her, though, at first, she refused to eat. Later, she accepted the nourishment, but only grudgingly. He bathed her and cleaned up after her. She was wrapped in silk negligees and doused in perfumes. The Beast spent hours painting her face and fussing with her hair. He said she had to become his "perfect little bitch."

Janet Bultaco learned to lay motionless, lifeless, expressing no emotion. Like any good stable horse at the sight of the whip, Janet Bultaco had learned to avoid the beating. She lay limp for him, an inanimate piece of meat, moveable, pliable. He could use her, but she would never give in.

That is what he wants from me. It's not about the sex. It's always about power. The Beast needs to dominate me.

That was their competition. *That is his game.*

Janet Bultaco had been imprisoned for eighty-seven days. Resisting, she would be kept alive; vanquished, she would be disposed of like the others. Bultaco resolved to endure whatever was forced upon her.

Like Sheherezade, I will withstand a thousand days. 'Til eternity runs out!

Sooner or later, the Beast would be apprehended. He would be held accountable, go before the system, and ultimately die for his crimes. A prosecutor would exact the world's revenge on the Beast. In her mind, Janet Bultaco was that prosecutor.

Shackled, she envisioned instead, Simon shackled in her courtroom.

Bultaco was handled, fingered, touched and stroked at his whim. Nothing of hers was left private. She imagined the Beast in prison garb in her courtroom as she formulated her arguments and cross-examinations. *See how much privacy there will be for you in a cell!*

Simon moved her about with his ropes and pulleys, turning her, twisting her, ever searching for even more humiliating positions. Janet Bultaco persevered, letting the text of her plea for the death penalty play out in her mind. *See how much comfort you find on Death Row!*

The Beast abused her and invaded her body crudely and roughly. He contemptuously spat his semen into her. Janet Bultaco closed her eyes to transport herself to the execution chamber. *See how you enjoy being on my table with my liquid entering your body!*

As the door to her chamber opened, Janet Bultaco braced herself. There was never any relief from the Beast. She no longer stared hatefully, that only amused him. Janet Bultaco instead gazed blankly off into space.

Simon came to her naked, proudly dangling his wand of torture. Their relationship was primal and wild he told her. The Beast was hideous. Scarred and gnarled, he truly was a beast, a detestable creature, no more.

"Good morning, Janeta. Today is an important day."

She could not speak. A gag was always in her mouth, except when she was fed. Speaking was not allowed even while eating. If she made even a sound, her gag was immediately replaced and the meal was over. Some manner of abuse would follow.

The Beast did not toy with her as he usually did. He took her quickly and roughly. Janet Bultaco, in her mind, replayed her summation for the jury. It had been practiced each of the last eighty-seven days.

Ladies and Gentlemen of the jury, anything but death for the defendant would be a gross miscarriage of justice.

"Today the Grand Game will be officially over," pronounced Simon.

The Beast spoke as he thrust himself against her. Janet Bultaco concentrated harder to keep herself in her courtroom.

You have heard from the loved ones of the deceased. Those poor dead women cry out to you from their graves.

"Today my total victory over the Higherpower and all his minions will be complete."

The Beast gave his final strokes and the evil semen entered her. Janet Bultaco remained limp, putting it out of her mind.

You must not allow this despicable animal to beguile you. You must do your duty!

"Ah, excellent as always, Janeta."

The Beast lay on top of her, breathing hard. She could feel his heart beating wildly. This was the most distasteful part of all.

I myself have experienced his craven torture. I have described it all to you.

The Beast usually rested on top of her, relaxed and breathing deeply. Frequently he fell asleep. Sometimes the drool from his mouth would run down her body. Occasionally, the Beast would rise and take her again.

Make no mistake, good citizens, he would do the same to your wife or daughter.

This time the Beast got up after only a few minutes. "A pity we have to end our relationship. But all good things must come to an end."

What?

Janet Bultaco's expression gave away her concern. She regretted having exhibited that weakness.

The Beast left the room and returned shortly with a few bottles and a syringe. Inserting the syringe into one of the bottles, he spoke to her calmly. "You should know that I usually do not enjoy this part. However, you are the Queen Bitch. So it will give me pleasure."

In the name of God, in the name of humanity, good citizens, you cannot allow this depraved creature to live!

"Do not think I am unaware of the loathing you feel for me. The seething hatred that swirls around in you, that gives you will to defy me. You should have more respect, Queen Bitch!"

The Beast stabbed one of the small bottles with the syringe, sucking up a light blue liquid. He held the syringe up and squirted a small amount of the liquid skyward.

You must do your duty and vote for the death penalty.

"You think your will transcends time and space. Your strength of character and mind can persevere against anything, that no force on earth can deny you your revenge. Ha, Ha, Ha!"

The whole world is watching you my fellow citizens, my fellow human beings. It is time for you to do the right thing.

"You are an intelligent bitch, Janeta. You know you are going to die. Yet, even now, you feel you are immortal."

He approached her with the syringe and stuck it into her thigh. She watched as his thumb pushed down and the pale blue liquid entered her.

Holy Mary, mother of God! It burns!

"Ah yes, Janeta. That is correct. Your time has come. I wonder, do you assume your hatred is so powerful that it will survive you? Vengeance is absolute. Justice will be done."

My God, is this how I will die?

"Yes, Janeta, you see it now, don't you. I have observed a hundred expressions from bitches about to die. And they have all melted away to nothingness. Do you think you can cheat death? Go to heaven?

Yea, though I walk through the valley of the shadow of death, I will fear no evil.

"You will not! You will become so much dust and nothing more."

Thy rod and thy staff, they comfort me.

"Dust Janeta, to be scattered by the four winds, indistinguishable from all the other dust in the universe."

Janet Bultaco felt the liquid pulsing through her veins. Her body was beginning to feel numb everywhere. *So, this is how it will end?* She never dreamed it could be so sudden.

My God, please hear me now. I have not always been a good Christian but I believe I have been a good human being.

"And when it is over, there is no more. You will not be remembered. You won't be missed. Everything will go on without you as if you had never existed. You can trust me on that, Janeta. I have been doing this for a long time."

Her body was stiffening. Janet Bultaco tried to move, to flex muscles, but the effort was getting increasingly difficult and ultimately impossible. Her mind was spinning and the light was beginning to recede from her. The vibrant eyes went blank. The stare, once so filled with hatred, drifted off to nothingness.

"The venom in your veins is quelled, is it not, my sweet. Your fury has taken its leave. Death is the eternal equalizer, Janeta. In death, we are all alike."

Simon undid the shackles and removed the gag. He hoisted the lifeless, though still breathing body over his shoulder. "About a hundred fourteen pounds, a few less than when you arrived." He carried his Janeta to the freezer where she would remain to die.

"In twelve hours you go to Processing where you will become dust. That is the way of the world. Death is the ending to every story."

Simon threw the body into the freezer, peering down a last time on a living Janeta. Disposal of the bodies was always an emotionless and tedious chore, but with the Queen Bitch he felt an unexpected satisfaction.

Even if only in part, an old debt was being repaid. "Sleep well, Janeta. Good bye, Queen Bitch."

There was only a moment of consciousness left. *I love you, John. Please avenge me!*

109

Kirsty Dunn was making final preparations for the six p.m. broad cast when the Fed Ex package was handed to her. She was busy and slipped the small envelope into her purse. *A present from Paul, no doubt,* Kirsty's smile had also landed her Paul Summerfield, CEO of Aspertec, a dynamic new biotech company.

Paul is always doing things like that, flowers, candy, and small gifts delivered to the set. A busy man, Paul sent them in his place, surrogates to express his love. Kirsty beamed. She would open the box when she had a chance.

The newsroom was buzzing this evening. A note, perhaps Simon's final note was the main story.

TO THE WORLD

A LITTLE TOKEN FOR YOU ALL
YOUR JUSTICE, A LITTLE SHORT DOES FALL
THE GAME IS DONE, MY REVENGE COMPLETE
WITH THE BEST OF ALL TIME, DID YOU COMPETE

FRET NOT, THAT YOU HAVE LOST
REGARDLESS OF THE COST

THERE'S ALWAYS ANOTHER DAY
AND ALWAYS ANOTHER GAME TO PLAY

SIMON

The note was sent to the Los Angeles Times. Rumor was that a body part from Janet Bultaco accompanied an identical note sent to the FBI. The FBI was not forthcoming. Speculation ran wild.

The night went by in an instant. Kirsty had forgotten about her gift, but remembered it when she was leaving. She reached into her purse for the Fed Ex envelope. *Dear Paul,* Kirsty thought as she opened it. Inside was a jewelry box just about the right size for a bracelet. *Bless his heart. He will have to be rewarded tonight for his thoughtfulness.* Kirsty flipped open the blue felt lid in anticipation. She lurched back in shock and horror. Someone had sent her a human finger!

The FBI labs confirmed that Kirsty Dunn had received Janet Bultaco's left middle finger.

Two days later, the FBI announced that they had received the right.

110

> We must live with the disheartening fact that not all killers will be apprehended. A brain surgeon does not save all of his patients. The tortured remains of victims cry out to us to capture their killers. But like the surgeon, we are not gods. We can only do our best. A good investigator sleeps at night.
>
> - Into the Mind of a Killer, John Hightower

He wrote the words. He believed the words. But he could not live the words.

The classical music played constantly in the small condominium. John Hightower was unable to sleep, and alternated between home and office looking for new perspective. What was that one small clue that was missed? *Study the fish, Higherpower. Study the fish.*

He was struck by the irony in his life. A distinguished career of some twenty years of catching notorious serial killers, and in the most important case of all, he was a complete failure.

We tracked the notes sent to us and to the Times, and the finger delivered to that young newswoman. As usual, our leads went cold. We got descriptions but descriptions of whom? Disguises that lead us to no one. You pay cash or use credit cards that lead nowhere. You never use the same vehicle twice. Rent them and leave them. We have your blood, your DNA, and so far that has given us nothing.

But I had my chances. Who shall I blame?

Exhausted, it occurred to John Hightower that the doorbell had rung repeatedly sometime earlier. Background noise to Beethoven's seventh, itself in the background. Suddenly it registered.

The mind is a mysterious, mystical and, until better understood, magical organ. Will we ever figure out the mind? Some never! His own was tired, overused and over worked, disgusted and dejected.

He retrieved the package left on his doorstep, a fairly large and somewhat heavy box. The urge was to tear at it quickly. Hightower had his fears. *There will be no prints, no fibers, nothing to help us I'm sure,* but there were the habits of a lifetime. He opened the box slowly and carefully.

It was cold; something was packed in ice and reminded him of a lobster dinner someone sent him once through some internet company. *Was it last Christmas or Thanksgiving, or was it the year before? The mind,* Hightower pushed the ice aside. His imagination ran wild. Was it from Simon? *Another body part? The box is too large for another finger, too small for another head. What if it's just a lobster?*

Hightower continued to carefully remove the ice. It was some kind of organ, but he could not tell if it was human or not.

The lab identified it as a human heart. Further tests concluded that the heart belonged to Janet Bultaco.

An envelope containing a greeting card was hidden in the box. The envelope was addressed to "My Old Friend." The card read:

HIGHERPOWER, MY WORTHY OPPONENT

LAST LICKS DONE, THE GRAND GAME CONCLUDED
YOU HAVE PLAYED WELL.
THOUGH DON'T WE EACH WISH YOU HAD DONE BETTER?

FOR JANETA, THE WHITE KNIGHT NEVER DID COME.
AN OBSTINATE BITCH, BUT STILL QUITE FUN.
TO THE WORLD SHE GAVE THE FINGER, TO ME HER BODY.
BUT HER HEART ALWAYS BELONGED TO YOU.

TILL NEXT TIME,

SIMON

111

I came to still woozy and not remembering much. Didn't have to though, I knew the drill. I was given a good healthy dose of ether, thrown into the back of some vehicle, brought to a secret dungeon somewhere, and here I was, strapped to a table.

The two of them were still blurry, and they were talking to each other like two love struck teenagers. I recognized Christine's voice; the other, I presumed was Simon.

"Did you do the bitch?" asked Christine's voice.

"Down the drain, my pet," answered Simon.

I assumed it was Simon's natural voice, and felt a certain irony in that I wasn't sure. All this time, I never heard the real Simon. Or saw him either; I strained my eyes for a look. Both naked, it was Christine, sure enough, and the other, well, Simon was a sight. Gnarled and scarred miserably over much of his body and face, it had to have been another disguise. But, it wasn't. The real Simon, it was finally plain how much he needed to be the master of deception and illusion.

"And now it's my turn, darling?" Christine begged him. "You did promise me."

Whatever it was, Christine would get it. How many times had she used that tone on me? And I could never resist her. No man could.

"Certainly, my sweet," answered Simon. "How can I refuse you?" Super Simon, woman hater, woman torturer, woman killer, *certainly, my sweet!* Impenetrable Simon, invincible Simon, they were all only mere bitches Simon, *how could I refuse you?* Unbelievable!

"Christine!" I called to her.

She walked towards me, as gorgeous as ever, a goddess, leaned over and kissed me on the cheek. "Hello, Frank," she said to me. At the same time, I felt a sharp stinging pain in my side.

Christine giggled, the same one I'd hear just after some raunchy sex. She proudly held up a toothbrush with a silver sliver of a blade imbedded in the handle.

"I taught her how to make that, Frankie. Used it to take the Queen Bitch. A very fast learner, our Christina, wouldn't you say?"

I didn't get a chance to answer. Christine put another slice into me.

"Christina, Christina," chided Simon. "You're hurting our Frankie. That's not civilized."

"You said I could do him." Christina used her hurt, disappointed voice, the one that could get you to agree to anything.

"She is the bloodthirsty one, is she not, Frankie?" Simon was laughing, then turned to Christine and delicately lectured her. "We do not maim our bitches, my sweet, and we only kill them because we have to."

Christine put her hand on me and began stroking me. That marvelous hand, how differently it felt. The little toothbrush kept waving back and forth ominously. Simon had that bleary eyed look of infatuation, and I feared he would give in to her.

"Simon," I said, half changing the subject, and the other half had to know. "Why have you done this? How?"

"How? With you so predictable, Frankie, what a question you ask. And, why? Why should be obvious too. You were one of the main profiteers in the Jaws case. You whipped up public fervor with your sensationalist articles. You made him horrific by giving him that name. You sent my brother to his grave. You, Frankie, were the worst of them all. But, you did make your name and quite a bit of money, didn't you?"

"What about the book, Simon?"

Simon began to laugh wildly. Christine smiled in response, though it appeared she didn't know why.

"If I wanted a book, Frankie, why would I get a piss poor writer like you? I could have had anyone. No, I need no book. Zodiac didn't have a biographer and there were hundreds, maybe thousands of books written about him. There will be even more written about me. I am the best of all time, The Master Of the Game. Isn't that right, my dear?"

"Yes, Simon, my love."

They hugged and kissed like honeymooners on their first night. What a lovely couple they made!

"It was all part of the Grand Game, Frankie. You were an important part, but just part of the game."

"And, now that your Game is over, you'll retire a legend, like you planned," Christine said coquettishly, while snuggling her face into Simon's neck. How many times had she done that to me? How God damned many times! And, how I loved it. "Return to the safety of obscurity where they can never find us," she cooed on. "We'll take our prey and no one will ever know."

"Yes, my sweet. That was the plan. But..." Simon's wheels were spinning. "There is the matter of Wycheck's bitches, Jana and Jenna. I did promise you that, Frankie."

"Leave them alone!" I screamed before Simon shoved a gag into my mouth.

"Ah Frankie, you know how I like to play, take the women. You are only here as a present for my little Christina. You are her bitch."

Christine snuggled closer and stroked him gently with her hands. "Simon, we have him here; Frankie is punished enough. You don't need to take his women."

"No!" he screamed, an amazingly swift change of emotion. Then just as quickly, calm again, "We must keep our promises. And besides, there is still Higherpower, anxious to play, and there is still much sport in him."

"Simon, you promised," pouted Christine.

"Yes, yes, my precious, I know, but there is so much fun still to be had, and we can play the next game together."

She seemed disappointed then cheered up. "All right, my love, we'll play if you like." Christine never wasted much time in arguing. She was a player not a litigant. They kissed passionately. It was disgusting.

"Now," announced Simon, "we still have our endplay to attend to. Would you care to do the honors for Frankie, my lovely Christina?"

"Can I play with him a little first?" She was waving the toothbrush like a Hibachi chef did his knife over a filet mignon.

"Christina!" Simon chided while shaking his head at me. Like, what am I going to do with her? She's so naughty.

Christine seemed disappointed again, but dutifully injected me with the blue liquid. No surprises, I knew what was going to happen, had it described for me often enough. In five minutes or so, I'd be completely paralyzed.

"Bye bye, Frank," Christine said snidely and gave me a little wave with the fingers of one hand. What a fool I was, once thinking she could be the woman in my life, replace Jane. What a damn fool! Another mistake, in a life full of them.

I could already feel the burning rush up my extremities. I refused to struggle as Simon described so many of his victims had. Fuck him! Fuck them both!

So, I guess that's that, my friend.

For myself, I leave this world without regrets. My life was what it was. I was weak and foolish, reckless many times, could have died often. Death finally caught up with me, that's all. But, I had my moments, did a few good things too. Life, we all pass through grappling and clawing, doing the best we can.

One regret though, if only I could see it. I envy you that, my friend, dear reader. To know how it all ends.

112

It was a cold ominous day on Santa Monica Bay. The spray of the cold ocean mist wore on his face, yet reminded him that there could be another life. The pleasure of breathing real air, and of thinking your own thoughts and not those pried from a killer's head.

The small sailboat bobbed helplessly on the water as Hightower ignored it in favor of his thoughts. *The last time we were here, my love, you got so sick. And you did it for me.*

She wanted to go for me, get me away from you, Simon, for a while.

The wind took the small craft well out to sea, its motion calming and soothing, though Hightower did not notice it. Wagner was playing in his head, "The Ride of the Valkyries." *Inappropriate! Right composer, wrong work.* Hightower forced himself to concentrate on "Sigfried's Funeral March" instead.

Four weeks and four days had passed since the receipt of Janet's heart. A lot had changed and even more hadn't. The world continued on its path unfettered and people carried on. Trains ran, planes flew, traffic was too heavy and the Dodgers were in third place. It seemed only John Hightower could not move on.

The Bureau, pressed with new priorities, was beginning to allow old ones to recede. Hightower had seen it before. Unsolved cases suffered the same fate as MacArthur's old soldier; they just faded away. It would be years before that happened to this cataclysmic one, but without progress, a man here, a priority there, the resources were already being siphoned off.

They crucified Tim Dawson, forced him out. He was the sacrificial lamb to the Bureau's failure, my failure. Dawson is better off, young and very talented and, therefore, much better suited outside of government service.

I myself am not properly configured for political hanging. So, they simply allow me to carry on.

The small boat was well off shore and John Hightower was forced to do some sailing. He pulled in the lines and tacked toward the land. *What caused me to take such an extreme turn in life, from all this beauty to chasing such horrific evil? How could I be here now with such a woeful task to perform?*

A heart is a small representation of a person. John Hightower did something he never imagined possible. He stole evidence, having taken a small piece of Janet's heart. *For cremation and burial, though I have no idea if that was what you wished.*

Kevin Fitzpatrick woke up Sunday morning to the smell of something burning on his backyard barbeque, Francine's breasts. Susan and Pam Berlanger's noses were sent to Mark Berlanger's attorney along with a note. "A contribution to the lawsuit. Don't fret, Furbanger. The government will pay. Simon." The Benchlys never received anything of their daughter. She was meaningless, never really part of your game.

John Hightower picked up the small container of ashes. *Less than half a thimble full! Not much to show for a life.* He searched for the right words to say. *I knew you for so long, and never really knew you, my darling Janet. We had so little time together, and that I wasted.*

Hightower carefully spilled the ashes onto his palm, and cast them upward into the wind. *A puff of smoke - no more than a puff of smoke!*

Sigfried received his redemption. Dear Janet, will you ever have yours?

He had written a small eulogy, but was unable to read it. The paper remained folded in his pocket. John Hightower was never good in such situations. He remained choked with grief and guilt. *Forgive me, my love. I failed you.* "Rest in peace, Janet," he uttered finally. It was all he could muster.

The small boat was turned and headed back to shore. *No hurry. Let the tide take me back.* John Hightower came this day to bury Janet Bultaco. He also buried everything else save a burning desire for revenge. *Not a thought of comfort or enjoyment will be entertained further. A savage killer is walking loose. That will not be tolerated while I live.*

So, now, ride Valkyries. Ride and carry your Sigfried to the heavens. So too, my will is reincarnated.

The small boat slowly drifted back to shore. This brief time on Santa Monica Bay concluded the thinking of what might have been.

There would be no further distractions.

It's been four weeks and four days. ALWAYS ANOTHER DAY, why the delay? TILL NEXT TIME, I'm ready. Make your play.

By these few precious ashes, I swear, Simon, you won't get away. I will not stop until I see you dead!

NEW GAMES

113

Recording G-4

"I have emerged powerful. From the mystical times, only a few have been bestowed with minds so mighty and intellects so sharp. I have honed the skills–the power to appear and disappear, to read men's minds and to cloud them, to predict events and to shape them.

I am on evolution's critical path, a direct lineage, undiluted, in every generation there is but one. Since before recorded time, my kind has come to challenge, to dominate, and to take our natural place in history."

Simon prepared a special dinner in celebration. Appetizer, escargots in brioche; a nice little endive salad; Chilean sea bass wrapped in rice paper with a cream of lemongrass and lime. And for dessert, a Grand Marnier soufflé that turned out perfectly.

How fortunate Simon thought himself, to have found his one true soul mate. He was one of a kind, what were the odds? Of all the bitches in the world, Simon had found the one who was worthy.

They were of like mind and disposition, he and Christina. She had become his student and accomplice, his companion and lover. And, she had proven herself. Christina had taken that pathetic Frankie, enjoyed him, and then disposed of him.

"Did you enjoy the way we sent them the Queen Bitch's critiquing fingers?" Simon asked Christina while placing the soufflé in front of her.

"Oh yes, terribly, my darling." There was a glint in her eye. They were one.

Christina picked up her spoon. She was a dainty eater, more sampling the meal than consuming it. *She is careful about her figure, and what a figure it is,* Simon thought. "The FBI had wanted to keep that little tidbit their secret. Won't they ever learn? I control the media, not they. A very nice touch with that Dunn woman, don't you agree?"

"Sheer brilliance. And the heart, too," she reminded him with enthusiasm, "let's not forget that. You really stuck it to Higherpower. Oh, and Francina's tits! Darling, that was genius."

"Thank you, my dear. And your soufflé?"

"Mmmm, scrumptious."

Simon checked her to see if she really liked it or was simply being polite. *Hard to tell,* he would continue to look for signs.

"A fair job all the way around," Simon graded his performance. "The Grand Game went pretty much the way it was planned. There was that aside for Rickford. A separate little game for him, but I must say, I enjoyed that quite well, too."

"Darling, only the best of all time could have done that. And for you, it was only a side play." Christina sipped her espresso and took another small spoonful of the soufflé. Simon watched her intently. *Does she really like it?*

"Only with the Queen Bitch did I fail miserably. Higherpower outwitted me there and I took a bullet. Well deserved, I could have died and perhaps I should have. For my carelessness!"

Christina put down her spoon and playfully chided. "My poor, poor darling, you obsess about everything. That was only a slight miscalculation. What matters is, you took her, you played with her, and you won the Game."

Simon smiled. It was a gross miscalculation, and a mistake, and even if it was minor, which it was not, it could never be forgotten, or forgiven. "Perhaps you're right, princess. And, let's give Higherpower his due. He was a worthy opponent, and I'm thankful for him. Higherpower gives my triumph meaning. A player is measured more by his competitor's skill than his own. I can hardly wait to play our next game, the Return Game."

Simon detected Christina's expression turning to disappointment. Only slightly, she was excellent at concealing her thoughts and emotions, but she could not hide them from him. "What, my precious?" *The same concern, that I stay too long, Christina prefers we go back into the safety of anonymity.* "I know, I know. I promised. But, what kind of champion would I be, if I didn't give Higherpower a rematch?" Simon stared into her face, studying, analyzing, scrutinizing. "Besides, we'll play together. What fun we'll have."

Christina smiled. "All right, my darling. We'll play together, we'll win, and it will be fun." It was decided. "Oh, I'm so full. You've made such a wonderful evening for us."

"My pleasure, my sweet."

"And now, love of my life, I am going to make your evening." Simon perked up in anticipation. "Hurry, let's both get ready. We are going to play your favorite game of all."

114

Simon sat cowering on the floor waiting for the inevitable. As young Peter Simmons did daily for most of his life. He could hear his mother's voice changing, turning colder in the next room as she prepared herself for the afternoon's entertainment, transforming herself from an indigent housewife into "Mistress Pleasure."

"Is Mommy's little bitch ready for punishment?"

The voice was good, improving, though far from perfect, but close enough to transport Simon back those many years. His stomach quivered in apprehension that turned instantly into paralyzing fear as the door bolted open.

"What are you doing on the floor? Miserable sot, get up on the table!"

Christine Taylor stood in the doorway, the perfect image of the Queen Bitch, Karen Simmons. Blonde wig, excessive makeup, tight fitting black leather corset with lace stockings, and catapulted up by six-inch stiletto heels she towered over the whimpering boy.

"I said, get up on the table!" The stick that was always in her hand came down on him again and again. Simon struggled to climb onto the chamber table, as Peter did his kitchen table.

"Mommy, please!" It was Peter Simmons voice, perfectly, resurrected from a distant past. "Don't hit me! I'm going! I'm going!"

"Faster!" snarled the Queen Bitch, as she increased her blows.

The intense pain, all but forgotten, was now allowed to reenter a body that had long since banished pain. Simon was no longer in his Castle and in complete control. He was Peter Simmons again and utterly helpless.

His mother peered down on him in disgust as she strapped him to the four legs of the table. Peter's eyes were clenched shut. He could not bear to look up at her disapproving face. She removed his clothes and replaced them with a nice little dress, fixed his hair, and painted his face. Karen Simmons turned her worthless little boy into her "perfect little bitch."

Peter lay on the table motionless. He would not resist, having learned long before that it was useless, and painful. At least an hour of torture was still ahead of him. He was careful not to add to the total.

Karen swatted and turned her bitch to swat some more. She was crude and rough, searching constantly for new ways to hurt, degrade, and humiliate. "I'm disgusted with you! A bitch is only good for the giving of pleashah, and you are woefully deficient there too."

Peter waited and persevered. The pain was great, her disdain worse, and yet the stirring began anew. After a time, Mistress Pleasure began playing with him. He knew it was wrong, was disgusted with himself. But it felt so very good.

Karen laughed as Peter's excitement began to show, encouraged it, while at the same time, punishing him for it. "What do you think you're doing?" she yelled, simultaneously stroking and swatting him.

He was ashamed and loathed himself for his weakness and lack of control. Peter clenched his teeth as the throbbing in him increased. He resisted mightily, but the pressure was rising with every repetition. Another tantalizing stroke, another more agonizing swat, and Peter could no longer contain himself. The release was explosive.

Karen stood by laughing and scowling at the same time. Peter hated her for it, yet he wanted so for her to love him. Karen left him strapped on the table for hours. "Lie here and think about how vile and disgusting you are! You're contemptible, a complete embarrassment to me! I wish I never had you!"

It was a game Karen played with him, one he was never able to win. Only the Queen Bitch ever won. Peter lay in shame and anger, anger that was compounded each day.

And yet, it felt so very good.

Hundreds of taken bitches later, and not one had come close to providing him that same fantastic feeling.

None, till Christina!

115

Simon was sleeping soundly when a sharp stinging sensation startled him awake. Christina had cleaned him up and removed all evi dence of their little game. She stood before him, Christina again, naked and gorgeous.

"Sleep well, my darling?" she asked, warmly and lovingly.

"Yes, my pet," Simon sighed, as he pulled new air into his lungs. In one mighty burst, all the tension had been expelled from his body, and he was as relaxed as he could ever recall. "Slept so very well." He yawned and tried to stretch, but was still restrained. "Let me up, my sweet, we must prepare for the Return Game."

"No, not yet, my beautiful Simon, not yet." It was then that he noticed the toothbrush in her hand, and realized the burning in his ribs was the result of a four-inch long deep gash. "I still have my present to give you." A devilish smile was on her face. "The best present of all, for the greatest of all time. Simon, I give you immortality."

He was puzzled. Christina made another cut, the pain from which he ignored.

"Remember, Simon, how you spoke of Zodiac, the best of all time, the only Master of the Game."

"Before me, my pet. I wear the crown now."

Another little slice. "Yes, but to be best is temporary. There is always another day and always someone to take the crown away. Zodiac knew when to quit. You do not."

Simon glanced over to the nearby table to notice several syringes, one filled with the blue liquid. "Christina, what are you doing?" She did not answer, only grinned; and it explained everything, leaving Simon only to curse himself for his ignorance. *How could I have been so stupid?*

How could she have hidden her intentions from me? "Christina, there are so many wonderful games for us to enjoy together. What a marvelous life we will have."

"No, Simon! I save you from yourself, and grant you your greatest wish. You will never be caught or found; you'll remain a mystery, the greatest of all time, Master of the Game; and, with time, your legend will only grow."

Christina cut him twice more, on the neck and on the cheek. Her eyes grew wider as the bright vermilion dripped down his face. Every part of Christina's body pulsed with excitement. The ruby red, how beautiful it was!

For a lifetime, she had given men great pleasures and had gotten few in return. Finally, Christina had found what she was searching for. The extraction of pain was her ecstasy, and the deliverance of death was divine.

"Shame, my love, that so much of your body is scarred and unusable to me. I'll just have to settle. And, as for our games together, I prefer my own games."

What a fool I've been! Simon focused his concentration and gave a mighty tug at the straps. Strength far beyond normal was far short of sufficient; his specially designed equipment was too perfect. *How ironic, a mere bitch, inferior in every way! Through the centuries, from the time of Adam and Eve, Samson and Delilah, Caesar and Cleopatra, always the same mistake, men have learned absolutely nothing.* "But, there is still so much I can show you," he offered, but there was not a taker.

"My love," Christina purred. "Please understand. I'm grateful for your tutelage and for you having awakened me. I now see my way so clearly. But, what I've learned is sufficient, and your money, I don't know where it all is, but enough. I'll manage. You are too compulsive, and set in your ways, Simon. You inhibit me. I must be free to travel my own path, seek my own destiny."

Master of the Game, greatest of all time, and I make the dumbest mistake of all time! "Christina, my love, I've enjoyed your present so much. The pain was exquisite. Promise me you'll do it again. Come now let me go. There is still one thing I must show you, the most important thing of all."

"Sorry darling, soon you'll disappear into history and legend. My gift to you, Simon's legacy will live forever." A quick wave of the toothbrush and Christina was holding Simon's ear in front of him. She waved it back and forth gleefully, then seemed pensive for a few minutes, scrutinizing the ear carefully. Simon watched her expression change as the plans formulated within her. And finally, a dark glint in her eyes and a twisted smile that frightened even him.

"No, actually my dear sweet Simon, I see no reason for you to receive such a gift. Why should you become eternal? You are a man. And, all men are evil. Men used me. You used me, and only for your "pleashah." You don't deserve immortality, only death.

But first, my love, I will play with you. Just a little."

EPILOGUE

116

From the Postscript

You may study serial killers for a hundred years, but never think you understand them. Because, you don't!

- Into the Mind of a Killer, John Hightower

John Hightower was confused. Both his mind and emotions were in a jumble. It had been nearly six weeks since he had cast Janet's ashes to the wind and he was once again on the living room floor. For the thousandth time, digging, searching for the one important clue Hightower knew had to be there.

Suddenly, he was startled, interrupted by the doorbell. Déjà vu, the Fed Ex man was on the other side of the glass panes. Hightower leaped to his feet and ran to the door.

Was it another "present" from Simon? The box was the same size, cold, and appeared identical to the one that contained his beloved Janet's heart. *What further torture do you have in store for me, Simon?*

Hightower opened the box carefully. His stomach churning, he pushed aside the packing material, then the ice. John Hightower was shocked. Simon had sent him something impossible. *A penis, never!* Hightower was befuddled. Everything was wrong and nothing made sense.

Two days later, the lab matched the tissue's DNA to the blood on the floor of Janet Bultaco's office. It was Simon's penis!

An envelope was found hidden at the bottom of the box. It was addressed to "My New Friend." The card read:

JOHNNY BOY,

TAKEN PAINFULLY, TEE HEE
THERE WILL BE MORE

CHRISTINA LIVES!

Finally, Hightower could piece it together. *The forgotten victim, Christine Taylor!* A wry smirk took over his face as he imagined the possible turn of events. Simon emasculated, killed by one of his victims, Hightower felt awkward that the thought tickled him so. *A touch overconfident, my friend, was there one victim who turned out not to be so helpless?*

What ironic justice!

Would that it had been sooner, in time to save you, my darling, and the others too. The thought quickly sobered Hightower's thinking. There wasn't any justice really, was there? Not when so many innocents were dead.

John Hightower sat on the living room floor, sipping his iced tea, trying to put order into his chaotic world. Yet he knew full well that one could never organize chaos. One could only struggle and carry on. That was the nature of the world, wasn't it?

It was over, ended so suddenly, not as Hightower would have liked or as he intended. But, what in life ever went as intended? If not this fateful turn of events, Simon could have killed and killed again. Until some quirky bit of luck or other twisted piece of fate intervened.

John Hightower was relieved yet frustrated, pleased yet unfulfilled, satisfied but not content. *My dear sweet Janet, I so wanted to kill him for you. Or, as you would have preferred, bring him to trial and let the system execute him.*

Simon paid dearly though, my love. There is that. Christina seems of the sadistic type; Simon must have suffered greatly. That's justice, in a sense, sardonic justice, but justice nevertheless.

John Hightower sipped the last of the tea and tried to recall a case where he was truly happy with the outcome. It was a long list and he could find no takers. With only the cessation of the killing to rejoice in, how could there be? Bittersweet was as sweet as it could ever get. That was the nature of his profession, wasn't it?

And, there was never a moment to rest. The line of killers was endless and each nipped at the other's heels. They were an affliction dredged from the depths of humankind, and relentless, gave no time for respite. No, he did not have time to dwell on things passed. There was a new killer to catch.

That was what John Hightower had to tell himself, that day, the next, and every day that followed.